D1136942

Discover more at millsandboon.co.uk

FROM BOARDROOM TO BEDROOM

JULES BENNETT

BLAME IT ON THE BILLIONAIRE

NAIMA SIMONE

MILLS & BOON

First Published in Great Britain 2020
by Mills & Boon, an imprint of HarperCollinsPublishers,
1 London Bridge Street, London, SE1 9GF

From Boardroom to Bedroom © 2020 Harlequin Books S.A.
Blame It on the Billionaire © 2020 Naima Simone

Special thanks and acknowledgement are given to Jules Bennett for her contribution to the *Texas Cattleman's Club: Inheritance* series.

ISBN: 978-0-263-27913-9

0220

MIX
Paper from
responsible sources
FSC
www.fsc.org
FSC™ C007454

This book is produced from independently certified FSC™ paper to ensure responsible forest management.

For more information visit: www.harpercollins.co.uk/green

Printed and bound in Spain
by CPI, Barcelona

FROM BOARDROOM TO BEDROOM

JULES BENNETT

For all of the unpublished authors out there…you can do it! Never give up doing what you love.

Prologue

"And the estate, businesses, and all holdings will go to Miranda Dupree."

"You've got to be kidding me." Sophie Blackwood refused to stay silent. She didn't know exactly what to do, what to say, but she couldn't just sit there and do nothing.

How in the hell did her father's ex-wife—his very young ex-wife—manage to sweep the entire inheritance? She was nothing but a gold-digging socialite.

Unacceptable.

Sophie and her father had never been close, but to will everything to the much younger woman who was no longer even his wife was a slap in the face.

Buckley "Buck" Blackwood continued to disappoint her even in death. Sophie glanced over to the woman in question who actually had the nerve to look surprised. Please, like she hadn't dug her claws so deep into Sophie's father... She knew this moment was coming.

Sophie shifted her focus to her brothers who were equally as stunned at the will that their father's lawyer, Kace LeBlanc, kept right on reading from, listing off each item, as if giving everything to an ex were perfectly normal.

Well, Sophie didn't have to stay and listen to this nonsense. She loved her brothers, but there was no love between her and Miranda.

Sophie was surprised her narcissistic step-monster didn't have a whole camera crew here to document this portion of her life. Being one of the star of *Secret Lives of NYC Ex-Wives*—New York's version of *The Real Housewives*—seemed to rule Miranda's life. The woman always had a crew following her, documenting every aspect of her glittery, flashy lifestyle.

This whole scenario really grated on Sophie's last nerve.

Miranda already had millions. She didn't need all of this other stuff from Buck—not the money and not the ranch. Granted, Sophie didn't need it, either, but damn it, she and her brothers were blood relations. Weren't they entitled to something?

Did nobody see the vindictive woman Miranda truly was? There had to be a way to prove she wasn't all high and mighty like so many believed. Sure, the reality show portrayed her as a nurturing, loving woman... Sophie didn't believe that front for a minute.

Channeling the growing pit of anger in her gut, she

met Kellan and Vaughn's furious stares as she exited the study of her father's estate.

The only people she cared about were her brothers. They were a team, they always had been. And she knew they would work together to get this travesty of a will overturned. But right now, she was too furious to think, or to concentrate on what their next steps should be. She just needed to get away from her father's house, where she'd never been happy and where she'd just had to sit through a new betrayal. Most people would have been remorseful after a parent's passing, and part of Sophie was sad. Buck was her father, but he'd always been a hard bastard to love. Turns out, that hadn't ended with his death.

As Sophie made her way out into the bright, sunny day, she slid her sunglasses off her head and onto her face. She needed a break. She just wanted an escape even if for just a few days. Royal, Texas, was such a beautiful town and Sophie absolutely loved it here. But like every small town, it was a hotbed of gossip, and this latest bombshell her father had dropped on them was bound to be the talk of the town for weeks. Everywhere she went, people would be whispering, speculating. The thought made her skin crawl.

But gossip can work both ways, she realized after a moment's reflection. If she played her cards right, maybe she could turn the situation to her advantage. All the talking everyone would be doing about the scandalous Blackwood inheritance would lead to lots of talk about Miranda, too. If Sophie could uncover anything— a scandal, or a secret, or maybe whatever bit of leverage Miranda must have held over Buck to get him to disinherit his own children—maybe she could use it to get the will overturned.

Sophie pulled out her cell as she settled behind the wheel of her sporty car. Time to get started.

One

Sophie barely recognized herself in the reflection of the mirrored elevator doors. Flying across the country, getting a complete makeover, and coming up with a whole new identity had been quite the feat.

But persistence paid off...or at least she hoped it would.

She'd traveled to New York to spy on Miranda. She had tried chasing down every possible lead in Royal... but none of them had panned out. After two months of failed attempts, she'd realized she needed to widen her net. If she was going to find anything, it would have to be in New York—and it would have to be in a different persona. No one was willing to spill secrets to the stepdaughter who was known to hate Miranda—but perhaps a new identity would let her slip in under the radar. Sophie had no other idea how to find dirt on her stepmother, so she'd taken a very hands-on approach.

For a week now, Sophie had taken on this new look and role, but she still hadn't gotten used to being someone else. She'd never been this deceitful or this scheming before.

But desperate times and all that.

As the elevator continued to climb toward the floors that housed Green Room Media, Inc. building, she wondered exactly what she'd be doing. She knew she'd landed the job as a temporary consultant, so she hoped this was a position that would get her close to some cutting room floor footage. Maybe she'd even come in close contact with some of the camera crew from *Secret Lives*.

She needed to find some juicy tidbit on Miranda. Something to hold over her or, better yet, to expose her for the gold-digging, conniving attention seeker Sophie believed she was. Something that would let Sophie challenge the will and put Blackwood property back in Blackwood hands, where it belonged. A woman who always flaunted her life and her material possessions all over television didn't need anything more.

Sophie and her brothers deserved their due inheritance. She didn't want to be a whiny child about it, but she'd grown up in Blackwood Hollow and the home held so many memories…memories that shouldn't have been just handed over to Miranda Dupree. Memories she and her brothers made with their wonderful late mother that Sophie wanted to carry over into her own family or her brothers' families one day. That legacy belonged to the Blackwood children, not a second wife. Sophie wanted to do this for her brothers; she wanted them to have what they deserved. They all had plenty of money… This wasn't about that. This was about family, which they'd never considered Miranda part of.

Sophie didn't believe Miranda's sweet and innocent public persona…not one bit. The woman wouldn't be on one of the most scandalous reality shows on television if she were that perfect. There had to be something. Unfortunately, Sophie had made a point of avoiding Miranda as much as possible during her father's short-lived second marriage. She just plain didn't know the woman well enough to know which closets to search for Miranda's carefully hidden skeletons. But surely they were around here somewhere, in the offices of the show that had been the centerpiece of Miranda's life for the past few years.

Secret Lives was a popular reality show based on divorced women living in Manhattan. Of course, ratings hinged on how many scandals the ladies could cause while displaying their lavish lifestyles. It was tacky and tasteless—but it was popular, and it came with a big staff of people behind it, all working to keep it going. That was where Sophie had found her "in."

Sophie had applied for a personal consultant position within the company that produced *Secret Lives*. The security in the place was top-notch, so she'd had to get creative on getting in. No way would a Blackwood be allowed in this office. Not with the death of Miranda's husband so recent. Just the word *Blackwood* would raise too many red flags and Sophie would be shut out before she could even get started.

A temporary job was the perfect opportunity to get inside.

The only glitch? Sophie's popularity from her interior design YouTube channel, *Dream It, Live It*, forced her to alter her look. Usually, popularity was a great problem to have—but for the time being, it was getting in her way. If she didn't have so many loyal followers, she wouldn't have had to go to such great lengths to disguise herself.

Nothing a little hair color, some carefully applied makeup, a sexy pair of cat-eye glasses, a polished jacket and skinny jeans couldn't fix. She typically wore fun dresses because she always found a dress to be much more comfortable than pants. So this outfit was definitely outside of her norm. So was the makeup. She much preferred a natural look, so the red lips were completely out of her comfort zone.

And the hair? She was kind of digging this style. A little fringe around her face and the bold shade of ashy blond made her feel a little sassy. The self-esteem boost was much needed because her nerves were all over the place.

She was hopeful and quite certain nobody would recognize her now.

So here she was, day one of her new job and fully embracing her new identity. Maybe blondes would have more fun.

Oh, and of course her name was the biggest adjustment. That was something she had to fully embrace and always be aware of because if someone tried to get her attention and she wasn't focused enough to recognize her faked name, her cover would be blown.

The elevator stopped and Sophie pulled in a deep breath.

No. She had to stop thinking of herself as Sophie. In this building, and for the next week, she would have to think of herself as Roslyn Andrews. She could remember that, right? A nice combo of Sophie's middle name and her grandmother's maiden name. No problem. At least she'd chosen something somewhat familiar. And she wouldn't have to get used to it for long.

She'd given herself a week timeline to get in, find the scoop and get out. She didn't like being sneaky—that was quite the opposite of her personality—but she also felt that she and her siblings had been wronged. So, one week. Surely she could do some quick snooping?

The elevator doors slid open and the posh offices of Green Room Media greeted her. The elegant white decor and semicircular desk in the middle of the spacious floor plan were simple, yet classy. The receptionist glanced up from his computer and smiled. She'd talked with him before when she'd come for her interview just days ago. They clearly needed someone fast because they'd hired Sophie on the spot.

"Ah, Miss Andrews. Welcome back. Are you ready for your first day?"

More than he knew. Would it be too obvious if she asked to view cut footage right off the bat?

"Let's do it," Sophie said with a smile. "Just tell me where I'll be."

Craig, she believed his name was, came to his feet and gestured toward the long hallway. "You will actually be working right alongside Mr. Townshend, you lucky girl. He's amazing, but he demands loyalty and precision. His personal assistant is out on maternity leave, but that's no problem. If you need anything, you can always come find me."

Working with Mr. Townshend? As in *Nigel* Townshend? She would be his temporary personal consultant? Sophie didn't know if she was thrilled or terrified to be put in the most inner circle of the entire company... and with the sexiest mogul to ever grace the covers of magazines. He was known as the British Billionaire Bad Boy. Any woman with breath in her lungs knew who Nigel was.

Sophie's heart fluttered and her stomach got a little schoolgirl giddy. Nigel was one very dominating, very powerful man. When Sophie had interviewed, she'd thought for sure she was just going to be a gopher or someone to answer phones. She'd hoped for more, but she also had to be realistic. She'd only been trying to get her foot in the door.

Well, she was in all right. Now she only had moments to mentally prepare to not only meet the sexy Brit but also to compose herself so she didn't come across as some nitwit who didn't deserve this position. She couldn't afford to be let go before she got what she came for.

Sophie hurried to catch up with Craig as he made his way down the wide corridor.

"Are you sure this is the position I'm here for?" she questioned.

Craig came to a halt so fast Sophie jerked to a stop to prevent running into him. He glanced around before leaning in and whispering.

"You didn't hear this from me," he started. "But *Se-*

cret Lives has dipped a little in the ratings and Nigel is taking it upon himself to find out exactly why. He needs fresh eyes to help him fix the situation. That's where you come in."

Well, that was no pressure at all. Nothing like being thrust right into the thick of things on day one. But at least it was a problem that didn't make her feel out of her depth. She did know a little about ratings; after all, she'd built her channel into something of a phenomenon. Maybe she could actually make a difference here, too, *and* get the scoop she needed. A win-win.

"Does he not have anyone who has tried to help so far?" Sophie asked, still positive this position was a mistake.

"His assistant would probably have been a good asset, but she's unavailable and Nigel wants someone from the outside." Craig lowered his voice even more. "I think the show is in jeopardy. He didn't tell me that directly, but... Well, I have some sources."

Oh, she had no doubt the receptionist knew all the ins and outs and was one of the best sources of gossip. Perhaps starting with a little break room talk over lunch would be a good starting point for her own project.

Things were already starting off better than she'd hoped. Surely if Sophie was dealing with the head honcho himself, she could gain access to all the cut footage. But she still had to be careful and calculated about this. There was no room for errors and no way could she raise suspicions. Above all, she couldn't run into Miranda. Even with the blond hair, glasses and completely different wardrobe, Sophie knew her step-monster would recognize her.

"Mr. Townshend is waiting," Craig said as he turned and put his hands on the gold handles of a set of white double doors. "Welcome to Green Room Media."

The doors swung wide and Sophie/Roslyn pulled in a deep breath.

Showtime.

When he'd asked for help, he hadn't expected a lush supermodel turned librarian. The sight of the curvaceous blonde with sultry glasses and a confident smile hit him right in the gut. He was also a fan of glossy red lips.

Those jeans should have been illegal, but he certainly wasn't complaining.

Bloody hell. He didn't have time for this distraction. He hadn't even had time to interview anyone for himself and had trusted his most loyal, dependable employees to do that. But he'd only asked for someone well qualified, professional and polished.

He'd certainly gotten that last part; he had to assume the rest of her credentials were just as impressive as the outward package.

Might as well embrace his new temporary consultant. *Temporary* being the key word. *Off-limits* was also another key word because he never ever fraternized with employees. He liked to date, but he'd never gotten too serious…much to his family's dismay and disappointment.

Most times the Townshends didn't understand why Nigel was in New York, growing his empire, and not back in England, settling down and working on new heirs. He loved his family, he truly valued them and missed them like crazy. But he wanted to branch off from the dynasty and create his own legacy. This company and his shows were bigger than anything he'd ever dreamed. He just needed to continue that trend of growth and success in order to show his family that his goals and dreams truly were worthwhile.

Pushing the family issues aside, Nigel kept his eyes locked on the striking woman in his office. Talk about a test in willpower. If she was going to be working alongside him for weeks or months to come, he would have to remember this was a professional environment. He demanded as much from each of his employees and he would never let them think that he was incapable of meeting those standards himself.

Nigel came to his feet and rounded his desk. He was the boss, time for him to act like one and put these adolescent hormones to rest. His family considered him the infamous black sheep for breaking away, and he was doing his best not to live down to that reputation. Just because a man didn't want to get married and produce a litter of children did not make him a failure.

Of course, his sister was getting married next week and he was a groomsman, so that certainly didn't help matters.

All the more motivation to turn these dwindling numbers around and get *Secret Lives* back on top of the rankings. Maybe then his family would be proud of the work he did.

"You must be Roslyn Andrews," he greeted, turning all of his attention to the new employee. "I'm Nigel Townshend."

Her smile widened as she crossed his office and extended her hand. "It's a pleasure, Mr. Townshend."

"Mr. Townshend is my father," he corrected. "You will call me Nigel."

With a delicate nod, she replied, "Alright, Nigel."

His name sliding through her lips was just as magical and potent as he'd expected. And all of his employees called him Mr. Townshend. He couldn't quite justify the reasoning behind his quick response to her calling him *Mr.* but here they were.

"I had no idea I would be working with you directly," she added. "Can I be honest?"

The combination of that sultry voice and the confident firm grip of her handshake assaulted every nerve ending he had. Her dark eyes flared when he slid his hand into hers.

Well, wasn't this interesting?

She snatched her hand back and adjusted the purse strap on her shoulder. He had to give her credit, though, her smile never faltered.

Self-assurance was a sexy trait. Add that to the alluring outward package and he might be in trouble with this one. Hell, he was already in trouble since they were on a first-name basis after a one-minute meet. He had employees who had worked for him for over a decade who still didn't call him Nigel.

"Please," he replied. "Honesty is our key policy."

She adjusted her tortoiseshell glasses. "I'm even more nervous now that I know I'm working directly with the boss. But, I promise not to let my nerves get in the way of doing my best work."

"I hope you've saved your best work for me because I need the best."

"No pressure," she joked. "I hope I live up to your standards."

"I have no doubt you'll do just fine. I've seen your résumé. The fact that you work in interior design actually appealed to me because I believe designers look at every detail in all aspects of life and that's exactly what I need. And, I'm not sure if you've heard anything, but I'm not difficult to get along with, though I've been told I have a dry sense of humor."

"I have two older brothers. I'm pretty good with holding my own, no matter the jokes."

With her honesty and sense of humor, Nigel could see they'd get along just fine...so long as he kept reminding himself this arrangement was professional and temporary.

How many times could he use those two words?

Probably not enough, because he had a feeling he needed to keep those in the forefront of his mind as long as Ms. Andrews worked by his side.

"Have a seat," he told her, gesturing to the leather chair opposite his desk. "Since I didn't sit in on the interview process, I'd like to get to know a little about you before we begin our day. Like I said, I've seen your résumé, quite impressive, and I've heard my crew speak your praises."

"I'm flattered."

She should be. They'd interviewed a slew of people for this position, but Nigel had put out very specific requirements. Interesting that the most striking, intriguing woman he'd ever met was the one who had landed in his office.

He worked with beautiful women every day. The entire cast of *Secret Lives* consisted of stunning ladies. But something about Roslyn seemed almost wholesome… which was quite refreshing in this field.

Nigel unbuttoned his cuffs and rolled up the sleeves of his dress shirt as he went back to his desk chair. Distance from her would help him keep his head in the game, so would focusing on the sole reason for her employment. He needed a new vision for the show and the only way he could see that happening was to bring in an outsider.

There was no room for attractions or office escapades. The last thing he needed was a sexual harassment lawsuit. Of course, bad press would drive up ratings, but he wasn't about to embarrass his family, put his own reputation on the line or degrade any woman.

He respected women and his new consultant would be no different. There's no reason he couldn't find her attractive and keep a level head about himself…right?

"I saw you recently moved to New York," he began, leaning back in his seat.

Roslyn nodded. "About a month ago. It was time for a change."

"You came from Texas?"

"I did. My family owns a ranch." She eased her purse onto her lap and crossed her legs. "My brothers still live there."

"So why the drastic change?" he asked.

A sadness swept over her face for a second before she tipped her chin and silently gathered herself together.

"My father recently passed and it made me realize how fragile life is. I'd always wondered what city life was like and I decided to take the risk."

Taking risks was certainly something he could understand and appreciate. He hadn't gotten this far without stepping outside the proverbial box and taking his own chances in business. He understood her need to be out on her own, away from her family, and he instantly admired her drive and independence.

"I'm sorry for your loss," he told her. "I have to admit, I'm impressed that you took such a leap."

"No time like the present," she stated with that same confident smile that punched him with another dose of arousal.

"You have a degree in design." Nigel glanced at the portfolio photos on his computer screen he'd been looking at before she'd arrived. "These are pretty impressive. Why the switch to media? Did you just want to make a change?"

She shrugged one delicate shoulder. "Why can't I do both? I've always loved design and I'm fascinated by media. Who knows? Maybe one day I can design living spaces and work areas for the stars. This is a good step in that direction."

Nigel leaned forward, lacing his fingers together on his desk. "Is that what you're hoping to gain here? The chance to meet celebrities and get your foot in the door?"

Roslyn opened her mouth, but he quickly held up his hand. "I'm not judging," he added. "I think it's brilliant."

"You got me," she laughed. "I'm always thinking

ahead. I figure if I'm going to take the leap into a new kind of market, why not make it a big one? I want to cover a wide variety and when I have my own company, I'll be well versed in all the things."

"That's exactly the type of asset I want on my team," he told her. "What's your favorite food?"

Roslyn blinked, then laughed. "Excuse me?"

"Favorite food."

"Um… I don't know. I guess sushi. Why?"

"I like to have dinner meetings and I want to make sure I choose something you'll enjoy."

He hated most kinds of sushi, but this was New York. Plenty of places served a wide variety that could accommodate both of them. For now, though, he wasn't quite ready to end this talk and he wasn't ready to dive right into work, though that's exactly what he should have been doing.

"Why don't I show you around," he said, coming to his feet.

Craig would've normally tour new employees, but Nigel had already blocked this morning off because he wanted to do so personally… Now he wished he had let Craig retain that honor.

"There are aspects of this company that you should know from day one," he continued. "I want you to be comfortable and think of this as your second home for as long as you're employed here. We're all friendly and, for the most part, we all get along."

Roslyn stood and eased her purse back onto her shoulder. "That's impressive with such a big corporation. I'm excited to be part of something so positive."

As committed as he was to making sure his staff all

worked well together, he wouldn't settle for anything less, Nigel needed a little more drama and action on the set of *Secret Lives*. The show couldn't afford to be all sweetness and niceness all the time. There needed to be a reason for viewers to tune back in, excited to see what would happen next—but right now, he just didn't have the answers.

He did, however, have a new consultant eager to see the offices and he might just have to take her to the penthouse suite and show her that breathtaking rooftop view. The penthouse was used on occasion for special events with the staff since it had a large boardroom table and full kitchen. But, it also had a private en suite that he would sometimes stay in when his office hours became too long and he just needed to crash.

His job right now was to save his show, and this woman may be one of the most striking and gorgeous consultants he'd ever seen, but he needed her and he wasn't going to do anything to jeopardize his show... especially by hitting on his newest hire.

"We'll start with the best part of the entire building." Nigel gestured to the lift in the corner.

"Your own private elevator?" she asked, with a half grin. "I'm impressed."

"There are perks to being the CEO."

And as the CEO, it was his responsibility to remain 100 percent professional, 100 percent of the time.

He worked with gorgeous women every single day. This shouldn't have been any different...yet it was.

Two

Sophie wasn't sure how to deal with her spiral of emotions as she stood next to Nigel in the elevator. She wished she'd known that she'd be working directly with him. She wished she'd known just how potent this powerhouse truly was. And she sure as hell wished she'd known just how her entire body would heat because this was a completely new territory for her.

Granted she didn't believe anything could've fully prepared her for that heavy-lidded stare, the strong jawline, the right amount of expensive cologne and that polished British accent.

Mercy's sake. She certainly hadn't counted on how sexy a conversation with a Brit would be. How did any woman in this office get work done? How was *she* going to get work done? She couldn't afford to get fired from her faux job because she was too busy fantasizing about the boss.

The man opened his mouth and a slew of inappropriate thoughts filled her head. But that wasn't why she was here. Though the eye candy certainly didn't hurt.

A man like Nigel Townshend wasn't just a panty-dropper, he was a billionaire bad boy with a bit of a reputation. He always had the sexiest women on his arm at award shows and debuts. He'd been known to date some of the hottest supermodels in the industry, but, to her knowledge, he'd never been seen with the same woman twice, which led her to believe he was a player.

And she was the total opposite, considering she'd never been with a man.

What would it be like to be with a bad boy? Maybe that was precisely what she needed. Perhaps she should give herself to a man who knew exactly what he was doing.

Then again, she wasn't about to announce to a man she just met that she was a virgin. She wasn't ashamed of the fact, and she certainly wasn't sorry she'd spent her years building her career and devoting every waking minute to growing herself as a successful businesswoman and YouTube sensation. There was no rule or timeline for sex, and she'd do it when she was damn well ready or when a man intrigued her enough to make her want to.

Unfortunately, her new boss intrigued her way more than he should. She could easily imagine him doing a clean sweep of papers off his desk and ripping her clothes off in a heated moment of passion. The clothes would be utterly ruined, of course, but she wouldn't mind sacrificing these skinny jeans.

Why were they called skinny jeans anyway when she clearly had curves and wore a size sixteen? If they were supposed to make her feel skinny, then they were failing.

Regardless, she'd much rather think of Nigel finding her irresistible. Maybe late nights would turn into lingering glances or sensual touching. Not that she thought he'd do anything inappropriate…but a girl could fantasize, couldn't she?

The elevator chimed as the doors slid open. Just in time to pull her from yet another delicious daydream about her new boss.

Good grief. She had enough issues right now. She needed to focus on the job her brothers had trusted her to get done. Getting down and dirty with the CEO of Green Room Media was not quite the angle she'd been thinking of. Besides, she'd promised herself to be back in a week and getting tangled in anything other than her plan would eat up time she didn't have to spare.

Nigel gestured for her to exit the elevator, and as soon as Sophie stepped out, her breath caught in her throat.

"I had the same reaction when I first saw the view," he told her, staying right by her side. "I admit, it never gets old. There's something so timeless, so classy and sexy about the New York City skyline."

From this rooftop penthouse with a wall of glass windows all around the perimeter, Sophie felt as if she could reach out and touch the sun. She had to agree, there was something sexy about this view. Something almost…

powerful, like because you were on top of the world that meant the whole world was yours to command.

Even with the wintery conditions outside, she was surprised by how bright the sky seemed to be from this angle.

Wanting to explore each part of this magnificent space, Sophie took one slow step after another as her eyes raked over the rich masculine leather furniture, the chrome fixtures, the simplicity of the lighting and the breathtaking sights of the city. This was definitely a man's space.

She told a slight lie when she'd said she was a wannabe city girl. She mostly stayed to the country life, a laidback style that fit with her personality and the way she designed. City life always seemed so noisy and rushed…not just the cars but everything and everyone else, too. She felt that people were too busy doing their own thing to truly listen to others.

Sophie enjoyed people, she loved chatting and getting to know more about them. How else was she supposed to grow and develop her brand? She had to purposely put herself out there, so over the years, she'd just defaulted to a social butterfly.

Hey, that bold move had paid off, hadn't it? Her You-Tube channel ranked in the top ten interior designers of the entire site and she could easily see herself climbing even higher.

"Come closer," Nigel urged, cupping her elbow and escorting her to the windows. "This is the place I escape to when everything downstairs becomes too much."

Sophie glanced from the city below to the man at

her side. "And here I assumed there wasn't a thing you couldn't handle."

Nigel's lips quirked. "Don't give away my secret."

"Anything you say is safe with me," she promised. "I'm not here to judge. I'm here to help."

She wasn't here to expose him for anything…unless he was involved in some scandal alongside Miranda. And even then, she didn't want to hurt anyone so she wouldn't do any harm to Nigel.

But Sophie couldn't start digging just yet. She had to ease her way in. Day two, she'd put more of a push on the plot since time was of the essence.

"I imagine there's quite a bit to escape from and many reasons to clear your head." She focused her attention back to the view. "Even the strongest people need to take a mental health break."

"The business can be cutthroat at times," he admitted.

"Too many divas to work with?" she joked, hoping he'd follow her lead.

"The ladies on the show?" he asked, raising his brows. "They're not terrible. A few can be demanding, but overall, they don't cause me too much trouble."

Not what she wanted to hear, but she'd barely gotten started.

Passing the time with Nigel certainly didn't make her angry.

"So, do you live up here?"

Nigel turned his attention toward her. "Oh, no. I've stayed here occasionally after long days of work, but I generally use this to take a break. We've had a few in-house gatherings and private showings up here for the show."

"I don't want to give the wrong impression," she began, hoping she sounded stronger than she felt. "I mean, you know you're an attractive man—"

"*People Magazine* thinks so."

Sophie couldn't help but laugh. "As I was saying, I'm not here for anything other than a great opportunity to learn and be an asset to your team and maybe grow my own skills on the side."

Nigel lifted one dark thick brow.

"Professional skills," she corrected, still unable to stop smiling. Oh, he was a naughty guy, and she couldn't help but like that quality.

"Believe it or not, I need a personal consultant and I take this company very seriously."

He shoved his hands in his pockets and cocked his head in that sexy, arrogant way. There was no doubt Nigel was a force to be reckoned with. He was known around the world, not just for his charm and good looks, but for the way he'd started a company and grown this reality show with high-class divorcees and launched these ladies to superstardom…including Miranda.

"But since we're being honest," he went on. "You obviously have to know you turn heads."

While she wasn't vain, she also wasn't one of those women who feigned being ugly or put herself down in the hopes of gaining compliments. She was also well aware that some men found a plus-size woman unattractive. Those were the men she didn't have time for in her life.

While it was gratifying to know that he didn't fall into that category, Sophie didn't want to get into this topic with Nigel. She couldn't afford distractions and she certainly couldn't afford a rumor of the new hire trying to get ahead by flirting, or more, with the boss. Rumors would just draw unwanted attention to her. Miranda couldn't know Sophie was anywhere near this office.

"Well, now that all of that is out of the way, is the attraction going to be a problem?" she asked, holding his gaze and forcing herself to face this head on. She'd always believed in honesty.

Well, except for her current situation, where she was lying about her name and why she was there. But some things were simply a necessary evil.

"No problem," he assured her with a crooked grin and that toe-curling accent.

Maybe other people were immune to Nigel and that sultry voice, but she was new here, new to him. She'd have to put up her strongest steel defenses to keep some resolve between them.

"What else should you be showing me?" she asked. "Maybe where my work space is? Or what projects you'd like me to review?"

He stared like he wanted to say something, but she raised her brows, a silent question waiting on him to answer.

"Craig set up an office next to mine," he told her. "If you're going to be working with me, then I need you close by. The space is not overly large, but you do have a window."

"My own office?"

Sophie certainly hadn't expected that. An office right next to Nigel? This position was better than she'd ever hoped.

Things were lining up almost too well for her. But she had to ignore the pull she felt toward her new boss and concentrate on what she came here to do. She didn't change her life and her looks just to snag a Brit. Getting the scoop on Miranda was priority number one.

"Does my office come with an elevator?"

Nigel's lips twitched once again, and she noticed every time he became amused his blue eyes twinkled. So silly to notice such things, but she couldn't help but study and try to figure out more about him.

"Sure. It's the one you used to get from the lobby to the reception area."

Sophie rolled her eyes. "Not what I meant," she joked.

She turned her attention back to the view. This was certainly a far cry from the Blackwood Ranch and its open skies with fields of green. Still, this was a different kind of beauty with all the steel combined with old structure. Her designer eye took in all the various shapes and colors. The snow seemed beautiful on the buildings and balconies. She wondered what a fresh snow would look like on the busy streets. Probably kids enjoyed playing in it and throwing snowballs.

The wintery white had her thinking about the recent home office she'd decorated in white and soft blues with various pops of green.

"Do you always study your surroundings?"

Nigel's question pulled her back as he stepped in beside her. Sophie glanced over her shoulder and shrugged.

"Occupational hazard. I love designing and creating, so my mind is always working."

"You're perfect for this position," he stated.

Sophie swelled with pride, but there was a niggle of guilt. She wasn't here because she wanted to ensure the greater good of *Secret Lives*. No, she needed to see those precious unedited outtakes with Miranda. Surely there were some that revealed behaviors or hinted at secrets the producers didn't want the public to see. There had to be something juicy there.

"With this being your first day, I won't bombard you too much. But tomorrow, you better be ready to work." Nigel gestured toward the elevator. "What do you say we go check out your office and then I'll have lunch brought in. Sushi?"

Sophie nodded. "Sounds perfect."

Nigel shoved his hands in his pockets and stared down at the magnificent skyline. He'd been a complete idiot to bring Roslyn up here earlier. He never fraternized with his staff.

But from the second she'd stepped foot in his office, she'd had a presence about her that had drawn him in. She'd been poised, confident, polished, sophisticated. She'd been witty and that smile had been like a heavy fist to his gut, knocking the air right out of him. She almost seemed too good to be true.

And she had been honest. Brutally so when she'd confronted him about the attraction between them. Part of him was impressed that she'd been so bold, while the other part had secretly wished she would've acted on her baser impulses.

Bloody hell. What had gotten into him? He couldn't act like this, not even in his thoughts. This company was his everything. He'd come to New York wanting to start his own legacy and he had done a damn good job of it. He couldn't just throw that stellar reputation away because he had the equivalent of a teenage crush. He had to regain control of this situation because Roslyn had been here for one day and he was already second-guessing getting involved with an employee.

He had bigger issues to deal with—like the fact *Secret Lives* needed a major bump in the rankings.

The cell in his pocket vibrated. There was never downtime where he was concerned, not in his position overseeing the company and not when working with several socialites.

He glanced to the screen and saw Seraphina's name.

Seraphina Martinez, or Fee to close friends, was one of the ladies on *Secret Lives*. She had a big lavish lifestyle and a giving heart. There was nothing low-key about her and she was a fan favorite. Especially after she came out with her bestselling cookbook, *Not Your Mama's Cookbook*.

Nigel turned from the skyline view as he answered the call.

"Fee," he greeted. "How are you?"

"I'm good, thank you. Listen, I just wanted you to know I've been thinking of your offer and I'm not sure I can accept."

Not what he wanted to hear. Seraphina had fallen in love with real-life cowboy Clint Rockwell and they were planning their future together…in Texas. When she's talked about leaving the show, Nigel had tried to entice her into staying in NYC by offering her an impressive package that came with marketing for her cookbook, more airtime and a nice sum of money.

"Now don't turn me down yet, luv," he told her. "We can make this work. I was hoping you'd consider a spin-off."

"A spin-off?" she asked. "Nigel—"

"Just think about it," he interrupted. "A Southern series showcasing you and Clint in this new chapter of your lives would be something the viewers would love."

Not to mention maybe that would be the angle he needed to save his show.

Nigel rubbed his forehead and pulled in a deep breath. He hadn't come this far in his career to allow setbacks to deter him. There was no room to be a failure or even to be mediocre. Staying in the middle of the road in prime-time television might as well be the kiss of death. Another show would come along and bump them right off.

Maybe exploring new territory was something they needed to try. The cast had gone to Texas to Miranda's ranch for the Christmas episodes that had actually caused a slight uptick on the rating's scale.

"Clint is everything to me," Fee went on. "We're a team now, but I'll discuss this with him. I'm not sure he wants all the cameras following us around Texas."

"Just talk to him," Nigel repeated. "I bet an episode centered around your wedding would be a killer series opener."

Silence greeted him on the other end and he knew Seraphina well enough to know she was considering this option. His mind rolled from one idea to the next.

This could be the key to those ratings he desperately needed to boost.

"I'm just not sure," she finally stated. "Clint and I really want out of the limelight. We want to start fresh. Those fires that ripped through Royal really put things into perspective for me."

The fires she referred to had ultimately brought her and Clint closer together, but only after putting them both in a lot of danger. The town really pulled through and continued to rebuild. They'd all been affected in one way or another.

"Think about it," he told her. "Talk to Clint."

"I will," she replied. "I know I still have some time left on my contract—"

"We'll deal with that later. See what Clint says first and get back to me. Let's not borrow worries just yet."

"Thanks, Nigel."

He disconnected the call and blew out a sigh. His mind circled back to his new consultant and he wondered if she would be able to offer insight to a new project should Fee agree to it. He didn't want to disclose this new information just yet…but he hoped he could talk Fee and Clint into a spin-off, that may be the answer to his problems.

Also, he wasn't about to spout highly sensitive inside business secrets to a brand-new hire. He missed his assistant right now. Merryl always knew what to do or the right things to say, but she was out with her new baby.

But even if the spin-off happened, and became a real success, Nigel wasn't ready to give up on saving *Secret Lives*. It was the main show he'd started all on his own once he rose to CEO at Green Media Room.

He'd come to New York to do something grand, not having anything to do with the Townshend name. *Secret Lives* was what he had to show for all those years of hard work. It was his baby and he would do everything to see it thrive.

With as sharp and witty as Roslyn was, and with her impressive résumé on design, he knew she had a brilliant mind. He planned on putting that to use and making sure his show remained on the air.

Could she be the miracle he'd been waiting on? Was she even capable of doing what he'd been unable to do himself?

He didn't have all the answers, but he knew one thing for certain… He was going to get more time with Roslyn and he couldn't wait.

Three

Sophie had been surprised when she'd gotten to her office the next morning and there had been no sign of Nigel. Craig had said something about an emergency and had given Sophie a list of things to read up on for now. Later, she was to sit in on a meeting with a few of the crew members from the show.

Perfect. A meeting was just the type of jumpstart she needed. No doubt the team would discuss the cast members and Sophie intended to take detailed mental notes on Miranda.

A couple hours later, there was still no sign of Nigel, and Sophie had to admit, she'd found herself thinking about him while she'd been reading the materials in preparation for the meeting.

The only way she could let Nigel in her mind, in

her life, would be as a stepping stone to carry out her plan.

Unfortunately, she hadn't expected these newfound responses. No man had ever heated her the way Nigel did. She'd never found herself wanting to throw away her innocence so fast, but Nigel pulled out a whole host of sensations she'd never known existed within her.

Maybe it was the bad boy power trip, or maybe it was the way he'd looked at her like he was imagining her naked. Maybe it was the way he could banter with her like they'd known each other for years.

Regardless, she'd never had an intimate relationship, let alone a fling. That was the main reason she'd had to be completely honest yesterday. She didn't want Nigel to believe she was here for him or give him the wrong impression of her true nature.

Well, her sexual true nature.

If she'd met him under different circumstances—where she wasn't lying to him, where she'd have had the time to actually get to know him—she might see where this attraction would lead.

But the fantasy was moot and she had to remain focused.

Sophie grabbed the documents and her cell off her desk and stepped from her office. The notes on marketing and upcoming filming ideas regarding *Secret Lives* had been interesting from a viewer standpoint… if she bothered tuning into the popular reality show. And she actually might religiously watch the show if Miranda weren't on there. The other ladies were in fact really interesting.

Sophie had watched a couple of times, but just the

sight of Miranda acting all sweet and kissing cheeks with her bling sparkling in the lights was enough to make Sophie gag and change the channel.

The meeting room was down two floors and Sophie made her way into the elevator with a few other employees she didn't know. They chattered about office gossip, none of which was useful to her.

When Sophie stepped into the meeting room, she found a seat at the end of the long table and smiled at the young man next to her.

"You're new," he said. "I'm Miles."

Sophie nodded. "Roslyn. Nice to meet you."

"These meetings are so silly," he muttered as he leaned into her. "Any of this information could be sent in an email, but Mr. Townshend is really cracking down. He's actually been on edge more lately. The ratings have dipped lower than ever."

Sophie kept quiet as Nigel entered the boardroom. His baby blues swept over the handful of employees before landing on her. A thrill shot through her and she had no idea how the man exuded such power in a room full of people and with just one simple look.

"I gather you all read the marketing notes," he began as he took a seat at the head of the table. "We're taking a new approach to the social media aspect and I want to make sure we're all on the same page."

Sophie listened intently as they went around discussing the new segments and how to best maximize the social media content. She watched as Nigel seemed to take to heart each employee's suggestions and she had to admire a man who didn't pawn staff meetings off on other employees or use them as a platform to spout his own ideas without listening to anyone else. He didn't patronize any of his crew members or make them feel like their ideas weren't worthy or of value. That spoke volumes for what he was like as a CEO.

Sophie also wanted to chime in along with everyone else and tell them they were going about this completely wrong. From personal experience, she knew what pulled people in and she knew how to dive into a certain market to really target the niche market.

Added to that, consulting was also about listening to all of the facts before offering up her opinion or suggestions. She was new and didn't want to step on toes on her second day, so she chose to just remain silent.

Sophie did take down notes on things she would like to discuss with Nigel in private. She'd recommend different angles on their current marketing plans. After all, she hadn't blown up on YouTube for nothing. She liked to think she'd done a few things right and knew how to grab the public's attention. Of course it didn't hurt she excelled at her career choice, but she'd had to market herself and become a brand to get that initial attention.

Her eyes darted back to Nigel and...

Speaking of attention. He stared at her in a way no man ever had before—like he wanted more than her thoughts. And in a room full of people.

Someone else started speaking, but Sophie didn't hear what they said. Nigel broke the spell by glancing away, but Sophie couldn't quite focus for the rest of the meeting.

Once they concluded, she gathered her things and headed back to her office. That meeting hadn't produced anything she could use to further her plan. In fact, very little was said about the show's stars at all. When filming was mentioned, it was mostly locations being brought up for upcoming shots and how they would be marketing the show by implementing new ideas.

So, since there was nothing she could do right now to dig into Miranda's dirty secrets, she decided to stay in the marketing headspace and pull together some ideas and suggestions for the show. Sure, she wouldn't be staying long, but it would still look suspicious if she didn't have *any* work to show for her time on the clock. She couldn't just ignore the fact Nigel believed her to be legit. So long as she kept up this charade, she could possibly find everything she needed.

Sophie had a spreadsheet she'd used when first getting started on YouTube—basically the dos and don'ts and what worked and didn't work when it came to brand promotion. The marketing field was like a strategic game and if the players didn't know what move to make next, the entire plan could be for naught.

She realized there was an entire team here, but Nigel had wanted fresh eyes and that's where she came in.

The moment Sophie stepped inside her office and circled her desk, she glanced toward the doorway and let out a yelp.

"I didn't mean to startle you."

Nigel leaned against the doorjamb, his arms crossed over his broad chest. His hair was just a bit mussed, as if he'd raked his hands through it after the meeting.

Clearly she'd been so focused on her own thoughts, she'd missed the fact he'd practically been right behind her when she'd come in.

"No, it's fine," she replied, laying her things down. "I'm actually glad you're here."

"Is that right?"

"I have some things I want to run by you regarding a few marketing suggestions," she replied, ignoring the way he just stood there, staring, like he'd rather be doing anything else than talking about work.

"Why didn't you voice your thoughts during the meeting?" he asked, his brows instantly furrowed.

"Well, my job is to listen to all of the material before tendering my opinion," she informed him. "Plus, it's my second day and I wasn't sure your employees wanted to hear that I think most of their ideas are wrong."

Nigel studied her for a moment before he let out a bark of laughter and dropped his arms. "I do appreciate all of this honesty you provide. But, if we're going to talk, I say we should do so over lunch. Meet me in the penthouse in thirty minutes."

"I need about forty-five," she stated. "Trust me. I've got something to share with you."

He stared at her for another minute. Sophie didn't miss the crackle of tension. Even if she was here as a ruse, she had to be up front because she'd never been good at hiding her feelings. There was only so much lying she could handle.

"Listen," she started. "The attraction here is…"

Nigel quirked a brow. "Yes, it is," he agreed with a smile. "But, I would never get involved with an employee. I'm strict about that. Especially now when my sole focus needs to be on the show."

Sophie nodded. "Okay, good. Because I didn't come

here for a fling or anything else. I just can't stand tension and I had to talk about the proverbial elephant."

"I appreciate your bold honesty."

With a shrug, Sophie sighed. "It can put off some people."

"Men?"

She nodded.

"Then they're fools."

There it went again...that crackling tension. She waited on him to say more, but he wouldn't. He'd already made it clear he didn't socialize with employees. Too bad he didn't know she wasn't a legit staff member. Though he probably wouldn't be too thrilled with her if he knew why she was really there. Maybe it was better this way. They couldn't be together, but at least she knew he wanted to be.

"I'll see you upstairs in forty-five minutes," she told him, needing to shut this moment down.

Nigel offered her a grin and nod, then he turned and was gone. Sophie blew out a breath the moment he stepped away from her office. Revisiting the attraction issue wasn't going to get either of them anywhere they needed to be. She had to remain focused and so did he. They both had outside issues that needed their full attention...though he didn't realize that.

And had she seriously considered getting into something—a fling—with her fake boss? Sophie was either sleep deprived or else she had completely lost her self-control when it came to Nigel because she'd gone this whole time without giving herself to a man. Was she really ready to jump into it all because of a sexy accent and some sexy stares?

No, she wouldn't lose sight of why she was here. Her job was to find what she needed to secure her and her brothers' family legacy. Nothing more.

If maintaining her cover meant that her business ideas helped Nigel and she assisted in making any part of his team stronger, that would just be extra.

Sophie figured by the end of this charade everyone would win.

Nigel was still smiling when Roslyn arrived at the penthouse suite. He should've kept this meeting in his office, all professional, but that was not what had come out of his mouth, so here they were.

The woman was quite intriguing. He didn't know her well, but everything he'd uncovered so far seemed so fascinating. The fact she'd basically called his staff incompetent both irked and amused him. He couldn't wait to see what she thought she knew that could beat the carefully crafted plans from the well-educated, experienced team he'd personally vetted for these positions.

Maybe her ideas held merit or maybe she was just full of herself. Either way, he admired her for having the confidence to speak up…as if he needed more reasons to find her attractive.

Today she wore a fitted pair of black ankle pants with a black jacket and red pumps. Those damn pumps matched her lips. She looked like a '50s pinup come to life and, like an idiot, he'd purposely put himself alone with her. But he had a feeling she could have shown up wearing sweats and sneakers and he'd still have found her just as striking because his attraction wasn't just to the exterior… She was damn smart and bold. Qualities he couldn't ignore.

And that was not smart of *him*. Not if he wanted to retain control over his emotions. He had to push aside his desires and the way his body responded when she looked at him. He already had one mess on his hands with the rankings of *Secret Lives*, he didn't need a scandal by having a fling with his consultant.

"I had lunch brought up," he told her as she stepped from the elevator. "There's quite a variety. I assume you don't eat sushi all the time."

"I do like other things, you know." She carried her laptop and cell and walked to the chrome-and-glass desk in the corner to put her things down. "But I skipped breakfast, so anything sounds great at this point."

While they made their plates, he took note of things she liked, things she overlooked. He found he wanted to know everything about her…and please her with this knowledge in the days to come.

"So, tell me, what do you know that my very well-trained staff doesn't? This is what I needed when I searched for a consultant. I need that fresh look on things from someone who isn't in the industry, but who still pays attention to all details."

They took a seat at the desk across from each other. Instead of starting on her lunch, Roslyn pulled up her computer and swiveled it around to show him a graph she'd created.

"This is fairly rough, but I plugged in a few numbers to give you an example of what I'm about to explain."

Intrigued, he ignored his lunch, as well. He watched as she pointed from one colored area to the next. She'd clearly pulled numbers from the latest rankings that had been just discussed at the meeting. How the hell had she been so fast?

"You can see that the targeted viewers are mainly on social media during these times. But your posts are going up during different times and missing their mark." She noted the difference, then clicked onto another screen and another graph. "The posts are good—but most of them are getting lost in everyone's feeds." She pointed out a few posts that had come the closest to hitting the time slots she'd highlighted. "Look at the difference in engagement—the uptick in likes, retweets, responses. If you put up the juicier posts—the ones with more exciting content—in these time slots, I think you'd see huge results."

Nigel stared at the screen and listened to everything she said. All of her thoughts made perfect sense...which made him wonder why his very well-paid team hadn't considered this strategy before. This was the first he'd seen anything like this.

"You did all of this in the few minutes since we spoke?" he asked, turning his attention back to her.

"Well, I admit I jotted most everything down, but I also made some mental notes, so I may have missed a few of the opinions," she admitted. "But, it was merely a matter of plugging numbers in. I've taken quite a few online marketing classes, so I just used what I've learned. It's a rough draft, like I said, but I can get more concrete examples before the next meeting if you'd like."

Sexy, sophisticated and smart. He was in a hell of a lot of trouble here.

"You've taken marketing classes?" he questioned after a moment.

She nodded and shifted her computer aside, then pulled her plate and bottled water in front of her. "I love design but I knew I wouldn't be able to grow and reach more clients if I didn't understand how the whole social media system works. I needed to know how to interpret all the ins and outs. No matter how good I believe my ideas are for decor, I won't get anywhere without understanding the dynamics of every aspect of business."

The more she talked, the sexier she became. She adjusted her glasses, not in a coy flirty way, but out of necessity as they started to slip. A wayward strand of blond hair landed across her forehead and she swiped it back, tucking her hair behind her ear.

"So basically you want to practice the 20/20/20 method, as well," she went on, oblivious to the fact the more she discussed business, the more turned on he became. "Not only posting during the right times, but also actively engaging with various followers. The rule is twenty new followers, twenty new comments, twenty new likes. Now, with *Secret Lives* being so successful, we can bump that number up. Viewers want to feel important, like they have that personal relationship or connection to the ladies."

She plucked a juicy strawberry from the plate, studied it and popped it in her mouth. Nigel had never been so jealous of a piece of fruit.

"I would recommend the cast of the show following the same method," she added. "They're your ticket to new viewers. If they aren't hyping up the show, nobody else will."

"They post quite a bit during the season," he replied.

"But what do they do in the off seasons? And are they posting the right content?" she countered. "Are they getting viewers intrigued for another episode? Hinting at scandal or something teasing to pull more people into watching the new shows?"

Nigel pulled up various social media accounts from the cast and scrolled through. He quickly saw that she was right—their content needed to be more tailored, more focused. He had his marketing team divided into specialty groups, each one focusing on one specific area. Yet in less than two days, Roslyn had managed to nail down exactly what they needed and even had a damn graph to prove her point.

After several moments of silence, Nigel placed his phone on the desk and pulled his own plate over. He picked at his food, rolling around all the information inside his head.

"If I overstepped—"

"No." He stared across the desk. Roslyn didn't seem insecure as she met his gaze, which just raised his admiration another notch. "You didn't overstep. These are things I need to know and you're going above and beyond in such a short time."

"Good. I didn't want to step on toes, but I was hired for a reason."

His respect for this new hire continued to climb. Maybe she wasn't too good to be true. Maybe she was just this amazing and he'd hit the jackpot.

With each moment he spent with her, he found her beauty taking a backseat to her brilliant mind. Looks would only get someone so far in life and Roslyn was proving to be a great asset on many levels.

Damn shame he didn't get personal with employees. Since his position was so prestigious and everything he'd wanted when he came to New York, he wouldn't jeopardize that for anything. He wanted his family in England to be proud of what he'd done. He didn't want them to think he just came here and bounced from one beautiful woman to another. Yes, he dated quite a bit, but he also didn't flounce it all over the media, and he never ever dated someone from the show...or his office staff.

Roslyn was exactly the type of woman he hadn't known he was looking for. If she weren't working for him, then he wouldn't have minded getting to know her on a more personal level and building trust. Trust was so hard to come by in this industry when most people were only looking out for themselves and how they could get ahead.

But while a more intimate kind of trust wasn't an option between them, that didn't mean he couldn't enjoy Roslyn's company, perhaps more than he did with any other employee.

"If you start with Seraphina's account, for example." Roslyn pulled up the page and turned her phone toward Nigel. "Even her bio could be catchier."

Nigel felt the brewing of a headache and shook his head. "Seraphina may not be part of the show much longer."

He hadn't meant to let that out, but his instinct told him Roslyn could be trusted. She'd gone to great lengths to prove herself and if he wanted someone to help him grow in the rankings, she would need all the pertinent information.

Roslyn's dark eyes widened. "Oh, um… I wasn't aware. Not that you needed to tell me."

"It's okay," he replied. "I actually just found out recently that she was considering leaving—though of course, we don't want her to go. I was on the phone with her this morning offering her another option. That's why I was a few minutes late to the meeting."

"Does she want to leave?" Roslyn asked. "What will she do?"

Nigel had kept asking her that very question. "She's moving to Texas with a cowboy she met while she was filming down there. She and Clint are getting married."

Roslyn smiled. "Well, that's great news for them and for the show. That's a huge marketing tactic and an angle that every viewer would love. A happily-ever-after for one of your favorite ladies is like gold."

"Which is why I want her and Clint to do a spin-off," he confided. "I've talked to her about it, but she's not sure Clint would be on board."

Roslyn's gasped. "Yes. A spin-off would be perfect. There's nothing more valued than a real-life love story and people put so much faith in such fairy tales."

"Fairy tales?" he questioned. "You don't believe in true love?"

Roslyn shrugged. "It's not often I see it in action. I mean, I love my brothers and they love me. Actually, my oldest brother has found love, but that's a rarity, in my opinion. I can't say I had love from my father and he certainly didn't have it for my mother. He cheated on her and made no qualms about it even after she passed away of a stroke. I guess I'm just jaded on the whole thing."

Interesting. For someone so passionate about her work, it seemed that Roslyn went the complete opposite way when it came to her personal life.

"So if a man showered you with bouquets of your favorite flowers, you wouldn't be tempted to fall a little in love?"

Roslyn laughed as she sat her phone down and reached for her bottled water. "A bouquet of flowers is so clichéd. If a man brought me a single stem with heartfelt words, that would mean more than an entire expensive bundle."

"So you need pretty words?" he asked.

"I don't *need* anything," she corrected. "I deserve someone who is honest and wants to open his heart to me alone. I just don't think that man exists."

Nigel processed her words, understanding pain masked by a wall of defense.

"And what about you?" she asked. "Do you believe in true love?"

"I don't think it's some type of unicorn myth, but I haven't exactly had time to devote myself to looking. Though my grandmother is more than ready to marry me off and start another line of Townshends."

"That sounds a bit archaic," she scoffed.

"You don't know my grandmother. The woman is a force to be reckoned with. I'm terrified of her."

Roslyn laughed. "Well, maybe you should be looking for Mrs. Townshend."

Or maybe he should work on figuring out how to get Roslyn out of his every waking fantasy. How could he even think about another woman with the way he wanted her?

And what Nigel wanted, he always got.

Now if he could figure out how the hell to get around his own rule of not getting involved with his employees all while saving his show, he could retain his sanity and stay in control.

Four

Sophie pushed away from her desk and came to her feet, adjusting her shirt over the top of her black pencil pants. She really wished she hadn't gone all out in the transformation. She missed the comfortable yet fashionable dresses that had become her trademark. A good maxi and flip-flops sounded perfect right about now.

But with it being winter in New York, she was happy for the extra layers. Mercy, that wind could be brutal. She certainly missed the warmth and sunshine back in Royal, but she truly felt like she was getting somewhere here…and she didn't mean with just Nigel.

A tap on her door frame had her lifting her head to see Craig. "Hey. Mr. Townshend called and wants you to meet him for dinner. He texted you the address and time, but he wanted me to follow up with you."

Sophie reached for her phone on her desk. "I didn't hear anything come through," she muttered.

She tapped the screen and, sure enough, there was a message from Nigel about dinner, but she'd also missed two from her brothers. Clearly she needed to check in.

"Got it." She smiled at Craig and waved her phone. "I forgot I put it on vibrate earlier."

"No problem," he replied. "So, how's everything going? Settling in okay?"

Sophie nodded. "Seems to be going really well."

"I overheard Mr. Townshend chatting with a few guys from the camera crew." Craig stepped into her office and lowered his voice. "He mentioned you and some of your ideas for capturing snippets for teasers for social media."

Sophie couldn't help but feel a swell of pride. Over their lunch yesterday, she'd not only discussed posts but also various ways to showcase small segments to continue to draw new viewers in. She was trying to appeal to all walks of life, no matter the stage a woman was at. Divorced, married, stay-at-home-mom, career woman, whatever. There was something in each cast member that could appeal to any potential female viewer.

But on the coattails of her pride came the guilt. While she may actually be good at her job, she hated being deceitful. Nigel and Craig and everyone else she'd encountered were so nice to her, making sure she felt like part of the team.

"Well, I just hope those ideas pay off for *Secret Lives*," she replied.

"Seraphina might be off the show." Craig cringed. "That won't be good."

So apparently it was still just at the rumor stage—Nigel must not have told anyone but her. She felt quietly honored at his faith in her discretion. Sophie might want to pull out all the gossip on Miranda she could, but she wasn't about to add anything to the mix or get into the lives of the other women. And there was no way she'd betray anything Nigel trusted her with…unless Miranda's name came into the mix.

"That would be a shame," she replied. "It seems all the women mesh really well together."

Craig shrugged. "I don't know. Between the ratings and the potential loss of one of the cast members, I just hope the whole show doesn't go under. But, that's just my nerves talking. We still have some great women."

"Do you have a favorite?" she prompted.

Craig smiled. "Doesn't everyone? I'm partial to Miranda. That whole Southern charm she has is so fun. Plus, she's probably the nicest out of the bunch." He grinned at her. "You look surprised—did you get a different impression of her? It's always difficult to tell on screen, but even when the camera is off, she treats the staff with respect and is always so friendly."

Ugh. Not at all what she wanted to hear. But that was just one opinion and Sophie had just gotten started.

"Nobody can be that sweet all the time," she countered with a smile to soften her doubts. "I bet you know some juicy dirt on all the cast."

Craig playfully raised a hand to his lips and mimed turning a lock before he shrugged.

"I knew it," she joked, but she wished he'd give up a little more information. "How long have you been here, Craig?"

"Three years."

"So you've definitely seen the ladies at their best and their worst."

He nodded and leaned his shoulder against the wall. "You could say that. There have been a few cat fights behind the scenes."

"Oh, I'm sure," she added. "Strong, independent women like that? There would have to be some alpha tendencies that clash."

"They do," he agreed. "For the most part, though, they get along. Maybe that's why the ratings have dipped. People expect more drama from such reality shows. These ladies usually pull for each other because they all understand what it's like to be a divorced woman trying to start over."

Or trying to dig her greedy claws into things that don't belong to her.

"Plus, they all really bonded over the fires that broke out while they were helping Miranda deal with her new inheritance after her ex passed away," Craig added. "All of that was something out of a movie."

Yeah, Sophie was well aware of what a nightmare all of that had been…and still was. The inheritance, the fires. Royal was still recovering and the Texas Cattleman's Club clubhouse is undergoing yet another renovation. Only a few years ago the entire place had been revamped and updated. With these recent fires, a portion of the beautiful main building had been damaged.

But Royal was a tight community. There may be drama and gossip, but when push came to shove, everyone pulled together.

Sophie's cell vibrated on her desk and she glanced to the screen.

It was her brother Kellan.

"If you'll excuse me," she told Craig. "I need to take this."

"Of course," he told her, pushing off the wall and heading to her door. "I'll let Mr. Townshend know you'll meet him later."

She waited until she was alone before she took a seat behind her desk and answered the call.

"Kellan. What's up?"

"Irina and I haven't heard from you for a few days. Any news?"

Irina and Kellan were madly in love after an affair that led to them realizing they were perfect for each other. Irina had been their father's maid, and had a dark past as a mail-order bride, but Kellan treated her like royalty.

"Nothing I can use," Sophie admitted.

The only thing she'd gained was a stack of steamy fantasies about her utterly delicious boss…but Kellan probably didn't want to hear that. Divulging the fact that she was working right alongside the hottest man who gave her all the feels and all the dirty thoughts might not be the best idea. And yet, who could blame her? It wasn't her fault she was having a difficult time focusing whenever Nigel was near.

"Are you doing okay?" he asked. "I worry."

Always the worrier where she was concerned—and even more so now that she was in New York undercover.

"I'm fine and I promise to let you guys know as soon as I see or hear anything useful," she vowed. "It's just taking more time than I thought. So far, Miranda is dubbed a saint."

Kellan snorted. "Doubtful. Maybe you haven't talked to the right people."

"Well, there are quite a few here," she admitted. "I'm working my way through."

Sophie kept her voice low since her door was open, but she hadn't heard any activity out in the hallway.

"I'm hoping to get into the film room and check out some of the cut scenes," she murmured.

"That might be the ticket, and the proof, we need. If she admits to manipulating Dad, or using some trick to push the will through, we'll be able to challenge it in court," Kellan agreed.

"How's everything in Royal?" she asked.

"Same. Irina is still planning our big belated honeymoon trip and I'm working on another deal with a developer in Houston."

Sophie loved that her brother had found such happiness with Irina. They'd come together after Irina had suffered an abusive marriage. Buck had rescued her by offering her a job and a way out, but Kellan was the one who had truly healed her heart. Kellan and Irina were meant for each other and Sophie was glad they'd finally come back together after years of knowing each other and dancing around the attraction.

The Blackwood children deserved their own happiness, but Sophie wasn't sure settling down with some perfect guy was in the cards for her. She certainly wasn't looking for love. Such an emotion didn't exist for everyone and she wasn't holding her breath that it would happen to her.

But lust? Yeah, that was not an issue.

Nigel made her want to throw out her vow to hold on to her virginity until the right man came along. She'd decided long ago there wasn't a right man or anyone she felt worthy enough to give that piece of herself to.

She didn't want to have sex just for the sake of having sex. Maybe she was in the minority with that line of thinking, but she didn't answer to anyone and she was proud of the fact she didn't sleep around to feel good about herself.

Nigel, on the other hand, had her envisioning flings and heated nights…and naughty whispers in her ear with that sexy British accent. Maybe if he'd come along sooner in her life, or if she were here under different circumstances, she would see just what could happen if she let herself go and let her desire guide her decision-making.

"Sophie?"

She jerked her attention back to the conversation. "Sorry," she replied. "I got distracted."

"You sure you're okay?" Kellan asked. "You don't have to do this. We can find another way to contest the will and make Miranda give up what's ours."

"I swear, I'm fine," she insisted. "Listen, I need to get back to work, but I'll be in touch."

"Love you."

"I love you, too," she replied before she ended the call.

Sophie glanced at the time and realized she only had a few hours before she had to meet Nigel. There were a couple angles she was working on for him and she wanted to finish up. The more she proved to be useful, perhaps the more he would trust her with the show's secrets. He'd already disclosed Seraphina's personal issue. He was bound to know *something* about Miranda that went beyond public knowledge.

Sophie's entire goal here had hinged on her finding useful gossip or some sort of concrete proof that Miranda had lured Buck into giving his estate to her. Sophie didn't believe her father had done so just because. But even if he had, Sophie didn't think she and her brothers should just be cut out of a family legacy.

Since Sophie was working so closely with Nigel, perhaps she should find ways to use that to her advantage. He would know these women better than probably anyone on the set. They trusted him and confided in him.

Sophie wasn't about to use her body to get information—she would never do something like that. But spending extra time with Nigel over dinners or coming up with new ideas to get into his office for extra minutes could lead to conversations she could use later.

After all… Nigel had clearly made it apparent he was interested. Maybe he would trust her with more and then she could get back to Royal…before she ended up losing her innocence.

Five

Nigel came to his feet when Roslyn entered the private room. He'd requested his usual spot on the second floor of Manhattan's poshest restaurant. He wanted no interruptions.

"I'm so sorry I'm late." Roslyn pulled off her red scarf and coat, then shook out her golden hair. "It takes quite a bit longer to get around the city than where I'm from."

"Country girl," he joked, gesturing for her to take a seat in the curved booth next to him.

The hostess took Roslyn's coat and scarf before leaving them alone.

The flickering candle and the tight bundle of white roses in a gold vase on the table set a romantic vibe, one he wasn't purposely trying to create. He'd wanted to spend time with her, and he'd wanted a good dinner. Why couldn't he have both? The decor wasn't his fault—it came with the room.

"I'll take your crazy traffic into account next time we meet," she told him.

"I'll send my driver next time," he replied.

"That's not necessary. I doubt you do that for your other employees."

True, but she wasn't just any employee. An argument he wasn't going to have now. He'd just send the car next time and she would have no choice but to allow him to make her life easier.

"Which reminds me of something I've been meaning to ask," she added, turning to face him. "Everyone in the office calls you Mr. Townshend, yet you told me to call you Nigel."

Busted.

"You're working closer with me than most of them do. Would you like a glass of wine?" he asked, instead of going in circles with an argument he'd ultimately win anyway.

"White, please. And nice dodge."

Nigel merely smiled with a wink as he got the waiter's attention and ordered drinks. Once they were alone again, he shifted toward her.

"Craig tells me you've been busy all day. I believe the words he used were *huddled over your computer and muttering to the keyboard*."

Roslyn smiled and tipped her head. "I may have been working on a few things."

"Such as?"

She turned and reached inside her bag and procured a folder. "I was hoping you'd ask. I went ahead and came up with some possible scenarios for some upcoming segments. Just a few things that would entice viewers to keep tuning in and expand your base."

Intrigued, and more than turned on at her work ethic and passion, Nigel eased closer. He wanted to get a look at what she'd brought, but he'd be lying if he claimed he didn't want to just get closer, to inhale that sexy floral scent that permeated from her. For such a country girl, she seemed to blend right in with this city life. She worked hard, hustled harder and had class, beauty and brains that just begged for anyone around her to notice.

Why was he torturing himself? Why didn't he just find another woman to spend time with…and one that would guarantee a satisfying ending to the evening?

Because none of the women he knew fascinated him like Roslyn Andrews.

Nigel listened to her talk, watched as she flipped from one graph to the next and even discussed pulling in a few celebrity appearances, perhaps at a cocktail party hosted by one of the ladies.

"Because if they hype up the event on their social media, you will instantly expand your viewer base," she finished.

Nigel extended his arm along the back of the booth. "Impressive."

Her smile beamed and her eyes sparkled. "I really think the solution to your problem is simple, but it will require a little grunt work."

Story of his life. He'd never met anyone who worked harder than him…until now. But her ideas and ingenuity were the exact match he needed not only to keep his show afloat but to rise higher than ever in the rankings.

"Let's take a break," he told her. "I skipped lunch and I'm hungry enough to order one of everything."

Roslyn laughed. "I'm not sure I'm that hungry, but I'd love an appetizer or bread to go with this wine."

They ordered and once they were alone again, Nigel wanted to dive into more about her personal life. There was a need to learn everything about her, which he couldn't explain, and wasn't even going to try. It had been a long time since a woman intrigued him like Roslyn. Everyone in the office who had met her so far had been just as fascinated and impressed by her work ethic and her drive... Her sweet Southern accent also went a long way in charming some of the men.

Nigel didn't like it, but he couldn't blame them. Roslyn was the complete package.

"So, you came to the city because you wanted a change after your father's passing," he began. "Are you enjoying the lifestyle here? Other than the traffic, that is."

"It's definitely an adjustment. I'm not sure I'd ever get used to all the chaos. Texas is a big state and I'm used to land and green grass with sunny blue skies." She hesitated before tipping her head and leveling his gaze. "Where are you from originally?"

She wanted to turn the tables? Fine by him. He didn't mind sharing his backstory, especially if that meant she was just as interested in him as he was in her. Maybe that was his ego talking, but he didn't miss the way she looked at him. He'd been hit on and charmed by many women—a man in his powerful position was prone to such things. Roslyn wasn't trying to seduce him with her pretty words or sexy clothes...yet she did all the same.

Everything about her turned him on and the differences between them kept tugging at him to uncover more. Because the more he found how different they were, the more he realized how much they complimented each other.

"My family is back in Cumbria, England," he told her. "Beautiful countryside and I love it when I'm there, but I also love the city. No reason I can't have the best of both worlds. I understand the appeal of vast land with green as far as the eye can see. That sounds like where I grew up."

"I bet you have horses," she guessed, curling her fingers around the stem of her wine glass. Yet, she never took her eyes off him as she smiled.

"We do," he replied. "It's something my grandmother and I always shared a passion in. When I go home, we always have a date at the stables."

"You've mentioned your grandmother before. I take it you two are close."

Roslyn shifted in her seat, causing the strands of her hair to brush against his hand behind her back. He couldn't resist sliding the ends between his fingers, his eyes darting to the golden strands.

"Your hair is so damn soft," he muttered before he could stop himself.

"Your grandmother."

"I've never felt her hair."

Roslyn laughed. "We were talking about your grandmother."

"We were, but I'd rather talk about you."

She hesitated for a second and the moment was broken. He pulled his arm back, not wanting to make her

uncomfortable or come across as a creepy boss. Hadn't
he told her he wouldn't get involved? How did she continue to pull him in? It was that damn mind of hers.
She was too fascinating, too intoxicating. He continu-
ally wanted more.

"Tell me more about this hometown of yours," he
said. "You know, Miranda also lived in Texas for a
time."

"I'm aware," she replied. "I made it a point to study
up on all the cast. I assumed that was part of my job,
right?"

"Always circling back to work." Nigel shook his head
and reached for his glass. "I've never met anyone who
cares about work as much as I do."

"Well, I care about my job and making a good impression," she stated. "I've always believed anyone can
make a difference, no matter how small their position
or their financial background."

She had the perfect words for everything. Literally
everything.

He'd been toying with an idea since the last staff
meeting, but he'd thought it too soon to jump the gun.
Now, though, he wasn't so sure. Maybe his idea was
exactly what was best not only for him, but for the
company.

"I want to run something by you," he told her.

"Okay. Are we back to discussing work?"

Nigel couldn't help but smile. "For the time being.
What do you say to working as the lead on the marketing for Serephina's wedding? I mean, not the actual wedding, but the marketing of the buzz around
the show? If you could draw something up that I could

show her, maybe we could convince her to air their nuptials—possibly into a new spin-off."

The idea rolled out of him as he continued on, hoping she would take this on. Roslyn's eyes widened, her mouth dropped open. After a moment, she regained her composure and took a sip of her wine.

"Well, I'm flattered you'd consider me for one of the most important episodes if that happens." She muttered the word as if rolling the idea around in her mind, thinking out loud so as to clarify her answer in some way. "I would love to draw something up for you. I hope that will convince Serephina to agree to the show."

A heavy weight lifted from his shoulders. Things seemed to be falling into place and Nigel was certain that everything he ever wanted was right in front of him.

"Who knows what will happen, but I'm confident with your plans and ideas. Fee will have a difficult time turning this down. She loves the other ladies and this show, and she still wants to see everyone succeed. I have faith in you that you're my key to getting this show back at the top of the rankings."

Something passed over her face, something he couldn't quite identify. After a moment, Roslyn squared her shoulders and gave a clipped nod.

"I won't let you down."

Sophie drained her second glass of wine and wondered yet again what the hell she'd gotten herself into. Agreeing to another project for Nigel? She didn't have time for all of this. She needed to get in and out of this job and this persona before Miranda knew she was here.

She needed to get back to her life in Royal and back to her legacy.

But she couldn't turn Nigel down. When he looked at her with that hope in his eyes, she knew how much he wanted this show to thrive. She saw how hard he worked, how invested he was in the program he'd created. Isn't that what she wanted? She wanted the life she worked so hard for, the life she was entitled to.

Nigel could've asked her anything and she would've agreed.

She reminded herself that the closer she pulled herself to the mogul, the better her chances were to find the exact information she needed. On the other hand, taking on a longer project may prove to be dangerous... from all angles. Still, she would stay until she got the ammunition she needed on Miranda and then Sophie would have to go.

"How was your dinner?" Nigel asked.

Sophie glanced down to her plate and was shocked she'd been able to eat a bite, what with the guilt and nerves fighting for top spot in her belly.

"Fine," she lied with a smile. "Much better than grabbing takeout and heading back to my apartment."

Her uptown penthouse was actually perfect. She'd spared no expense when looking for a short-term lease. She'd had to pay for the entire month, but she would be out long before that...she hoped.

The glass walls she had offered her a spectacular view of Central Park, and with the snow they'd had lately, every time she looked out her windows, she felt a little bit of giddiness. She didn't have snow in her part of Texas and the blanket of white always took her breath and inspired her for future designs.

"We can dine together every night if you prefer not to eat alone," he replied, placing his napkin on the table.

"This isn't a date."

"Of course not. You know I don't date employees." Nigel quirked a brow. "Did I imply it was?"

"Actually, yes."

He laughed and shrugged. "I like your company, both professionally and personally. You're not immune to all of this, either."

There went those nerves again. And when he'd toyed with the ends of her hair? Revved up all of her sexual urges with the simplest of ways. Still, he didn't get involved with his staff, or so he kept saying, and she couldn't throw away her virginity on a man she was lying to and essentially using.

Except, she wanted to. Mercy how she wanted to.

She was so out of her league here. The flirting, the charm... She was a complete innocent in every sense of the word.

"Dating would certainly complicate things," she finally stated. "I mean, I'm only working for you temporarily and for all you know I have a boyfriend back in Texas."

Nigel reached for her hand, stroked his thumb along the top of her knuckles, and stared directly into her eyes so intently that she'd swear he could see into her soul.

Oh, boy. He may keep saying he didn't date employees, but he hadn't said anything about making said employees ache with desire.

"If you have a man in Texas, then he's a fool for letting you come here alone."

Oh, that low British accent had her toes curling in her Ferragamo pumps. There went that belly flutter again.

"Do you hit on all of your employees?" she asked.

"I've never made a pass at any woman I worked with," he explained. "I've never wanted to."

Until now.

The words hovered between them and she wished she could ignore the blaring bells and red flags waving in her mind. If this were another time, another place, if she could show him her true identity and start over, then maybe this attraction could lead to something more.

But the harsh reality was she was only here to take down her ex-step-monster. She'd gone to drastic measures to do so and she couldn't get sidetracked now— not when she'd promised her brothers. And besides, how could they build anything real between them now? She couldn't keep up the facade forever, and the more deeply they got involved, the more betrayed he'd feel when he learned she'd been lying to him all along.

"I have to attend the CBN Awards Ceremony on Friday. I was going to go alone because it's not a big deal and I know this is last minute but…" That thumb continued to stroke her hand and he eased just a touch closer. "Join me."

"Nigel, I—"

"I'll send my personal stylist to your office tomorrow morning," he went on. "Choose anything you want and I'll make sure hair and makeup are informed you'll need their services. They'll come to you, so don't worry about that."

Was she living in some warped version of *Pretty Woman*? Turning into someone she wasn't and getting a makeover to go out and be draped on the arm of the hottest man she'd ever met?

If her brothers had any idea Nigel Townshend was hitting on her, or the way he kept looking at her and touching her, they'd have had her on the jet back to Texas before she could even say *Pretty Woman*.

"I'm not sure how it would look—my going to an awards show with you," she replied. "Especially since I'm new and we just started working more closely together."

Not to mention the fact if the cast of *Secret Lives* was there, Miranda would recognize her right off the bat. Glasses and blond hair would only cover so much.

"Won't you want to go with the ladies from the show?" she asked. "You know, like a united front?"

"This isn't a ceremony for them," he replied. "It's for directors, producers, creators. It's a small affair, but I'm expected to attend."

Miranda wouldn't be in attendance? He was offering up a free dress, hair, and makeup, and a night of schmoozing?

Beyond all of that, Sophie had never felt such a pull, such an instant bond to another man. How could she just ignore all of that? Yes, this was the worst possible timing considering the circumstances, but she was in the thick of things now, so…

Sophie smiled. "I'd love to go."

The smile that spread across Nigel's face had her wondering if she'd just sacrificed every part of her sanity… and her heart.

Six

"Okay, Nigel," Lulu said, as she stepped from her en suite. "I'll try to hint around to Fee about her wedding. I agree it would be amazing to make it a special episode of the show."

"Thanks, Lulu," Nigel replied. "I knew I could count on your support."

She disconnected the call and slid her cell into the pocket of her robe.

Lulu Shepard may be one of the stars on *Secret Lives*, but her life was crumbling. Her very best friend, the one she confided in and went to when she needed a trusted soul, was leaving the show.

Seraphina had found love and was moving to Texas to begin her life. Lulu was happy for her, but selfishly she wanted her friend to stay in her life, as a constant, reassuring presence. Though she did love the idea of the wedding being aired for the world to see. The love Fee and Clint found should be shared and celebrated at any opportunity.

But after the wedding…what would Lulu do with Fee so far away? Their luncheons would be reduced to texts and occasional calls. Even now, Fee was away more than she was home, spending as much time as she could with Clint in between packing up her life in Manhattan. It was almost enough to make Lulu wish she'd stayed longer in Texas… But no, it was better that she'd left.

This show was such a huge part of her life and she loved every aspect of it. She truly had no idea what she'd do if the show failed or if she didn't have that constant in her life anymore.

The doorbell rang and Lulu glanced to the time. Nearly ten o'clock. Who would be stopping by this late?

Clearly someone the doorman knew, but he hadn't buzzed her to let her know, meaning it was either a neighbor or the guest was on the list to be allowed up unannounced.

That narrowed down her suspects to just a handful.

She crossed her penthouse and looked out the peephole. The one person she both wanted to see and wanted to avoid stood on the other side.

Kace LeBlanc.

She tightened the knot on her silky robe and pulled in a shaky breath as she slid the lock and opened the door.

"Kace."

Those warm brown eyes landed on her and she felt the jolt just as fiercely as if he'd reached out and touched her.

She'd done some reckless things with Fee and the

cast of the show, but none had been as reckless as starting to lose her heart to Kace. The man was the opposite of her, he lived in Texas, he irritated the hell out of her... But she couldn't deny there was still something about him that turned her on in ways she couldn't explain.

She'd seen a different side of him when they'd helped clean up from the fires in Royal. He'd not been so cocky and arrogant. He'd been...strong, powerful, commanding in a ridiculously sexy sort of way as he'd worked to get things organized and put the town back in order.

And she'd ultimately given in to that attraction. Who could blame her? There was no way she could keep denying herself, denying him.

"What are you doing here?" she finally asked.

His eyes raked over her state of undress and she shivered once again. Who knew a stare could be so potent?

Kace took a step forward, urging her back until he was inside and could close the door behind him.

"I'm in town for business," he told her. "I was walking to my hotel and the next thing I knew, I ended up here."

"Without calling or texting?" she asked, irritated that he could get to her on every level. "That's rude, Kace, even for you."

He took one step closer. "Are you going to turn me away?"

Lulu crossed her arms to keep from reaching for him. "No. No, I'm not."

The smile that spread across his face had her wondering what the hell she was getting in to.

"Did I tell you how stunning you look tonight?"

Sophie didn't need the words. She could tell by the

way Nigel kept close to her side, the way his eyes would roam over her as if he knew exactly what she looked like out of this sultry red dress that fit her every curve.

When she'd seen all of the options for her to try on, she'd fallen in love with this one immediately, unable to stop herself from imagining how Nigel would respond to the sight of her in it. He hadn't disappointed. She should've turned him down, she should've stayed focused on her task and not gotten swept up in all of the glitz and glamour and limo rides with a sexy man.

Yet here she sat in the back of his car as they maneuvered through the city streets. He shifted in his seat and his leg brushed hers, as if she needed the reminder of how close they'd been all evening.

Throughout the entire night, Nigel had constantly touched her in some way—his hand on her lower back to guide her, his thigh aligning with hers beneath the table at dinner, a simple hand holding hers as he led her to and from the car.

"There wasn't a man in that ballroom who wasn't mesmerized by you," he went on. "I'm glad you were my date."

"So this *was* a date?" she asked, trying to search his face as the flashes of the lights off the streets and buildings slashed across his features.

"What if it was?"

Be careful.

The voice rang through her head, but she ignored it. There was nothing careful about being this close, this attracted to the man she was deceiving.

She'd never misled a single person in her life and

here she was lying to the one person she actually wanted to get to know on a personal level.

But there was so much chaos going on in her life, how could she even think about something personal with Nigel? Their lives were worlds apart and he didn't even know her real name.

"I thought you didn't get mixed up with employees," she countered.

He slid his fingertip along the slit in her skirt…the one that extended all the way up her thigh. Sophie shivered as her eyes darted from his hand to his face.

"I never have," he agreed, with a level gaze. "Maybe I've changed my mind…if you're interested."

Up and down that fingertip went. He touched her nowhere else, but she couldn't suppress the arousal that spiraled through her. She needed to put a stop to this… She'd needed to stop him long ago, such as when he'd asked her to join him for dinner or when he'd stared at her in the penthouse office like she was the most delectable thing and he was a starving man.

"Nigel—"

His finger stilled. "Should I stop?"

Sophie pursed her lips as a silent sparring battle took place between her awakened wants and common sense.

But she'd put her career ahead of her personal life for so long. Couldn't she just take what she wanted? Just this once? Who said she had to save herself for the right man? What if that perfect one never came along? What if Nigel *was* the right man?

"You're thinking," he murmured. "I can practically see you arguing with yourself."

"Sometimes I just want to ignore what's right, what's

expected of me." Her thoughts spilled out before she could keep them inside. "Do you ever have that guilty feeling that you're being selfish?"

Nigel's eyes dropped to her lips. "Every decision I make is on purpose. So, no. I don't have regrets."

Of course, someone as powerful and confident as Nigel wouldn't second-guess his actions. He likely had his life all laid out to perfection with no worries of consequences.

Sophie had always prided herself on her own strength, but sitting in the back of a dark car with her faux boss had her willpower shrinking. Even before tonight, he'd mesmerized her and made her wish for and want more than she'd ever allowed herself.

Why couldn't this be easy? Why couldn't she have met him under different circumstances? Why did she have to choose between holding true to her legacy and the promise to her brothers and going after what she desperately wanted?

Before Sophie could say anything, the car came to a stop and moments later, her door opened. The driver extended his hand to assist her and as soon as she stepped out, she realized they weren't at her penthouse, but back at Green Media.

She glanced back to Nigel as he exited the vehicle.

"That will be all, James."

The driver got back into the car and drove away.

"How am I going to get home?" she asked.

Nigel smiled. "If that's where you want to go, I'll have him come back."

"And my other option?"

"Coming up to the penthouse with me."

She took one step toward him, silently telling him she wanted just that. She wasn't sure why he brought her here, maybe he wanted to do some work later, maybe he wanted her to feel like they were on neutral ground since they both worked here…she had no clue.

Her imagination went into overdrive and she wasn't so sure she was ready for more than this sexual banter and heavy tension. But if not now…when?

They were clearly attracted to each other and they were both adults. She was tired of always working. Even with her fake work she was working.

While she loved her job, it had always come ahead of her own personal life. Like now. Even her faux job was getting in her way.

Sophie adjusted her clutch beneath her arm and pulled in a shaky breath.

"I could use a drink first," she admitted, shivering against the cold.

Nigel removed his suit jacket and draped it around her shoulders. Now she was fully enveloped by his scent, his warmth. Another stepping stone on this path they'd started down together.

A glass of wine sounded good right about now. Who knows, maybe they could start talking and she'd find more information on Miranda, because so far her search had turned up nothing useful. Wasn't that why she was here? To get some sort of proof that her stepmother swindled her way into the will and deceived Buck?

Or maybe Sophie was here at this moment to do something for herself. To finally give in and take what she'd denied herself for so long. Because right now, she wanted to be here for Nigel and absolutely nothing, or no one, else.

"A drink," he repeated with a crooked grin. "I can manage that."

She'd never been more aware of any man in her life than she was in that elevator on their way up to the penthouse. There was plenty of room, yet he stood at her side, with his hand beneath his jacket at the small of her back where her dress dipped low and exposed her bare skin.

That woodsy cologne of his had tantalized her all evening. She'd never been turned on by a man's scent before, but, well, everything with Nigel was becoming her first.

The door slid open and she stepped into the penthouse. As she walked through, the lighting automatically lit up her path. The view of the city below drew her to the wall of windows. The swirling snow shone bright as it caught the various lights from buildings and the streets below.

"I never thought I'd be so mesmerized by snow."

Nigel's dress shoes shifted across the hardwood floors. "You look good in the city. This life suits you."

If he only knew how much she missed her old self. Her boots and flip-flops, her long, flowy dresses. Pants were of the devil and she was so over them. Give her a nice maxi or A-line sheath any day over skinny jeans and tailored jackets.

She missed the ranch and wondered what all was going on now. She missed her French-inspired home in her luxurious gated community. And she desperately missed her own bed.

A flash of an image with Nigel in her bedroom

pierced her thoughts. He could never be there. He could never know she was truly a Blackwell. If he ever discovered why she was truly here, he'd never forgive her and he'd never believe she hadn't set out to deceive him.

If he could have only known the real Sophie without this deception getting in the way...

"You prefer red or white?"

Sophie glanced over her shoulder to Nigel at the bar in the corner. She offered a smile and gripped the lapel of the jacket, pulling it tighter around her chest.

"I think you know by now I prefer white."

He picked up the stem he'd already poured. "Just making sure," he said, returning her smile.

As he made his way over to her, Sophie tried to put her worries, her betrayal out of her mind. She took in the sight of her date bringing her a glass of wine, thought of how quickly he'd wrapped her in his jacket, remembered how he'd been impressed with her ideas and gave her credit for them without stealing them as his own when he very well could have.

Nigel was a noble man, a man she could easily fall for...was already falling for.

This date was going far beyond what she'd envisioned.

Date. She really shouldn't let that term settle in because actual dating wasn't possible for them. A date would imply there could be more, but other than attraction and flirting...this was all there could be.

Unless she was up front with him with as much as she could be and still not ruin her quest for the downfall of Miranda.

"I'm not naive," she told him as she took the glass. "I'm also not going to deceive you."

Well, not any more than she had to.

Nigel held onto his tumbler and raised his brows. "Is there something you think I've misunderstood?"

She pulled in a breath and took a sip of her wine before she exposed a very personal truth. "I've been focused on my career and trying to grow my design business, so my social life has taken a backseat."

More like it wasn't even in the car.

"I want to be the best at any job I do," she went on. "So dating hasn't exactly been on my radar."

"I'll take it as a compliment that you made an exception for me."

Sophie rolled her eyes. "You would," she laughed before pulling in a deep breath. "What I'm trying to say is that I realize you called this evening a date and I'm positive you brought me up here hoping we could extend our...um..."

"Oh, now you're shy?" he asked. "You've been so blunt and honest since you came to work for me. Don't stop now."

"Fine." She squared her shoulders and tipped her chin. "We've already agreed there's an attraction, so I won't pretend you don't hit every button for me."

"Is there a but?"

"But," she went on, "you need to know one vital piece of information before you decide anything else about me."

He took a sip of his own drink and took another step closer to her. "And what's that?"

"I've never been with a man before."

Seven

Nigel stared at Roslyn and waited for her to laugh or tell him she was joking. But those bright eyes continued to hold his and she didn't even offer a hint of a smile.

An innocent. He honestly didn't know any adult who was still a virgin. Yet the one woman he'd been craving for days—even though it sure as hell seemed much longer than that—stood before him as vulnerable as she could be. Quite the juxtaposition to her bold, confident personality in every other aspect of her life.

She hadn't had to tell him, yet she'd trusted him with her most personal piece of information.

"I totally understand if you want to end with the drinks and call your driver to come get me."

Without a word, Nigel took the glass from her hand and sat both of their drinks on the accent table. Turning back to face her, he stepped closer to her and framed her face until she had no choice but to look directly at him.

"I've said this before, but I've never met anyone like you."

Her eyes studied him. "I can't tell if that's a good thing or a bad thing."

"Good," he laughed. "Definitely good."

"So... I'm staying?"

His body stirred and he had to force himself to move slowly. He'd never had to worry about this before, but he found that her being a virgin wasn't a turn off at all... quite the opposite, actually.

"Everything from here on out is your call," he told her, grazing his thumb across her plump lower lip.

He'd never relinquished control of anything in his life, but found that's exactly what he wanted to do with Roslyn. He not only wanted her comfortable, he wanted to follow her lead, to learn with her as she expressed herself and explored her passion.

Nerves settled deep and he had to tamp down the anxiety over the thought that he was taking advantage. He wasn't about to do anything she didn't want, but he had questions.

"Were you that focused on work you didn't take time for yourself?"

"I want to make a name for myself," she told him. "Personal life could always come later."

Or now.

Nigel leaned in and slid his lips across hers. Her swift intake of breath and the increased pulse at the base of her throat only increased his need to make her feel everything she'd deprived herself of.

The fact that he was the first one to even make her think about giving herself up in such a way was more than an ego boost…it was a bloody treasure.

"So why are you here with me?"

She licked her lips and he knew the act stemmed from nerves and not some practiced ploy. "Because I can't help myself," she murmured honestly. "I've never felt drawn to someone the way I've been drawn to you. I know it's not right since you're my boss and I've tried to ignore what I feel."

Nigel eased the jacket from her shoulders and tossed it aside. "What do you feel?"

He tipped her head and braced one arm around her lower back to hold her firmly against him.

"Attracted, desired." Her eyes dropped to his mouth. "Aroused."

For someone so innocent, she knew all the right words to say. She raised her hand, hesitated, then placed it on the side of his face.

There was that hint of insecurity. He'd never seen even an inkling of that in the office. She'd always been confident and strong. Even in the minor position she'd been hired for initially, someone like Roslyn was too big in life to be a simple consultant.

"Don't be afraid," he told her, even though fear pumped through him. He wanted everything to be perfect for her. Roslyn deserved more than for him to swipe off the top of his desk and lay her out.

She'd never done this before and he had to respect her reasons why…even if they were foreign to him.

Nigel took her hands in his and stepped back. Then he led her to the oversize leather sofa and urged her down. As she sat, those expressive eyes stared back at him. He'd have given anything to rip that excuse for a dress off her body and explore her tempting curves with his eyes, his hands, his mouth, but he didn't want to rush or frighten her.

Self-control was key here.

Roslyn started to reach for the top of his pants, but he pulled away. Confusion flashed across her face as she stared back up at him.

Nigel dropped to his knees in front of her, circling her waist with his hands, and leaning in to brush his lips across the swell of her breasts where her dress dipped.

"Trust me," he murmured over her heated skin. "Let me make you feel good."

"I'm feeling pretty good already," she sighed, settling deeper into the sofa.

The flare of her hips beneath his hands had him eagerly roaming down and pulling the skirt of her red dress back up over her shapely legs. He shifted his focus between her eyes and the dark skin he revealed inch by inch. He didn't want to miss a single part of her experience.

Roslyn stared down at his hands, her mouth open, her lids heavy. Desire looked good on her and he planned on making sure she knew just how desirable she truly was.

Anticipation pumped through him, knowing no other man had ever touched her in such a way. The experience seemed heightened, the intensity raised to a dizzying degree. He was too far gone, and from the little pants and sighs, so was she. Obviously she wanted this just as much as him.

Nigel glanced down to peek at the black lacy panties visible from beneath the slit of the skirt. He slid his thumb over the delicate material, right at the point where he knew she ached.

Her gasp had him smiling. So responsive, so passionate. She was utterly perfect, and he hadn't even pleasured her yet.

When the snug dress wouldn't move anymore, Nigel gripped her hips and tugged her into a half-laying position. Better. Now he could shift the dress a bit more and expose the rest of those lacy panties.

His breath left his lungs as he finally took her in from the waist down. He'd never seen a sexier sight and he ached to touch her, to taste her.

Roslyn's hands threaded through his hair as she continued to stare back at him. The want and need he saw looking back at him had Nigel ready to give her anything she wanted…and more.

Unable to wait a moment longer, he leaned down and slid his lips over her, where the lacy seam met skin. She trembled beneath his touch and Nigel continued to hold onto her hips as he explored her with his mouth.

Those fingers in his hair tightened, pulled, and only further aroused him. Roslyn had all this pent-up passion and he was about to make her come undone.

He curled his fingers over the scraps of material at her hips and slowly eased the panties down her legs. She still wore those bedroom heels and he most definitely wanted those to stay in place. He was a sucker for a woman in heels.

"Nigel," she whispered.

He stilled, raking his gaze up her body until he met her eyes. "You trust me?"

She bit her lip and nodded. Nigel slid one fingertip over her, earning him a soft moan.

He eased farther down, settling his shoulders between her parted legs. She continued to thread her fingers through his hair, as if she couldn't stop touching him. He was so damn aroused and turned on, but this moment, this night, was all about her. He never believed selfishness had any place in the bedroom and he sure as hell wasn't about to start now.

While he'd love nothing more than to shed this suit and show her exactly how much he wanted her, that would do Roslyn no good. He wanted her to see exactly how great this could be, how perfect her first sexual experience should feel.

No pressure, right?

His lips barely grazed her center and her hips bucked. The need for more had him sliding one finger into her.

Roslyn cried out and he absolutely loved the sounds she made…loved knowing he was the one making her come undone.

When he replaced his finger with his mouth, Nigel knew he'd never experience a sweeter, more erotic moment in his life. Roslyn moaned as she arched into his touch.

Nigel pleasured her until she gasped his name and fisted her fingers in his hair, pulling tighter than before. Her heels locked behind his back, the point of her shoe dug in and he didn't care one bit.

This. Was. Everything.

Roslyn had a passion that he'd never seen in another woman. She had an abandon that proved she wasn't

ashamed to be herself, to expose the most intimate side
of herself.

Nigel waited until her trembling ceased before he
kissed her inner thighs and eased up. When he glanced
down, he took a mental picture, never wanting to forget this for a second. Her hair had come undone, now
spread all around her. Her eyes were closed, her mouth
open, a sheen across her chest, her breathing rapid.

Roslyn looked exactly like what she was…a woman
well loved.

But he had no clue what to do now. Nigel had never
been in this situation before. He'd never been so bloody
attracted to a woman, and a virgin at that. And she still
was a virgin.

Damn it. He was more scandalous than the stars of
his show. If anyone found out he'd taken his brand-
new hire to bed, his reputation would be shattered. It
would give weight to every doubt and reservation his
family had expressed, every time they'd told him that
New York wasn't his place and he should come home
where he belonged. He'd built a life for himself here
that he could be proud of—how could he risk throwing that all away?

And yet how could he resist this woman who had
given him this beautiful gift? Besides, she was showing him such trust—surely he could show a little trust
in return that everything would work out.

Nigel pushed aside any thoughts that didn't center
around Roslyn. Because right now, and for the foreseeable future, all he wanted was to continue showing this
woman just how much she was desired.

Eight

Sophie pulled in a shaky breath and attempted to sit up and right her dress.

They had just broken all the rules. This could hurt the business he loved so much and it could jeopardize her plan to protect her family's legacy. But she wasn't sorry this had happened. How could she be? Nigel had just pleasured her in the most intimate way and he hadn't even fully undressed her.

He slid his hands over her thighs, up to her waist, and pulled her forward.

"I don't know what to say," she muttered, feeling reality crash back down.

"You don't have to say anything," he replied with a naughty grin. "Believe me, this was my pleasure."

Speaking of...

"Don't you want—"

"Oh, more than you know." He cut her off with a low laugh that seemed to hold more frustration than humor. "But this was about you. I've wanted you since you stepped foot into my office. I can't resist you, Roslyn."

There it was. The reason she couldn't fully enjoy her first sexual experience. Nigel didn't even know her real name. Guilt and disappointment spiraled through her. She'd finally chosen to give herself to someone, and her pleasure had been robbed by her lies. She had nobody to blame but herself.

How could she let this go any further? Clearly Nigel cared for her on some level. He'd taken his time, he'd made love to her with his mouth, and now he looked as if he was perfectly content with nothing more.

Why couldn't she have met him before the deceit? Why couldn't she just tell him who she was and why she was here?

Because her brothers were counting on her and she couldn't let them down. Miranda had no right to take ownership of a family legacy that meant nothing to her anyway.

"I may be inexperienced," she told him. "But I'm not naive or dumb. You've got to be…frustrated."

Again, he let out a throaty laugh. "I'll admit to being a trifle uncomfortable."

His smile slowly faded and those lingering eyes continued to hold her in place. Another burst of arousal slid through her, coupled with fear of all the unknown components that made up this warped relationship.

At some point, this was all going to blow up in her face and they were both going to end up hurt. The longer she stayed, the more involved they became, the more Sophie knew there would be no good way for this to end.

Nigel sighed and came to his feet. He raked a hand over his mussed hair and stared down at her, then offered a soft smile.

"You look good spread out over my couch," he told her. "I've envisioned you several times, in several ways—spread across my bed, in my shower, on my desk."

Sophie adjusted her dress and stood, tugging the material down to cover her thighs. "You've been busy," she joked, though her nerves were even more out of control than they'd been before he'd pleasured her.

"I told you, I've never met a woman like you." He tucked a strand of hair behind her ear and raked his thumb over her chin. "Nobody has been able to distract me from work before and nobody has ever made me want to put them first in everything. You've put some spell on me."

Sophie swallowed, unable to form words to follow his declaration. This was getting too deep, too intimate... But she knew tonight was just a stepping stone for the future. She wasn't innocent enough to think they'd just stop here.

"I could say the same," she replied, still recovering from his touch. "I just didn't expect any of this."

She had to tell the truth where she could. Maybe he'd even turn out to be understanding. After all, he'd have to see that her attraction to Nigel had nothing at all to do with her plan to reveal Miranda for the ruthless gold digger Sophie believed her to be.

But what if he took it badly? What if he threw her out…and then called Miranda to tell her everything? She couldn't bring herself to risk it.

Lying to his face made her miserable. She'd never felt so guilty, so ugly. But she'd already started this and she would see it through.

"The new responsibilities I've given you have nothing at all to do with this attraction," he told her. "I need you to know that. In a very short time, you've proven to be a worthy asset."

Sophie smiled. "I didn't think you gave me an extra project to get in my pants. But I'm glad to know you find my ideas of value."

At least she could be a little proud of the effort she'd put into this faux job. If she'd learned anything from her father, it was how to work hard no matter the occupation.

She just wished her father would've thought more of her and her brothers and shown some real care toward them—in his life or in his death. Money and assets aside, she didn't know why he wouldn't leave them a part of his legacy. Why he would throw it all at Miranda like she deserved more in her blingy, snobby life. The woman mainly stayed in New York with her friends and outgoing lifestyle. Her place in Royal was just a getaway.

Even though Sophie and her father had had a strained relationship, having everything removed from her life where he was concerned seemed so final, so heartbreaking. Like she just had to sever any ties she had with him. He was her father, she still loved him and she had nothing of his to hold on to.

"I'm glad you decided to go to the ceremony with me tonight," Nigel interrupted her thoughts, reaching for her hand and lacing his fingers with hers. "You may not believe me, but I typically go alone."

Sophie tipped her head. "I do find that hard to believe."

Nigel wrapped his arms around her, pulling her in closer to his solid, powerful body. "And I find it hard to believe no man has captured your attention or your heart yet."

She stilled. "Is that what you're after? My heart?"

Nigel slid his hands over her backside and squeezed. "I'm not looking to fall in love, not when I'm busy building an empire and a name for myself. But I wouldn't mind some companionship while you're in town."

"A fling?" she asked.

"That's such a juvenile, crass term."

He slid his lips over hers, so softly she had to grip onto his shoulders to keep herself grounded in the face of the tenderness.

Sophie eased back and studied his face. "Then what do you mean?"

"There's no reason we can't enjoy each other's company," he told her. "I like being with someone whose body isn't the only sexy part. You're a match to my business mind and that's refreshing in this industry. You challenge me to be better and that's quite an admirable trait."

Again, she was flattered he found her useful and formidable, and that he noted she was smart. That meant so much to her because she did pride herself on being an educated woman.

"Is that all you want my company for?" she asked.

"Hell, no." He slid his hands up over the curve of her hips to settle at her waist. "I want to be the man who continues to awaken this inner vixen. I want to be the man who shows you what intimacy can be. I'm a jealous bastard and I hate the thought of any other man being any of those things to you."

Sophie shivered at his commanding, authoritative tone. She'd learned vital information about Nigel tonight: he was a giving lover and he was a force to be reckoned with. As strongly independent as she prided herself on being, she couldn't ignore his advances and she didn't want to.

But why couldn't she enjoy Nigel's company while she was here? She was a grown woman and didn't need to make excuses for going after what she wanted. She wasn't going to hurt him or Green Room Media. All Sophie wanted to do was find some juicy dirt on Miranda and then she'd be on her way.

But Sophie needed to find the scoop sooner rather than later. Her week was nearly up, and she had nothing to take back to Texas other than the best sexual experience she'd ever had. She wasn't ready to go, the thought of leaving had knots of anxiety and tension balling up within her.

Emotionally, she couldn't afford to keep up this charade. Even though she'd devised a sneaky scheme, she truly wasn't a ruthless person and she didn't like stooping to this level. But, if she left, she'd be leaving Nigel and she wasn't ready.

"You seem to still be thinking."

Nigel's words cut into her thoughts and she redirected her attention to him.

"Maybe I wasn't persuasive enough," he added, bending down to run those talented lips along her exposed neck.

Sophie dropped her head back and curled her fingertips into his shoulders. Did anyone ever say no to this man?

"I'm yours," she muttered, helpless against his persuasion. "For as long as I'm here."

She didn't know if she should hurry and get out before she got hurt or take her time and enjoy the ride.

"We haven't received confirmation of your plus one."

Nigel pinched the bridge of his nose and closed his eyes. He could handle the cat fighting and nit-picking of the ladies from *Secret Lives* without breaking a sweat, but when it came to his grandmother, he somehow resorted to a child being scolded.

"I haven't sent in my plus one, yet," he replied, blowing out a sigh.

"Yes, I'm aware. Hence the nature of my call."

Dame Claire Worthington never failed to choose sharp, witty words and there wasn't a soul in the family, or anywhere else in Cumbria, that dared cross her. In addition to being strict and demanding, she was also loving, loyal, respected…and that's why he hated letting her down.

Nigel turned from the wintery view of the city to face the leather sofa…the one he'd had Roslyn spread out on just last night. He'd told himself that he'd come up here to think and get away from the office for the day, but perhaps he just wanted to return to the scene of the best night of his life.

He had no clue what was happening with his new temporary employee, but he knew he wanted more from her...professionally and personally. Why couldn't he have both? He made the bloody rules and owned the company. He wanted her to stay on permanently, not just because he wanted her in his bed, but because she'd already brought so much to Green Room Media. Workplace romances happened all the time—there had to be some kind of protocol they could follow to keep everything scandal-free.

"Nigel."

"Yes, yes," he stated, shifting his attention back to his grandmother. "I know. Plus one."

"The RSVP was due in by today. I'm sure it slipped your mind with as busy as you are with your city life, so that's why I called. You can just tell me you'll be bringing a date to your sister's wedding and I'll make sure catering gets the accurate number."

As if an inaccurate count of his one date, or lack of, would throw off the filet Oscar-style menu. His grandmother made it no secret he was only getting older and that she disapproved of the fact that he still hadn't settled down, let alone started working on producing the next generation of little Townshends.

His grandmother was old school and British...there was no arguing with her and she damn well knew it. But for all that, she certainly wasn't the pearl-wearing, tea-sipping elderly woman. She worked hard all her life, raised her children without a nanny and ran their horse farm alongside her husband. She understood his reasons for wanting to build his own empire and the move to NYC, but she wasn't backing down on his settling soon to start a family.

"You are cutting this close," she added. "The wedding is next week, you know."

"I'm aware."

His sister was marrying the love of her life…or so she said. They'd chosen Valentine's Day as their wedding day, which was just a little too cutesy for him, but she hadn't asked his opinion.

Nigel had met his soon-to-be brother-in-law a handful of times when he'd gone home and the guy seemed like he'd fit into the Townshend family perfectly. But Nigel was in no hurry to bring home a woman. It would take someone special to get him ready to introduce her to the rest of the clan.

An image of Roslyn flashed through his mind.

No. Hell, no. First of all, when he brought a date, they wouldn't expect her to be someone from the office. Second, he couldn't bring Roslyn because…well…

Why not? She would actually be the perfect candidate. She was poised, she could definitely hold her own and there was nobody else he'd want on his arm.

Nigel couldn't prevent the smile that spread across his face. His family would have no way of knowing Roslyn was from the office. If she came as his plus one, it would give him another opportunity to get to know her on a deeper level. He wasn't ready for that commitment his grandmother was after, but spending more time with Roslyn would give him more insight to her. A fake relationship for the sake of his family wouldn't hurt anything, right?

After that, he could explain they broke things off and nobody would have to know.

That is, if Roslyn went along with this crazy plan.

"And for pity's sake, wear a tie," Dame Claire scolded. "I know you have your own style, but this is a black-tie affair."

"Yes, ma'am." Ideas rolled through his mind on how to approach Roslyn with his proposal. "I promise I won't do anything to embarrass you or the family."

"Oh, please," she chided. "Nothing embarrasses me, but I do have standards. I expect you and your date to be here no later than Wednesday. The wedding is Saturday."

"I'll be there," he vowed.

"You *both* will be here," she corrected.

Nigel laughed. Of course she'd assume he was bringing someone simply because she said so. He told her to give everyone his love before he disconnected the call.

He stared at the phone another second and finally shot off a text before he could think better of it.

Going up against a persnickety, hardheaded old grandmother called for drastic measures.

Meet me at the office penthouse.

He hit Send, then quickly added another text.

I need a favor.

It was Saturday night, so maybe she was out on the town, but he didn't think so. Roselyn worked hard and seemed to put her career above socializing. He didn't want to discuss his family's drama and wedding issue via text. And he just wanted to see her…the wedding was just the perfect excuse.

Nigel didn't want Roslyn to think he was a complete jerk who only wanted to get her undressed. He'd meant what he'd said when he told her that he respected her and planned to take his time.

Time would prove to be the ultimate foreplay, especially since she'd already said yes to his advances. And a trip to his home? He couldn't wait to take her back to the place where he had grown up, where he'd dreamed. He'd continue to charm her with the grand estate of Shrewsbury Hall. The home itself rivaled Buckingham Palace with all the rooms, windows, ornate architecture and decor.

Roslyn would love his childhood home if he could get her there. He couldn't imagine any interior designer not falling in love with the rich history and all the stories behind each room and heirloom.

Nigel had to talk her into being his plus one first. Coming off their encounter last night, he hoped fate was in his favor.

Nine

"Meet your family?"

Sophie knew getting physically involved with Nigel was risky, both to her heart and her mind, but flying all the way to Cumbria, England, to be his plus one at his sister's wedding? And for Valentine's Day?

That was more than just taking a step in a dangerous direction—it was practically bungee jumping off a cliff. Meeting the family, attending a wedding that would equate to something from royalty and pretending to be his girlfriend for the sake of duping his family?

More lies might just do in her mental state and she wasn't sure she could keep all of them straight.

"I know this is out of nowhere," Nigel stated, raking a hand through his hair, clearly stressed.

She'd only known him a short time, but she'd never

seen him this flustered. Clearly he was in a bind and wasn't any more comfortable asking her than she was being invited. She also had to assume that he wouldn't have come to her had he'd had another choice.

"My grandmother is quite persistent," he added, his dark eyes pleading with her.

"But, what about my job here?" she asked, still reeling from the out-of-the-blue request. "I mean, what will everyone think? First I'm hired as a consultant, then I'm put in charge of heading up the marketing for the wedding episode that may or may not happen, then I go to an award ceremony with you and now a family wedding back at your home?"

Her mind was spinning just saying all of this out loud. Talk about a whirlwind experience. But the biggest issue for her was the thing she didn't dare say aloud— between getting swept up with Nigel and his charm and sex appeal, and her inability to deny him anything, she was running out of time to uncover information on Miranda. Every angle she'd tried ended up a dead end. Everyone she spoke to absolutely loved the woman.

"I know it looks crazy... It *is* crazy," he amended, reaching for her hands. "Nobody here has to know about where we're actually going. I can say I have you going on a trip to scout potential locations for the show."

More lying. For someone who used to pride herself on honesty, she'd fallen down the rabbit hole of deceit and she wasn't sure she'd find her way back out anytime soon.

If she went away with him, Sophie knew they'd pick up where they'd left off the other night... That both thrilled and terrified her. She'd never wanted anyone the way she wanted Nigel and that was what scared her most. How could she ever let him go?

Nigel's strong hands held hers as he continued to stare at her, imploring her with his eyes.

"How long will we be gone?" she asked.

A toe-curling smile spread across his face. "Five days."

Five days in an English countryside estate with a man she was quickly falling for, during which she'd have to pretend to be his girlfriend so his family would get off his back. Seriously, what could go wrong?

Sophie had lied to get to this point and now she was taking this acting skill on an international tour. What would her brothers think when she told them about this venture?

Maybe she should keep this part to herself. She didn't want to use Nigel. That part kept niggling at her. She may be lying in her position here, but she wasn't lying about her growing feelings or attraction. She wasn't that good of an actress. But all of these emotions were completely unexpected and causing issues she hadn't planned on.

"I don't want to pressure you," he told her. "I just didn't want to ask anyone else."

The fact he trusted her with meeting his family and only added to her shame. He was being so transparent with his life with her, as far as she knew, and she was a complete phony.

Yet she couldn't say no. She wanted to spend more time with the man who made her wish this were all real. He made her daydream about a real relationship, a real attraction…a real affair instead of one based on lies.

"I'll do it," she told him. "I'll go to England."

Nigel's shoulders relaxed as he stepped closer her and gripped her hands to his chest. "You will love my home and my family. Dame Claire can be overwhelming at times, but she does everything out of love."

Sophie wasn't sure how she'd deal with a large, loving family and a doting grandmother...especially one with a title. Sure, she and her brothers were close, and she'd loved her her mother, but the relationship with her father just left her feeling broken.

What would her life be like if she had a close relationship with her father? Maybe the outcome of the will would've been different and Sophie and her brothers would have had their legacy given to them.

She only had her brothers now and they were depending on her. Even though Kellan had said she could come home, she didn't want to let them down. She wanted to be the one to make everything right. She wanted to give them back what had been taken away.

"What should I pack for this wedding?" Sophie asked, ignoring the blaring horns and red flags in her head.

Nigel quirked a brow. "I've got everything covered. My jet will be ready to go Wednesday morning and your dresses and jewelry will be on board."

And Sophie fell just a little deeper into this *Pretty Woman* scenario.

Central Park was absolutely gorgeous in the winter. Freezing, but breathtaking and so picturesque.

Sophie huddled deeper into her coat as she walked along the curved path through the park. The brisk air gave her a freshness that she didn't find in Texas heat. Besides, she'd wanted to get out of the office and take a much-needed break.

She'd tried calling Vaughn, but she'd only gotten his voice mail. She stopped at a park bench that had been cleaned off and took a seat, pulling out her phone to call Kellan.

She had to tell them what she'd be doing, but she'd been stalling, struggling with her guilt. In all of this snowballed mess, she had to be honest with someone. She couldn't exactly leave the country without letting her brothers know. She respected and loved them too much to lie... She'd done enough lying as it was.

Sophie dialed and wrapped her arm around her midsection to hold in the warmth of her coat. Kellan answered on the first ring.

"There's my favorite spy."

Sophie inwardly groaned, hating the nickname, even though this had all been her idea. "Good to hear your voice, too."

"Found out anything yet?"

"I'm getting closer," she stated, which was partially true. She was actually going to a meeting later with two members from the camera crew. If anyone knew about behind the scenes shenanigans, it would be them.

"I hope to have some information within the next few days," she added. "But I called to tell you that I have to do a bit of traveling. I'll still check in and keep my eyes and ears open, but... I'm going out of the country."

"Out of the country?" he repeated. "How does that fit into the plan when Miranda is going to be in New York for filming?"

Yeah, she was still trying to figure that out herself. In her original plan, she would have already left New York by now with the sought-after evidence in hand. As it was, she would have to dodge Miranda if she popped into the office, but Sophie had seen the upcoming shooting schedule and there was no reason for Miranda to be at Green Room Media for the next few weeks.

"I can't do anything to raise suspicions," she defended. "I was asked to travel, so that's what I'm doing."

Swirls of snow fluttered around and mesmerized Sophie as she clutched the cell. For someone so accustomed to heat, she really was enjoying her time in NYC during the winter. Maybe she should visit more often. Perhaps she should even incorporate some of her videos here for inspiration… Well, once she could go back to being Sophie Blackwood, posh interior designer and not Roslyn Andrews, temporary consultant and wannabe mistress to Nigel Townshend.

"And going out of town is a direct order from the boss?" Kellan joked.

"Pretty much," she muttered, as die-hard runners braved the cold and jogged by. "Listen, it's only for five days and I promise I haven't lost sight of the prize."

"I'm sure you haven't. But, Darius said that Miranda invited him to Blackwood Hollow. I don't know what she has up her sleeve."

Sophie gripped her coat and the cell as dread settled into her belly. "He's coming there?" she exclaimed.

Darius Taylor-Pratt was their half sibling…a secret revealed after their father had passed. Even in death, her father continued to work his controlling hands in their lives.

"Apparently," Kellan replied. "She may be trying to pit him against us, but I'll keep my eye on things here. Don't worry."

"What the hell is she plotting?" Sophie muttered.

Frustration and confusion settled in alongside her guilt and she wondered if any of them would come out of this entire situation unscathed. And all because her father had been selfish or blinded by his young ex-wife and decided none of his children deserved their legacy.

Miranda sure as hell didn't deserve it, either. Buckley had been twenty-six years older than his bride. Why else would a beautiful young socialite marry a wealthy older man if not for the money she could get out of him? Miranda made no apologies for liking the finer things and Sophie knew the woman was just gathering a nest egg for the rest of her lavish life. And now she was pulling in Darius.

Sophie hated sounding spoiled and the issue truly didn't come down to money, but the fact Miranda just didn't deserve a dime of what should have been theirs. She didn't deserve the family home that held so many memories of Sophie's childhood. Sophie's brothers deserved to keep the estate, to pass down to their children one day.

"Does Vaughn know Darius is coming?"

"Yeah. We talked this morning. You know he doesn't like all this family drama, but he does want to know what's going on."

Sophie still didn't know why her father had never confessed there was another heir. Maybe he'd wanted them to find out after his death so he wouldn't have to deal with the questions, the repercussions. Or maybe he had wanted them to all be in an upheaval, perhaps pitting against each other. She truly had no idea what his ultimate plan had been for his children.

Sophie came to her feet and sighed. "Don't keep me out of the loop just because you're worried. I'm doing this grunt work and I deserve to be included as soon as you know anything."

"I promise to call you when I learn more," he vowed. "So, where are you going that's taking you away on business?"

Sophie didn't want to lie anymore. She was tired of it. Even though she knew she'd take backlash from Kellan and Vaughn, she had to be up front, because that's what she expected from them.

"Cumbria."

"What the hell for?"

Sophie cleared her throat and made her way back down the path. "Nigel is taking me for his sister's wedding."

"Excuse me?"

"You heard me."

"Damn it, Sophie. You're getting in too deep there. You need to just come home and we'll figure out something else. Traveling with Nigel Townshend to his home is a bad, bad idea."

Sophie bit the inside of her cheek, trying to quickly come up with the right words to reply, but Kellan beat her to it.

"Oh, no. Don't tell me you're sleeping with your fake boss."

"I'm not sleeping with him." *Not yet.* "He asked me to be his date because his grandmother is always on his back about not settling down. He figured if I went, they would at least leave him alone for a few days and he could enjoy his sister's celebration without getting hassled."

"Uh-huh. And you're telling me he's not interested in you?"

Oh, he was more than interested. Her body still tingled from just how interested Nigel Townshend was. There was nothing about her feelings for Nigel that she'd be sharing with her well-meaning brothers.

"Listen, I know what I'm doing and I'm a big girl. You worry about finding the scoop on our long lost sibling and I'll work on Miranda."

"I don't give a damn about Miranda right now," Kellan growled. "You can't get caught up in a love affair with Nigel. You're vulnerable, Soph. You're grieving and totally out of your element. Besides, Miranda will know what you're up to if she catches you anywhere near her showrunner."

"Stop worrying about my mental state. I'm fine," she assured him, even though she was worried herself. "And nobody is going to catch me. I barely recognize myself in the mirror with all this blond hair and these glasses."

It was true. She missed her dark hair. The blond did horrid things to her skin tone, but a dye job was worth the sacrifice if she could get some blackmail material on Miranda.

She might come across as all mama bear on the screen, doting on her costars and always trying to help, but nobody was that squeaky clean and wholesome. There had to be some proof that Miranda had done something underhanded to get the Blackwood money—

something that would justify getting the will thrown out. Sophie wasn't sure how she could make this work to their advantage, but she had to try. No way was she giving up her childhood home that easily. If they could just get Miranda out of Royal for good, they could all move on to the next chapter of their lives. They hadn't gotten along with the woman when she'd been married to their father, so now that he was gone, there was no reason for her to stick around.

"I'm heading back to work," she told her brother. "Keep in touch and don't make me beg for information."

She disconnected the call and made her way back to Green Room Media. She had a meeting to get to, a trip to prepare for and a stepmother to bring down.

All in a day's work.

Ten

Nigel settled into his seat as the jet taxied down the runway. He glanced at Roslyn, trying to figure out why she'd been so quiet and reserved on the way to the airport and since boarding.

Maybe he'd been too demanding by asking her to be his date. Maybe she'd felt pressured, like her job would be on the line if she refused. That wasn't the type of man he was, nor was it the type of man she deserved. He wanted her to know she mattered, she was valued. Not someone he considered disposable if she didn't comply with his wishes. And certainly not who could be bought.

Bloody hell. Since when did he try so hard to impress a woman? He actually cared what Roslyn thought of him. Oh, he'd always prided himself on caring for his dates, his relationships, but no other woman had impacted him like Roslyn.

He admired her talents, her brilliance, and he couldn't ignore the sexual pull, the desire and passion he'd witnessed. The combination continued to make him wonder if there was something else smoldering beneath the surface…and he couldn't wait to explore.

Bringing Roslyn to his family's estate was risky, but hell, he'd taken risks his entire life… Why stop now when the reward could be so memorable and thrilling?

When the plane lifted, Roslyn gripped the seat and closed her eyes. A minimal act, but one that hinted at why she'd been so closed off since they'd boarded. Well, he'd finally found her flaw. He had honestly wondered if she was too good to be true…and if fear of flying was her only drawback, he was in real trouble.

Nigel didn't want a commitment or love or anything crazy long-term, but he enjoyed Roslyn and couldn't help but want to see where all this went.

He came to his feet and crossed the cabin to the other white sofa, taking a seat, and her hand. He squeezed, earning him a quick glance.

"What was that for?" she asked.

"You looked like you needed it. Why didn't you tell me you were afraid of flying?"

Roslyn lifted a shoulder and glanced down to their joined hands. "Pride? Fear of admitting I'm flawed? It's silly, actually. I mean, flying is the safest form of travel, or so the saying goes."

Nigel shifted in his seat and took both of her rigid hands in his. "Relax," he told her. "I've never been in a crash yet."

Roslyn rolled her eyes and gave a half grin.

"That's better," he murmured with a smile. "But, seriously, having a fear is nothing to be ashamed of. Why didn't you ask me to sit with you and hold your hand?"

"I've never asked anyone to hold my hand when I've been afraid," she countered. "Talk about humiliating."

"Everybody is afraid of something."

She quirked her brow and leveled his gaze. "And tell me what your fear is? Besides your grandmother."

Nigel laughed, but she wasn't far from the mark. He'd never discussed his true anxieties or insecurities with anyone before.

"Failing my family," he finally admitted. "They were all stunned when I wanted to move to New York and start my own brand and work in television. I need this show to continue to succeed not just for me but for them. And then there's my personal side. Settling down, marrying, and starting the next generation of little Townshends is actually expected of me and I know my family is disappointed that I've waited this long. I could always find a woman and start a family, but that's not what I want. My parents were married a long time before my mother passed from a stroke. I want love. I'm just not sure when it will find me. I'm just so swamped with work and growing the brand."

Nigel stopped himself before he went on too much. He already sounded like a fool for believing in love. Roslyn had already said she wasn't sure the emotion truly existed and he wasn't so sure there was someone out there for him, either.

At what point should he give up and just find a woman he'd want to be the mother of his children? Did he actually have to love her in a way old romances said a husband should love a wife? What was even normal these days, anyway?

"Family really means that much to you."

Roslyn's murmured words pulled him back.

"Family is everything," he stated. "That's why I'm going to all this trouble to bring a date."

Her wide smile made her eyes sparkle. "And here I thought it was because you couldn't stand being away from me."

Nigel moved closer, settling his hands on either side of her hips until she had her back pressed against the leather couch.

"That, too," he said before he slid his mouth over hers.

She moaned against his lips, sliding her hands over his shoulders and threading her fingers through his hair. Just the simplicity of her touch had his arousal pumping through him. He had to remind himself that she was still innocent, but he also couldn't ignore how passionate she was.

When Roslyn arched that curvaceous body against his, Nigel slid his hands beneath the hem of her silky blouse and found warm satiny skin.

Roslyn tore her mouth from his and dropped her head back, his name coming out on a whisper from her lips.

"Tell me what you want," he demanded.

He wasn't going to do anything she wasn't comfortable with, but he wanted her more than he wanted his next breath…and they certainly had plenty of time on this flight for him to show her just how much he needed her.

"Tell me," he repeated, easing back to watch her face, to look for any hesitation that might indicate she wasn't ready for more.

Her eyes met his and she smiled…and his body responded. There was nothing in her eyes but hunger, desire and anticipation.

His hands shook as he slid her shirt up and over her head. When he tossed it to the side and reached for the straps of her lacy black bra, she reached up and framed his face with her hands.

"You're nervous," she stated with a soft smile. "That's adorable."

Adorable. Not a word anyone used to describe him since he'd probably been a toddler.

And nervous? Nigel wasn't about to admit any such thing…no matter how true the statement. They both needed this. They both had been dancing toward this moment since she sashayed into his office in those hip-hugging jeans and killer heels, dazzling him with her beauty and impressing him with her knowledge and her mind.

Instead of answering, he dipped his head to graze his lips over the swell of her breasts just above the outline of that sexy-as-hell bra.

Roslyn eased down as he reached behind her back and unhooked the garment. She jerked it from her arms and lay on her back, staring up at him, her eyes silently pleading for him to take her.

Definitely no hesitation here. This woman knew what she wanted, knew *whom* she wanted. Nigel may not understand why she'd waited so long to give herself to a man, but he was damn happy she'd chosen him.

He didn't know what this said about her true feelings, but he couldn't analyze that right now. He wanted her and she sure as hell wanted him.

With her blond hair all fanned out around her and her body completely exposed from the waist up, Nigel didn't hesitate to remove the rest of her clothes, including her shoes. Once she laid bare beneath him, he came to his feet and made quick work of shedding his own things.

There were certainly perks to owning your own jet. Privacy being the key.

The way her eyes raked over him had Nigel hurrying even more. He procured protection from his wallet and covered himself before settling over her.

Her hands trembled as she slid her fingertips up his arms and over the curve of his shoulders.

"Looks like we're both nervous," she told him with a shaky smile.

This might as well have been his first time, too, because he did not want to screw this up. He wanted Roslyn to experience everything she deserved and more. Her satisfaction hinged on his every touch, his every move. Everything that happened here would be with her forever…and he knew this experience would be lasting for him, too.

Believing in someone was key in his life and he knew he had her trust if she had decided to give her virginity to him. The idea humbled him and made his confidence grow even deeper toward her.

Nigel was about to ask again if she was okay, but her knees came up on either side of his hips and she wrapped her legs around his waist. Nigel leaned down and covered her body, her mouth, still without joining them completely.

Taking his time was what he should have been doing, but all Nigel wanted to do was be one with her, to finally feel her heat and know her pleasure…to take everything she was willing to give.

Later they could explore. Between his own wants and her arched body and soft moans, Nigel knew they were both just as eager.

He lifted his head slightly, wanting to see every emotion she displayed as he slid into her.

Roslyn didn't disappoint.

Her mouth dropped open a second before she bit her lip, her lids fluttered shut, and she tipped her head back, pressing her breasts into his chest.

She. Was. Perfect.

Nigel moved carefully at first, more than aware of each sound or expression she made. They settled into a rhythm so effortlessly, as if they'd done this before… or as if they were meant to be.

The thought was silly, but there was no other way to describe the manner in which they fit and moved so beautifully.

She whispered his name on a plea as the rhythm of her hips quickened. Nigel followed her lead. She may lay beneath him, but all control was in her hands.

Roslyn's fingernails bit into his back as her climax took over. She arched, tightened her knees against his hips, and let out a cry of passion. Never before had he seen anything so erotic, and yet vulnerable.

Her abandon had him losing control even further and following her into his own release. Nigel gripped her hips and slid his mouth over hers to connect them in every way possible.

The hum of the engines and the heavy breathing in his ear were the noises in the cabin as his body came down from its high.

Nigel eased up, glancing at Roslyn who had the widest smile on her face, her eyes completely locked onto him.

"If you were trying to distract me from flying, you did a hell of a job."

Nigel laughed and pulled away from her, taking her hands to bring her up to his side.

"Well, since we have several more hours, I say we take this to the back bedroom so I can make sure you are completely relaxed."

Roslyn came to her feet and held out her hand. "Show me the way."

Eleven

Cumbria, England, was exactly like Sophie had imagined. Rolling snow-covered hills and little cottages dotted the landscape alongside the curvy road. The entire trip from the airstrip toward the Townshend estate was picturesque and she couldn't keep her eyes off the scenery. It was like being transported back into another time. One where life was simple and carefree. Much like the life she enjoyed back in Royal.

Perhaps she and Nigel weren't so different after all. He'd admitted how protective he was of his family, and he was clearly going to great lengths to please them… something she could totally relate to.

More and more she was seeing how compatible they were.

After that memorable plane ride, it was a wonder

she could focus on anything but her tingling body. She couldn't stop herself from a constant replay of every single arousing touch. Those hours only pulled her in deeper to his world, making her want more, making her wish things were different.

Nigel reached over to take her hand and gave a gentle squeeze. "Nothing to worry about. My family will love you. We just have to pretend like we're in love."

She didn't even know how to unpack that whole statement, but she should at least attempt.

Nervous? She had far surpassed nervous when it came to meeting his family. His grandmother went by Dame for crying out loud.

And pretend? Yeah, she'd gotten that down pat and honestly deserved some Oscar for her performance.

Love? No, there was no love here. A good healthy dose of lust and sex, but not love. She couldn't allow herself to think along those lines because she was already falling, and at some point, she'd have to guard her heart from tumbling completely out of her control. She just didn't know where to draw the boundary lines.

"Do you want to talk about what happened on the plane?" she asked as she turned from the postcard-worthy view to face him.

He steered the car around another sharp turn before flashing her a grin. "What do you want to talk about? I had a great time. Best flight of my life."

She wondered how many times he'd used that bedroom for other women he whisked off around the world. Jealousy had no place here, after all she was lying to him and they'd made no promises to each other. Still, she couldn't help where her mind wandered.

"Maybe I should have brought you on my plane sooner," he joked.

Sophie got a nasty pit in her belly. "Do you seduce many women on your private jet?"

"Don't go there," he growled. "I'm not a playboy like the tabloids want people to believe and I certainly don't seduce women in my jet."

"You had my clothes off before we reached cruising altitude," she countered. "You seemed pretty experienced."

"I haven't been a monk, but I swear that I have not taken any other woman to bed on my plane."

He sounded so sincere and Sophie really had no reason to disbelieve him. But the whens and wheres of his former affairs weren't really the issue here. Of course, he'd had women and relationships before her. He was a sexy, powerful man. Good grief, they weren't even in a relationship and she already had the unhealthy girlfriend mentality. They'd had sex and she was his pretend girlfriend for the rest of the week. Sounded simple enough, right?

But nothing was simple about her emotions or sex. If she'd thought she was falling for him before, the intimacy on the plane had only exacerbated the issue. Now she didn't know if her feelings stemmed from the man she finally gave herself to or if they came from the fact he truly was a genuine guy and not the playboy the media played him out to be.

Any other thoughts or words died in her throat as Nigel turned into a long drive where the grounds were surrounded with tall evergreens covered with a blanket of crisp white snow.

As he turned the last curve of the drive, the trees opened up to reveal a vast two-story brick-and-stone home. There seemed to be windows everywhere and juts of bay windows on both floors. Sophie imagined many reading nooks in those bays.

The home looked old, but not unkempt. The estate went right along with her original impression of the town—everything about this place was like she'd stepped back in time. She couldn't wait to explore the inside, get inspired for even more future designs, and learn of the history behind such a manor.

A large pond sat in front of the home and she could only imagine summertime here with the grounds blooming with colorful flowers. But even with the freshly fallen snow, the estate was breathtaking.

She'd uploaded some old material to her YouTube channel for the next month so she didn't have to worry about keeping up while she was undercover. But she would certainly be taking mental notes from this place for ways to incorporate new and old into any living area.

"Welcome to Shrewsbury Hall," Nigel told her as he circled the drive and pulled to the front entrance.

She'd heard him say that name before, but seeing the vast home made her realize it was certainly worthy of such an upstanding title. And she'd thought her family had money. This place could hold three of her own French provincial home. The mansion also made her father's ranch estate seem small.

A man in a wool coat and hat immediately came out and opened her door. Sophie pulled her coat around her chest and thanked him.

Nigel came around the car and shook the man's hand. "Thank you, William."

"Glad to have you back home, Sir Nigel."

Sir. Of course, he'd be addressed as such.

"It's good to be here." Nigel nodded toward the home. "Is everyone inside?"

"Dame Claire is waiting on you with bourbon and some snacks. She figured you'd be hungry after your flight and would need to relax with a drink."

"You mean she's ready to grill my girlfriend and me?" Nigel asked.

"That, too, sir."

Sophie was still reeling from the *girlfriend* comment when Nigel took her hand and led her up the stone steps to the front entrance. The architecture alone was drool-worthy and Sophie couldn't wait to see the interior. She could only imagine the videos she could shoot from here…if she were actually here as herself and had the opportunity to do such things.

She missed her design shoots, but since going undercover, she'd had to back off just a bit. She still replied to comments and answered her DMs on her social media accounts, but she was itching to get back to new material…and Shrewsbury Hall was the absolute perfect backdrop.

Too bad she wasn't here as Sophie Blackwood, interior designer.

Hell, she wasn't even here as Roslyn Andrews, consultant. She was here as an imposter of an imposter. Good grief. It would be a miracle if she didn't need therapy after this entire ordeal.

And after the hit to her mental state—and, inevitably, to her heart—she had better find some seriously juicy dirt on Miranda once she returned to New York.

"From what you've said before, I wouldn't have taken your grandmother for the bourbon type," Sophie muttered as they reached the door. "I assumed tea and cookies, or biscuits as you call them."

Nigel laughed. "Don't try to stereotype her. You'll never find a box that fits the personality of Dame Claire Worthington."

Sophie didn't know whether to be afraid or amused, but before she could decide, Nigel opened the double doors and swept her inside.

All air caught in her lungs as Sophie took in the magnificent foyer that extended up to the second floor. Straight ahead was a fountain with a curved staircase flanking either side.

The chandelier's beaming lights bounced off the marble floor, the fresh floral arrangements at the base of each staircase were perfectly placed in large marble urns. Not only was the entrance something from a royal magazine but the fragrant aroma from the wintery mix smelled so inviting.

This setting could have easily been ripped out of a fairy tale and Roslyn wished more than anything she could let herself get swept away into this fantasy life.

"There's my city boy."

Sophie turned her attention to a tall striking woman with a stylish pixie cut. The silver-haired lady had on a pair of jeans and a bright green sweater paired with little silver sneakers. Not at all the image Sophie had had in her mind of the *Dame*. But her relaxed style did put Sophie a little more at ease.

Nigel's grandmother came up and wrapped her arms around him before easing back and turning her focus, and affection, to Sophie. She found herself enveloped in a strong embrace and caught Nigel's smirk and smile over the shoulder of Dame Claire.

"Welcome, welcome," she greeted, pulling away from Sophie. "I'm Claire."

"It's a pleasure to meet you, Dame Worthington. I'm Roslyn Andrews."

Nigel's grandmother waved a hand and shook her head. "None of this Dame nonsense. Those titles are so archaic. Call me Claire. And while you're at it, tell me how you managed to capture my workaholic grandson's attention to get him to bring you here."

"Can we at least take our coats off and get settled before you start grilling her?" Nigel asked. "And you ordered me to bring a date, so don't pretend to be surprised."

"As if you ever listen to me," Claire muttered. "You've never brought a woman here in your life, so I'm already impressed with this one."

Sophie removed her coat and handed it to a man who seemed to appear out of nowhere, along with two others, to take their things.

Nigel had never brought a lady home? That was rather interesting. Did he mean it when he said he just wanted her here as a guise or did he actually want to spend alone time with her and have her meet his family?

Sophie didn't know what all the answers were and she couldn't wrap her mind around it now. If there was a chance that Nigel had truly wanted to share more of his life with her, then she feared the guilt would consume her. She wished she could go back and tell him everything, wished she could start fresh. Maybe then what they shared could actually be real.

But she couldn't go back and she definitely couldn't tell him the truth now.

"William said you had bourbon," Nigel said after the staff took their things.

"Your favorite," Claire replied with a wink.

"Oh, please. You introduced me to that brand when I turned eighteen and told me not to settle for anything less."

Claire laughed. "Guilty. So come on in and let's chat."

She wedged herself between Nigel and Sophie, looping her arms between them, and led them into another massive room with high ceilings. The fireplace on the far wall crackled with a warm fire and a tray of fruit, cheese, cookies, and other finger foods was set out on the table between the large leather sofas.

"Is Ellen here?" Nigel asked.

"She'll be along later. Your sister is very eager to see who you brought home."

Sophie settled onto the sofa next to Nigel and across from Claire. She hadn't realized she'd be this nervous to meet his family, but after their romp on the plane, she was a bundle of mixed emotions.

"Now, tell me how you met," Claire said, clasping her hands like a proud grandmother.

"At the office," Nigel piped in. "You know I have a policy about not dating employees, but Roselyn changed all of that."

They'd discussed their story and decided to keep it as close to the truth as possible.

Claire's eyes darted between them, then landed back on Nigel. "Do you always work? Wait, don't answer that. I know you do. Do you at least take this poor girl out to dinner?"

"Of course," Nigel replied, reaching for a lemon square. "We've had several work dinners."

"Nigel Phillip Townshend," she scolded.

He laughed. "I'm kidding. Relax."

Claire turned her focus to Sophie. "You must be a saint to put up with him. He's given me every one of my gray hairs, I tell you."

Sophie settled her hand on Nigel's knee. "Ignore him. One of the first things he asked when I started working with him was what my favorite food was."

"For work meetings?" Claire asked, raising one perfectly shaped brow.

"For a real date," Nigel chimed in. "I knew the second I saw her I wanted her as more than my consultant."

"Office romance. Well, it's your company and I think it's romantic…so long as you keep romance in the relationship and not just in the form of a spreadsheet."

"I like her," Sophie laughed, glancing to Nigel. "You had me afraid to come."

Nigel cringed and Claire let out a burst of laughter. "Did he, now? I'd love to hear what picture he painted of me."

"I'd like to know what he said about me, too."

Sophie turned to the entrance of the living area as a beautiful, curvy woman came striding through. Her long dark hair fell in waves over her shoulders and she looked as if she'd just come in from riding a horse given her tight black pants, tall brown boots, and bright red fitted jacket.

"Ellen, you're just in time." Claire came to her feet and kissed the woman who had to be her granddaughter on the cheek. "Nigel's girlfriend was just dishing on workplace romance and what he truly thinks of his family."

Nigel muttered a curse under his breath and rose to greet his sister. Sophie stood as well, nervous at encountering another family member. Maybe she could knock these little meetings out one by one and not be so nervous come the day of the wedding.

"Workplace romance?" she asked, eyeing Nigel. "Well, aren't you all candy hearts and bouquets of flowers."

"Actually, Roslyn doesn't like bouquets," he said. "She thinks they're clichéd."

She turned to him. "You remembered that?"

His eyes shifted from her eyes to her mouth and back. "I remember everything you've ever said to me."

Sophie's heart picked up and she knew then, Nigel wasn't faking a relationship. He meant what he'd said. And she knew in that moment he was getting in just as deep as she was… But did he know? Was he aware of how he looked at her with his emotions in his eyes?

Dread filled her stomach at the thought of Nigel getting hurt in the end. She had never wanted to crush anybody except Miranda. All she'd wanted to do was come to New York, scope out some cutting room floor footage and talk to some crew members. She'd wanted to be in and out in a week's time.

Yet here she was, spending the next five days in

England pretending to be Nigel Townshend's girlfriend when she really wanted to be his everything in real life.

"Wait a minute," Ellen said, staring at Sophie. "You look familiar. I think I know you from somewhere."

Sophie froze as Ellen's brows drew in and she pursed her lips in thought. Sophie had not come this far to be outed, but her disguise wasn't foolproof and Ellen was smiling like she might just know Sophie's dirty little secret.

Twelve

With Nigel out of the country, Lulu was set on getting Fee to agree to the spin-off—or at least the wedding episode for *Secret Lives*.

"If that's really what you want to do, I'll stand behind you," Lulu told Fee.

The cameras moved around but Lulu ignored them. She'd gotten more than used to having her entire life filmed. Today she was having lunch with Seraphina as they chatted about Fee's upcoming move to Texas. While she hated losing her best friend, she understood how much Fee loved Royal and the people there—not just Clint, though the love Fee had for her fiancé was certainly something special.

When the cast and crew had been there for Christmas at Miranda's estate, they'd all fallen a little in love with the charming town. And after those devastating fires, Lulu more than understood Fee's need to be with the man she loved in his hometown.

After all, hadn't they all wanted to land a cowboy?

Unfortunately, the only one who'd caught her eye, and gotten on her last nerve the entire time she was there, was Kace the snarky lawyer... The snarky lawyer who'd shown up at her penthouse just to talk a few days earlier. Sure, like they'd ever *just talked*. At this point, they couldn't be alone for two minutes without clothes falling off. Mercy, the things that man could do with his hands.

"Everything okay?" Fee asked, reaching for her water glass.

"What? Oh, yes. Sorry." Lulu smiled and pushed thoughts of Kace aside. "Just thinking."

"About anyone I know?"

Fee's eyes twinkled, her smile all-knowing. Lulu didn't keep secrets from her best friend, but she wasn't about to voice anything about Kace on camera. Sure, her admission to her attraction to the sexy Southern attorney would get ratings going, but she wasn't ready to share her feelings with the world or Kace. There had been enough footage of the two of them bickering during the cleanup from the fires last month. By the time this show aired that they were filming today, who knows where she'd stand with him. Would she tell him her feelings? Would he admit to his?

"Let's concentrate on you and your new love," Lulu stated, giving her friend a wink. "I say we throw a big going away party. I'll host and we'll do it on my rooftop terrace."

Fee lifted her glass in a mock toast. "You know I'm always up for a party."

"Perfect. I'll get everything together."

And playing the dutiful hostess would give her the distraction she needed from one Kace LeBlanc.

Lulu waited until the cameras left to pull out her begging for the wedding episode and questioning her friend about the spin-off. She loved Fee and didn't want to put her on the spot for all viewers to see.

Fingers crossed Fee would be in agreement for both. Nigel was counting on Lulu to make all of this work out and she didn't want to let him down.

"That was weird how my sister insisted she'd seen you before," Nigel stated, gesturing for Sophie to enter their second-floor suite.

Sophie's heart still hadn't gone back to a regular rhythm after that close call. The scrutiny with which Ellen kept staring had had Sophie ready to hop back on Nigel's jet and head back to New York.

"Weird," she agreed, for lack of anything else to say.

As she eased past him and into the room, Sophie gasped at the view. A wall of patio doors leading out onto a private balcony drew her across the room, ready to take in the beauty of the land from above.

Heavy gold drapes outlined each side of the doors and she was positive no royal palace was arranged more beautifully. Her decorator eye would take in all the details of the room later, but she wanted to step onto the balcony and look over the snow-covered grounds.

"It's freezing out there," Nigel said when she unlatched one of the locks.

"I just have to see it for a moment. I'm imagining the beauty in the summer."

She shoved open one door and took in the crisp fresh air. Sophie blinked against the bright white covering of snow that stretched over the grounds for as far as her eye could see. The evergreens were accented with winter and she hated that she'd missed seeing this place all decked out for the holidays. She imagined perfectly decorated Christmas trees with gold-and-white stockings hung from each of the fireplaces, dinner parties with glamorous dresses, and champagne fountains.

She turned from the view and came back in, latching the lock behind her.

"You grew up here?" she asked.

"I lived here my entire life, except for my schooling, until I moved to New York." Nigel shoved his hands in his pockets and glanced around. "This is actually my room, not a guest suite."

Of course, they would be staying in his childhood room. If that didn't add another layer of guilt, nothing would. She wanted to come clean with him; she wanted to tell him everything. But how could she and still stay loyal to her brothers?

It was supposed to be so simple. A few days at Green Room Media, snooping for exclusive footage, chatting with some camera guys. In theory it all sounded like a perfect plot...but somehow the execution had gone astray and now she risked breaking her heart and hurting the one man who made her want to forget this entire vendetta.

"Quite the little prince," she joked. "Though I imag-

ine you stood on your balcony and had the best imagination as a child. I know I would."

He smiled and started to cross to her. "And what
would young Roslyn have imagined?"

Young *Sophie* would have loved this room. "She
would have pretended to be a queen overlooking her
land, protecting her castle and her family."

Not so far removed from grown-up Sophie.

"Really?" He closed the gap between them and took
her shoulders in his hands. "That little girl wouldn't
have dreamed of a knight coming to rescue her from
the tower?"

"I've never needed to be rescued," she countered.
"I'm the one who would save the day. Always."

Wasn't that what she was ultimately doing now? Sacrificing to save her family's legacy?

And who knew what would happen now that Darius was coming to Royal and Miranda wanted to connect with him.

One thing Sophie knew, she refused to let Blackwood
properties, holdings and finances stay in the hands of
a gold-digging socialite who probably already had her
sights set on another unsuspecting wealthy man. Sophie
couldn't figure out why she hadn't already remarried,
but maybe the perfect billionaire hadn't come along, yet.

"You're very protective of your family," he stated,
sliding his thumbs up along her neck and jawline. "I
admire that."

He had no idea the lengths she'd go to.

"You and your sister must have a special bond," she
replied. His touch had her body tingling and trying to

concentrate on the actual conversation was difficult. "Since you are part of the wedding."

"We've always been close. She's older than me, so my grandmother doubled the pressure on her to settle down and have children." Nigel laughed. "Now that she's closing in on that goal, Grandmother has turned her attention solely on me. You've been warned."

Sophie reached up and gripped his wrists, returning his grin. "I can handle myself for a few days. Besides, I don't mind playing your girlfriend. You're not exactly an ogre."

Nigel's low laugh curled those nerves tighter in her belly. "I'll take that as a compliment. You're pretty sexy, too."

After the way he'd worshiped her body on the flight over here, she didn't need the words. She was well aware of how he thought of her. During their time on the jet, Sophie had pushed aside all of the outside problems facing them, all of the lies and deceit. She'd focused on them, on the pleasure and desire.

But reality hit hard now that they were here and she had to maintain the facade. Sophie only hoped she could get through these five days without Ellen circling back to how Sophie looked familiar.

"You know, we don't have to be down for dinner for a while," Nigel said, backing Sophie toward the four-poster bed.

"If we lose track of time and miss dinner, your grandmother will reprimand both of us."

Nigel shook his head. "If she thinks there's a chance you're going to help with the next generation of Townshends, she'll lock us in here and to hell with all dinners."

The idea held its temptations…but she knew it was nothing more than a fantasy. Even without the deception hanging between them, Sophie was sure this world wasn't for her. The Townshends were pretty much as powerful and wealthy as royalty. And even though the Blackwoods were wealthy in their own right, the differences were vast. City and country life were quite different. Nigel may have grown up in this gorgeous countryside town, but he was all city. He was larger than life, someone who needed that hustle and hard work. Royal, Texas, wasn't for someone who needed that rush of moving from one project to the next.

Sophie, on the other hand, loved her laidback lifestyle back home. She loved the ease of her work, the thrill of designing for others at her own pace.

Nigel kissed her neck and Sophie realized how silly and foolish she was being by thinking there would ever be anything more between them. Instead of a foundation for a true relationship, they had a fling, they had a farce for the next few days, and they had her lies. Not exactly future-building material.

"I thought we were faking this relationship," she murmured, thrusting her fingers through his hair.

"Only some parts." His lips moved over her heated skin. "I want you. Nothing about that is a sham."

She couldn't argue, not when she wanted him just as fiercely.

In a flurry of hands and stolen kisses, their clothes fell to the floor. Sophie stumbled back onto the bed and Nigel followed her down, pressing his weight against hers and into the soft thick pile of blankets.

Sophie hadn't known she had such passion inside

her until she met Nigel. Never before had she wanted to forget her goals and give everything, including and especially her body, to one man.

"I'll be right back."

Nigel eased off the bed, leaving her to watch as he crossed the room. The brightness from the daylight filtered in through the glass doors, casting a glorious glow on his magnificent form.

She didn't even try to turn away or hide the fact she was blatantly staring.

Nigel rummaged around through his luggage until he pulled out a box of condoms. Sophie laughed.

"Wow. Feeling optimistic, aren't we?"

He shrugged. "Hopeful. Besides, we're here for five days."

"Are you planning on us leaving this room?" she asked as he stalked back toward her. "You do have a wedding to be in."

"Oh, I wouldn't miss my sister's wedding." He sat the box on the side table and climbed back on the bed. "I also wouldn't miss the chance to explore this body again. I don't think I appreciated it enough on the plane."

"Oh, I'd say you appreciated me more than enough," she laughed. "Maybe it's my turn."

With a bold confidence she'd never felt before, Sophie came up to her knees and pressed her hands on his bare chest. She shoved him back onto the bed and straddled his lap.

"I think you've had enough control for once."

Leaning back against the headboard, Nigel placed

his hands behind his head and smiled. "I'm not about to argue with a beautiful woman."

She had no idea what she was doing. She only knew she wanted total power over him for this moment, so she let her desires guide her.

Sophie reached across to the nightstand and grabbed a condom. There was no hiding her shaking hands as she tore open the wrapper and carefully covered him.

He never took his eyes off her.

That intense stare added to her nerves…and her arousal. This man could be so potent without saying a word or even reaching for her. The way he looked at her, like she was the most important thing in his life, was so foreign to her. She could tell he was falling for her, even if he hadn't said so or maybe he didn't even realize it himself.

But she couldn't, wouldn't, dwell on emotions right now. Nigel had awakened something inside her and she wanted to spend their time together not worrying about the issues back home. For the duration of her stay here, she would play the dutiful girlfriend and sultry lover.

Those would be the easiest lies she'd ever told.

Bracing her hands on his chest, Sophie joined their bodies. The moment they connected, she let out a sharp cry. This was so much different than what she'd experienced earlier. She didn't know if it came from the dominance on her part or the position, but Sophie closed her eyes as sensation after glorious sensation rolled through her.

Nigel's hands gripped her hips and she lifted her eyes to focus on him. Yeah, there was that look, the one she could identify—something stronger than lust…something she feared would get them both hurt.

Ignoring the impending broken heart, Sophie placed her hands on either side of his head and leaned down. Her hair curtained them both as she slid her mouth over his. She wanted everything he had to offer and more. She wanted to consume him, to join with him in every way. The ache in her body grew as her hips pumped against his. The spiral of euphoria slithered through her as she tore her lips away and cried out.

Nigel gripped her backside as his own body jerked and trembled. Sophie watched as the pleasure overcame him, and she wondered if anything could ever compare to this moment.

She didn't believe so. All she could do was enjoy these next few days, because when they got back to New York, she was going to have to finish her plan and head home as soon as possible. The longer she spent with Nigel, the more she worried he might just be the one she hadn't known she was looking for.

Thirteen

Nigel didn't know why he was so damn nervous, but he stood outside of his suite door and adjusted his bow-tie. He hated these bloody things, but since he had to stand up with the groom, he had to wear one.

He'd left Roslyn to get ready on her own while he'd gone to see if anyone needed help with setting things up for the ceremony. Ellen had decided to get married in the grand ballroom of the estate and there were bustles of wedding planners, florists, caterers, and who knows who else all around the east wing on the main level.

Nigel had ended up in the study, reading texts from Seraphina telling him she was so sorry, but she and Clint had made the decision not to film a spin-off. She went on and on about how she knew this would not be what Nigel wanted—assuring him that she'd had a lengthy conversation with Lulu about the prospect of a new show—but Fee wanted to let him know that she was certain it wasn't for her. She would be happy to talk contract removal once he returned home.

Nigel cocked his head from side to side, trying to alleviate some of the pressure of this bloody buttoned-up shirt and tie. He had no clue what to do about Fee's contract right now, and that was something he'd have to put on the back burner—at least for today.

His sister was getting married and Roslyn was no doubt going to looking breathtaking. He'd had five gowns for her to choose from that his personal stylist had assured him any woman would love.

He tapped his knuckles on the door and then reached for the knob. The moment he pushed it open, every thought vanished as he took in the sight of Roslyn across the room, standing in front of the floor-length mirror.

Her eyes met his in the reflection as she fastened one earring. Her honey blond hair fell in waves over one shoulder and the ruby red strapless gown fit as if the designer had all of those luscious curves in mind.

The material draped down in the back and scooped low in the front. A little flare at the bottom only accentuated Roslyn's pinup shape.

"I hope you like it," she told him, turning to face him and smoothed her hands down the front of the dress. "I know it's a little flashy for a wedding, but someone told me red was your favorite color."

Flashy? More like elegance and sex all rolled into one. The dress, the woman… It was all utterly perfect.

Nigel moved on into the room and smiled. "You've been talking to my grandmother."

"Maybe."

Nigel stopped before he reached her, afraid if he got too close they may never leave this room. The sight of her had him forgetting any issues with *Secret Lives* and the dealings back in New York.

"I don't think it's customary to show up the bride," he told her.

"Oh, I doubt I could do that," Roslyn laughed. "I haven't seen Ellen's wedding dress yet, but I'm certain she's going to be stunning."

"I'm positive I won't be able to take my eyes off you. Maybe we could skip the ceremony and just hit the reception."

When he started to reach for her, she skirted around him with another laugh.

"You're a groomsman," she reminded him. "I'm pretty sure your family would notice if you weren't there."

"With the way you look right now, I don't really care what my family thinks." He took a step toward her, his gaze raking over her once more before landing on her eyes. "I couldn't imagine being here without you."

Roslyn's smile faltered and she glanced down to her hands.

Nigel reached for her, curling his hands around her arms. "Everything alright?"

Her dark eyes came back up to his. "I need to tell you something."

Good conversations never came from that starting point. Nigel smoothed his thumbs across her skin, toying with the thin straps across her arms.

"You look worried," he told her. "Whatever it is, you can tell me. I trust you."

She opened her mouth, then closed it. A moment later she pasted on a smile that he knew she'd forced.

"I just…"

Worry rolled off her in waves so Nigel leaned forward and slid his lips over hers for a second before easing back.

Roslyn licked her lips and sighed. "I think I'm falling for you."

Well, that wasn't what he'd thought she would say and he had to admit, he wasn't surprised. Scared like hell that the words were out in the open, but not actually surprised. He wasn't oblivious to how she looked at him, how she touched him.

"I know it's wrong," she went on in a hurry. "We're supposed to be faking this while we're here, but—"

"Roslyn." He had to stop her. "You're intriguing, you challenge me, you're sexy as hell and I enjoy our time together. I just… I can't offer love. I'm married to this show, to growing it even bigger. A relationship with love and commitment… I don't know when I could offer that. You deserve more than I'd be able to give you."

Roslyn closed her eyes and shook her head. "I should've kept my feelings to myself," she muttered.

"No," he countered. "I'm glad you shared what you're feeling. I just…can't say the same. I care for you, but love isn't something I can do."

She returned her anxious gaze to his, but Nigel kissed her forehead. He wished he could give her everything she deserved, everything she wanted. But love was huge and he couldn't commit to something so strong, so permanent right now…not when he was in limbo of making or breaking the show he'd worked so hard to produce.

"Besides, there's plenty about me you don't know," he retorted. "Let's enjoy the day and then we can work on taking things slow once we get back to New York."

"I don't think New York and slow belong in the same sentence," she stated. "But, I agree. We should enjoy today and then we'll talk later."

Nigel wrapped her in his arms and wondered if she was the one. His grandmother had already fallen in love with Roslyn, but Nigel wondered if all of this was too good to be true.

Were they meant to be? He'd known her such a short time, but he couldn't ignore the strong pull or the deep connection they'd already formed.

But he also had to remember that the show came first for now. There was too much going on, too many people depending on him and his social life; his *love* life would not be taking top priority.

Sophie swayed in Nigel's arms in the ballroom. Try as she might, she couldn't forget the overwhelming guilt she'd felt when he'd told her he wanted to get to know her more. She'd opened her mouth and her thoughts, her feelings had come tumbling out and she couldn't take them back.

She'd wanted to come clean about everything. She hated lying to this amazing man, but instead of telling him the full truth about her background, she'd told him her honest feelings instead.

How could she love him, though? How could she

make such a claim when he didn't even call her by her own name?

She'd taken something so beautiful, so mind-blowing, and turned it into something ugly and fake. What would he say when he found out why she'd infiltrated his company to spy on a woman he likely considered a friend?

Sophie gripped his shoulders and closed her eyes as the soft music enveloped them on the dance floor. He would no doubt hate her once he discovered who she truly was and she deserved nothing less.

But she would relish this fantasy moment for as long as she could. She didn't want to ruin his sister's wedding. But once it was over, she was going to have to tell him. If he wanted to get to know her more, if there was even an inkling of a chance for them, he'd need to know the truth before things went any further.

First, she'd have to talk to her brothers because all of this started when she'd vowed to find dirt on Miranda. There was overwhelming evidence that nothing sinister existed on the woman. Maybe she wasn't a monster like they thought. It was a possibility they had to consider, but then what would they do? Sophie still wanted the childhood home and estate to go back to her brothers. The home had to stay in their family…it just had to. But if they couldn't challenge Miranda in court, what other option did they have?

She would have to figure out what the next move should be once she spoke with Vaughn and Kellan.

Miranda aside, Sophie couldn't lie to Nigel anymore. Her feelings far surpassed anything she'd expected and now that she was in so far, she couldn't keep deceiving him. Once he discovered who she was, Sophie would just have to accept any backlash she received.

The song came to an end and Sophie pulled back. "I'm going to grab a glass of champagne."

Nigel drew his brows together. "Everything okay? You seem like you're not all here."

She hadn't been *all here* since she'd started this whole charade, but she nodded.

"Why don't you dance with your grandmother while I take a breather?"

He stared another moment before nodding and releasing her. Sophie gathered the skirt of her dress in one hand and maneuvered her way off the dance floor. Somewhere in the back of her mind, she'd logged the beauty of the reception with all the lighting and crystal beading draped from the elegant table arrangements and the chandeliers suspended from the high ceilings, casting a kaleidoscope of colors across the marble floor.

There were gorgeous people everywhere dressed in stunning gowns and sharp suits. And Sophie felt like such an imposter...likely because she *was* an imposter.

She'd barely stepped away from the dancers when a member of the wait staff came by with a tray of champagne glasses. Sophie smiled and grabbed one, needing something to hold to occupy her shaky hands.

"Thank you for coming."

Sophie spun around to see Ellen smiling and holding her own glass.

"Of course," Sophie replied. "You had the most beautiful wedding I've ever seen."

Her satin gown was positively radiant, showcasing a vintage vibe with a lace overlay. It was strapless with a flare from the waist and a delicate train. Her headpiece was a simple diamond headband with a sheer veil that trailed the length of her train. Three strands of crisp white pearls adorned her neck.

"I mean, thank you for coming home with my brother," Ellen clarified. "I've never seen him this happy and I'm pretty sure I have you to thank."

"Oh, well, he makes me pretty happy, too."

"You're good for him," Ellen said, then took a sip of her champagne. "I hope he'll come home more often— and bring you with him. I've always wondered what it would be like to have a sister."

"I have two brothers, so I know how that feels," Sophie replied with a laugh.

But the guilt continued to mount. Her lies had trickled so far off course from the simple plan she'd initially concocted. Now she was lying to sweet, innocent people, intruding in this family event where she didn't belong. She'd likely be in photographs of this day and when Nigel or Ellen saw them, they'd have to relive this all over again. The betrayal and the deceit.

Ellen reached for her hand. "Then I do hope we can get to know each other more. I swear I feel like I know you from somewhere, but it must just be how quickly we connected. You know how with some people, you just have that instant click."

Yeah, that must be it.

"Anyway, I'm just really glad my brother found someone he actually wanted to bring home," Ellen went on. "He's always so busy working, maybe you can convince him to take more time off and visit his family."

"I'll see what I can do," Sophie promised with a smile.

Ellen leaned in and gave a one-armed hug before turning back to the reception and her guests…leaving Sophie alone with her drink and thoughts bouncing around. Even though this was all based on lies, Sophie had very good intentions, but she didn't know if anyone other than her brothers would see that.

Even a glass of champagne wasn't making Sophie feel better or helping her forget her problems. Once this magical day was over and she and Nigel were on their way back to New York, she would have to talk to him. She might have started this whole vendetta against Miranda, but the entire plan had snowballed and what could have potentially been the greatest thing in Sophie's life was now likely ruined to the point of no return.

Nigel swirled his grandmother around on the dance floor and caught Sophie's eye. When he sent her a wink, her entire body jolted from love.

She did love him. There was no denying the truth now that it stared her in the face…literally.

Now she had to figure out if she could clean up this mess she'd created, manage to reclaim her rightful inheritance, and hold on to the man she didn't know she'd been looking for. Oh, and wait to see if he could fall for her because he was still unsure.

Sophie didn't see a way to get out of the impending broken heart and she had nobody to blame but herself.

Fourteen

Sophie bundled her coat closer around her neck as she made her way from the car to Nigel's jet. They'd spent another day at Shrewsbury Hall after the wedding, but now they needed to get back to work.

And she needed to get back to reality...which meant she needed to tell Nigel the truth.

Sophie figured once they were settled in for their flight would be the perfect time. He couldn't storm out and maybe she could get him to see how all of this had gotten out of her control.

Not that she would make excuses. There were none. She'd blatantly lied to him and each time he called her Roslyn, she felt...well, like she was her own dirty little secret.

How could she have expected to prove Miranda was evil when Sophie had been doing evil herself?

Sophie boarded the jet as nerves curled through her. She'd spoken with both of her brothers last night and they supported her decision to tell Nigel. They'd agreed that maybe there was no dirt to be found on Miranda. They would have to find another way to get their property.

Settling into one of the white leather sofas, Sophie fastened her seat belt as she waited for Nigel to finish speaking with the pilot. She wasn't nearly as nervous about flying this time, perhaps because she had too much on her mind. No matter how many times she rehearsed her speech, she was terrified to just let those words out in the open.

Nigel stepped through to the cabin and his eyes immediately locked with hers. Her time was up.

"Are we all set to go?" she asked.

Nigel sighed and settled back against his seat. "We're all good."

"You don't sound good."

He lifted a shoulder and glanced back at her as he laced his fingers in hers. "I hate leaving my family. It never gets easier. That's the real reason I don't visit more. My grandmother thinks it's because I work so much, but that's not it. I can carve out time, it's just difficult to come here and then have to leave again."

Sophie understood that need to be close to family. She loved her brothers with her entire heart and couldn't imagine living in another country where she couldn't see them anytime she wanted.

"Do you ever think of moving back?" she asked.

"Not really," he admitted. "I mean, I love it here, but

I've made a home and a life in New York. I need to visit home more often, though."

"Your grandmother and sister would love that," Sophie told him. "Family means everything at the end of the day."

"I agree. Which is why I'm hoping you'll join me when I return next month."

"What?"

Sophie stilled. Return with him? He couldn't mean that. He couldn't really want her to come back. First of all, this was just pretend and second of all, in a month, they likely wouldn't be speaking.

Her heart hurt because he stared at her with such hope in his eyes while he waited on her answer.

"My family seemed to take you in as one of their own and if we're getting to know each other more and more, it only seems right that you come back with me." He shrugged. "I mean, if you want to."

Roslyn closed her eyes just as the plane took off down the runway. Her breath caught in her throat but the fear she had of flying took a backseat to the fear she had of breaking Nigel's heart.

She simply couldn't do it. Not now. Not when he was pouring out his raw, honest feelings. He may not have been using the *L* word, but he was already inviting her back and that spoke volumes.

He literally was handing her everything, and if she told him the truth now, she would be throwing it all right back in his face. He would hate her.

There had to be a better way.

"I've got you," he murmured, squeezing her hand when the plane tipped up. "Just breathe."

He thought she was being silent and avoiding speaking to him because of her fear... If only he knew.

If only he knew her real name, her story...would he still want anything to do with her?

Sophie opened her eyes and shifted to face him. "I'd love to come back with you, but first I want you to meet my family. Well, my brothers. Then we'll see if you still want me to join you."

Nigel's smile widened. "You think I'm going to meet your brothers and get scared off? Are they that bad?"

"They're wonderful." But the truth was brutal. "I just want you to know everything about me before we go any further."

He stared at her another minute and Sophie wished she could just get up the courage to tell him the truth right now like she'd mentally prepared herself to do, but she couldn't.

"I'd love to meet your brothers," Nigel told her as he leaned in and slid his hand across her cheek and through her hair. "I want to know everything about you, Roslyn Andrews."

Sophie Blackwood.

It was on the tip of her tongue, but she said nothing like the coward she was.

How could she ever accuse Miranda of anything at this point? Sophie had betrayed Nigel day after day and she'd had the nerve to call it love. But she did love him. She'd made a mistake that she couldn't take back and there was no way she could've ever seen this disaster coming. Never before in her life had she purposely set out to hurt someone, to blatantly lie to someone's face. Going into this whole charade, she knew she'd be lying, but she honestly didn't think the end result would be so painful for so many.

The guilt and shame settled heavy in her heart as Nigel kissed her. The intimacy poured out of him and she just hoped he could find it in his heart to forgive her.

"Do you have a second?"

Nigel turned from his office windows and faced the doorway where Miranda stood.

"For my biggest star? Of course."

Miranda laughed as she stepped in and closed the door at her back. "I know I can always count on you for an ego boost."

Nigel truly did love each of the *Secret Lives* ladies in different ways. Miranda was genuine and loving. Always eager to help others. He couldn't imagine anyone not feeling drawn to her, though he'd heard about her difficult relationship with her ex-stepchildren.

Nigel knew Miranda and the Blackwood siblings didn't get along, but he really never understood why. Then again, he didn't know the Blackwood kids, either.

He'd never had one problem with Miranda and he respected her as a businesswoman and an asset to his show.

"What are you doing in New York?" he asked. "If you'd told me you were coming, I would've arranged lunch."

"Oh, don't worry about that." Miranda tucked her red hair behind her ear. "I was in town for a few meetings with some potential investors for Goddess Inc."

Goddess Inc. was Miranda's baby, which happened to be the country's fastest growing fitness empire. The woman was a force and she had already made a huge impact in the industry.

"I can have dinner arranged for us," he told her. "I have a new consultant that I'd like to introduce you to. She's got some great ideas about the show and how to boost ratings."

"I'd love to meet her," Miranda stated.

Nigel shoved his hands in his pockets and leaned back against the window ledge. "So, what brought you by? I know you didn't just pop in to say hi."

Miranda adjusted the clutch beneath her arm and shook her head. "I'm worried about Fee. With her leaving the show and all."

Nigel pulled in a deep breath. "As much as none of us want to lose her, change can sometimes be a good thing."

"She told me you asked her to consider a spin-off."

"I did and she decided to just make a fresh start with her new life, without all of the cameras." Nigel shrugged. "I can't blame her. I don't like it and I want her to change her mind, but I can see why she'd want to just enjoy her new marriage without any added stress."

Miranda pursed her lips. "Are you looking to replace her on the show?"

He'd thought about that. He actually wanted to discuss that with Roslyn, but since they'd gotten home from England yesterday, he'd been so busy playing catch up. Work that he hadn't been able to handle through emails and long-distance phone calls had become a bit of a pile, so he hadn't had the chance.

"I haven't decided on that just yet," he answered honestly. "We may see how things go without. I hope

I can talk Seraphina into making a guest appearance every now and then."

At least they could work out the rest of her contract doing things that way.

"Let me set up dinner reservations and we can talk more," he told Miranda as he reached for the phone.

"Oh, no." Miranda waved a hand. "I actually have to get back to Texas. I have a few things still to clear up after Buck's death."

"Well, next time you're coming to town, you'd better give me a heads-up," he warned with a smile.

"Of course I will," she promised.

Miranda crossed the room and kissed his cheek. "I'll see if I can talk to Fee about those guest appearances. It might sound sincerer coming from a friend and not the man writing her checks and talking about contracts."

Nigel nodded. "I'd appreciate that."

Miranda left his office almost as quickly as she'd come. He really didn't know what to do about Fee leaving. A few weeks ago that news would've stressed him out and had him losing sleep. But since meeting Roslyn and having her occupy most of his thoughts, work wasn't as stressful.

Part of him felt like a teen with a crush. Which was absurd since he was well into his thirties. He didn't want Roslyn to be too good to be true. The fact she gave herself to him for the first time spoke volumes for her character and her feelings toward him. He knew she couldn't have been intimate with him had she not felt so strongly about him.

He was supposed to meet her brothers soon. Roslyn promised to have them come to New York and they'd all meet at her penthouse for dinner. He was excited to get to know all facets of her life, but he didn't know why she'd seemed so worried. Her family couldn't be complete monsters. Besides, he wanted to try to explore the idea of more with her. He'd told her he couldn't love her, he didn't have it to give, but that had been fear. He wouldn't have taken her home if he wasn't feeling something stronger for her.

Nigel wanted to see just how far this would go and there was nothing that would change his mind.

Fifteen

Sophie stepped from her office just as a flash of red hair caught her eye.

The gasp escaped her as she turned back into her office and quickly shut the door.

Miranda was here? Why? Did she know what Sophie was doing? Had she come to rat her out?

Sophie leaned back against the door, trying to listen, but she heard nothing. With her breath caught in her throat, Sophie closed her eyes and tried to remain calm. If Miranda had revealed her secret and Nigel knew the truth, he'd be in here any second.

Craig's muffled voice echoed down the hall followed by Miranda's laugh. Good, she was moving away from Sophie and Nigel's offices.

Just keep going. Get on that elevator and get the hell out of here.

Sophie had known there was a possibility Miranda might show up at the office, but considering Sophie had planned on getting in and out in a week, she hadn't been too worried.

Now, well, she'd been here a couple weeks and knew she was tempting fate with each additional day she stayed.

Sophie had texted her brothers and asked how soon they could get to New York. She'd told them everything and pleaded with them to help her with Nigel. Maybe that was still a coward's way out to have backup, but she was desperate to hold on to the best thing that had ever happened to her.

Hopefully Vaughn and Kellan could be here tomorrow and Sophie could get all of her lies out in the open and tell Nigel exactly who she was and why she'd deceived him. She had to make him understand that every part of what happened between them was real—especially the part where she was falling in love with him.

Until all of this mess was over, Sophie wasn't going to be able to relax. And now she had to watch out for more Miranda sightings. Perhaps she should stay in her office or, better yet, feign sickness and head to her penthouse where she could hide out until she could confront Nigel.

Either way, Sophie was walking a thin line and at any second she could fall off and get lost in her web of deceit.

Nigel had just eased into the back of his car when his cell rang. He'd spent twelve hours at the office today trying to formulate a game plan for some grand going away party for Seraphina. Of course, the event would be aired, but the show needed to be the grandest of all. A black-and-white cocktail party at the Waldorf? A luau in Hawaii? He wasn't sure what would be the best, but he did plan on getting Roslyn's take on several ideas.

As his driver pulled away from the curb, Nigel answered his phone without looking.

"Nigel Townshend."

"Always so professional."

He smiled at his sister's teasing tone. "Aren't you supposed to be on your honeymoon?"

"I'm in Morocco now," she told him. "We just arrived after a couple days in Spain. It was beautiful, by the way, thanks for asking."

Nigel laughed and settled into his seat. He dropped his head back and closed his eyes. He'd take even a second of relaxation at this point. Trying to figure out ways to save his show from plummeting into an abyss while losing one of their top cast members was quite stressful.

Which was just another reason he couldn't wait to see Roslyn. She always made things seem better, brighter.

"So why are you calling your brother when you should be spending time in newly wedded bliss?"

"Are you alone?" she asked.

"I just left the office, so I'm with my driver." Alarm bells went off in his head. "What's going on? Are you okay?"

"I'm fine, but I'm worried about you."

"Me? Why?"

Ellen sighed. "You remember how I kept saying Roslyn looked familiar to me?"

"I do."

"I don't know how to tell you this," she murmured.

Nigel sat up and gripped his cell. "Just say it," he demanded. That trickle of fear down his spine had him on edge.

"Her real name is Sophie Blackwood."

Blackwood. As in… Miranda's late ex?

"She's actually a famous designer," Ellen went on. "I was watching one of my favorite YouTube channels on the plane and that was when it hit me. She has a massive following on her channel *Dream It, Live It*. I've watched so many of her design videos that I should have recognized her right off the bat, but she's altered her look. She's not a blond naturally and she doesn't usually wear glasses."

Nigel rubbed his forehead as his sister's words settled in.

"Are you positive?" he asked, hoping she wasn't, but knowing she was or she never would've called.

"Yes. I'm sorry."

Nigel's chest constricted. His driver continued toward Roslyn's penthouse. No, *Sophie Blackwood's* penthouse.

Why the deception? Because of Miranda? To get back at her for some reason? He didn't know the answers, but he sure as hell deserved them…starting with why she had used him, going so far as to tell him she was falling in love with him.

Going so far as to sleep with him over and over.

Nigel clenched his jaw and willed himself to remain calm. He had to talk to Roslyn…or whatever the hell she wanted to call herself. He had to hear her side, though he couldn't imagine there was a defense strong enough to make him forget what she'd done or warrant forgiveness.

"Nigel," Ellen said. "Are you still there?"

"I'm here. I'm on my way to her penthouse right now."

"I'm sorry," she said again. "I don't want you hurt."

Hurt? Yeah, he was, but bloody furious might be closer to his current mood.

"Will you text or call me later?" she asked. "I'm worried about you."

"I'll be fine," he lied. "Thank you for telling me—you did the right thing. Go enjoy your honeymoon and we'll talk when you get back."

Nigel disconnected the call and immediately typed in *Dream It, Live It* in his phone's browser. His heart sank when a smiling brunette popped up onto the screen. She casually leaned against the side of a pale yellow sofa. She wore a pretty floral dress with very little makeup and she was actually barefoot and holding a glass of wine. She had her head tipped just so and a perfect smile for the camera.

This was his Roslyn.

No. This was Sophie Blackwood with millions of followers. She was clearly a major success—and not at all in need of a job. Yet, she'd come to Green Room Media and infiltrated herself as a consultant, going so far as to sleep with her boss...and for what? Obviously something to do with Miranda, but Nigel didn't know why he'd gotten involved in this family drama.

He clicked through the different thumbnail photos of the videos. She certainly did look different with all that rich dark hair.

Bloody hell. She looked sexier, more natural.

And he still got that tug of arousal when he saw that smile and those curves. No amount of betrayal could turn that off.

"Sir, should I wait?"

Nigel realized the car had come to a stop. He shoved his phone back into his pocket and reached for the handle.

"I'm not sure how long I'll be," he replied. "Just don't go too far."

"Yes, sir."

Nigel had no clue what would happen once he confronted Ms. Blackwood. Right now she felt like a total stranger. He'd told her he wanted to get to know her more on a deeper level, but he'd had no idea he didn't know her at all. He hadn't even known her damn name.

Everything over the past few weeks had been a lie and Nigel wasn't leaving here until he got the answers he deserved.

The guard had alerted Sophie to a visitor and Sophie granted him permission to come on up. She glanced around the penthouse and onto the balcony where she'd set up a late-night dinner. She knew Nigel had been working so hard.

She wanted to do something for him to let him know she admired the way he juggled everything. She also wanted to pamper him just a bit.

Vaughn and Kellan had reluctantly agreed to come tomorrow, so this would be the last night Sophie would have with Nigel before he discovered the truth. She just wanted one more magical evening with the man she loved before she potentially lost him forever.

A heavy lump of guilt settled in her throat. Time was running out and she would have to make the most of every moment tonight.

When the elevator chimed and slid open, she glanced across the penthouse as Nigel stepped out. He'd clearly been raking his hands through his hair. The stress of the show was getting to him. She offered a smile, but it dropped into a worried frown when he didn't return the gesture.

"Rough day?" she asked.

"You could say that."

Sophie crossed to the island bar and grabbed the drink she'd made for him.

"I thought you could start with a nice bourbon before dinner," she told him, handing him the tumbler of amber liquid. "I've set us up over next to the balcony so we can still see the beautiful view, but not freeze."

Nigel tipped back the drink and sat the glass back on the bar. He shoved his hands in his pockets, but remained silent. Work must have really kicked him down today. She'd never seen him so worn or quiet.

"I have good news," she told him. "I got in touch with my brothers and they can be here tomorrow. I'd love for us to all do a nice dinner if you think you can leave the office early enough."

She turned toward the island to start filling the plates with pasta.

"Your brothers," he repeated slowly. "Would that be Vaughn and Kellan Blackwood?"

The plate dropped from her grasp and shattered onto the floor.

"And that would make you Sophie," he added.

Sophie glanced over her shoulder. Nigel held up his phone to show her a muted video from her YouTube channel.

"I had no idea you were so popular until I discovered this," he went on. "Sophie Blackwood, a YouTube sensation and brilliant interior designer."

Sophie gripped the edge of the counter. "Give me a second to explain."

"A second? Oh, I think you'd need much longer than that, don't you? I mean, you've clearly been planning this for a long time." He dropped his arm and shoved the phone back into his pocket. "How long would you have gone on with this charade, *Roslyn*?"

Tears pricked her eyes, but she needed to put up a strong front and not be seen as weak. She needed him to understand her actions, her reasoning. He understood family loyalty, didn't he?

"That's why I wanted you to meet my brothers," she explained. "I wanted to tell you everything with them here so they could help me explain what we were up against."

Sophie started to step toward him, but glanced to the shards of the broken plate near her bare feet.

"You're going to cut yourself."

Nigel muttered a curse under his breath and stepped over the mess, the broken plate crunching beneath his shoes. He gripped her by the waist and lifted her up and over, setting her down safely a good distance away.

Even in his anger, he was still a gentleman. How

could she not be in love with him? He obviously cared for her or her actions wouldn't have hurt him so much.

That sliver of information gave her hope. She knew he'd be hurt no matter how he discovered the truth, but she just wished she could've been the one to tell him. Now the betrayal seemed so much harsher.

"Who told you?" she asked.

Nigel shook his head. "That doesn't matter. You're the one who lied and used me."

Sophie recalled the flash of red yesterday.

"Miranda," she murmured.

"What?"

Sophie held his gaze. "Miranda told you, didn't she? I saw her at the office yesterday."

Nigel's eyes widened. "You saw her and didn't say anything? Afraid of getting caught?"

"I have valid reasons for everything I did."

The muscle in Nigel's jaw clenched and he propped his hands on his hips. "Miranda didn't tell me anything, so clearly she doesn't know you're here."

In that case, Sophie had no idea how he found out, but it really didn't matter. All that mattered was that she'd hurt him. She had to find a way to make him understand why she'd done this. Would he believe her if she told him she'd give up the vendetta against Miranda for a second chance with him?

At this point, no. The shocking news was too fresh, the pain too raw.

"My father's will left everything to Miranda," Sophie started. "My brothers and I got nothing."

"So you're seeking revenge as some sort of poor little rich girl?"

Sophie swallowed and blinked back unshed tears. "I know that's what it looks like, but the money has nothing to do with it. Miranda doesn't deserve anything from my father. She just married him for the fortune— the ranch and all of its history mean nothing to her. She has my childhood home and everything else that should remain in the Blackwood family."

Nigel stared at her from the slit in his lids. "So you came here to what? Find dirt on Miranda and then blackmail her into giving you back what you want? That sounds petty and childish."

"No, it sounds like my brothers and I want our home back. We want to be able to keep that in the family," she cried. "Miranda doesn't care about Royal like we do. She has her own life, her own empire. My brother and his wife are expecting a child and we want to carry on the Blackwood legacy."

Sophie stared at him, waiting for some sign that he understood where she was coming from. That he might get her loyalty wasn't a bad thing even if she'd made a bad choice.

"And did you find what you were looking for?" he finally asked.

Sophie crossed her arms over her chest. "No. I didn't find anything negative on Miranda. And I certainly wasn't looking to fall in love."

Nigel let out a humorless laugh and turned from her. "Don't throw that word out, not now. You don't know what love is. You don't lie to the people you love and you sure as hell don't deceive them."

Sophie took a few steps forward, close enough that

she could reach out and place her hand on his rigid back. He stiffened even more, but he didn't turn to face her.

"I never meant to deceive you," she stated. "When I applied for the job at Green Room Media, I wanted to talk to people, get some scoop against Miranda. I never ever thought I'd be working that closely with you."

"Yet you did." Now he did turn, causing her hand to fall away. "You got close to me. You slept with me and for all I know that was part of the plan."

He shook his head and raked both hands over his messy hair. "Once you realized you'd be working one-on-one with me, I'm sure that just fit right into your deceit. I mean, who better to get gossip from than the CEO? No one in the company has spent more time with Miranda than me. Giving your virginity was above and beyond, though."

"Stop," she ordered, the pain slicing her heart too deep. "I never wanted to be with a man until I met you. I knew in the end you'd find out who I was, but by the time I realized I loved you, it was too late for there to be any easy way to come clean. I was afraid of ruining things between us, so I didn't know how to tell you the truth. But you have to know that I couldn't have given myself to you had I not fallen so hard."

"All of this is so convenient," he mocked. "You just land a job with me, have access to nearly everything regarding the show and you get a free trip to Cumbria. I can't believe I was so naive not to trust my gut when I wondered if this was too good to be true."

"We don't have to be over," she said, her voice softening as the gnawing ache threatened to constrict her. "I know you're angry and confused and hurting. I also know I don't deserve to ask anything of you, but I'm asking that you take time and think before you just throw me out of your life."

"You think any of this is up to me?" he snarled. "I'm not the one who threw this all away. You did. You could've told me at any point over the past weeks who you really were, but you opted not to. Or, hell, at the very least you could've told me when you claimed you started falling in love with me."

"Looking back, I see that," she admitted. "But that would have meant letting down my family—choosing you over the promise I made to them. I told my brothers I would follow through and find the information we needed. I didn't want to let them down."

Maybe appealing to the side of family loyalty would get him to see she wasn't a complete monster.

"I'm the same person you were with in Cumbria," she told him. "I never lied to you about my feelings."

"You're not the same person at all," he countered. "I didn't even know your name."

Shame consumed her and she nodded. "But you know my touch and you know I love you. If you think back to our time together, you'll see that. You remembered what I said about that single stem, you know my food quirks, you know how well we mesh on a business level. We work together perfectly from every angle. Once you get beyond the shock and the anger, I hope you'll realize that no matter what happens, I'll always love you."

He said nothing, just continued to stare at her. Sophie wanted so badly to reach for him, to have him wrap his arms around her and tell her that he didn't hate her, that they would work this out.

But that was foolish thinking. His forgiveness was something she didn't deserve.

"I don't need to meet your brothers," Nigel finally said. "Needless to say, you're no longer welcome at Green Room Media and you're no longer part of my life. So go back to Texas and deal with your family drama there, but leave me out of it."

Without another word, he turned and headed to the elevator. Sophie watched as he stepped in and didn't even look back at her. She kept waiting, hoping for something else, but there was nothing. He'd literally cut her out just that fast.

The moment the doors slid closed behind him, Sophie let the tears fall. She'd brought all of this upon herself. There was nothing to show for her efforts—no dirt on Miranda and no relationship with Nigel. She was literally going back to Royal empty-handed, alone and in worse shape than when she'd arrived in New York.

Sophie turned toward the kitchen and stopped when she noticed the broken plate. Clearly the only thing she was good at lately was destroying everything around her. She only wished her heart would be as easy to clean up as this dish.

Sixteen

In the five days since he'd seen Sophie, Nigel still couldn't bring himself to go up to the penthouse of his own office building. The one space he'd always gone to for solace now held memories too painful to revisit.

He stared out the window of his office, watching the snow swirl around, remembering how the flakes would stick to Sophie's lashes.

Sophie. The name seemed to fit her, yet it was so strange to think of her that way. Like a bloody fool, he'd watched too many of her videos. Maybe he was just a masochist, but he'd wanted to see the real Sophie Blackwood in her element.

She'd positively shined and was so personable, so fun.

He hated to admit that he recognized in her the woman he'd started falling for. He'd thought Roslyn had been just a facade, but Sophie was the same, just like she'd said. And yet there was such a difference that he couldn't put his finger on. He tried yet again to push the thought away and refocus on work.

The gray skies didn't help his mood right now, neither did the fact that he couldn't pinpoint a location to have the farewell party for Seraphina. He wanted to make things as easy as possible for her and Clint.

His cell vibrated on his desk with an incoming text and Nigel glanced over his shoulder. Ellen's name popped up.

On a sigh, he grabbed his cell and opened the message.

I haven't heard much from you. I'm worried. Nana doesn't know anything because she just messaged me about "that nice American girl" coming back next month and doing a girls' luncheon.

Bloody hell. His grandmother would be heartbroken over all of this. Perhaps he should stick to the original plan of just telling her they broke up. He didn't want to tell her that Roslyn was really Sophie and that she'd lied to them all.

Granted, he'd taken Sophie home under the pretense of her being his girlfriend so he'd lied, too.

This entire situation was a mess. So much deceit, so much pain.

Nigel typed back a quick text, telling his sister he was fine and just busy at work and that he'd take care of Nana.

He hadn't even put his phone down when it rang and Miranda's name appeared.

Nigel swiped the screen to answer.

"Miranda. What can I do for you?"

"I hope this isn't a bad time," she replied.

Considering he was wallowing in his own self-pity party, this was the perfect time for a distraction...unless there was more bad news.

"You're not leaving the show," he commanded.

Miranda's soft laughter came through the phone. "No, I'm not. I'm not calling about work. I'm calling about your personal life."

"Is that right?"

"Listen, I've never stepped foot into your private affairs, but I need to now," she went on. "I know Sophie was in New York trying to find something damning on me. I also know she was working for you."

Nigel crossed his office and sank down onto the leather sofa. "Did you know the entire time?"

"I found out before I left the office," she stated. "I pondered what to do with the information."

Nigel dropped his head back on the cushion and pulled in a breath. "So that's why you are calling me? She didn't find out anything, if that's what you're worried about. There's nothing negative about you to be found here, no matter how hard she looked."

"Well, I appreciate that, but that's not the reason for my call."

Nigel really didn't want to talk about Sophie to anyone. He'd even dodged talking to his own sister during these past several days.

There was no question he'd been falling in love with

Roslyn, even though he'd tried to deny his feelings because he'd wanted to wait. The fact was, he'd been falling from day one. The pain wouldn't be so crippling and crushing if he'd just wanted her for sex. He missed her. He missed her smile, the way she'd hold his hand, her quick wit and sharp mind... He missed everything.

"I'm the last person who should come to her defense, but I am," Miranda went on. "Sophie and her brothers feel like they were wronged in the will after their father's death. I can't blame them for that. They've always thought I was after the Blackwood fortune. I wasn't, but given the way things happened with the will, their suspicious do make sense."

"Not to anyone who knows you," he informed her. "You don't have a callous bone in your body."

"Well, Buck left me strict orders before his death and I'm just trying to respect those wishes," she said. "Sophie is loyal to her family, Nigel. I truly believe she never meant to hurt you in any way."

Stunned, Nigel listened as Miranda defended her former stepdaughter. Nothing about that should have surprised him, though. Miranda was always the peacemaker, the one who would jump in to help anyone with no questions asked. She had a natural need to see those around her happy...even, apparently, those who were set on destroying her.

"I'm not sure why you'd want to help her out," Nigel said.

"Honestly, I'm helping you both," Miranda replied. "You know how gossip spreads. I learned that you took Sophie to England to Ellen's wedding. That tells me you really like her. I've never heard of you wanting to take someone home, let alone for a family wedding."

"It was a front to keep my grandmother off my back about settling down," he mumbled.

"That may be part of it," she agreed. "But don't discount your feelings. You don't have to tell me what they are. Just be honest with yourself. Enough lies were told and I wanted you to know the type of person Sophie really is. Her father wasn't the easiest man to love and he wasn't always the best to his kids, but he's trying to right a wrong from the grave and unfortunately, he's using me to do it—setting up enough of a mystery that the kids see me as an enemy."

Nigel had no clue what was all going on with that mess. But he knew Miranda's kind heart just wanted to make peace. He also knew she wouldn't have called if she didn't believe Sophie was a good person.

"You can do what you want, but I just had to share my thoughts," Miranda added. "And, if you were wondering, Sophie is going to be working on the Texas Cattleman's Clubhouse renovations. She's doing so free of charge and paying for the decor she uses. That information isn't public knowledge because she didn't want people to know. I believe that speaks to the type of woman she is."

Miranda said her goodbyes, leaving Nigel even more confused with his thoughts and his jumbled emotions. He had no clue what to do right now, and for the first time in his life, he felt utterly out of control.

All he knew was that he wanted this ache to cease. How the hell did he get over the one woman he wanted, but shouldn't?

* * *

Lulu smiled across the table at Kace.

"So, what do you say?" she asked, barely able to contain her excitement.

She'd asked Kace to lunch…not a date. This couldn't be a date. It just couldn't.

But the sexy cowboy attorney from Texas might just be the best add-in to *Secret Lives* if he'd simply agree to make a few guest appearances. When the show had filmed in Royal, the viewers had positively eaten up all the Southern charm those men had.

Of course there had only been one man who charmed Lulu enough to capture her attention and he sat right across from her still battling himself with the answer.

"Did you ask Nigel or the other women about this?" he finally asked.

Lulu picked up her water glass and took a drink. "I wanted to see what you said first. As for the other ladies, they'll totally be on board."

Who wouldn't? The man was a walking fantasy in a Stetson and shiny boots.

"Is this for the show's ratings or because you can't stand to be without me?" he asked with a smirk.

"The ratings, though I'm not sure we have it in the budget to pay you *and* your ego."

Kace eased back in his chair and propped one large strong-looking hand onto the table. Lulu couldn't ignore the desires just the sight of his hand pulled from her.

So what if her intentions to get him on the show were because she wanted him around her more? She was human with basic needs. Maybe they'd been at each other's throats at one time, but sex changed everything.

"Just say you'll do it and leave the rest up to me," she urged. "Unless you hate the city life."

He let out a low sexy laugh. "New York isn't exactly my speed, but it's doable every now and then."

Lulu barely resisted the urge to leap over the table, straddle his lap and hug him. "Does that mean you'll do it?"

His kissable lips twitched. "If you can line up everything and get all the working parties to agree, I'll do it."

Lulu let out a slight squeal and clapped her hands together. "Perfect. You won't regret this."

Kace leaned across the table, taking her hands in his as he lowered his voice. "Make no mistake. You'll owe me."

And that sounded like the most delicious promise ever.

Seventeen

Sophie stared at her sketch pad and what she'd laid out so far, then she stared back at the nearly completed room. The architect and contractor had done a marvelous job of restoring the burnt portion of the clubhouse. Now she was trying to find a way to keep the decor true to the rest of the clubhouse, plus add in some special touches to really celebrate the reopening of this wing.

"Looks like some things still need decorated."

Sophie nearly dropped her sketch pad as she spun around at the familiar voice. "Nigel," she gasped. "What are you doing here?"

He casually leaned against the doorway that had yet to be trimmed. With a gray T-shirt and worn jeans and even a pair of cowboy boots, he fit in perfectly. She'd never seen him in boots and she couldn't help but smile.

"Are you relocating to Texas?" she asked, nodding to his new attire.

With his hands in his pockets, he shrugged. "I figured I should at least try to look the part. I draw the line at the hat, though."

How could he have her smiling when looking at him hurt so much? But as conflicted as she felt, she knew he was here for a reason. She only hoped she was that reason.

"Did you come here looking for me or are you filming in Royal again?" she asked, unable to stand the anticipation.

"Maybe both," he replied.

Nigel pushed away from the door and took a slow walk around the open space. He didn't say a word as he continued to survey everything…which consisted of drywall, paint cans and etched glass windows.

Maybe he'd come to drive her crazy and make her pay for what she'd done to him. Although, she didn't know how much more she could suffer because living without him had been pure hell these past few days.

"I hear you're doing the decorating," he finally said as he focused his attention back to her.

Sophie clutched her pad to her chest. "I am. I wouldn't trust this to anyone else."

"I've seen your videos—you're good at what you do," he replied. "They're lucky to have such talent."

Stunned at his accolades, Sophie simply said, "Thanks."

Nigel took one step, then another, until he came to stand within inches of her. His eyes roamed over her face, her hair, before landing on her eyes.

"You dyed your hair back," he murmured, reaching out to smooth a strand behind her ear.

Sophie shivered at his touch and leaned in just enough to feel his warmth. "I wanted to get back to myself now that I'm home."

She didn't know how long they were going to do this small talk and dance around the proverbial elephant in the room. Seeing him again only reminded her of all that she'd had that she'd then thrown away…not that she'd thought of anything else since returning to Royal.

"I like this better," he told her as he dropped his hand, but didn't take a step back.

The familiar woodsy scent of his cologne enveloped her, making her recall laying against his chest and sleeping when they were in England. Making her remember when he'd first wrapped her in his jacket on that snowy night.

So many memories made in such a short time. Nigel had packed such a powerful impact on her life and embedded himself so deeply into her heart.

"Why are you here?" she asked, unable to stand the silence and the nerves eating away at her.

"I'm here for you."

Fear ebbed away as hope flowed in. Sophie wanted to reach for him, but she needed to hear what he had to say. What had made him come all the way here instead of calling or texting? What happened in the five days after she'd left?

Because since she'd been back, all she'd thought of was where she could've righted her wrongs. But once she was caught in that downward spiral, she'd been completely out of control and she'd had no way to stop.

"I got a call from Miranda," he added.

Sophie blinked. "Miranda? What did she call you about?"

"You. She came to your defense without hesitation."

Seriously?

Sophie didn't know what to say to that remark. She'd never known Miranda to want to help her out. Of course, there was all those people who sang her praises and swore that Miranda was practically a saint, but Sophie hadn't experienced that side of her. Truth be told, they'd never really interacted much, not even when Miranda and Buck had still been married.

"What did she say?" Sophie asked.

Nigel smoothed a hand over his jaw and the back of his neck. He seemed so exhausted, which only matched her own situation. She hadn't slept for replaying the past few weeks over and over in her head. She wondered if he'd been awake all night thinking of her, too.

"She basically said that you had valid reasons for coming to New York."

How the hell had Miranda known Sophie was in New York? Had she seen her that day?

"I found out that Craig mentioned my new consultant when he was chatting with Miranda," Nigel went on. "I had actually talked to her about meeting you, obviously not knowing the truth, and then Craig was talking about how amazing you were and how you could be on the show because you're just as stunning as the others. I mean, you know how Craig gossips. He ended up showing Miranda a photo."

"She could've called me out right then," Sophie murmured. "Why didn't she?"

"I'd say she knew why you were there at that point," he told her. "But when she called me, she explained how you and your brothers feel cheated with the will and everything."

"We *were* cheated," Sophie reiterated. "We still don't understand why we were cut out."

"I get that." Nigel gave an understanding nod. "I don't get why you continued to lie to me, not once we started getting so close, but I know why you initially came to New York. You were trying to save your family's legacy. Believe me, I above anyone else understand the importance of showing family loyalty."

"I still don't understand why she came to my assistance," Sophie thought out loud.

Nigel reached for her arm and slid his fingers down to hold her hand. "Maybe because she's not the monster you all think she is. Maybe because she wants to see you happy. I truly believe she wants to fix her relationship with you and your brothers."

Sophie wasn't so sure about fixing things, but she also wasn't so sure that Miranda was out to take everything. She'd seemed just as surprised at the will as the rest of them. Maybe that hadn't all been an act.

"And her call made you come?" Sophie asked.

He squeezed her hand. "Her call made me think a little more about what this must have been like from your point of view. For years I've been somewhat of a black sheep for leaving England and not marrying or settling down. Family is important to me, even though I'm not jumping in to produce heirs."

Sophie smiled. After having met his grandmother and sister, and seeing where he came from, the archaic sounding trait wasn't so bizarre after all.

"Honestly, I couldn't stand being without you," he finally said. "The office was lonely, even though my staff is bustling all over the place. Every time I looked at events for the show coming up, I wondered what you would think or how you would change things. I can't even go up to my penthouse because I see you displayed on that couch. And now I can't go back to England because Nana thinks we're a couple."

Sophie smiled. "Is that all?"

Nigel took another step forward until they were toe-to-toe. He framed her face with his hands and leaned in, barely a breath from her mouth.

"No, that's not all," he whispered. "I love you and I want you. I won't ask you to give up your life here. I'd never do that. I'll fly back and forth if need be. I don't give a damn at this point, I just need you."

Sophie's heart nearly exploded. She never thought he would forgive her, and she sure as hell never thought Miranda would be the one to turn him around.

Had Sophie been wrong all this time? Was Miranda really just misunderstood and wanting to make things right?

Sophie wrapped her arms around Nigel's waist. "I need you, too. I've been miserable knowing that I hurt you. I just, I didn't know what to do and my loyalty was so torn—"

Nigel covered her lips, cutting off her sentence and any other thought she may have had. Nigel was here, he was holding her, kissing her and loving her. None of this was a dream and while she didn't deserve his forgiveness, she wasn't going to turn him away. She'd never take him for granted again.

Sophie eased back, sliding her fingers through his hair. "I swear, I'll never lie to you about anything ever again."

Nigel smiled. "That's good, but I hope you know what you're getting into with me."

"I have a pretty good idea."

"Maybe we'll need to make you an extra on the show," he stated. "I'm sure ratings would skyrocket with the most sought-after designer."

Sophie laughed. "Well, we'd have to marry and divorce since the show is about exes."

Nigel shook his head. "I'm never letting you go, but I'm sure I can sneak you in somehow."

He continued to stare at her and Sophie had never felt so excited and anxious and thrilled all at the same time.

"And you still have to come back home with me next month," he added. "My grandmother will grill you on babies and weddings."

Sophie met his gaze and grinned. "I'm open to both."

Nigel kissed her again, then wrapped his arms around her and picked her up, spinning her around.

"I'm never letting you go again," he told her. "I hope you don't mind a houseguest because I packed a large suitcase."

"Stay as long as you like," she told him.

"How about forever?"

Sophie kissed him again and knew she'd been given a second chance at her first love. Nothing could steal her happiness now.

* * * * *

BLAME IT ON THE
BILLIONAIRE

NAIMA SIMONE

To Gary. 143.

One

Honor thy mother and father.

Grayson Chandler smothered a sigh. With all due respect to Moses, but if he'd been stuck listening to Grayson's mother nag on and on and about his lack of duty, loyalty and wife, the prophet might've asked God to nail down the specifics on that commandment.

Swearing. Out.

Muzzling. Out.

Faking a coronary episode to avoid her complaining. Gray area.

For a moment, a flicker of guilt wavered in Grayson's chest. But at the moment, he was caught in his mother's crosshairs. Pit bulls with lockjaw had nothing on Cherise Chandler. She didn't let go of something—whether it was a project, a subject or a grudge—until she was done with it.

Which didn't bode well for him.

He was thirty years old and president of KayCee Corp, one of the most successful global tech start-up companies in the country and he hadn't been a child to be controlled long before he left his parents' house. For years, he'd answered only to himself, owed no one else explanations or justifications.

Yet none of that mattered when it came to the crystal blue gaze that could make him feel like the little boy who'd been busted hiding a stray dog under his bed for a week.

Hell.

Parental guilt trips were a bitch.

"Grayson, your stubbornness is becoming ridiculous," his mother said, a note of irritation in her voice. She shifted closer and a small frown marred her brow. "You've proven your point with this little business venture of yours and Gideon Knight's. But your father needs you now, your *family* needs you. It's time to stop playing at CEO, step up and take your place at Chandler International. It's your responsibility. Your duty."

He clenched his jaw, trapping the vitriolic stream of words that scalded his throat. *This little business venture. Time to stop playing.* As if striking out on his own without the emotional or financial support of his Chicago old-money, well-connected family was the equivalent of a rousing game of Monopoly. With those few words, she'd dismissed years of his and Gideon's hard work, relentless determination and resulting success.

He should've been used to this casual disregard. Of his accomplishments. Of him. As the second son, the "oops baby" of Daryl and Cherise Chandler, he'd been an afterthought from birth. But somehow, his skin had never grown that thick.

Another black mark in the "Why Grayson Isn't Jason Chandler" Column. Right under rebellious. Selfish. And disloyal.

Didn't matter that he'd had a hand in founding a tech platform that served major businesses and assisted them in tracking their shares with its unrivaled software. Didn't matter that his business was one of the most successful start-ups to hit the financial scene in the last five years.

None of it mattered because it wasn't Chandler International.

Dammit.

Grayson shoved his hands in his tuxedo pockets and glanced away from his mother's scrutiny. Guilt and shame knotted his gut.

He was throwing a pity party, but at least he was *alive.*

Jason couldn't say the same.

And because his mother had lost her son—her favorite son—Grayson imprisoned the sharp retort that weighed down his tongue.

"I take my position at and ownership of KayCee Corp as seriously as Dad does with Chandler. I also understand my obligation to our family. But as I've told both of you, my company is my legacy just as Chandler is Dad's."

"Don't be deliberately obtuse, Grayson. It's not the same—"

"Mother," he interrupted, voice cold. "Now isn't the place or time for this conversation."

She parted her lips, but after a second snapped them closed. Oh yes. Only proper decorum and being potential fodder for gossip trumped getting in the last word.

"Cherise, it's so wonderful to see you again," a feminine voice intruded.

The pleasant, soft tone shouldn't have scraped him raw, leaving an oily slide of disgust. He didn't need to glance behind him to identify the woman. He'd be able to identify that dulcet tone, that light floral scent anywhere.

Identify it, then crucify it.

"Adalyn," his mother crooned, a smile erasing her frown as she moved toward Adalyn Hayes with outstretched arms. "Don't you look beautiful?"

Grayson shifted to the side, studying his mother as she warmly embraced his ex-girlfriend. The woman who'd almost become Mrs. Grayson Chandler.

The woman who'd stabbed him so deeply in the back he still had phantom pains from the scar a year and a half later.

She hadn't changed at all. Still stunningly beautiful with oval-shaped green eyes, delicate features, pretty mouth and long sleek hair as dark as a raven's wing—or as dark as her heart. A midnight blue gown that glittered as if stars had been sewn into it clung to her small breasts and willowy frame before flowing over slender hips to pool around her feet.

No, she hadn't changed a bit. But he had.

That beauty no longer stirred desire inside him. Those embers had long turned to dust, incapable of being lit ever again.

"Grayson," Adalyn purred, turning to him and linking her arm through his mother's. "I didn't know you would be attending the gala this year. It's wonderful seeing you."

"Hello, Adalyn."

Damn if he'd lie just for the sake of pleasantries.

"I've missed you," she murmured as if his mother had disappeared and just the two of them existed in the crowded ballroom of the North Shore mansion. "We need to get together for dinner and catch up with one another."

"I love that idea," his mother chimed in, patting Adalyn's hand. "We've missed you, too. I was planning a dinner party for next week. You and your parents are invited. I'll call your mother to officially issue the invitation."

The conversation sounded benign, but something seemed…off. Too jovial. Too neat.

Too false.

"Matchmaking, Mother?" he asked, infusing a boredom into his tone that didn't reflect the cacophony of distaste and rage roiling inside him like a noxious cloud. "You don't think this is a little beneath you?"

"Not when you insist on flitting from woman to woman, behaving like a male whore," she snapped, and no, it wasn't the first time he'd heard those words.

Manwhore. Playboy. Embarrassment. But again, that damn not-so-thick skin. The barbed insult pricked him like the cockleburs that would sting his fingers when he visited his grandmother's horse farm as a child. Back then, he'd plucked them off and rubbed away the nip of pain. Now, with his ex a witness to his mother's disdain, those nips drew blood.

Deliberately curling his lips into a mocking smirk, he bowed slightly at the waist. "Thank you, Mother. Now tell me what you really think because I sense you're holding back."

She scoffed, returning her attention to Adalyn who watched him with a gleam in her eyes. A gleam that heralded trouble. For him.

"You're thirty years old and it's time to put away such childish behavior. The future CEO of Chandler International needs a good woman by his side supporting him. The board will not endorse or accept a man whose name and picture ends up on those dirty little gossip websites as often as the business section."

He stiffened. The smile he gave his mother was brittle, felt close to cracking right down the middle.

"Well then I guess it's a good thing I don't intend to be the future CEO of Chandler International. Which makes the board and my love life nonissues. Now, if you'll excuse me, I see several people I need to speak with." Bending his head, he brushed a kiss over his mother's cheek. "Mother. Adalyn."

Without waiting for the diatribe about his rudeness, he pivoted and strode away from the two women, the noose that had slowly been tightening around his neck loosening with each step.

He should've seen this coming. His mother had been less than subtle about her wishes for him to settle down and marry. Especially in the last six months.

Since Jason had died.

The thought of his brother lanced him through the chest, a hot poker that hadn't cooled in the time since his death. With a thirteen-year age difference and the knowledge that Jason was the favorite between them, they hadn't been close. But Grayson had loved his older brother, respected him. And the tragic randomness of a brain aneurysm had only made Jason's death harder to accept.

But Grayson hadn't had time to grieve before his parents had started pressuring him to leave the business he'd created and return to the family company. The Chandlers were American royalty, and with the heir now gone, the spare had to step up and perform his duty. Which meant helming Chandler International and, according to his mother, committing himself to a woman from a respectable background.

The knot that had started to relax around his throat tightened again, and he jerked at his bow tie. God, the thought of being back under his father's thumb, having to answer to Daryl Chandler and the board full of men just like him... Of having his independence stripped from him... Of having to live by the constricting rules that governed being a Chandler, one of Chicago's oldest and wealthiest families...

He was already suffocating.

Fuck, he needed air.

Charging across the ballroom, he didn't stop until he exited the cavernous space filled with the glitterati of Chicago. They were supposed to be his friends, his business contacts, his people.

And all he wanted was to escape.

Escape them all.

Two

The last place Nadia Jordan belonged was this gorgeous North Shore mansion that wouldn't have been out of place in the French countryside. And as the security guard skimmed a glance over her dark brown hair that no doubt looked like she'd been dragging her fingers through it—because she had been—and down her leather jacket and faded jeans to her tennis shoes, he no doubt agreed.

But in her defense, it was a Saturday night, and she'd been on her way back home from one of her brother's travel league baseball games when she'd received the emergency call from her supervisor that had brought her here. As the older sister and guardian to a teenage boy, her idea of an emergency included a hospital, an asthma attack or broken limbs. But obviously she and her boss, the vice president of operations with KayCee Corp, had very different ideas of what constituted a crisis. His involved a high society gala, a white tuxedo shirt and spilled shrimp cocktail.

When she'd received the call, she'd wanted to tell him

she was off the clock. He could button up his jacket for the rest of the night. But being a rural transplant from Tatumville, Georgia—and yes, it was as small as it sounded—she'd been lucky to land the job in Chicago as secretary in one of the country's hottest tech firms. And with a brother who was involved in every extracurricular activity his new high school had to offer, as well as his college tuition bills on the very near horizon, she literally couldn't afford to say no to her supervisor's sometimes wacky requests.

Being a secretary hadn't been her dream job. Nursing held that honor. But leaving for school and entrusting her brother to her mother's seriously lacking maternal care hadn't been an option. Nadia had cared for Ezra since their mother had come home from the hospital with him, even though Nadia had only been seven. Sacrificing for him so he could have a stable home and a chance at a successful future hadn't been a hardship. She would do anything to ensure he had the opportunities she hadn't.

Which explained why she stood in the foyer of an ostentatious mansion, holding a garment bag with a clean dress shirt, waiting for a black-suited security guard to grant her entrance.

"Ma'am, your name isn't on the guest list," he informed her, scanning the screen of the tablet he held.

She fought not to roll her eyes. *No shit, Sherlock*. She belonged in a world with linoleum and mass-produced light fixtures. Definitely not this alternate universe with gold and marble tiles and mammoth crystal chandeliers. "I know. My supervisor, Mr. Terrance Webber, is the guest. I'm his secretary, and he asked me to bring an item by for him." She held up the garment bag, silently explaining the "something."

"He assured me he would leave a note with security so I could bring this to him. I shouldn't be long at all."

"A moment, please."

"Sure." She forced her lips into a smile, when she really wanted to lament the fact that she could be curled up on her living room couch, covered from chin to toe with an afghan, settling in for an evening of campy B horror movies.

Several moments passed as the guard spoke into a headpiece, and she tried not to gawk at the over-the-top evidence of wealth surrounding her. A gilded staircase that could've graced any classic Hollywood movie set curved to a second level. Paintings that appeared old, and therefore expensive, were mounted on the walls and a huge fireplace inlaid with more gold damn near covered a far wall.

So this was how the one percent lived.

Enlightening.

And intimidating as hell.

Finally, the guard ended his conversation and glanced down at her.

"Mr. Webber is currently in the first men's room in the east wing. He instructed you to meet him there." He turned and pointed toward the rear of the foyer and a corridor that branched off to the right. "If you'll follow that hall to the end, make another right. The men's restroom is the last door on the left."

"Thank you."

Relief poured through her as she marched forward, ready to have her errand done so she could return to real life. Which didn't include this uncomfortable tumbling in her stomach.

Well, her life in Chicago didn't include it. In Tatumville, she'd been intimate with this feeling—this sense of not belonging, of not being worthy. When you were the daughter of the town Jezebel, who was also a drunk, people tended to stuff you in the "won't amount to much" box. But when Nadia and Ezra left her hometown and started over in Chicago, she'd vowed never to let anything, or anyone, make her feel that insignificant again.

The music drifted away until she could barely hear it as she traveled down the hall. Her cell phone buzzed in her jeans pocket, and she paused to fish it out. A grimace crossed her face as she read the text.

Terrance Webber: Where are you, Nadia? I need the shirt ASAP. They're about to serve dinner.

Inhaling a deep breath, she held it for several seconds, then slowly released it. Being snippy with the boss was a definite no-no.

Nadia: I just arrived. I'll be at the restroom in a minute.

She typed the reply and started walking, tucking the phone in her back pocket. The sooner she got this over with the bet—

"*Oof.*"

The air barreled out of her lungs as she slammed into the wall that had just sprung up in the middle of the corridor. She stumbled back several steps, and the garment bag tumbled from her fingers. Big, strong hands gripped her forearms, steadying her before she could follow Mr. Webber's shirt to the floor.

"Thank you. I'm sorry about…that…"

Her words dried up on her tongue as she met a unique gaze. Heterochromia, it was called. She'd looked it up soon after starting her job. One vivid, sky blue eye, and one forest green. Startling and beautiful. And only one man she knew possessed it.

Grayson Chandler. President of KayCee Corp. Her employer.

And the man she'd been secretly lusting after for over a year.

Oh, God. Surely You couldn't be so cruel.

But as Grayson cocked his head to the side and skimmed his gaze from her face, down her body and back up, she had to admit that yes, indeed, God might have a mean streak. Otherwise, why else would He allow her to come face-to-face with this beautiful man while she looked like something that had been dragged over home plate a couple of times?

He bent down and snagged the forgotten garment bag from the floor. Standing, he offered it to her, a smile quirking the corner of his mouth. Wow...that mouth. Full, sensual with a deep dip in the center of the top lip. Her fingers itched to trace it, to test the softness. She shivered, and from the narrowing of his eyes, she didn't think he missed it.

"I've heard of Cinderella showing up late to the ball clothed in a beautiful gown. But not with her dress in tow." He held the bag out to her, arching an eyebrow. "I think you need an upgrade in fairy godmothers."

"Yes, well, Cinderella was high-maintenance," she murmured, accepting the luggage.

A sharp bark of laughter escaped him, and from the slight widening of his eyes and the surprise flashing through the blue-and-green depths, it seemed the crack of amusement caught him off guard. Join the club.

"And you're not high-maintenance?" he asked, slipping his hands into his tuxedo pants.

The movement opened his black jacket, offering a glimpse of his pristine white shirt stretched across a broad, powerful chest and flat abdomen. Heat tangled in her belly, and she fought the urge to cover it with her hand. As if that futile gesture could contain it.

"You would be the first, then," he said. Before she could respond to that loaded statement and the hint of bitterness in it, he continued. "I've never met the anti-Cinderella before, and I have to admit I'm curious. After you change, will you allow me to escort you to the ballroom?"

Mortification swelled inside her chest, scorching a path up her throat and pouring into her face. It figured that when she stepped into a fairy tale and met Prince Charming, instead of being the bejeweled, beautifully gowned princess, she was the poor scullery maid. Only thing missing was the ash on her face.

Clutching Mr. Webber's shirt tighter, she hiked up her chin. She might be embarrassed, but damn if she'd show it. "Actually, I'm only here to drop off this shirt for my supervisor. He's the guest, not me."

He frowned. "It's Saturday. Aren't you off the clock?"

She shrugged. "Technically. But when the boss calls…"

"Are you getting paid overtime for this little errand?" he pressed.

She didn't reply. They both knew the answer. And judging by the darkening of his eyes, from irritated to thunderous, he didn't like it. Why did that send a thrill tripping down her spine? Especially when it was *Grayson's* employee who had delivered the order for her to be here? She refused to analyze the first or share the second.

"What's your supervisor's name?" he asked. No, *demanded*. The hard, flat tone brooked no refusal. Again, that trickle of excitement, only this time it sizzled, arousal hardening her nipples, clenching her belly…pooling heavy between her legs.

She didn't do controlling men. Not after the childhood she'd experienced and all the things she'd witnessed between her mother and her "boyfriends." In many ways, Grayson reminded her of those men. Rich. Handsome. Pillars of the community. Respectable. Untouchable. Except for furtive meetings with her mother in the alleys behind bars or in the back seats of expensive cars.

Yes, he bore more than enough resemblance to those

hypocrites that she should shy away from him. But from the first, Nadia had been drawn to his lovely mismatched eyes, the sharp angles of his cheekbones, nose and jaw. The carnal perfection and temptation of his mouth. The tall, elegant frame with wide shoulders and chest, a tapered waist and long, powerful legs.

But unlike those men who'd ignored her mother on Main Street but couldn't get enough of her on back streets, Grayson seemed to possess a core of integrity. The few times they'd run into each other since she'd started working at KayCee Corp, he'd been nothing but respectful, his gaze not dipping to linger on her generous breasts or her equally generous ass. He'd never uttered sly innuendo or propositioned her. It'd been…refreshing. And had only deepened her schoolgirl crush.

Yet none of that justified her reaction to that implacable, disobey-and-bear-the-consequences tone. Or explained why she imagined him clasping her chin in his big hand, holding her still for a hard, hungry kiss while cuffing her arms above her head.

Arousal rippled through her, and she clenched her thighs.

"Cinderella," he said, stepping closer, while she stared up at him like prey caught in the unblinking stare of a predator on the hunt. "His name."

"W-why?" she stammered. *Oh, for God's sake.* She tipped her head up, drawing her shoulders back. "Why do you want to know?"

Why do you care?

"So I can have a very civil conversation with him about taking advantage of his employees and not compensating them for their time. To discuss how not to abuse one's position of power over another, including expecting them to be at one's beck and call."

"There're a lot of 'one's' up in there," she grumbled.

Shaking her head, she ignored the curl at the corner of his mouth, and the warmth it caused to slide through her veins. Like liquid sunshine. And all because she'd made him smile. Somewhat. *Good Lord, woman. Get it together.* "I can't do that. One, I need my job, and two, it's no big deal." Even though it kind of was.

"Oh, but it is," he purred, mirroring her thoughts. "And you don't have to worry about your job, Cinderella. Who-ever he is wouldn't dare to fire you."

The arrogance and satisfaction in his assurance shouldn't have been sexy, but damn, it *so* was. Even the fact that he didn't remember her, though they'd met a handful of times, couldn't diminish the desire he stirred in her. Did it sting? Oh yes, and more than a little. But she worked for his company, not for him directly. And if life had taught her anything, it was to be realistic. Men who were constantly photographed with sophisticated, slender, gorgeous social-ites, actresses and models wouldn't notice a small-town, curvy, unassuming secretary.

So yes, him not recognizing her made sense. Still hurt, though. Every woman—even Cinderella—longed to be memorable. Especially to the man who starred in her every dark, sweaty, erotic dream.

"I appreciate your concern, but my lips are sealed, and I really need to—"

"What would it take to unseal them?" he murmured, and she stiffened, shock winging through her as his gaze dropped to her mouth. And stayed there.

Nervous, she sank her teeth into her bottom lip, and something flashed in his eyes. On another man, she would've labeled it lust. But not him. Never *him*.

"Tell me what I need to do. What you need me to give you," he added.

Her apparently filthy mind supplied answer after an-

swer, and none of them had to do with clean shirts, bosses'
names or uncompensated time.

She cleared her throat. "I don't—"

The hallway plunged into darkness.

"What the fuck?" Grayson snapped.

Yes. What the fuck indeed.

Three

"Any word yet?"

Grayson glanced down at the woman sitting on the floor of the hallway. The light from his cell phone revealed her back pressed to the wall, her long, entirely-too-gorgeous legs stretched out in front of her and crossed at the ankles. Jesus, what this woman did for denim…

Dragging his attention away from the siren's call of her thighs, he returned it to the cell in his hand. "Citywide blackout," he replied, his voice rougher, more abrasive than usual. Unexpected, and inconvenient, lust clawed at him. "I wasn't able to get any calls out, but I managed a couple of texts. According to my friend, the police are advising everyone to stay where they are. Which won't be a problem for us. It seems the tech guru who owns this mansion installed a state-of-the-art security system that has now malfunctioned, locking us all inside." Grayson shook his head. He'd met the man earlier. The guy epitomized the definition of "book sense but no common sense." As the grandiose house and the money spent on it testified. "So until the blackout is over, and power is restored, we're trapped here."

Quickly, he typed out a text to his parents, but it didn't go through. Damn. But at least he knew they were safe somewhere in this building.

"Shoot," she muttered, thrusting her hand through her thick brown hair.

No, not brown. That was a woefully inadequate description for the beautiful blending of auburn and shades of copper and chestnut.

"Yes, I'm afraid you're stuck with me for the foreseeable future," he drawled, lowering to the floor and setting his cell phone between them, so the flashlight app created a small, dim circle of light. Drawing his legs up and propping his wrists on his knees, he glanced at her. "Look on the bright side. I could be your supervisor."

He chewed up the word *supervisor*, angry still at the thought of the nameless, faceless man. What spoiled, selfish asshole made his employee traipse all the way out to the Gold Coast to bring him a shirt on the weekend? She still hadn't revealed his identity, but he intended to find out. And when he did, Grayson would enjoy throwing around his last name to put the fear of God in the man. No, the fear of a Chandler.

"Good point," she agreed absently. But then a smile lit her face, and a peculiar and *unwelcome* catch snagged in his chest. Forget the light from his phone, the beauty of that smile could illuminate the entire building. Hell, the Chicago skyline. "Oh, thank God. He's safe."

"Who's safe?" he asked, because screw it, he was curious about her. Any woman who showed up to the DuSable City Gala in a leather jacket and skinny jeans was way more interesting than one in a gown and jewels.

At first, he didn't think she'd answer, but after a moment,

she said, "My brother. I left him at his baseball game, but he's at a friend's house instead of on the road."

"Did you try reaching your parents? Just in case he wasn't able to contact them?" Almost as soon as the words exited his mouth, he wanted to snatch them back. Emotions flickered across her face, there and gone before he could decipher them. Well, except for one. Pain.

"It's just my brother Ezra and me," she said, tone flat.

He recognized that particular note. Too well.

"I'm sorry," he murmured, curling his fingers into his palms until the short nails bit into the flesh. It was either that or erase the distance between them and cup her too-lovely face. "I know the pain of losing someone, too."

Her eyes, as dark as espresso, softened. She shook her head. "No, I'm sorry for your loss." If he hadn't been studying her so closely he might've missed the slight shift of her hand from her lap. As if she, too, considered touching him, but decided not to at the last moment. "My parents aren't dead. They're just not…here. I'm my brother's guardian, and we moved to Chicago a little over a year ago. It's just us."

More questions piled into his head, his curiosity about this beautiful woman insatiable. That in itself should've alarmed him. The last woman to elicit even a tenth of this magnetic pull had left his heart and pride battered and bruised.

Still, she'd satisfied a small piece of his curiosity. That honeyed drawl. Definitely not a clipped, flatter Chicago tone. She hadn't mentioned where she'd moved from, but he'd bet his favorite bottle of Glenlivet that she'd lived somewhere hot and south of the Mason-Dixon Line. The slightly exaggerated vowels and soft consonants flowed over his skin like a heated caress. He had the insane urge to strip naked and let it touch every inch of him.

He shook his head as if he could somehow dislodge the

thought. Yet…he couldn't stop his gaze from roaming over her features. When he'd first bumped into her, he'd focused on steadying her and keeping her from falling backward. But when she'd lifted her head, he'd been struck dumb for the first time in his life.

Years ago, he'd started boxing as a way to release aggression and get some exercise. He clearly remembered the first time he'd had his bell rung by a sparring opponent. The other guy's fist had plowed into Grayson's stomach, blasting the air from his lungs, leaving his legs rubbery and his head spinning. When he'd peered into this woman's dark brown eyes and beautiful face, he'd been back kneeling on that mat again.

Long-lashed eyes that turned up at the corners. Regal cheekbones to match the almost patrician slope of her nose with its flared nostrils. Below, her wide, full, utterly perfect mouth had him fighting the urge to press his thumb to it. Just to feel the softness of that slightly heavier bottom lip that formed a natural pout. That mouth would inspire both worshipful poems and dirty limericks.

Then there was her body.

Even the worn leather jacket, simple white T-shirt and ripped skinny jeans couldn't detract from the lushness of her curves. If anything, the plain clothes emphasized the miracle that was her body. Tall, even in gym shoes, the top of her head brushed the underside of his jaw. Strong but slender shoulders. Beautiful, firm breasts that would more than fill his hands—and God, did he want to find out for himself if that were true. A tucked-in waist that accentuated the wide flare of hips that had his palms tingling to cradle her—hell, degenerate that he was, he wanted to dig his fingers into her…leave his prints behind on that flesh. Impossibly long, thick legs and that ass. He briefly closed his eyes. God only gave asses like that to those He really loved… He must love the *hell* out of her. Round. High. Flawless. Made to be adored.

Yes, Grayson's first glimpse of her had pummeled the sense from his head and ignited his body like a struck match tossed in a pool of gasoline. Not even Adalyn had garnered that reaction from him.

And sitting here with this woman in a private world carved out of darkness, he couldn't deny that he wanted her. Wanted to feel her breath on his lips, his skin. Wanted to taste her mouth, taste that golden almond skin, discover its flavor for himself. Wanted to feel those abundant curves pressed to his larger, harder frame, adhered to him by sweat and lust.

The clawing desire also had him mentally scooting back.

Nothing that powerful could be good. Especially for him and his addictive personality. During his teens, it'd been the excess afforded him by his parents' wealth and social status. Later it'd been women. Then he'd poured that intensity and driving need into founding and building KayCee Corp. And then into Adalyn.

Yeah, he sensed that he could become wildly addicted to the woman next to him, whose vanilla and earthy scent— like fresh wind after a summer storm—reached out to him, tempted him. Hell, a woman whose name he didn't even know.

And that scared the hell out of him.

And yet…

"What's your name?" he demanded.

Her hesitation was brief, but he still caught it.

"Nadia," she said.

"Nice to meet you, Nadia," he murmured, stretching his hand out toward her. "Grayson."

Again, she paused. But then, she slid her palm into his. And when an electrical charge sizzled up his arm and straight to his cock, he instantly regretted touching her. Only pride kept him from jerking his hand away.

He shifted his gaze from their clasped hands to her eyes, expecting to see the same shock. Instead he glimpsed resignation. And shadows. His gut clenched. Experience had taught him that secrets lurked in the shadows. Lies lived there.

Slowly, he released her, returning his hand to his knee. Resisting the urge to fist his fingers and ease the residual tingling.

Or capture it.

Turning away from her, he stared straight ahead into the enveloping dark. "Why don't you want me to know your name?" he finally asked, casting aside the socially acceptable tact that had been drilled into him since birth. "Do we know each other?"

Her sharp but low intake of breath glanced off his ears, and he faced her again, openly scrutinizing her face for any telltale signs of deception. But she was good. Aside from that gasp, her expression remained shuttered. Either she had nothing to hide or she was damn good at lying.

He couldn't decide which one to believe.

"No," she whispered. "We don't know each other."

Truth rang in her voice, and the vise squeezing his chest loosened a fraction of an inch.

"And I guess, I didn't see the point of exchanging names. If not for this blackout or you being in this hallway instead of the ballroom, our paths wouldn't have crossed. And when the power is restored, we'll become strangers again. Getting to know each other will pass the time but it's not because we truly want to. It's not…honest."

Her explanation struck him like a punch. It echoed throughout his body, vibrating through skin and bone. *Honest.* What did he know about that?

In the world he moved in, deception was everywhere—

from the social niceties of "It's so good to see you" to the cagey plans to land a business deal. He wasn't used to her brand of frankness, and so he didn't give her platitudes. Her honesty deserved more than that.

"You're right," he said. "And you're wrong." Deliberately, he straightened his legs until they sprawled out in front him, using that moment to force himself to give her the truth. "If not for me needing to get out of that ballroom and bumping into you here, we wouldn't have met. You would be outside, unprotected in the parking lot or on the road. And I would be trapped in the dark with people I wish I didn't know, most likely going out of my mind. So for that alone, I'm glad we did connect. Because Nadia…" He surrendered to the need that had been riding him since looking down into her upturned face, and clasped a lock of her hair, twisting it around his finger. "Nadia, I would rather be out here with you, a complete stranger I've met by serendipity, than surrounded by the familiar strangers I've known for years in that ballroom."

She stared at him, her pretty lips slightly parted, espresso eyes widened in surprise.

"Another thing you're correct and incorrect about. True, when the lights come back on and we leave here, we probably won't see each other again. But in this moment, there's nothing I want more than to discover more about Nadia with the gorgeous mouth, the unholy curves and the underwhelming fairy godmother."

Maybe he shouldn't have pushed it with the comments about her mouth and body, but if they were being truthful, then he refused to hide how attractive he found her. Attractive, hell. Such an anemic description for his hunger to explore every inch of her and be able to write a road map later.

Her lashes fluttered before lowering, hiding her eyes. In her lap, her elegant fingers twisted. He released the strands of her hair and checked the impulse to tip her chin up and order her to look at him.

"Why did you need to escape the ballroom?" she asked softly.

He didn't immediately reply, instead waiting until her gaze rose to meet his.

Only then did he whisper, "To find you."

Four

Nadia struggled to compose her features. To not let the yearning tangling in her to reflect on her face. Especially with Grayson's piercing scrutiny attempting to peel away her carefully constructed protective layers. She'd spent years erecting them and couldn't afford to let him see the insecure woman who raised her brother the best way she could, constantly afraid she would screw him up in some way as their mother had with her.

But *oh God*, did he tempt her to lower her guard. To surrender to the quiet invitation in those amazing eyes.

Still, Grayson Chandler, president of KayCee Corp, one of the most successful tech start-ups to explode onto the financial scene in years, the golden son of the revered Chandler family, *couldn't* want her. Not Nadia Jordan, formerly of Tatumville, Georgia, daughter to Marion Jordan, the town's notorious man-eater and drunk.

It had nothing to do with her self-esteem—or lack of it—regarding her body. If her mother had bequeathed anything to her, it was a confidence in her curves. Because Nadia had inherited her build from Marion.

From the time Nadia had been old enough to understand what was happening, she'd witnessed the lust and appreciation men possessed for Marion's large breasts, wide hips, thick thighs and not-so-small behind. Those rich pillars of the community might ignore her in public when standing next to their wives and daughters, but in the dark, in secret, they couldn't get enough of Marion's brash laugh, her flamboyance, her casual sensuality, and of course, her body.

And when Nadia hit puberty and started to fill out, their dirty leers had transferred to her. Almost everyone in her hometown had expected her to follow in Marion's footsteps. Like mother, like daughter. Earlier than she should've, she'd learned to dodge grasping, searching fingers, to avoid deserted hallways and dark corners where teen boys and older men could trap her.

It was why she'd escaped Tatumville as soon as she could. To move to a place where she wasn't seen as her mother's daughter. To give her brother a chance to grow up out from under that censure.

So no, she didn't have body issues. Still, she'd seen the pictures in society and gossip magazines and blogs capturing Grayson with women who were the anti-her.

And then there was the matter of his wealth.

He might not know all of her background, but from her clothes and the conversation they'd shared, he had to know she was not only from the other side of the tracks, but that those tracks were miles away.

She didn't trust rich men. Too many times had she witnessed her mother not only using those kinds of men for money, favors or gifts, but also allowing them to use her, too. Nothing they gave Marion had been free, and in Nadia's experience, rich men did nothing without expecting something back.

Staring at Grayson with his *"To find you"* ringing in her ears, she forced herself to remember those lessons. She tried to resist the small but insistent whisper in her mind asking what would be the harm in letting go just once in her life? Who would it hurt if she took something for herself?

"You don't strike me as the kind of man to believe in that fated nonsense," she finally said, resenting the rasp in her voice.

"I'm not," he agreed. "I don't believe in ideas like destiny, blind faith or unconditional love. I forge my own path, make my own choices and live by them. And there are always conditions, strings attached to everything. Nothing in this life is free," he said, echoing her own thoughts. "You know what I do believe in, Nadia?" She shook her head, and the intensity in his gaze seemed to deepen. "What I can touch, see…taste. If I can't, then I don't trust it."

"And yet…." She trailed off.

"And yet," he continued. "It might not have been you who dragged me out of that ballroom. But I'm here. And I'm not alone."

Alone.

That one word resonated inside her, expanding until it rang like a struck gong. A man like him shouldn't be alone. It struck her as…wrong.

"It seems to me that someone who attends a gala that even peons like me know about isn't often alone." She cocked her head. "Unless he wants to be."

"You know what they say about assuming, Nadia." He tsked, but she didn't miss the thread of steel in the teasing. As if he were warning her to back off the topic. Which perversely only heightened her desire to pursue it.

"Well then don't let me assume, Grayson. Enlighten me. Tell me something about yourself. Something nobody knows. Something that will stay here in this hallway. Between you and me."

He studied her for a long moment, and Nadia met that blue-and-green gaze, no matter how much she might want to duck her head and avoid it. And, she didn't rescind her request. She waited, her chest tight, hoping he would answer. Even if it was some bullshit that every gossip outlet knew. For this moment, she could pretend it was only for her.

"I hate this pretentious, fake, incestuous fishbowl," he finally murmured, drawing his legs back up and propping his arms on his knees again. Turning from her, he stared straight ahead, but a small muscle ticked along his jaw. "No, not a fishbowl. A shark tank. A tank full of predators waiting for the slightest sign of weakness so they can tear you to pieces. Do you know how exhausting it is to be constantly on guard?"

"Yes," she whispered. God, did she. "But, you know, the thing about sharks? We see them as ruthless, single-minded killers, when they're not. They're important to the ocean's ecosystem. In a way, they're protectors. Smaller fish depend on them for survival. I could make the argument that if they didn't exist, neither would the weaker, more vulnerable species."

He shifted his gaze back to her, and a faint smile played with his lips. Heat rushed into her face. Thank goodness for the dark so he couldn't see the evidence of her mortification. Unfortunately, her mouth wouldn't stop running.

"I watch a lot of Animal Planet," she mumbled. "But maybe, you're in that tank to protect the defenseless so they can thrive."

The smile disappeared. And she regretted whatever she'd said that had caused it to vanish.

"I've been called a lot of things in my life, but protector has never been one of them. You make me sound noble, and I'm not," he said, that vein of harshness entering his voice again. This time, it might've induced her to back away from the subject—if not for the presence of something else there, too, something that tasted of desperation, of…pain.

It drew her to him.

The press painted Gideon Knight and Grayson Chandler as light and dark, the yin and yang of KayCee Corp. Gideon was the intimidating, merciless owner, while Grayson was the golden, charming half. But the glimpses of him she'd received tonight…

Who was Grayson?

Those glimpses promised that more lurked beneath that affable mask. It was the *more* that had her reaching out to him. Had her settling her hand over his.

"In my experience, people who warn you that they aren't noble are the ones with good hearts. It's the ones who brag about being righteous and moral that you need to watch out for."

Grayson's gaze dipped to her hand, then slowly lifted until it met her eyes. A shiver rippled through her, and he didn't miss it.

"My heart isn't good, Nadia. I'm selfish. Greedy. Spoiled. And if you knew the thoughts in my head right now, about you, you would remove your hand from mine," he warned.

She didn't. Even though her heart thudded against her sternum, she didn't heed his warning.

"Go on and ask me," he murmured, and her breath caught in her lungs at the sin in his voice. "You're thinking it. I can see that in those pretty brown eyes. Ask me what thoughts are in my head."

Here in the dark, the caution that ruled her life started to unravel. That small, low whisper encouraging her to take grew in volume, in strength. In this hallway, cut off from the real world, with only the man she'd fantasized about for company, she was Eve reaching for the apple even knowing she shouldn't.

Knowing that traveling down this path with her em-ployer would be one of the biggest mistakes of her life…

She bit the apple.

"What are your thoughts about me?" she asked, the ques-tion barely there.

"Are you sure?" he pressed. When she nodded, he did, as well. "You bumped into me earlier, but only because I'd already stopped. I couldn't move. Watching you walk is pure sex. The confident stride of those legs that mesmerize a man. Give him thoughts of how they would clasp him in their strong embrace. The sensual sway of hips I want to dig my fingers into while I press you close and take your mouth that was created to be claimed, corrupted. That's what you are, baby. Corruption. Sin. Desire in flesh. And I want to kneel in front of you and beg you to consign me to your hell. Because I want to burn in you. With you."

Oh God.

Desire, scorching hot and out of control, blazed a path from her belly, up her chest and to every limb of her body. Consuming her. With just words, he caused her nipples to tighten, her sex to spasm in need. Thank God she was sit-ting, because her trembling legs wouldn't have supported her. Not when the blood in her veins had become liquid lust. Not when the breath in her lungs had evaporated into smoke.

I want to kneel in front of you… Because I want to burn in you. With you.

Now, she could do nothing but picture him on his knees in front of her, that proud head tilted back, his amazing eyes fixed on her. His fingers clasping the tab of her zipper and steadily lowering…

She closed her eyes, not to block out the image but to dwell on it.

"Nadia." Gentle but firm fingers pinched her chin and lifted her head. "Look at me," Grayson ordered, and she did. When she stared into his amazing eyes, he nodded. "Your turn. Tell me something nobody knows. Something that will stay here in this hallway," he said, lobbing her words back at her.

Brave. She'd always prided herself on not backing down from any challenge. Especially because it'd almost always meant going without something—food, rent, money. But here, brave meant being selfish. It meant grabbing ahold and taking for herself…for once.

And God, did she want to take.

Could she do it only for tonight? Slap the time-out button and live brashly, without a thought for the consequences? Who would she hurt?

Maybe just herself once morning dawned or the lights came back on. But she was prepared to walk out of here accepting that when she returned to work on Monday, she would go back to being the nameless, faceless employee on the twentieth floor.

If she could have this slice of time with Grayson, then she'd deal with the hurt of becoming invisible again.

"I like tequila shots," she whispered. "What no one knows is you're like that hit of tequila. Potent as hell, hot and strong like the first punch of alcohol to the stomach— and I'll gladly get drunk on it, on you, even knowing I'll be hungover and remorseful in the morning."

The silence between them thickened and heated. His grip on her chin tightened, and the slight pressure drew a gasp from her. His eyes. They seemed to glow with the same need that snapped inside of her. His skin tautened across his cheekbones, his sensual, full mouth flattening into a firm line.

"Do you understand what you do to a man like me when you say that?" he growled.

"A man like you?" she rasped.

"I told you," he said, voice rough, harsh. His hand shifted

from her face and up into her hair, gripping the strands. "I'm greedy. Selfish. And will take without conscience what you're offering me." He tugged on her hair, and pinpricks of pleasure danced across her scalp. She sank her teeth in her bottom lip to trap a moan. "What are you offering me, Nadia?"

"Me," she breathed. "For tonight. All of me."

As if those words snapped a fraying leash on his control, Grayson swooped down and crushed his mouth to hers. *Oh God.* She hadn't been prepared. Maybe she'd believed she was. But foolish, foolish her—she wasn't.

Not prepared for the intensity, the hunger, the *ravishing.* She felt silly even thinking that antiquated word, but no other could describe how he consumed her. Dragged her under with the thrust of his tongue, the hard but sensual molding of his lips to hers.

His holds in her hair and on her chin tightened. He tugged her head back farther, and his thumb pressed firmer just under her bottom lip. Both helplessly and willingly, she opened wider for him, for the plunging and tangling of his tongue. For his possession. A possession she not only welcomed but craved like her next breath.

He had become that vital.

His mouth abandoned hers, and with a disappointed whimper, she followed him. But he shifted his grip to her jaw and held her still. He trailed a sizzling path from her lips, down her throat and to the crook between neck and shoulder. There, he nuzzled her, and she gasped as a jolt leaped from that spot to her taut nipples, through her knotted belly and down to the already damp and spasming flesh between her thighs.

Reaching for steady purchase to cling to in the erotic maelstrom, she dug her fingernails into his shoulder. And held on.

"Come here," he murmured, his hands dropping to her

hips and drawing her toward him. Over him. In breathless seconds, she straddled his rock-hard thighs. Slowly lowered herself until the long, thick length of his erection pressed against her denim-covered sex. A low, shaky gust pushed out of her lungs. Damn. He was... Screw it. He was big. And for a woman who hadn't had sex in well over a year? Intimidating.

But for a woman who'd never indulged in sex where she didn't need to worry if the man would gossip about her afterward?

Exhilarating.

Liberating.

Rolling her hips, she stroked her sex over him. A full-body shiver worked its way through her, and she groaned at the stunning pleasure. Layers of clothes separated them, but they didn't prevent her from *feeling* him. His width, his hardness, his strength.

Sinking her teeth into her bottom lip, she ground against him, rubbing, rocking over his flesh, getting lost in the swells of desire that threatened to quickly drown her in the release that already loomed wonderfully close. Jesus. She was going to embarrass herself by coming quickly just from some fully clothed dry humping, and she couldn't bring herself to care.

"I like that you're using me for your pleasure, baby," he praised in a silk-and-gravel voice that both slid over and abraded her skin...her nerve endings. "But don't hide from me." He pressed his thumb to her lip and gently tugged it free from her teeth. "I want to hear every sound, every word of your need for me. Don't keep anything from me."

Oh God. He was temptation, a sinful lure enticing her to fall in the most spectacular of ways.

With deft hands that spoke of skill and practice, he removed her jacket and shirt. Seconds later, she sat on his lap, his rigid dick between her thighs and his beautiful, bright gaze on her half-naked body. She resisted the urge to lift one arm over her plain bra and cross the other over her stomach.

No, she might not be ashamed of her body, but that didn't prevent insecurities from creeping in with their sly reminders that she wasn't like the women he'd been pictured with. Though Nadia worked out and ran—not just for health reasons but because it was also a great stress reliever—she would never have a cut six-pack unless she drew it on her abs with a Sharpie. Her flatish, soft belly carried faint stretch marks, and her breasts... Well, they were firm, but their weight would always make them sag a little rather than sit high on her chest like perky B cups.

"Don't even think about it," Grayson snapped, his eyes sparking with blue-and-green fire. Stroking his hands up her arms, he squeezed her shoulders, before continuing his journey south until he cupped her breasts in his big hands. "Maybe I should've been more specific when I told you not to hide from me. Not sounds, not words and definitely not this gorgeous body."

"You're certainly bossy, you know that?" she said, arching an eyebrow but leaving her hands on his shoulders. "Does that usually work for you?"

"Yes," he rumbled, whisking his thumbs over her stiff, aching nipples. "And it does for you, too." He pinched the tips, wringing a low cry from her. "Doesn't it, baby?"

She didn't answer but lowered her head and took his mouth, swallowing his wicked chuckle. He didn't let up playing with her body, tweaking and tugging her nipples until she ripped her lips from his and threw her head back. More than anything, she wanted him flesh to flesh, no barriers. Reaching behind her, she unclipped her bra and yanked it off. An almost feral growl tore from him, and he hefted her breasts, lifting one to his mouth and sucking deep while continuing to toy with the other.

Every flick and circle and suckle agitated the insatiable creature she'd become. She tunneled her fingers through his hair, gripping, caught between clutching him close so he couldn't turn her loose and pushing him from her, unable to bear the brutal sting of pleasure.

Switching to the other mound, he rubbed the wet tip, but slid his free hand down her torso, over her stomach and beneath the band of her jeans. Her audible catch of breath echoed in the hallway, and she stilled as his fingers slipped underneath denim and cotton, resting on top of her sex.

Lifting his head, he met her gaze. "Yes or no?" he asked.

Desire burned in his mismatched eyes, but so did resolve. His stare assured her that he wanted her, but if she said no, he would back away.

"Yes," she said, the answer firm and sure.

She wanted his touch. *Him.* Releasing her hand from his hair, she dipped it under her pants as well, covering his fingers with hers. "Yes," she repeated.

She tilted her hips, and their combined touch glided over her flesh. Twin thick groans saturated the air, and she couldn't contain the cry that slipped from her lips. Together they stroked her, slid through her folds and down to the small, tight entrance to her body. On the tail end of a curse, Grayson abandoned her breast to wrench the button on her jeans free and tug down the zipper, granting them more room.

Fingers tangled, side by side, they caressed her opening. But it was him that pushed inside, stretching her with a familiar but almost-forgotten burn. And now, with his fingers buried deep, she wondered how she would go on without it.

In a duet that was as dirty as it was beautiful, they coaxed a tune from her body.

"Touch yourself," he commanded, and she obeyed, untangling her fingers from his and slipping beneath his palm to slick a caress over the swollen button of nerves. She jolted, whimpered.

He gave a soft chuckle. "Do it again, Nadia. We're going to take you there together."

Shivering, she circled the nub, again and again, his rough praise and encouragement pushing her to rub harder, more, harder, more...

"Oh God," she croaked, then splintered.

She cried out, quaking from the inside out. Grayson replaced her fingers with his, making sure she received every measure of the orgasm rippling through her. She went limp, falling into his body and wanting nothing more than to curl against him, lethargy weighing down her limbs.

Like she was a rag doll, he lifted her from his lap, damn near ripping the tuxedo from his powerful frame. Then he stripped her of her remaining clothes and arranged her on the makeshift pallet he made of his suit. He loomed above her, the dim light from his cell phone still managing to highlight the corded strength in his arms, chest, abs and thighs. His cock. Her lungs locked down all available air in her lungs at the sight of the heavy column of flesh rising from a dark nest of hair. The desire that had settled to a hum low in her belly sparked and crackled, the flames leaping to hot life. He was sexy, perfect...beautiful.

Thank God this wouldn't go beyond tonight. Because she had the unnerving sense he could also very well be heartbreak.

Grayson tore open the small foil packet he'd retrieved from his wallet and rolled on the protection. The virile, erotic sight caused all her unsettling thoughts to scatter. All thoughts except him finally being inside her.

Lifting her arms to him, she murmured, "Grayson."

An invitation. A plea.

"Gray," he rasped, crawling over her and settling between her thighs.

"What?" She moaned as his weight pressed into her.

"Gray," he repeated. "Those close to me call me Gray."

But we're not close, hovered on her tongue and from the sharpening in his blue-and-green gaze, maybe he expected and anticipated her protest. Sex didn't make them close, didn't grant her privileges.

But this was a night for pretend. For fantasy.

Both caused her to whisper, "Gray."

Satisfaction gleamed in his eyes, and he settled more firmly over and against her, every rock-hard, unforgiving plane of his body pressed to her softer, rounded curves.

"What did you say you were willing to give me, Nadia?" he growled, his erection at the entrance to her body.

"All of me," she rasped, then gasped as he surged inside in one long, smooth, powerful thrust. "Take all of me."

And he did.

Not holding back. Not allowing her to hold back.

He slid his hands under her ass, angled her up and, withdrawing in a slow drag that lit up nerve endings like fireworks, he then plunged back inside her. Stealing her breath. Words. Sanity.

Circling her arms and legs around his neck and hips, she clung to him, let him hurl her into the storm he created with each flex, each parry and thrust, each branding kiss.

The man was a sexual act of God.

He powered into her, taking her body, giving her pleasure…breaking every notion of what sex really was. Because she'd had sex before, but as he buried himself in her again and again, riding her until her thighs trembled and her breath stuttered, she could admit to herself that this… this exceeded all of it.

This, she'd never experienced.

And already, even though she'd promised herself there couldn't be a repeat, she craved it again.

"Gray," she cried out, fearing and welcoming the end that swelled dangerously near.

"Let go, baby," he ordered, his voice harsh with the same need that clawed at her. "Let go and give it to me."

As if all she needed was his permission, she did as he commanded. She let go. And ecstasy whipped through her like lightning. Illuminating her, searing her, sending her flying.

Above her, his hoarse shout dimly filled her ears, but she was already falling into the darkness, embracing it.

Knowing in the morning, she would have only memories to hold on to instead of Grayson Chandler.

Five

"Thanks, Pete," Grayson said to his longtime driver as he alighted from the gleaming black Lincoln Town Car. Shivering a little against the cool October Monday morning, he shut the door before the other man could. "I should be finished by six tonight, but if I'm staying later, I'll call a cab."

"Yes, sir," Pete drawled, touching the brim of the black cap that Grayson insisted he didn't need to wear. "But just give me a call when you're ready. Look what happened the last time I wasn't around to drive you. Blackouts. Trapped in locked-down mansions. You're obviously not safe without me."

"Cut it, old man," Grayson rumbled, but grinned at the chauffer.

Pete was more than a driver. When Grayson was a child, the older man had been his best friend, pseudo-uncle and confidante. Hell, it'd been Pete who'd sat Grayson down and explained the more intimate details of sex. Which had been a vast improvement over his father's uninspired "For

God's sake, cover your dick, Grayson, and don't get any gold-digging whores pregnant" speech.

"Have a good day and try to keep Gideon from turning anyone into a statue with that black-eyed stare," Pete teased, rounding the hood of the car. With another mocking touch to his cap, he ducked inside the car and pulled off.

Grayson shook his head, chuckling, but also wishing his friend hadn't mentioned the blackout or being trapped in that damn North Shore mansion. He'd spent all of yesterday and last night attempting to exorcise that evening from his mind. More specifically, trying to remove memories of Nadia and the hottest sex of his life from his mind.

So far, he'd failed. Epically.

Maybe if he hadn't woken up alone, cold and half-hard on a marble floor, with her scent still saturating his clothes, his skin... Maybe if he didn't bear the scratches of her desire on his shoulders and back... Maybe if his dick didn't rise to attention every time a passing thought of those espresso eyes flickered in his head...

Maybe then he could pass off that evening as an unexpected and pleasurable incident.

But today wasn't that day.

As the day before hadn't been. And tomorrow wasn't looking too good, either.

Clenching his jaw, he ignored the low-grade throb in his body. As a boy and then a young man who'd lived most of his life by someone else's rules, he guarded his control like a dragon jealously protecting treasure. Now more than ever, with his parents trying to snatch his life away again and force him back into the world he'd been so desperate to escape.

Waking alone and with no way to contact Nadia, no way to see her again—it had threatened that need to determine his own fate. Because although he'd agreed to one night, he'd lied. After tasting her delectable mouth, caressing that gorgeous body, he wanted more.

Those hours in that hallway had been the most honest, unfiltered interaction he'd had in years. He craved the sincere honesty as much as the hot-as-hell sex. And while the hunger to reinitiate contact with a veritable stranger for conversation should have been an ear-splitting blare of caution, he couldn't deny—at least not to himself—how much he wanted it.

"Good morning, Mr. Chandler," the lobby security guard greeted him from behind the large black desk.

"Good morning, Gerald. And welcome back," Grayson paused in front of the desk. "How's your wife and the new baby?"

The young man beamed, his joy evident in his wide smile. "They're both doing wonderful. Thank you for asking, sir."

"Good. Congratulations to you both." Grayson nodded, then continued toward the bank of elevators, a disquieting emotion sliding under his rib cage.

The guard's obvious delight in his family had Grayson flipping back through his own memories. Had his parents' gazes ever contained that gleaming sheen of pride, of happiness at the mention of him? Not that he could remember. For his brother, yes. Even a couple of times for his sister, Melanie. But not for him.

Just yesterday, disappointment and anger had colored his mother's frosty tone when he'd declined her invitation—order—to attend a family brunch. He'd already been raw from the previous night and sitting down with his mother and father with anything less than full, emotional body armor was foolish. And contrary to what they believed, they hadn't raised a fool.

Resentment, weariness and, yes, pain flickered in his chest, but he ruthlessly smothered them. Feeling *anything* was not only futile, but messy. Refusing people access to your heart, to your soul, prevented them from handling it like fruit in the supermarket bin—squeezing, bruising, then abandoning it.

He jabbed the call button on the elevator a little harder than necessary, willing it to hurry the hell up. As if by getting on the lift and traveling the twenty-five floors to his office, he could leave these morose thoughts in the lobby.

"...a little something, Gerald. Congratulations to you and your wife."

Grayson froze as the soft voice with a hint of a rasp reached him from across the lobby. The elevator finally arrived, but the doors opened and eventually closed without him moving toward it.

That honeyed drawl. New and too damn familiar. He'd heard it in his head last night when he'd jerked awake in his bed, hard and hurting.

It wasn't possible.

Since she'd been on his mind only minutes ago, he was probably having an aural hallucination...

Slowly, he pivoted, his gaze zeroing in on the guard's desk—and the woman standing in front of it handing a small gift bag to Gerald.

Even across the lobby, she appeared tall, the nondescript black heels adding only a couple of inches. Rich chestnut hair was tamed into a painfully neat ponytail. A dark brown suit that seemed a size or two too big hung from her frame, nearly obliterating the curves beneath. From the hair to the wardrobe, nothing about this woman was similar to the woman he'd spent an unforgettable, sex-drenched night with.

Nothing but that melodic accent, which sent all his blood rushing south.

Forgetting everything—the meeting he had scheduled with Gideon, the conference call with a prospective client—he retraced his steps toward the security desk. Before he reached his destination, she turned, a smile curving her lips. Then she lifted her gaze. Met his. And her smile disappeared.

Shock vibrated through him, the echo of it growing louder until only white noise filled his ears.

Nadia. In his building.

His gaze dipped to the familiar green and white badge clipped to the lapel of her jacket. A KayCee Corp employee.

Shock morphed into anger edged with the bitter taste of betrayal.

His employee.

Saturday, she'd pretended not to recognize him, but she'd known who he was all along. Why hadn't she said something? Had she planned to use their night together against him? Blackmail him?

One of his personal codes was never to become involved with employees—ever. Not only was it unprofessional and a legal suit waiting to happen, but with his position of power, no relationship would ever be equal.

But by remaining silent, she'd unwittingly made him violate his own rule. She'd stolen his choice away. That knowledge burned, fueling the already scalding fury at her duplicity.

"Nadia," he greeted, ice coating his voice. Alarm flashed in eyes he'd laughably thought of as honest. Good. She should be worried. He scanned her badge. "Nadia Jordan. What a surprise meeting you here. And with that badge on."

"Mr. Chandler," she said, striding forward and erasing the space separating them. Her chin hiked up, the defiant gesture belied by the crossing of her arms under her breasts. As if protecting herself. "Good morning."

"Good morning," he repeated, arching an eyebrow. "So formal. But then again, it appears you're very good with pretenses," he drawled. "As far as this one goes—" he deliberately scanned her from the top of her scraped-back hair to the tips of her plain shoes "—it's a good one. I almost didn't recognize you."

She dropped her gaze, but a moment later, her shoulders straightened, and she returned her eyes to his. "I didn't—"

"What? Lie? Be very careful how you finish that sentence," he warned, anger slipping into his voice and replacing the mocking tone. "Especially when it isn't a party guest you're talking to now, but your employer."

Something that could've been guilt flashed across her face.

Could've been. Probably wasn't.

"I didn't lie. We didn't—don't—know each other. I've worked for KayCee Corp for a year, have spoken to you a handful of times, and you didn't even know my name."

"So we're going to play semantics?" he growled, leaning closer. Close enough that her fresh, earthy scent filled his nostrils. "Is that your game? Be care—"

"Grayson."

He jerked his head up at the sound of his name spoken in the crisp, cultured voice he'd grown up associating with displeasure and chastisement.

Hell.

He inwardly groaned. Grinding his teeth together, he shifted his glance over Nadia's shoulder.

"Mom."

Cherise Chandler's ice-blue stare swung from him, to Nadia, then back to him, dismissing the other woman. "I've been trying to call you all morning."

Yes, and he'd been ignoring her all morning. In the last few months, his mother had taken to blowing his phone up and always with the same subjects: returning to Chandler International, marriage, duty. He was…tired.

"I'm sorry I missed them," he lied. "I didn't mean for you to come all the way down here, though." Truth.

"Well, how else was I supposed to invite you to lunch with us?" she asked.

Us? For the first time he glanced behind his mother and noticed the petite woman standing with her. Adalyn. *Jesus Christ.* How much worse could this damn Monday get?

"Adalyn." He nodded in his ex's direction.

Adalyn smiled, taking the curt greeting as an invitation to approach him, place a hand on his chest and rise on the tips of her stilettos to brush a kiss across his cheek. Only manners bred into him since birth kept him from stepping back and wiping the imprint from his face. From the glitter in her green eyes, she guessed it. She'd always been fond of games.

He'd never divulged the true reason behind their breakup to his parents. Adalyn hadn't cheated, but in some ways, it would've been less devastating to him if she had. Still, he'd given his parents the old "two different people" excuse, not so much to protect Adalyn's reputation but to shield himself from their scorn. His father would've called him a fool, and his mother would've gifted him with her patented "You're a disappointment" look and the "marriage is about more than love" speech.

No, he'd kept his mouth shut. But now, with Adalyn using this opportunity to wheedle back into his life, he regretted the decision. His father and mother might have scoffed at him, but at least they would have known why he couldn't abide this woman's presence.

"I was so delighted when your mother called and invited me to come see you this morning. Like I said Saturday, it's been such a long time. I would love to catch up with you," she fairly purred.

At one time, that sensual tone and pouty mouth would've had him ready to find a private place. But that had been before he'd discovered her love had been an act. Before he'd discovered he was just a walking, blue-blooded bank account to her. Before she'd shattered whatever he'd had left of his belief in the inherent integrity of people.

She'd been a brutal but effective teacher.

"I'm afraid lunch isn't possible today," he said, switching his attention to his mother and not bothering to address Adalyn. "My schedule is full."

"Nonsense," his mother dismissed his excuse with a wave of her hand. "We're family, and you can move meetings around. I've already made an appointment for twelve at—"

Anger, frustration and, yes, he wasn't too proud to admit it to himself, desperation, coalesced inside him, and before he could question the logic of his decision, he moved forward, closer to Nadia. He slipped an arm around her lower back, his hand resting on the lush, feminine curve of her hip. She stiffened, but he ignored it, silently praying that she didn't pull away from him.

"No, you misunderstand. Lunch isn't a business meeting. I already have plans with Nadia." He paused, then pushed out, "My girlfriend."

A silence filled with "what the hell?" reverberated between all of them. Beneath his hand, Nadia damn near vibrated with tension, fury, shock—most likely all three. And he couldn't blame her. He'd just thrown her under a runaway bus, rendering her the sacrifice on the matchmaking altar. In the deafening seconds that passed, he could've rescinded his announcement, passed it off as a joke, but he stayed silent, hoping she'd go along with him.

"Don't be ridiculous," Cherise snapped.

"You can't be serious," Adalyn spat at the same time, dropping the butter-wouldn't-melt-in-my-mouth act.

Both women glared at him, then switched their glowers to Nadia. The need to protect her surged within him, and he shifted closer, his hold tightening.

"Of course I'm serious," he replied, tone silken and heavy with warning. "Why wouldn't I be?"

Adalyn sputtered, red flooding her face, but she pressed her lips together, wisely remaining silent. His mother had no such compunction.

"She's not exactly your type, is she, Grayson?" she scoffed, her gaze scouring Nadia. Cherise then settled a hand on Adalyn's back. A smirk curved his ex's mouth.

He frowned and parted his lips, a hot retort jumping on his tongue. But Nadia beat him to it.

"*She* isn't a type at all," Nadia said dryly. "But a person who just so happens to be standing here."

"So you are seeing my son?" Cherise demanded, as imperious as a queen speaking to a peasant.

Again, he opened his mouth to warn his mother about her tone, but once more, Nadia beat him to it.

"That's what he said," she said. Then with such sweetness Grayson would need to make an appointment with his dentist, she added, "He's not in the habit of lying, is he?"

He swallowed back the growl that shoved against his throat. She'd thrown his own accusation about lying back in his face. God, he didn't know whether to snarl at her or murmur "well played."

"Grayson, I need to speak with you." Cherise paused and shot a meaningful look at Nadia. "Alone."

"I'm sorry, Mother," he apologized again. "I don't have time right now. Gideon is probably waiting in my office." Leaning forward, he brushed a kiss across his mother's cheek. "I'll call you later. Adalyn." He nodded abruptly at the other woman, then turning, he strode back across the lobby, his arm still around Nadia's waist.

This time when he punched the call button for the elevator, seconds passed before the doors slid open, and he guided her inside. Only when they started to rise, did he drop his arm and shift away.

And tried to ignore that he could still feel her, as if the prolonged contact had branded the sensation of her into his skin.

He wished he could ignore her, forget that the scene downstairs had happened. But he couldn't. As angry as he remained that she'd lied to him—and he still couldn't stop the nagging need to know *why*—he'd dropped her right in the middle of a family issue without her permission.

That made him a desperate asshole, but an asshole nonetheless. He already knew how he looked in her eyes—a hypocrite.

A year ago, he wouldn't have had any problem telling his mother to back off, to stop the matchmaking. But that had been before Jason died. Before Grayson witnessed his stalwart mother fall apart in grief. Causing her any more hurt when she'd lost the son of her heart…

Maybe it made Grayson a coward and a hypocrite, but he couldn't do that to her. But neither could he let her or his father rule his life again. He'd labored and sacrificed for this company, for his freedom.

God. He clenched his fingers into a fist at his side, staring ahead at the sealed doors.

He was so goddamn lonely.

And other than Gideon, trusting in someone had burned him in the past. So Grayson took only what he allowed himself to have. Those few hours of sex, pressed close to someone and pretending they were intimate. Pretending they were sharing more than just pleasure. Pretending that in the morning, he wouldn't escort them from his home with no promises.

He glanced at the silent woman next to him. In that hallway, he hadn't needed to feign anything. And maybe that's why he couldn't eradicate the inane sense of betrayal.

For once, he hadn't been faking it. And she had been.

Focus, he ordered himself.

He had to fix the problem he'd created that now involved her. And unfortunately, he saw only one way out of it.

The elevator drew to a halt on the twenty-fifth floor, and he moved forward, cupping Nadia's elbow.

"This isn't my floor," she objected, stiffening under his hand.

"We have to talk," he said in way of explanation. "I can hit the emergency button on this elevator, and we can do it here and chance the fire department being called, or we can go to my office and have privacy. Your choice."

"That's a choice?" she muttered but moved forward.

"I never claimed you would like either option," he said, not bothering to keep the bite from his tone.

He guided her down the quiet hallway toward his office. Not many people had arrived yet, but those that sat behind their desks threw him and Nadia curious glances. He could just imagine the gossip that would erupt behind them as soon as they passed.

Moments later, he paused next to his assistant's desk. The older woman regarded both of them, but nothing in her expression or voice betrayed any curiosity. Only one of the reasons he valued her. She was the very definition of discretion.

"Mrs. Ross, would you please notify..." He trailed off, frowning. "Who is your supervisor?" he asked Nadia.

She arched an eyebrow, and he swallowed a growl at the not-so-subtle reminder that he didn't know a damn thing about her. "Terrance Webber."

He nodded, familiar with the VP of operations. And now he knew who to have a talk with about requiring their employees to work when they weren't on the clock or financially compensated. Although he would now make sure Nadia would be for Saturday night.

"Would you call Terrance and let him know Ms. Jordan is in a meeting with me and will be a little late arriving?

And also, call Gideon and tell him we need to move our meeting back a half hour."

His friend wouldn't be happy, but the delay couldn't be helped.

"Yes, sir," Mrs. Ross said. "I've updated your calendar. You have a conference call scheduled for ten thirty. Lunch with the Forester Group at twelve thirty and an appointment with legal at two. I've also emailed you the messages you've received so far this morning, listed in order of urgency."

"Thank you." He reached into his briefcase and pulled free a couple of paperbacks. Settling the books on top of the desk, he pushed them toward his assistant. "For Jack. You mentioned he just started the J.D. Robb In Death series. I saw these and picked them up for him."

A warm smile spread across the woman's face, lighting it up. At sixty-three, she should've been readying herself for retirement, not still working. But her husband had been injured on his job five years ago, and even with his insurance, the bills had piled up. Not that she seemed to mind being the breadwinner of the family; the woman was devoted to her husband.

"Thank you, Mr. Chandler," she murmured. "He will love these." Clearing her throat, she gave him another smile. "I'll make sure you aren't disturbed."

Nodding, he headed toward his office, still clasping Nadia's arm. Once he closed the door behind them, he released her. What he had to propose would be unprofessional enough without any more unnecessary touching.

"Please, have a seat," he invited, waving toward the two arm chairs that flanked his wide glass desk.

"If you don't mind, I'd prefer to stand. Since I won't be staying long," she added. "You're either going to fire me for Saturday or order me to pretend the scene downstairs didn't happen. Neither should require much time." She emphasized her point by peering down at the slender watch on her wrist.

Her reminder of the night of the blackout rekindled the fury simmering inside his chest. "That's where you're wrong, Nadia," he snapped. "I can't fire you because I had inappropriate relations with an employee."

Hell, "inappropriate relations." Such an anemic description of the cataclysmic sex they'd had. Even standing here with her, frustration and anger a hum in his blood, he couldn't deny the presence of the third emotion swirling in his body. Lust. For the plush mouth set in a firm, unsmiling line. For the full breasts that had filled his palms to overflowing. For the long, thick legs that her ugly skirt couldn't hide. For the sex that had clutched him like a lover's embrace.

"My actions could be misconstrued as sexual harassment or coercion. It doesn't matter that you hid the fact that you are my employee." He cocked his head, studying her impassive face through narrowed eyes. "Care to explain to me why you didn't enlighten me about our association? Whether I recognized you or not, you damn sure knew me. And you. Said. Nothing. Why?"

She didn't immediately reply. Instead, she mimicked his gesture, tilting her head, as well. "Does it really matter now?" She flicked a hand toward the desk behind him. "Do you need me to sign a contract or affidavit swearing not to sue you or the company for sexual misconduct?"

"No," he snapped. *Yes.* The businessman inside him snarled at the same time. Jesus, she had him arguing with himself. "I want an answer to my question."

"I don't have one to give you, *sir*," she replied evenly. Stubbornly.

"You mean, you don't want to give me one." When she remained silent, continuing to meet his glare, he bit off a curse and dragged a hand through his hair, pivoting. After several seconds, he turned back around, scrutinizing her. So many questions ran through his head. *Who are you? What were your motives? Did you use me? Were you faking?*

No.

Her motives for remaining in that hallway with him might've been self-serving, but those lust-soaked moans, those hoarse whispers... Those had been real.

"About downstairs..." He exhaled a deep breath, focusing on the main reason why he'd escorted her to his office. "I'm sorry I dragged you into the middle of it. But now that I have, I need your help."

For the first time since entering the office, an emotion crossed her face. Surprise. Quickly chased by suspicion. Smart woman.

"My help?" she slowly repeated. "What kind of help could you possibly need from me?"

"For you to be my fiancée. I need you to agree to marry me."

Six

Nadia stared at Grayson Chandler. No, gaped. Because she couldn't have heard him correctly. He hadn't just... proposed to her. Between leaving her house this morning and arriving at work, she must've been in a car wreck and was currently in the hospital, hopped up on morphine and she was dreaming.

Dreaming of coming face-to-face with him in the lobby when that had never happened before.

Dreaming of being an awkward witness to the tension-filled confrontation between him, his mother and the gorgeous woman who obviously had biblical knowledge of him.

Dreaming of him introducing her as his girlfriend.

And now dreaming of him announcing that he wanted her to marry him.

Damn good drugs could be the only explanation for this hallucination.

"Nadia?"

She blinked, and no, Grayson still stood there, and so

did she. The prick of her fingernails against her palm further solidified that all of this was indeed real.

"What did you say?" she whispered.

He sighed and thrust his fingers through his hair, half turning away from her. His profile as sharp as freshly hewn marble and utterly perfect.

And she really shouldn't be admiring the striking angles of his cheekbones, the arrogant blade of his nose and the criminally sensual fullness of his mouth. Not when he'd apparently lost his mind.

"Not for real, Nadia," he said, returning his blue-and-green gaze to her. God, those eyes. She'd somehow convinced herself they couldn't possibly be that vivid, that penetrating and stunning. She couldn't have been more wrong. Though she wanted to glance away from the intensity of his stare, the unique beauty captured her. "I don't need a real fiancée, nor do I want one. I'm asking you to pretend that we are a happily engaged couple for several months. Long enough for my mother to forget this idea of fixing me up with Adalyn Hayes."

"Wait." She threw up a hand, palm out. "Your ex, Adalyn Hayes?"

His gaze sharpened. "Yes. How do you know about her?"

When she first started working at KayCee Corp, she'd inhaled everything she could uncover about him. Still, she doubted announcing *"Because I have a humiliating crush and looked up everything about you"* would go over well. Shoot, it mortified her just to admit it to herself.

"Who doesn't?" She deflected his question with a shake of her head. "So you two are getting back together?"

He frowned. "No. But unfortunately, my mother doesn't seem ready to accept that hell will have a freak blizzard before I marry Adalyn."

She blinked. "Well."

"So will you help me, Nadia?" he pressed, moving forward, and she just managed to check the urge to backpedal, maintaining the space between them.

She needed that distance, *required* it. Otherwise his sandalwood and mint fragrance would wrap around her and influence her to do foolish things. Like bury her face against his chest. She'd fought that same impulse in the longest elevator ride known to mankind. And had barely won the battle. She wasn't pushing her luck in this office.

Again, she shook her head. "I still don't understand. This must be a one-percenter thing, because normal, poor people don't do this. Why not just tell your mother that you're not interested?"

Something flashed in his mismatched eyes. Before he said a flat, blunt and enigmatic "Right now it's not an option," she'd known he wouldn't reveal anything to her.

Turnabout was fair play, she guessed. After all, she'd dodged his question about why she hadn't admitted to knowing him. Maybe if he'd been the flirtatious, warmer man she'd been trapped with, she might have felt safe confessing her reasons. But she couldn't tell this cold, guarded version of Grayson that she'd selfishly wanted a night for herself, that he'd been her fantasy come to vivid life. That for once she hadn't considered the consequences. That she didn't think he would recognize her if their paths crossed again.

No, she couldn't share that with this familiar stranger. Would he use that info against her in some way? Fire her? Or worse...mock her?

"I'm sorry, but I—"

"Don't you want to know what saying yes entails?" he interrupted her, his steady gaze assessing. Analyzing. And she didn't like it at all. "Five hundred thousand dollars. If you agree to be my fiancée for four months, I'll give you half a million dollars. And another two hundred and fifty thousand after a staged breakup."

She gasped, shock pelting her like icy sheets of rain. "Seven hundred and fifty thousand dollars?" she wheezed. "For four months?"

He shrugged a wide shoulder. "Call the extra quarter of a million bonus pay." Studying her, he murmured, "So what is your answer, Nadia?"

Good God, what she could do with all that money. Pay off debt, move to a better neighborhood, splurge a little for both Ezra and herself, have actual savings. To a successful business tycoon and billionaire like Grayson, seven hundred and fifty thousand dollars might be pocket change, but to her? To Ezra? It meant a complete change in circumstances, in lifestyle. Hell, in *life*.

But who would believe you two are a couple? Even his mother refused to accept it.

The soft, scoffing whisper ghosted across her mind, and she felt the lash of truth.

Grayson was a Chandler. They were American royalty, like the Rockefellers or the Kennedys, possibly richer and with a more sterling reputation. A woman from a tiny, obscure Georgia town who was the daughter of the town Jezebel and didn't even know who her father was didn't belong with a man who could date his ancestors back beyond the Mayflower.

He needed someone like his ex—urbane, sophisticated, moneyed, connected, gorgeous…thin. No one looking at Adalyn Hayes would question why they were together. Next to women like Adalyn, Nadia would seem like a deviation, a charity case from the other side of the tracks.

Then, there was the night they'd spent together. Ducking her head, she crossed her arms over her chest. Both to hide the inconvenient puckering of her nipples at the thought of him naked on top of her…inside her…and a feeble gesture to protect herself from his piercing scrutiny. She couldn't deny the unrelenting arousal that his presence ignited. Even when he stared at her, cool and calculating, offering three-quarters of a million dollars. Being in close proximity to him for months spelled *Danger* with a capital *D*.

He would be a menace to her reason, her control and, as much as she loathed admitting it, her heart. That treacherous heart that insisted on forgetting that rich, handsome men expected the world, and when they didn't receive it, left wreckage behind.

She refused to be wreckage for anyone else again. Ever.

"Your offer—" *bribe* "—is generous, but I'm going to turn it down."

Though his expression remained passive, his eyes glinted with anger. "Why?" He slowly perused her from head to toe, and she ordered herself not to fidget as he regarded her thrift store suit made for a woman a little bigger than her own size sixteen and shoes that weren't fashion forward but comfortable. With a growing man-child under her roof and the bills to match, the shoes weren't only all she could afford, but they were also her armor. And damn Grayson Chandler for causing a sliver of embarrassment to slide between her ribs.

"You don't need the money?" he asked.

Bastard. "No, because I'm not a whore," she ground out.

He arched an eyebrow. "I don't believe I mentioned sex being included in our arrangement."

Of course he hadn't. Heat rushed up her neck and poured into her cheeks. The night of the blackout had been an aberration for him. He might have professed to admire—no, adore—her curves then, but today, except for that insulting scan down her body, his gaze hadn't wavered from her face. She hadn't glimpsed so much as a glimmer of desire in his eyes. Frustration, yes. Anger, oh, plenty of it. But not the need that had flared so brightly in his gaze less than two days ago.

Like she'd said, an aberration.

Though mortification singed her face, she hiked her chin. "You're right, you didn't. But there's more than one way a woman can prostitute herself," she said. Her company. Her pride. Her soul. "And sorry, but I'm not willing to do it. So, if that's all…"

"Do you want more money? Is that it?" he pressed.

Fury mingled with her humiliation, and both loosened her tongue. "You're my employer, as you pointed out earlier. When you roped me into that scene downstairs, it wasn't like I could've disagreed with you and not feel like I was jeopardizing my job. But now that you've assured me that you won't fire me, I feel very safe in saying, Hell. No." She pasted a fake, too-bright smile on her face. "Now, if *that's* all…" she repeated.

Not waiting for him to dismiss her, she pivoted on her chunky heels and exited his office. Gratefully, Mr. Webber had meetings for most of the day and didn't ask her about hers with Grayson. And she didn't volunteer any information. By the time she clocked out for the day nine hours later, her head throbbed with a low-grade headache. A couple of aspirin, a glass of wine and a bed with a Netflix series called her name. They were the only things that could possibly salvage this day.

Just as she exited the elevator and stepped into the almost deserted lobby, her cell phone rang. She smiled, already knowing who waited on the other end.

"I'm leaving now," she said to her brother in lieu of a greeting. "And I'm cooking spaghetti and meatballs," she added since one of his favorite questions was "What are we having for dinner?"

Ezra laughed, and she could clearly picture his wide, easygoing grin and sparkling dark eyes. From his laid-back and affable manner, no one would guess they had grown up in the same house with the same neglectful mother. Or that he'd seen things in his seventeen years that no child should.

Though they shared a mother, it was anyone's guess who his father was, just as Nadia would have a better chance of winning the lottery than finding out the identity of hers. She and Ezra had the same brown eyes and facial features from their Caucasian mom. But where Nadia's lighter, caramel skin and loose curls and waves hinted at a father with Spanish or even biracial heritage, Ezra's darker tone and tighter curls that he'd twisted into locs denoted an African-American or Afro-Latino father. Didn't matter to Nadia. He was her brother, bonded by blood and experience.

She loved him as if she'd birthed him herself. And protected him just as fiercely.

"See? I wasn't even calling you about that, but it's good to know." He laughed again, and she grinned. "I couldn't wait until you got home. I had to call you now."

Nadia halted midstride across the lobby, pausing in front of the security desk. Nerves tumbled and tugged in her stomach, her fingers tightening around the phone.

"What is it?" she breathed.

"I got in!" Ezra crowed, his excited shout blasting in her eardrum. "I got into Yale!"

"Oh, my God!" she shouted before quickly remembering where she was. The evening shift guard quirked an eyebrow at her, and she jabbed a finger at the cell she still held at her ear. "He was accepted into Yale!" she explained as way of apology, and at only a slightly lower volume. The guard mouthed congratulations, and she gave him a thumbs-up.

"Who are you talking to?" Ezra teased. "Please tell me you didn't just tell a complete stranger that your little brother was accepted into college?"

"Not a total stranger," she scoffed. Then she chuckled. "Okay, kind of one. But he's happy for you, too. Ezra," she whispered, pride, joy and such an immense surge of love swelling inside her. "I'm so happy for you. So damn proud.

You'll be the first in our family to attend college. And not just any college. *Yale*."

"You should've been the first, Nadia," he said, loyal to the end. "You're brilliant and could've easily gotten into any school you wanted. But instead you stayed at home. Because of me."

Blinking against the sudden sting of tears, she waved a hand in front of her face and battled back the moisture. She continued out of the building and stopped on the sidewalk. Closing her eyes, she tilted her face up to the gray-and-purple sky that still contained the last rays of sun. Yes, she'd sacrificed her dreams of a degree in nursing for him, but she'd never regretted it.

"And I'd do it again," she murmured. "Now," she cleared her throat of the emotion clogging it. "Spill. Give me everything."

He read the acceptance letter, delight coloring every word, his normally relaxed voice pitched high with exhilaration. "And, Nadia, they awarded me a partial scholarship!"

"That's amazing!" But worry sank its fangs into her delight, poisoning it. Partial scholarship. The annual tuition for Yale was almost fifty thousand dollars. When he'd first applied, they'd been counting on him receiving a full ride. With his grades, it was possible. But even with the help of the aid he was receiving, she still had to come up with twenty-five thousand.

And she couldn't help him. When Nadia had been eighteen, she'd tried to get a car loan only to discover that her mother had been using her name and social security number for everything from bills to credit cards for years. If Nadia applied for loans on his behalf, and on the off chance received them, the interest rate would be so high, she would be repaying that loan even *after* she died. And she hated for Ezra to incur debt even before he graduated college.

Jesus. They were barely making ends meet as it was. And tuition didn't include books, food and other necessities…

"That's okay, sis," Ezra said, as if reading her mind. "It's just an honor to be accepted. I understand if we can't afford for me to go. There are plenty of great colleges here in Chicago. And—"

"Ezra." She broke in on his sweet but heartbreaking speech. "No, stop it. You're going to Yale. I'll come up with the money."

"But how, Nadia?" he demanded, the stubborn nature they both shared making its appearance. "If you'd just let me apply for loans…"

"No," she said, adamant. His young life shouldn't begin choked by debt that would take decades to pay off. "I'll handle it, okay? I don't want you to worry. You should be celebrating right now! So forget spaghetti. When I get home, I'm treating you to a deep dish at Pequod's. Be ready," she ordered. "And I mean it, Ezra. I'm proud of you. Congratulations."

"Thanks, sis." He coughed, cleared his throat. "And I love you."

She gasped even as tears stung her eyes again. This time she let a few tears roll before carefully wiping them away. "Good God! Did the zombie apocalypse hit and nobody told me? You actually said the *L* word!"

He sighed. "And you wonder why you don't have dates. You insist on talking."

She loosed a loud bark of laughter, startling the couple walking past her. Their pace kicked up a notch. "Oh, you're going to pay for that one. Don't be surprised when you wake up one morning eyebrowless."

With his chuckling still traveling through their connection, she hung up. As her arm dropped to her side, her hilarity ebbed, then disappeared, allowing entrance for reality and the dread accompanying it.

Only one option would completely cover Ezra's tuition and expenses.

Dropping her phone in her purse, she turned and headed back inside. All the way to the elevators and then the ride to the twenty-fifth floor, she reminded herself why she couldn't turn tail and run in the opposite direction. She conjured images of Ezra—as a gap-toothed six-year-old with a mess of unruly curls; at eleven, wide-eyed and big for his age on his first day of middle school; at fifteen, when he walked into her bedroom, clutching the ragged piece of notebook paper their mother had left behind explaining how she'd moved on with her new man.

Nadia's little brother had experienced too much—suffered too much—to not receive everything life had to offer.

She stepped off the elevator and retraced the path she'd taken that morning beside Grayson Chandler. His assistant's desk loomed large and empty, so she strode to the closed double doors of his office and knocked. Maybe he'd already left for the day, too. God, she hated the thought of having to do this all over again tomorrow...

"Come in."

The deep, commanding timbre reached her through the doors, and she couldn't contain her shiver. Not fear or revulsion. Far from it. It was a dark, wicked sensation that knotted her belly even as it pooled low beneath her navel.

Oh, for the love of...

She had to get it together before she walked into this office and committed a cardinal sin. Like throw herself at his feet and beg him to touch her, make her explode under his knowing fingers, brand her with his mouth and his...

You're here for one reason alone. Ezra.

With those words ringing in her head, she twisted the knob and entered the lion's den.

Grayson sat behind his desk, his focus on the computer monitor. A small frown creased his brow, but nothing could detract from his almost overwhelming masculine beauty. Trepidation struck her again, full force in the chest. How could she ever hope to pull this off? What made her think she could go through with this or that people would believe it?

He glanced up, noticed her standing in the doorway and the V of his eyebrows deepened. "Nadia?" He rose from his chair. "What's wrong?"

"Wrong? Nothing."

But he'd already circled his desk and stalked across the office toward her. The predatory stride did something totally inappropriate to her lungs and her sex. As if the two were mystically joined, and Grayson's sexual magnetism had flipped the switch to activate the connection.

She shook her head, closing the door behind her. "Really, nothing's wrong. I just…" She exhaled a hard breath, and he drew to a halt inches away, his disconcerting and too-damn-perceptive gaze roaming over her face. "I wanted…"

"You've changed your mind," he finished for her, his stare hooded, full lips absent of the gloating smile she'd expected. Instead, his face remained an inscrutable mask that revealed none of his thoughts.

Again she asked herself, who was Grayson Chandler? And the fact that she couldn't pin the answer down unnerved her.

"Why?" he asked.

"Does it matter?" she replied. Going through with this charade meant giving him access to her time, her personal space and even her body if they were to pretend to be a loving couple. She had to shield some parts of herself from him. And her life with her brother was one of those parts. Grayson couldn't have that. "Is the offer still open?"

He didn't immediately answer but continued to scrutinize her as if she were a column of profits and losses that refused to reconcile. She wasn't, though. She was just a desperate woman willing to sacrifice her pride for the one she loved, but not her soul.

Not her heart.

Never that.

He crossed his arms over his wide chest. "It is. Are you sure you want to do this, Nadia? Are you sure you can handle all it entails?"

"Yes."

No. Hell no.

"I'll pretend to be your fiancée for four months, and at the end we break up. Money exchanged. We resume being employer, employee." Although, how she was supposed to return to being a random secretary instead of "the boss's ex-girlfriend" she had no clue. It seemed unrealistic to think everything could go back to normal, but she'd cross that bridge when she came to it. Maybe while she played fiancée, she would also search for another job. "What wouldn't I be able to 'handle'?"

"Since it's my parents and Adalyn that we're trying to convince, that means attending dinner parties, galas and other social events. It means bearing the brunt of the scrutiny and attention and not wavering. It means…" His voice lowered, and she tightened her thighs against the pull deep inside. "It means not flinching when I put my hands on you. It means moving into my touch, making every photographer and media outlet believe you want it—my touch, my lips. Make them believe you want me. Can you do that?"

Could she do that? Pretending to want him wasn't hard. The most difficult part would be keeping him from knowing how much she craved him.

No, the most difficult part would be guarding her heart so it didn't mistake fiction for fact, desire for affection.

She'd made that mistake once. Had let herself forget that most rich men only crossed the tracks for one thing. Women like Nadia were good for dirty little secrets, but not to openly court, not to marry. For a moment, she believed that rule hadn't applied to her, but she'd been cruelly reminded.

She'd never forget again.

But dammit, why did he have to describe what he expected in detail? Now she couldn't evict the images of him lowering his head to nuzzle her throat or brush her mouth with those beautiful lips.

"I can do it," she said, forcing a firmness into her voice that was more bravado than certainty. "Can you?" She'd asked it in jest, in challenge, but underneath, she truly needed to know.

"Can I convince anyone that I'm hungry for you? Can I make people believe that I might be holding your hand, but I'm five seconds away from dragging you over to the nearest flat surface and making you come until we're both sweating and shaking?" A tight smile barely curved his lips. "Yes, Nadia, I can do it."

Oh. Damn. His words seemed to seep into the air, burrow into the walls, camp out on the furniture of his sitting area. They inhabited the room, inhabited *her*, so she breathed them, wallowed in them, drowned in them.

"Promise me one thing," he murmured, his blue and green eyes shadowed, his jaw like stone. "Don't fall in love with me."

She blinked. Then laughed, the sound hard, strangled. "Well don't you think highly of yourself." Was he serious? Fort Knox had nothing on the fortress hiding her heart. "I don't think that will be a problem."

"Good," he said, still in that soft tone with the underlying thread of steel. "Because I don't want to hurt you. Do you make my dick hard? Yes. But that's where it begins and ends. I don't want a relationship. So don't let me hurt you, Nadia. Protect yourself from me."

Her breath caught in her throat. She made him hard.

That wasn't anything special. He wanted her to remember her place and stay in it. To not have delusions of grandeur where he was concerned. Contrary to the fantasy fairy tales peddled, princes didn't fall for scullery maids.

Fine with her. She didn't believe in princes and their false professions of love anyway.

"Like I said, that won't be a problem," she assured him. "And since we're setting boundaries and rules. I have two." She ticked up a finger. "One. As you mentioned earlier, sex isn't on the table. Which I'm fine with." The low thrum between her legs sent up a plaintive *Are we really, though?* Ignoring her traitorous and greedy body, she continued, "But that means it's off the menu with everyone else, too. I refuse to be a pathetic side piece in the public's eye." Been there, done that. No thank you on a repeat. A scowl darkened Grayson's face, but again, she moved on. "And two, at the end of the four months, *I* break up with *you*." She paused. "That's a deal breaker."

She didn't go into why it was important to her that she be the one to end this relationship, fake or not. Redemption, maybe. Or pride. It was one thing to look like Cinderella with Prince Charming. It was another thing to be dumped by Prince Charming and return to the cinders and ashes.

The scowl eased and something uncomfortably close to understanding darkened his eyes. She fought not to squirm or, worse, explain herself.

Finally, he nodded. "Human Resources has your banking information, so I'll transfer five hundred thousand there from my personal account tomorrow."

"No." She shook her head. "I only want two hundred and fifty thousand." Just enough to cover all four years of Ezra's tuition and a little extra for incidentals.

Once more, displeasure creased his brow. "The agreement was for half a million now and an additional quarter million when the four months were up."

"No, we didn't agree on that because I turned down the original offer. The terms of our new arrangement are two hundred and fifty," she argued.

"Who in the hell turns down that much money for a lesser amount?"

"That would be me. Take it or leave it." When she walked away from this it wouldn't be feeling like a gold digger. She stretched her arm out toward him. "Deal?"

He studied her palm before closing the distance and enfolding his big hand around hers. It was just her hand but, God, she felt…surrounded. That small gesture reminded her of how he'd wrapped his larger frame around her body, holding her tight as he thrust inside her with care and ferocity.

"Deal."

Why did that one word sound like a warning?

A hard squeeze of her fingers shattered her thoughts, and she glanced from their connected hands to his hooded, sensual gaze. "You have secrets, Nadia Jordan. And I'm going to enjoy uncovering each and every one of them."

Now *that* was definitely a warning. She jerked her hand away from his, not caring how he interpreted the action. Pride demanded she deliver some pithy remark and casually stroll out of the office. But self-preservation… Well it screamed louder than pride at the moment.

With a jerky nod of her head, she wheeled around and damn near charged out the doors, not daring to look back.

Best not to tempt fate…or her shaky resolve.

Seven

The ballet.

She was going to the freaking ballet.

Standing in front of her small closet, Nadia squeezed her eyes shut, pinching the bridge of her nose. She counted to ten and once more surveyed the contents. Jeans, shirts, blouses, skirts and a couple of dresses—all clothes suitable for work and casual time outside of the office. But nothing in the cramped mess came within even centimeters of appropriate fashion for the *ballet*.

God, every time she said it aloud or in her head, her stomach rolled and pitched like a ship in a storm. Unless she could count the number of times she'd watched *Fame*—and honestly, did that even count?—she'd never been interested. But apparently not only did the elite of Chicago attend ballets, they hosted parties *before* them.

When Nadia had decided to take part in this relationship charade, she'd figured on having at least a few days to become accustomed to the idea that her life wouldn't be hers for the next four months. But no, Grayson had called the following morning—this morning—to inform her they were attending a pre-ballet cocktail party at his parents' house.

God, what had she been thinking to agree to this?

Ezra needs to go to college debt-free.

Right. If she kept repeating that to herself, maybe she could make it through this evening and the long ones ahead of her.

Sighing, she reached inside the closet and withdrew her black "any-do" dress. The dress that would do for any occasion whether it was a wedding or funeral. Holding it up, she peered at the modest neckline, cap sleeves and knee-length hem. Simple and perfectly respectable.

Perfectly boring.

Well, there wasn't anything she could do about it. Unfortunately, her budget didn't allow for a shopping spree on the Magnificent Mile. Tossing the dress on her bed, she bundled her hair on top of her head and glanced at her watch before slipping it off and setting it onto the bedside dresser.

Five thirty. She had an hour and a half before Grayson picked her up. Between now and then, she had to shower, put on makeup and get dressed. She would definitely be cutting it close, but—

The loud, obnoxious buzz of the doorbell interrupted her thoughts. Frowning, she hesitated before treading out of her bedroom and down the hall. Who could that be? Ezra had travel ball and wouldn't be home until after nine. And other than his friends, no one else would drop by unannounced.

Because she no longer lived in Tatumville, she peeked out the small window bracketing the front door. A beautiful woman in a perfectly tailored forest green pantsuit stood on the doorstep. Confusion and curiosity warred as Nadia opened the door.

"Can I help you?" Nadia asked.

The woman, who appeared to be several years older

than Nadia, smiled, and a sense of familiarity niggled at her. Did she work for KayCee Corp? Is that where Nadia had seen her? Had to be. It was doubtful Nadia would've met this woman of obvious sophistication and wealth at one of Ezra's ball games or at the neighborhood supermarket.

"Nadia Jordan?" she greeted.

"Yes." Nadia nodded, arching an eyebrow. "And you are?"

"Melanie Chandler. Gray's sister." She dipped her head in the direction of the tiny foyer behind Nadia. "May I come in?"

"Oh. Um, sure." Though a barrage of questions pinged off her skull, she stepped back, granting Melanie entrance. "I'm sorry if I forgot that you were coming over. I don't remember Grayson mentioning—"

Melanie arched an elegant eyebrow, and in that moment, she looked so much like Grayson, Nadia wondered how she hadn't immediately guessed her identity. Though Melanie's eyes were sky blue, she and Grayson shared the same strong facial features and confident bearing.

"Why am I not surprised?" Melanie shook her head, then glancing over her shoulder, waved at someone behind her. "In here, Pete."

In moments, an older man with white hair, dressed in a black suit, strode up Nadia's short, narrow walk. He carried several garment bags and a smaller case. With a smile in Nadia's direction, he entered her home and stood next to Melanie. Her small foyer suddenly seemed tinier and shabbier with these two in it.

"Where should I put this, ma'am?" Pete asked Nadia.

"I don't know what 'this' is," she said, flustered and a little annoyed at the sense of being ambushed. "Anyone want to tell me?"

Melanie sighed then crossed her arms. "Let me guess, Gray not only didn't mention my arriving, but also didn't mention that he instructed me to bring over several dresses for you to choose from for tonight?" Nadia's expression must've reflected the icy punch of shock ricocheting through her because Melanie huffed out a bark of laughter. "Well this is…awkward. Why wouldn't he tell you since he asked me to come by?"

"Probably because he knew I would've told him I'm not a paper doll that needs to be dressed since I've been doing it quite well on my own for all these years," Nadia gritted out from between clenched teeth.

Mortification seared her, probably branding her cheeks a neon shade of red. Yes, she wasn't wealthy, but dammit, she wasn't a charity case, either. *He'd* asked *her* to go along with this charade. And now having his own sister show up on her doorstep with clothes because obviously what Nadia had to wear wasn't good enough… He might as well as have said *she* wasn't good enough.

Face still burning, she straightened her shoulders and met the other woman's gaze. "This is really nice, but not necessary."

"Wait, before you toss us out of your house—which you're well within your rights to do," Melanie said, holding up a hand. "I realize my brother's method might bear all the sensitivity of a goat, but his heart is in the right place. You're someone he cares about, and he wants to make sure you're comfortable and confident tonight. While you are a beautiful woman, and I can see why he's so taken with you, a gorgeous dress never hurts. Besides… You haven't seen the shoes, Nadia." Melania smiled, an almost avaricious glint in her gaze. "The. Shoes."

In spite of the lingering hurt and embarrassment, Nadia laughed. Melanie didn't appear to be covered in the same condescending ice as her mother, and she didn't deserve Nadia's anger.

Capitulating, Nadia waved toward the small living room. "These better be some shoes," she muttered.

Pete walked ahead of them carrying the small pile of luggage, and Melanie looped her arm through Nadia's.

"One thing you'll learn about me really quick. I don't kid about stocks, world peace or footwear."

Chuckling, Nadia let herself be led forward.

An hour later, she stood in front of the cheval mirror in her bedroom. And stared.

This can't be me.

She lifted her arm, about to press trembling fingers to the glass, but at the last minute, she aborted the gesture. Sheepish, she glanced over her shoulder to see if Melanie had seen the foolish move, but the other woman was busy packing up her makeup case. Returning her attention to the mirror, Nadia again gaped at the woman gazing back at her.

Though she'd initially been upset with Grayson for his high-handed tactics, now she…

Oh hell, she felt like freaking Cinderella.

Instead of hiding her abundant curves, the deep silver dress accentuated them. The boat neck flowed into a formfitting top that glided over her breasts and stomach. The rich satin skirt gathered at her waist before falling in stunning draping to the floor. Melanie had parted her hair down the middle and then gathered the thick strands into a bun low in the back. The pointed toe of stilettoes sprinkled with twinkling rhinestones peeked out from under the dress's hem. Diamond studs that'd had Nadia nearly hyperventilating graced her ears and an impossibly thin silver necklace with a diamond nestled in the dip of her throat encircled her neck.

Forget Cinderella. She looked like a goddess.

It both delighted and terrified her.

Yes, in this attire she might look like she belonged more

than she would've in her black wedding/funeral dress. But no dress, shoes or jewelry could change the fact that she *didn't*.

A wave of panic blindsided her, and she pressed a palm to her chest. What if she humiliated herself and Grayson? She didn't know how to mingle with people who might as well as be from another planet instead of a different part of town.

From one moment to the next, she was once again standing in her old house in Tatumville with Jared informing her he wouldn't be escorting her to his parents' anniversary party because it was doubling as an engagement celebration for him. To the woman worthy enough to wear his last name. Not her. Not Marion Jordan's daughter. Nadia might be good enough for a secret roll in the sheets, but not to introduce to his family and friends...

Pain, sharp and bright, sliced into her, and she gasped at the agony of it. Even now, almost two years later, that memory still contained the power to bring her to her knees. Of all the lessons she'd been taught in her life, that one had nearly devastated her.

It was also the one she could never afford to forget.

"Nadia?" Melanie's reflection appeared behind her. Gentle hands cupped Nadia's shoulders. "Are you okay?"

"Yes, of course." Nadia forced a smile to her lips, and in the mirror, it looked as strained as it felt. Turning away from the condemning visual, she faced Grayson's sister. "Thank you so much for all your help. I can't believe you worked that much magic in an hour."

"Please," Melanie scoffed, squeezing Nadia's shoulders before releasing her. "Like I had to do much. You're gorgeous, Nadia." Melanie tilted her head to the side, studying her. "I have to confess, when Gray asked me to pick up dresses and shoes he'd chosen and to come over and assist you for tonight, I was curious. It's a first. You're obviously different."

"I know." Nadia waved a hand. "I'm poor. Can't tell a salad fork from a dessert fork. Thick. Come from peasant stock instead of American royalty…"

"Yes," Melanie agreed, but with such a matter-of-factness, Nadia couldn't take offense. "All that is true. But I was thinking, you're different because my brother gives a damn. He's never asked for my help before, and he's never chosen a woman's evening gown to my knowledge. The fact that he cares about you being as comfortable as possible makes you…more." She paused, and the corner of her mouth quirked. "And the salad fork has longer tines but a shorter handle. The dessert fork is the opposite. Shorter tines, longer handle."

"Thanks," Nadia murmured. And not just for the flatware advice. Melanie's words whirled in Nadia's head. *My brother gives a damn. The fact that he cares about you being as comfortable as possible makes you…more.*

The charade. Grayson needed to make the charade as believable as possible. It was all a part of the act.

Silently repeating those reminders, she picked up her purse from the bed. Just as she finished fastening the band, the doorbell rang. The knotting of her stomach belied the words tramping through her head. Nerves because of the evening ahead. Nothing else.

Liar.

"Here's your wrap." Melanie laid a matching length of satin over Nadia's arm. "And I'll see you there." Squeezing Nadia's hand, Melanie disappeared out of the bedroom.

Dimly, Nadia heard Melanie greet Grayson, and though Nadia's mind ordered her to get going, her feet refused to cooperate. Closing her eyes, she inhaled several deep breaths. She could do this. For Ezra, she could do anything, face anything. Even the cliquish, Chicago social elite—and Grayson's mother.

With an image of her brother walking across Yale's illustrious campus planted firmly in her mind, she exited the bedroom and strode down the short hallway toward the front door.

Grayson stood with his hands in the pockets of his pants, his back to her. But maybe he heard her carpet-muffled footsteps or caught the frantic slamming of her heart against her ribcage… Either one, he turned and faced her.

And God, did he look amazing.

The perfect American prince in a tapered black suit that practically worshipped his tall frame. A stark white shirt emphasized the golden tones of his skin, while a light blue-and-gray pinstriped tie that appeared to be silk even to her untrained eye, drew attention to the hard wall of his chest. A pocket square of the same pattern and color as the tie peeped out of his jacket and a gold, black-faced watch adorned his right wrist.

She'd encircled her fingers around that strong wrist as his full mouth had sexed hers. She'd stroked that chest. Brushed her lips across it while he'd plunged into her over and over again. Faint twinges of pleasure echoed deep and high in her body.

Fake fiancée. No sex. Ezra's tuition money.

Drawing in a breath, she halted several feet away from him.

"Well, I'm ready," she needlessly announced, running her palms down her thighs in a nervous gesture she regretted revealing. She raised her gaze to Grayson's and resisted the urge to fidget. She waited as his hooded, blue-and-green inspection swept over her from the middle part of her hair to the jeweled toe of her shoe. After an insurmountable amount of time—okay, seconds—his scrutiny returned to her face. His expression remained as neutral as ever, but his eyes...

The minimal amount of air left in her lungs made a break for it. Driven away by the gleam lighting his stare like flashes of dry heat. That was...good.

Good for the pretense. To help convince people that he did indeed find her attractive.

But, oh God, not so good for her resolve to remain distant. When he looked at her like that—she nervously fingered the small diamond pendant at her throat. When he looked at her like that, he almost made her believe, too.

And that was dangerous.

"You are stunning," he stated, and the flinty tone contradicted the blaze in his eyes that had flames dancing along all her exposed skin. He withdrew his hands from his pocket and approached her. She almost dipped her head. Anything rather than study the careless sensuality in his confident prowl. "Here." He extended his palm toward her, and in the middle sat a small, black box. "I can't have my fiancée showing up at our first public event without her ring." His lips curled in a sardonic twist as he lifted the lid.

She should've been blown away by the huge, multi-carat diamond nestled in the bed of white satin. The thing could've funded a small developing nation. But it left her cold. Probably because *it* seemed cold. A statement piece, not jewelry lovingly and carefully chosen for a woman he planned to spend the rest of his life with. Or shoot, maybe it was the kind of ring he'd bought Adalyn at one time. If so, that was incredibly sad.

"Thank you," she murmured, as he removed the jewelry and slid it on her left ring finger. The rock weighed her hand down, and wasn't that just apropos? This whole sham of a relationship was an albatross around her neck. "It's lovely."

The half smile deepened, as did the hint of a snarl. "Lovely," he repeated, rubbing his thumb over the square-cut gem. "Most women would've been gushing over a five-carat diamond, but I get a 'lovely' from you. Maybe if I told you it was yours to keep after the four months are up, you could manage more enthusiasm," he said.

"That isn't part of our bargain," she replied, stung by the implication in his admonishment. "And I'm so sorry my response didn't meet your standards. Should I throw myself at you and squeal with glee? Or maybe get down on my knees in gratefulness."

Something dark and...hungry flickered in his eyes, and she stiffened against the spark of need igniting deep inside her, tingling in the tips of breasts, clenching between her legs.

He shifted forward until a mere breath separated them. Lifting her hand at the same time he lowered his head, he brushed his mouth across the ring, and she barely stifled a groan at the whisper of those full, soft lips she remembered so well ghosting across her skin.

"When you get down on your knees for me, Nadia, it won't be out of gratitude," he said in a silken tone that caressed her flesh even as it triggered every feminine warning in her body. This wasn't a threat.

It was a promise.

"We should go," she breathed, tugging her hand free.

For a heart-stopping moment, he didn't release her, and in that same moment, she didn't want him to. She wanted him to drag her closer, consume her mouth like he had in that shadowed hallway and possess her, claim her. Mark her.

But then, he did let her go, and she exhaled. Relieved.

Or at least that's what she tried to convince herself she felt as she let him settle her wrap around her shoulders and they headed out of her house.

Relief.

Not disappointment.

Eight

"**P**rime property, Grayson," Harold Denson boasted. Grayson gritted his teeth as his father's friend droned on and on about a deal that must be invested in. Why the other man thought Grayson cared remained a mystery.

"Ready to be snatched up and developed. I was telling your father about the project, and he told me to talk it over with you since you will soon be stepping up to head Chandler International. I was happy to hear that, and if I must say so, it's about time, too. That tech business you've been fooling around with has been profitable, I'll give you that. But it isn't Chandler. Without your brother—"

"If you'll excuse us," Nadia interrupted from beside him. The hand she settled over his chest stemmed the surge of anger strangling him. Between his father obviously announcing to anyone who would listen that Grayson was returning to the family company and the insensitive mention of Jason, he needed space, air, a drink. And to get away from this ass.

"I'm so sorry to steal Grayson away from you, but he promised me a tour of his childhood home before we leave for the ballet."

"Oh, of course! Grayson, show this young lady how the other half lives. Just don't get lost, you two," he added with a chuckle and a leer over Nadia's breasts and hips that had Grayson's fingers curling into his palm. Older man or not, friend of his father's or not, the man needed a quick lesson in how to respect women. Especially the woman on Grayson's arm.

"Thank you," Nadia said with a smile. She covered his fist with her other hand, squeezing lightly. "How about we start with the library?"

"Sure, baby," Grayson murmured, allowing her to lead him away. The library was in the opposite direction, but at this point, he didn't care. He just needed to be...away.

Focusing on the twist at the back of her head, he imagined loosening it and tunneling his fingers through that wealth of thick strands. Just the thought of wrapping them around his wrists and tugging, hearing that low, hungry moan, diverted his attention from the stranglehold of frustration and sadness he'd felt since stepping foot in his parents' home.

Jason was everywhere. In the pictures mounted on the mantelpiece over the formal living room's fireplace. In the framed degrees hanging prominently in the receiving room.

In the empty space beside their father as he held court with his guests. Everyone knew Jason's spot had been at Daryl Chandler's elbow.

Grayson briefly squeezed his eyes shut, then reopened them, zeroing in on Nadia again as if she were his lodestone. His true north that guided him away from the dark abyss of regrets that just waited for him to slip and plummet into its depths.

"Here." Nadia held out a glass of ruby-red wine, her

knuckles grazing his chest. "You look like you could use this."

"Only if it has a shot of whiskey in it," he growled, but he sipped the alcohol. Grateful for the private corner she'd found and the distraction of doing something with his hands. Because they would either be wrapped around Harold's neck or cupping Nadia's ass. Both would give Grayson immense satisfaction—touching Nadia even more than choking his father's friend—but both actions would also get him into trouble he didn't need.

"Do you really want a tour of the house?"

"No," she said, lifting her own glass to her lips.

He shook his head, raising the wineglass for another sip and studying her over the rim. Part of him desperately wanted—no, needed—to call bullshit. Even Adalyn, who'd been born to a wealthy family had been awed by the Gold Coast greystone mansion. Soaring three stories up, the majestic home had been in his family for four generations. With huge bay and picture windows dotting every floor, stone steps leading up to several entrances and towering peaks, his childhood home resembled a Victorian house deposited in the middle of Chicago.

But Nadia had strolled past the tall iron gates surrounding the property and the gurgling fountain with just a passing glance. Once inside she hadn't gaped at the vaulted cathedral ceilings, the grand foyer with the winding staircase, the priceless art decorating the walls or the cavernous rooms with huge fireplaces, antiques and crystal chandeliers. No, Nadia had only given his family's prosperity and affluence fleeting attention. Just as she'd done with the ring.

Why her obvious lack of enthusiasm for the piece of jewelry still grated, he didn't know. Couldn't explain. It just...did. He peered down at her left hand and the diamond setting that cost more than some people's yearly salary. When he'd bought the ring, his intention had been to ensure everyone who saw it understood his serious intentions. In his circle—or his parents' circle—money spoke much louder than words. But Nadia, it seemed, didn't care about what it said.

Yes, he wanted her awe. For her to be excited. Or hell, just affected. Because if not, that made her different. And he didn't trust "different"—it unnerved him. He couldn't get a handle on it, couldn't analyze and add it up. It meant she wouldn't stay in the neat box he'd created for her.

The last thing he needed was for her to be more than any other woman.

The last thing he needed was for her to be…different.

"You didn't like the ring."

Hell. Where had that come from? And yet, he couldn't stop himself.

"Why?" he pressed.

She studied him, her espresso gaze unwavering. "In my experience, rich people wield their money like a weapon. Protecting themselves and those they deem worthy and waging war on everyone else. They arm themselves with money to bring people to heel. When you've been on the receiving end of that short leash, how many dollars a person spends on their home, car, clothes and even you, doesn't matter much."

Grayson stared at her, each word an indictment against him, his family, his world. They were all guilty—especially him. Wasn't he paying her to lie? To pretend to be someone she wasn't for his benefit?

He shook his head as if the gesture could rid him of the thought and the unsettling pinpricks of guilt. She could've turned him down. Hell, she had, but then had returned to *him*, accepting the bargain. And it was just that—a bargain. One they both profited from. Just like other women in his past, she wanted money from him. Only this time, he was going in with his eyes wide open. No feelings attached. No fervent promises of love. No commitments.

It was the most honest transaction he'd ever entered in his life.

"If money doesn't matter, then what does?" he drawled, mocking her. "Love? I hate to break it to you, Nadia, but the two are mutually exclusive."

"Tell me something," she murmured, and when he didn't reply, she continued, "Was that ring for me…or for you?"

A disdainful response hovered on his tongue, but remained stuck there, something deep inside him refusing to loose the vitriolic words. Instead, he stared down into her upturned face, spying a knowledge in those dark eyes that made him want to remind her of who he was—her employer, the man paying her a quarter of a million dollars, a fucking Chandler…

He wanted to beg her to stop peering inside him and seeing the secrets, the wounds he zealously guarded.

"Grayson," an all-too-familiar voice interrupted his and Nadia's visual showdown.

He tore his gaze away from his fake fiancée to meet the green one of his ex-fiancée. Adalyn smiled, and the sultriness in her eyes stirred nothing in him but irritation.

"I haven't had a chance to speak to you all evening," she said.

"Hello, Adalyn," he replied, nodding.

Objectively, he noted the sleek length of her raven hair and her petite figure encased in an off-the-shoulder cocktail dress. Without conscious thought, he compared her to Nadia with her tall, lush body showcased to perfection in the silver dress that had his hands itching all night to touch her. He'd cupped those hips. Dug his fingers in the soft flesh there as he drove into her.

Because he could—because this charade granted him permission—he slid an arm around Nadia's lower back and rested his fingers against that enticing curve. Pressing his fingertips into it, melding the present with his vivid memories.

"You remember Nadia. Nadia Jordan, this is Adalyn Hayes," he murmured. Turning his attention to his ex, his voice hardened, losing the warmth it'd contained when speaking to Nadia. "Adalyn, Nadia Jordan, my fiancée."

Adalyn flicked a look at Nadia and then down at her hand. Unless Adalyn had gone spontaneously blind she couldn't have missed the diamond on Nadia's finger. Her mouth flattened briefly before regaining the polite society smile that could mean anything.

"Yes, I'd heard the news about your sudden engagement. It's the hot topic of conversation this evening. Congratulations," Adalyn said, the sweetness in her smile nowhere near the dagger-edge sharpness in her eyes. "How exciting." She settled a hand on his chest, and it required every bit of his control not to flinch. "I remember holding that title once, as well. Fiancée to Grayson Chandler. The experience was...thrilling," she added, her tone lowering, as if inviting him to recall the intimate times they'd shared.

Unable to stand her touch another second, especially with Nadia's warm body tucked against his, he stepped back. Adalyn's arm dropped to her side, and he didn't miss the glint of anger in her gaze.

"Nadia, right?" Adalyn asked, swinging her attention away from him. But Grayson stiffened, a surge of protectiveness sweeping through him. He'd witnessed Adalyn's cutting disdain in action. No matter that his and Nadia's relationship wasn't real. He wouldn't allow Adalyn to slice her to pieces with that razor she called a tongue. "I almost didn't recognize you from the last time we met. Your dress is lovely." Adalyn tapped a French-tipped finger against her bottom lip, her eyes narrowed. "Is that Michael Kors?

I'd heard he'd incorporated a few pieces in his collection for…healthier women."

The petty bitch.

Grayson shifted forward, anger blazing his path. "Adalyn…" he growled.

"Actually, I'm not certain who the designer is," Nadia interrupted, wrapping an arm around his back and leaning closer. She chuckled, the sound light, soft and so sweet, he tore his glare away from his ex and glanced down at her. With her head tipped back, she returned his gaze, her lovely mouth curved into a smile that held not just affection, but a sensuality that Adalyn damn sure couldn't miss. Even knowing her expression was feigned for the other woman's benefit, his breath snagged in his lungs and his cock stirred, hardening.

She was—damn, she was dangerous, the smile on that made-for-sex mouth a fully loaded weapon.

"Can I be honest?" she asked, treating Adalyn as if she were a close friend. "I'm not really into fashion. But thank goodness I have a man who knows me so well, he chooses gowns that I'll love. Or more importantly, that he loves to see me in."

Nadia trailed a finger down his chest, and his shirt might as well as have disintegrated under the teasing caress. He forgot about silently applauding how she deftly fielded Adalyn as fire trailed in the wake of her touch. Not caring how it appeared, he grasped her wrist and lifted her hand to his mouth, brushing a kiss across her fingertips. Surprise flared in her eyes. But so did desire. And the sight of it had an electrical current traveling through his veins.

Adalyn's laugh carried an edge, like shattered glass. "Well, isn't that sweet? And, I apologize if I offended you, Nadia. But can I be honest, as well?" She didn't wait for Nadia to reply but dipped her head as if about to confide a secret. Again, Grayson fought the urge to step in front of Nadia, to shield her from Adalyn. "I know tonight has probably been a little overwhelming for you, but you'll have to forgive us our curiosity. This relationship came out of nowhere. Usually, Grayson is constantly in the society columns and gossip sites. But we haven't seen him with you once. Almost as if he's been keeping you under wraps. Hiding you."

Adalyn's implication was clear. That he was ashamed of Nadia. His fury returned tenfold, and he couldn't contain the menacing rumble that rolled out of him. Even Adalyn had the sense to back up a step.

"You're right, Adalyn," he agreed, voice quiet, carrying a warning. "There is nothing 'usual' about Nadia. She's unlike any woman I've been with." He allowed the *including you* to remain unspoken. "I selfishly wanted to keep her to myself before subjecting her to the BS that goes along with being my wife. She's that special to me." Sliding his hand from her hip and up her spine, he cupped her neck, drawing her closer until she rose on her toes. Until her breasts pressed into his side. "Now that you've experienced the other side of my life, are you ready to leave me?"

"Never," Nadia said in that same teasing lilt, but her eyes... Those dark eyes held all the confusion swirling inside of him over how far he was taking this exhibition of affection.

"Good," he murmured. Then brushed his lips over hers.

But it wasn't enough.

That small hit of her taste had him ignoring Adalyn and the roomful of people, including his parents and sister. He returned to Nadia's mouth for more. For a deeper sampling. To thrust his tongue past her parted lips—whether parted in shock or desire, he didn't know—and take what his memories wouldn't let him forget. Reacquaint himself with what his logic assured him couldn't possibly be as good as he remembered.

Logic could go fuck itself.

She was every carnal wish and wicked sin wrapped in beauty and light.

She was the one to break the kiss. The one who retained a modicum of propriety and restraint. Not him.

That quick, she'd gone to his head, and he'd gotten drunk on her.

Goddamn.

He lifted his head, noticed the stares, heard the murmuring. Adalyn had disappeared at some point during the kiss, but he could almost feel the weight of his parents' displeasure. In spite of the playboy reputation he bore, he didn't do this—lose control, make a spectacle of himself—ever.

This woman. She flayed to pieces every resolve, every vow he'd made. He couldn't go there with her. Deliberately, he conjured an image of himself a year ago after he'd ended his relationship with Adalyn. How broken he'd been. How disillusioned he'd been. Adalyn hadn't only cracked his heart down the middle, she'd stolen his ability to trust himself, his judgment.

His ability to trust, period.

And Nadia, though she might desire him, she only wanted from him what every other woman did.

What he could give her.

He could never lose sight of that.

Never.

"Grayson," Nadia whispered.

But he couldn't look at her. Couldn't meet that gaze. Because, despite the reminders of why he had to tread carefully with her—with himself—if he glimpsed desire in those beautiful eyes, he might seek out the nearest room with a door and lock. And damn the consequences, he would lay her out and take everything she would offer him. Then demand more.

"We should get ready to leave for the ballet," he said,

grasping her elbow and leading her toward the living room entrance.

He had to reestablish the grounds of their arrangement.

This relationship was fake. It had an expiration date.

Nadia Jordan was his end game.

She could be nothing else.

Nine

"Mr. Chandler, your father is here to see you," Mrs. Ross announced on the other end of the line. "He doesn't have an appointment, sir."

A faint spurt of humor echoed through him at his assistant's reminder that was more directed at his father than him. Her disapproval hummed beneath the cool tone, but it would be lost on Daryl Chandler. He was the kind of man people shuffled their schedules for. The kind of man who demanded it.

Leaning back in his office chair, Grayson closed his eyes, pinching the bridge of his nose. Sadly, he wasn't shocked at this visit. Well, correction. He was surprised his father stood on the other side of his office door instead of his mother. After the performance Grayson and Nadia had put on at the cocktail party three nights ago, he'd expected this "intervention."

"You can send him in, Mrs. Ross," he said, setting the phone down.

He rose and rounded the desk, standing in front of it. Preparing himself. That he braced himself as if readying for battle spoke volumes about his relationship with his father.

Seconds later, his office door opened and Daryl Chandler strode through as if his name was engraved on the gold plate instead of Grayson's.

To Grayson, his father had always been bigger than life. He'd inherited his height and big, wide-shouldered frame from Daryl Chandler—a throwback to the ancestors who had worked the railroads instead of owning them—and though his father probably wouldn't easily admit it, Grayson had inherited his business acumen, too. But ever since he'd been born with a defect—his different-colored eyes— Grayson had been flawed and second best with his father.

There'd been a time when Grayson had lived up to his father's opinion. Like when, as a teen, he'd decided to have an impromptu party on his father's yacht. Or when he'd been caught smoking weed on the private school grounds. But those stunts were in the distant past. Over the years, he'd proven he could control not only himself, but his life, and run a successful company.

None of that seemed to matter to his father, though.

When would it cease mattering to Grayson?

"Good morning, Dad. This is a surprise."

His father arched a still-dark eyebrow. "Somehow I doubt that, Grayson." He lifted an arm and waved it toward Grayson's desk. And for the first time, he noticed the manila folder in his father's hand. "I won't make this long."

"Of course." Curiosity and a weighty sense of foreboding expanded inside Grayson's chest. This was the first time since he and Gideon founded KayCee Corp that his father had visited the offices. This one didn't bode well.

He led Daryl to the two armchairs in front of his desk. He lowered into one and waited for his father to settle. A steely pair of green eyes studied him, but Grayson wasn't that rebellious teen anymore. He was a thirty-year-old man who'd matured, carved out his own future and lived on his own terms. If his father waited for him to squirm, he might need to cancel his meetings. Wasn't going to happen.

"I believe you can guess why I'm here," Daryl began, resting the folder on his thigh. Grayson tried not to stare at it, but at this moment, the innocuous light brown file loomed like the real threat in the room. "After that... undignified display the other night, your mother and I thought it best if I paid you a visit."

Undignified display? To what did he refer? His engagement? Or the kiss? "I'm afraid you're going to have to be more specific, Dad. I attended as Mother requested with my fiancée. Which part offended you?"

Daryl scoffed, irritation flashing in his eyes. "Take your pick, Grayson. Showing up with that woman. Springing this joke of an engagement on both of us and making us accessories to it because you knew we wouldn't cause a scene in front of all our friends."

Though anger tightened his gut, Grayson propped his elbows on the arms of his chair and templed his fingers beneath his chin. "An accessory?" He snorted. "You make my relationship sound like a crime. Which, I suppose you see it as one. Still, the time when I had to bring the woman I'm seeing by for approval has long since passed—if it ever existed." He shook his head. "I will apologize for not letting you and Mother know about the engagement in a more private setting, though. It hadn't been my intention to embarrass you."

Just waylay any more matchmaking attempts by his mother.

His father waved aside the apology with a flick of his hand, dismissing it. "Considering the number of women you run through, all captured by those unseemly gossip sites, we're thankful you haven't brought them to our home."

The barb struck true, no doubt as Daryl had intended. But Grayson refused to let him see the effect. "But when you contemplate giving a woman our last name and bringing her into our family, she certainly requires our approval. And this Nadia Jordan does not meet the standards of anyone who will be a Chandler. Not even remotely." His father picked up the envelope and extended it toward him. "Take it, Grayson. Read it."

Though he wanted to tell his father to forget it, Grayson reluctantly accepted it. Knowledge meant power. And though his and Nadia's relationship was fake, he would protect her, shield her from his parents, if need be.

He opened the folder and removed the thin sheaf of papers, scanning the top sheet. An investigative report on one Nadia A. Jordan. Surprise reverberated through him, discordant and ugly. Well, hadn't his parents been busy?

Several minutes later, he lifted his head and met his father's gaze, hardening his expression into a mask that he hoped revealed none of the thoughts whirling through his head. Father unknown. Neglectful mother with a reputation that must've made being her daughter a nightmare. Arrested for shoplifting. No college education. Wrecked credit.

His parents would read this report and see a poor, uneducated woman from nowhere trying to get her greedy hooks into their son.

Grayson saw a woman, who in spite of the kicks and punches life had thrown, had risen every time to not just continue, but to thrive. A life that might have bent her, but from the passion and defiance she'd shown him, hadn't broken her.

He saw a survivor.

"Is this supposed to change my mind?" he asked, tossing the report onto his desk. "So, she wasn't born with a building named after her family? That doesn't make her unworthy to wear the illustrious Chandler name," he drawled.

Red surged into his father's face, the only sign of his rising temper. "You're damn right that makes her unworthy. If you want to screw her, fine. But marry her? A thief? And from that GED, a high school dropout? The daughter of a whore? And God only knows if she falls far from the tree. No, Grayson. Marriage to her is out of the question."

"You want to stop right there, Dad," Grayson said, voice flat. A tone he'd never used with his father before. He had no intention of marrying Nadia, which made this whole discussion moot. But no way in hell would he allow his father to denigrate her. As if she were something on the bottom of his shoe. "You have your opinion of Nadia, but you don't get to talk about her like that to me. Ever." He struggled to remain respectful, but if it'd been anyone else but Daryl Chandler uttering these insults, they would've been picking themselves up off the floor.

Again. His anger made no sense.

But it didn't have to.

"This is what I'm talking about, Grayson," Daryl snapped, shooting to his feet. He paced away from Grayson, who also stood. "I can see why some of her... charms would grab your attention. But stop thinking with your dick," he growled, striding back toward Grayson and halting in front of him. "This is about more than you, it's about family, about loyalty, about living up to the Chandler name and all that it entails instead of dragging it down as you seem intent on doing."

How? By living when Jason didn't?

The question clanged in his head like the rattling of a ghost. A ghost that refused to be exorcised.

"So forget my own happiness, my own future?" he asked quietly, now referring to more than Nadia. To his company, to making his own choices, to living an existence out from under the smothering burden of a legacy he hadn't asked for. "How much do you expect me to sacrifice?"

"Whatever it takes," his father shot back. Inhaling a deep breath, he shoved his hands into the front pockets of his gray suit, visibly calming himself. "We all sacrifice, Grayson. Particularly now that Jason..." He cleared his throat, his gaze briefly shooting to the floor-to-ceiling window behind Grayson. When he returned his regard to Grayson, his eyes reflected none of the emotion that had wrapped around Jason's name. "I can't helm Chandler International forever, nor do I want to. It's a birthright passed down from father to son, and it is now your turn, your privilege, your *destiny* to lead and build it into even more than I have.

"And you need the right woman at your side. The *right* woman, Grayson. And as high-handed as your mother might be, she's right. Adalyn is a perfect choice. She's from an exceptional family, has been educated at the finest schools, is beautiful and knows our world. Also, her father and I are in the middle of discussing a very lucrative business deal. It would mean expanding both Chandler International and The Hayes Group into a power to be reckoned with in the national and global financial markets. I'd prefer not to anger Thad Hayes by having my son rebuff his daughter, which would result in the failure of this venture."

"Now who's the whore, Dad? You want me to pimp myself out for a company expansion," Grayson growled.

"I want you to do what's right," Daryl snapped. "It's not like you and Adalyn aren't compatible. You were engaged before, so there's no need for the theatrics."

"Were," Grayson ground out. "And there's a very good reason why I didn't go through with it."

His father shook his head. Pulling his hand free of his pants pocket, he glanced down at his watch. "I have to go. But get rid of the girl, Grayson. And start courting Adalyn. If you must be photographed like a common reality

TV star, then it should be with her, not a plaything. And," he narrowed his eyes on him, "I expect you to attend the next Chandler board meeting. The directors need to understand that you will be stepping in as CEO and become familiar with you."

With that order, his father turned and strode out of the office, leaving Grayson alone. And angry. Saddened. And so goddamn powerless.

And he resented his father for that.

Hated himself even more.

Family duty and loyalty strangled him, crushing him under its burdensome weight. As the "spare," he hadn't been his parents' first choice.

But now, he was the only one left.

Ten

"Ezra, can you get the door?" Nadia called from her bedroom. She'd just emerged from the shower and answering the doorbell in a short, threadbare towel didn't seem like a great idea. On Saturdays, she tended to go casual, but not *that* casual.

"Yeah, I got it," her brother yelled back. As was their custom, on Saturday mornings she cooked a big breakfast, and he cleaned up afterward. Since her bedroom was off the same hallway that led to the kitchen, she heard him tramp down the hall toward the foyer.

She shimmied into a bra and panties, then tugged on a black, V-neck sweater and her favorite pair of boyfriend jeans that were faded from multiple wears and washings. As she searched for a pair of socks among the endless singles, a knock echoed on her door.

"Come in," she said, triumphantly retrieving a matching pair.

A second later, Ezra opened the door and poked his

head through, his dark locs swinging against his handsome face. His handsome, frowning face. "There's a guy here to see you."

Her heart thumped against her rib cage. She hadn't made many friends in the short time she'd been in Chicago and hadn't dated once. So the "guy" could be only one person.

"Okay, I'll be right out," she said, infusing a calm into her voice that belied the tumble of nerves in her belly.

Still frowning, Ezra backed out of the door. Moments later, she emerged and padded down the hallway toward the front of the house. Though the thin carpet masked her footsteps, Grayson still looked up as she approached, his blue-and-green gaze steady on her. She almost faltered, the power of those eyes like a physical blow.

Though days had passed since the cocktail party, and their contact had been minimal, she still felt his mouth pressed to hers and tasted the hunger in that kiss. She dreamed about that kiss. Even now, she forced her hands to remain by her side so she didn't lift one and press fingers to her lips. As if she could somehow capture it.

In the middle of his parents' living room, she'd yearned to wrap her arms around his neck and demand a deeper touch that would fill her empty places. She'd longed to be burned by the pleasure that had haunted her body, her mind. The desire that had flared so hot between them during the blackout hadn't abated, hadn't dimmed. Before that kiss at the cocktail party she could convince herself that the out-of-the-ordinary circumstances had stirred the combustible heat between them.

The kiss had razed that opinion to ashes.

But it'd also reinforced her emotional walls with steel. If one kiss could level her... As much as she'd believed she'd loved Jared, he hadn't ignited the out-of-control need to surrender herself that Grayson did.

It was...terrifying.

Because Grayson, with his innate sensuality, dark emotions that seemed to seethe just under the surface, had a dominance that could strip away the control she'd fought so hard for. He could render her vow to never lay her heart and soul out for a man to use again to cinders.

She couldn't permit that.

She didn't know if she would survive intact.

No way in hell would she risk finding out.

She repeated that warning in her head as she took in his tall, lean frame in black slacks and a cream-colored sweater that probably cost more than her living room furniture.

"Grayson," she greeted, drawing nearer. His sandalwood and mint scent reached out to her, and she cursed herself for inhaling deeply, savoring it. "This is a surprise." She halted next to her brother. "I don't know if he introduced himself, but this is my brother, Ezra. Ezra," she nudged him with her elbow, "this is Grayson Chandler, my...uh, friend."

"Friend, huh?" Ezra snorted, rolling his eyes, appearing all of his seventeen years. "Okay, we'll go with that." He stuck out a hand toward Grayson. "Nice to meet you, Mr. Chandler."

"You, too, Ezra. And it's Grayson." Grayson shook her brother's hand.

"So what are you two crazy kids up to today?" Ezra questioned, crossing his arms and glancing back and forth between her and Grayson.

"Please," she scoffed, shoving his shoulder. "Get out of here and finish the dishes."

"Fine," he grumbled, then pivoted and headed toward the rear of the house.

Once he'd disappeared, she returned her attention to her "fiancé."

"Grayson, what are you doing here? Did we have something scheduled?"

He shook his head. "No, I stopped by to see if you were free today."

"For?" she pressed. "What's the occasion? A dinner party? A charity event?"

"Neither. I—" His lips snapped shut, and a muscle leaped along his jaw. Several seconds later, he said, "Do you trust me, Nadia?"

"Not even a little bit." Truth, but not all of it.

When it came to him, she trusted herself even less.

A ghost of a smile flirted with his mouth. "I deserve that. And respect it. But will you give me a pass today? Take a chance on me."

Take a chance on me.

The simple words shouldn't have been a temptation. But for her, they were. In the past, when she'd trusted people, they'd either disappointed or devastated her. She didn't go in blind anywhere; she required a map, seven different exits and an escape hatch. Yet...

Yet, as she met his mesmerizing eyes, she wanted to place herself into his hands, let him alleviate the exhaustion of always being in control. Even if just for a little while.

"Okay," she murmured. "Give me a few minutes. I'll be right back."

He nodded, his expression revealing nothing. But she caught the flash of something in his eyes. Something she believed could be relief. That was probably her imagination, though. Her trying to convince herself she wasn't in this confusing place of emotional quicksand alone.

Sighing, she returned to her room and then quickly applied a minimal amount of makeup, tugged on her ankle boots and grabbed her jacket. At the last second, she picked up the ostentatious engagement ring and slid it on her finger. Moments later, she slipped back out of her bedroom into the hallway.

"...says you're a friend, but I can guess what kind of

friend you are." Ezra's voice drifted to her as she treaded closer. Ahead, her brother stood in front of Grayson, his back to her. Though Grayson had him by several inches, Ezra straightened his shoulders and tipped his head back. "I don't know what kind of thing y'all have going on," he continued in his drawl. "But she's my big sister. And she's been through enough for a lifetime. I don't want you adding to it."

Silently, Nadia groaned. Love for her brother and his overprotective streak poured through her, but she also longed to yank him up and shove him back toward the kitchen. She could take care of herself without him threatening would-be boyfriends. Still... Damn, she adored the kid.

"I don't plan on hurting your sister," Grayson promised, his voice solemn, no hint of amusement. He could've easily patronized the teen, but sincerity rang from his words. And part of her believed him. The only problem was, most people usually didn't *plan* on harming other people. They just did.

"Good." Ezra nodded. "She's all I have and she has been taken advantage of and hurt too many times in the past. She needs someone who'll take care of her for once instead of the other way around. Especially after Jared—"

Oh God.

"I'm ready," she called out, moving down the hall at a desperate clip. Jesus, why would Ezra bring up her ex-boyfriend? Both Grayson and Ezra turned to face her, and guilt flashed across her brother's face. But it quickly morphed into a stubbornness she was well acquainted with. "You." She jabbed a finger in his chest. "Dishes. And if you go out tonight, make sure you call and let me know."

"Sure." He kissed her cheek, then glanced back at Grayson, giving him that chin tip that seemed to be a part of the masculine language. "Nice talking to you, Grayson."

When he once more disappeared into the kitchen, she shifted her gaze to Grayson. "I'm sorry about that," she said with a small wince. "He's a little overprotective."

But Grayson shook his head, his stare flicking over her shoulder in the direction her brother had gone. "He loves his sister and is watching out for her. There's nothing to apologize for." Nabbing her jacket from her hand, he held it up, and she slipped her arms through the sleeves. "You're lucky to have one another," he murmured, his large hands settling on her shoulders. His fingers lightly squeezed, before releasing her. "Let's go."

Though questions about his enigmatic statement whirled inside her head, she went.

"I should be annoyed with you right now," Nadia muttered, sinking into the chair that Grayson pulled from the restaurant table.

A delicate glass vase filled with water and floating, lit candles in the shape of lilies cast a warm glow over the white linen. Folded black napkins that reminded her of origami sat next to sparkling silver flatware. A breathtaking view of Lake Michigan through floor-to-ceiling windows, its gently lapping waters gleaming orange, pink and purple from the setting sun, provided a stunning backdrop. Even though other diners and the low hum of conversation surrounded them, their corner table, partially shielded from prying eyes by a wall of lush greenery, exuded the illusion of privacy. And from the curious looks they received upon entering, she clung to that illusion.

By himself, Grayson would draw attention. But with her by his side? The looks seemed sharper, the whispers louder. Part of her wanted to rise from the table and walk out. She'd been on the receiving end of hushed talk behind hands enough to last a couple of lifetimes. But the other half of her—the half that brimmed with defiant anger—

met their furtive glances. Yes, she'd dared to enter their cushy, exclusive turf. But she wouldn't lower her eyes in apology for being there.

Grayson ordered wine for both of them, and as their waiter hurried away, he turned to her. "Annoyed with me?" he repeated, the corner of his mouth quirking as he settled in the chair across from her. "Whatever for? Didn't we just spend a great day together? Buckingham Fountain. The SkyDeck. The Riverwalk. Navy Pier. Fried Twinkies."

"Yeah." She sighed. "Extra points for the fried Twinkies. They're probably the only reason I *should be* annoyed and am not full-blown irritated." He arched an eyebrow, and she sank her teeth into her bottom lip, fiddling with the napkin on the table. "I sound like an ungrateful shrew, and I'm sorry. Thank you for an amazing day I wasn't expecting. Ezra and I have been in Chicago for a little over a year, but between work and his schedule and, well, life, I haven't had the opportunity to explore the city. Today was wonderful. So again, thank you."

"You're welcome, Nadia. It was my pleasure," he murmured. Cocking his head to the side, he studied her. "Now tell me what you're not saying."

She huffed out a ragged laugh that abraded her throat. "It's...this." She leaned back and waved a hand up and down her torso, indicating the royal blue long-sleeved sheath dress that both glided over and clung to her breasts, hips and thighs. Beneath the table, black knee-high stiletto boots of the softest leather embraced her calves and feet. Yes, Grayson had escorted her all over Chicago in a laid-back, surprisingly *fun* tour of his city. He'd gifted her with a day that had made her feel free and special. But... "The dress for the cocktail party, this one—they're not part of our bargain," she finished.

It went deeper than not wanting to be the recipient of his charity. So much deeper.

"But it is part of our bargain, Nadia," Grayson contradicted. "I asked you to play the part of my fiancée. And that includes making you look the role, as well. And that's my responsibility since the arrangement was my idea, not yours. What kind of man would I be if I didn't take care of the needs of the woman I supposedly love? Not just emotional and sexual needs. But her material needs, as well? And not because I owe her anything, but due to it simply being my pleasure."

She didn't have an answer. Couldn't formulate one because her mind had stopped functioning at "emotional and sexual," fogged over by the heated arousal pouring through her. She, more than anyone, comprehended how well he fulfilled a woman's desires, satisfied her body.

"You're still not being completely honest, though," he continued, those piercing eyes glittering like gems in the light of the candles. "Tell me. Is your aversion to receiving gifts a general issue, or is it specific to me?"

She stared at him, the width of the square table seeming to shrink to that of a postage stamp. Suddenly, he was too close, his presence too large, too compelling. Too…tempting. Everything in her screamed to avoid that gaze, to keep silent. That she didn't need to divulge more to him—didn't need to give him more of herself—than what was required to pull off the relationship charade.

But trapped by his enigmatic, fascinating eyes, she couldn't squelch the impulse to confide in him. Even if it was just this little thing.

Because all she could afford with this man was "a little."

Defying the voice that warned that even a small amount was too much, she murmured, "It's both, I suppose."

Their waiter appeared with their wine. She gladly sipped from her filled glass, appreciating not just the sweet flavor of the Riesling but the temporary reprieve it provided. Moments later, the waiter left them again after taking their dinner orders, and she set her wineglass down on the table. Lifting a fingertip, she traced the slender stem, focusing her attention on it instead of Grayson.

"I grew up in a small town in Georgia. The kind where there's still a dime store, a pharmacy that also sells ice cream and a church on every corner. As you can imagine, everyone knows everyone and their business. For some, this could be the perfect place to grow up, but when your mother is…" She paused, the scraps of familial loyalty and respect her mother hadn't destroyed not allowing her to call Marion Jordan a whore. "Popular with men," she substituted, "your life can be hell."

She shifted her regard from the glass to his face, searching for a reaction to learning who her mother was. Surprise? Revulsion? But his stoic expression revealed none of his thoughts. The absence of a reaction gave her the courage to continue.

"My mother didn't work. She was taken care of by the men she 'dated,'" she said, using Marion's term. "Mostly wealthy men. They paid her rent, her bills, and yes, bought her jewelry and clothes. That's how Ezra and I survived— off the gifts of these men. But that's only when my mother decided to share the wealth. When she would remember to buy groceries or clothes for us, when she wasn't spending the money on herself. Once, when I was sixteen, I was so desperate to feed my brother, I stole a loaf of bread and jars of peanut butter and jelly from the store."

Her voice didn't waver as she confessed her one and only crime to him, and she didn't lower her gaze. The store security guard, the gossips in her town, the judge had all informed her she should've been ashamed of herself. But she hadn't been then and wasn't now. She'd done what needed to be done so her little brother didn't go to bed hungry, his stomach cramping with pains because he hadn't eaten in two days. Their mother had vanished on one of her many disappearing acts, probably with some man at a hotel where she ate while her children starved.

No, Nadia had accepted the probation and the town's scorn and the whispers of "the apple doesn't fall far from the tree," and apologized to Mr. Carol, the grocery store owner, but she'd never bowed her head in shame.

She wouldn't start with Grayson.

"I learned those gifts came at the price of my pride in taking dirty money, knowing what my mother did to earn it. The price was our sense of security, our independence. As soon as I was old enough—and as soon as I could find someone willing to hire me—I got a job at a gas station convenience store in the next town over. It meant spending time begging for rides or biking it the thirty minutes there and back, it meant less time with my brother so I could provide for us, it meant not finishing high school and graduating with a GED, it meant passing on college. But it also meant not depending on another rich man's 'gifts and generosity.'"

Silence reigned between them for precious seconds. Her heart thumped against her rib cage, the pulse ponderous in her ears. In this instant, staring into his unique eyes, she tried not to cringe under the vulnerability clawing at her. She felt more exposed than she had when he'd stripped her clothes from her body in that dark hallway.

Not only had she confessed that her mother had been the town whore, but Nadia had also admitted that she had a criminal record and was a high school dropout. Not exactly fiancée material compared to the women he dated.

"What did you want to go to college for?" he asked quietly, taking her aback with the question.

"Nursing," she said. "Maybe because I've always been the caretaker in my family." She lifted a shoulder in a half shrug. "It just wasn't meant to be. And besides, Ezra is the genius in our family. He's—" She bit off the rest of the sentence, almost spilling about him being accepted to Yale.

Though she'd shared some of her past, she still didn't trust him with her family. "He's brilliant. Special," she added.

"And you aren't?" he challenged, a snap in his voice. She frowned at the scowl that creased his brow, at the flash of anger in his narrowed gaze. He propped an arm on the table and leaned closer. "Baby, from what you've told me, you practically raised yourself and your brother. You sacrificed your childhood so he could have what little security a teenager could manage to give him when his real parent couldn't be bothered. You packed up from the only home you ever knew to move thousands of miles away to a strange city. You're a fighter, a survivor. A GED doesn't make you any less brilliant, any less special. Not going to college doesn't mean you're not as smart, not as driven or successful as other people. In my eyes, it requires more intelligence, more grit to carve out the living you've made for both yourself and Ezra than to just accept all the advantages of being born with wealth and opportunities as your due. One takes character, determination and strength, the other the Russian Roulette of birth and luck."

She couldn't speak. Could only *feel*. Surprise. Delight. Gratitude. Sadness. They all swirled and tumbled in her chest, swelling in her throat.

No one—absolutely *no one*—had ever called her smart, strong or a survivor. And for this man to say those words…

She dodged that intense stare, instead ducking her gaze to the pale gold contents of her wineglass. God, she wanted a sip. Anything to distract her from the weight of his scrutiny, from the almost terrifying depth and power of her own emotions. But she didn't dare attempt to lift the glass with her trembling hands.

"Nadia," he said, and though she avoided his eyes, the vein of steel threading through the tone brooked no disobedience.

She lifted her regard back to him, immediately becoming ensnared in the blue-and-emerald depths.

"I'm going to continue to give you gifts. Not because I owe you or as a debt I expect you to repay." He reached across the table and wrapped his long fingers around hers so they both held the glass stem. The warmth and strength of his grip was an embrace that enfolded her entire body, not just her hand. "I'm not going to stop because you deserve them. The girl you were, the teen who grew up too soon and the woman who bears all the responsibility of the world on her shoulders but too little of the beauty. That's what I want to give you. It's my honor to give you. Some of that beauty. Let me."

Again, she couldn't speak. Didn't dare nod. No matter how much she longed to. God, the temptation to relinquish control just for once and let someone—no, not someone, *Grayson*—carry the burden and care for her swept through her like the sweet warmth of a spring day. It lulled her, coaxed her to lie down, to let go.

Who would it hurt?

Her.

In the long run, it would devastate her. Because she could so easily come to rely on him. And the day would come—four months from now to be exact—when he would be a non-factor in her life. When he would disappear, leaving her aching for him—yearning for his shoulder to rest her head on, his chest to burrow her face against—instead of facing the world.

No. Grayson might not be Jared, but he was still a handsome, wealthy man who could make her believe in fairy tales.

Patching up the chinks in her armor that his words and her longing had created, she sat back in her chair, placing much-needed distance between them. Picking up her wine, she sipped, wishing the alcohol would transform into something stronger.

Their waiter chose that moment to return with their plates of steaming food. Thank God. Several minutes passed while they dug into their entrées. In spite of the emotional storm brewing inside her, she moaned at the first bite of tender, perfectly cooked medium-rare sirloin.

"Oh, my God." She closed her eyes, savoring the blend of spices and loosed another near orgasmic groan. She lifted her lashes. "This is so good it should be criminal…"

Her voice trailed off. How could she speak when her lungs refused to release any air?

Grayson stared at her, and the heat in that gaze seared her, sent flames licking over her, engulfing her. His hooded contemplation dipped to her mouth, and she sank her teeth in her bottom lip to trap her gasp. As if he'd heard it, his scrutiny rose to hers.

She wanted to rear back from the intensity and heat— and also tip her face toward it as if his desire was the sun, and she longed to bask in it.

Jerking her attention back to her meal, she concentrated on cutting, chewing and swallowing. Ignoring the tingle in her nipples, the twisting of her belly and the yawning ache between her thighs.

"Can I ask you a question?" she murmured as their plates were cleared away.

He nodded. "Of course."

Though he'd granted her permission, she still hesitated. "Why are you going through this whole charade? In your office, you told me telling your mother you weren't interested in her matchmaking wasn't an option. But why? I know we don't know each other that well, but you just don't strike me as the kind of man who would…" God, how to finish that sentence without offending him?

A slight smirk curled the corner of his mouth. "What? Allow others to manipulate me?"

"Yes."

He chuckled, but the sound was dark, sharp and humorless. "I'm not. Usually." He grasped his glass of wine and raised it, but instead of drinking from it, he stared into the golden depths. "What do you know about me, Nadia?"

She lifted her hands, palms up. "Like I said, not much."

"Really?" He arched an eyebrow. "You haven't looked me up at all?"

"Not really." It wasn't a lie—exactly. She'd obsessively followed any online item about him before the night of the blackout. Now, it seemed almost as if she were betraying him. Which was utterly ridiculous.

"My family is well known. They're a part of Chicago history and trailblazers in the financial industry. First steel, then railroads, then real estate, then they diversified in everything from insurance to media. Chandler International was—is—a powerhouse in the corporate world. And since my great-great-grandfather started the company over one hundred years ago, a Chandler has always sat in the CEO office. And until six months ago, my brother Jason would've continued the tradition."

A shadow crept over his face, dimming his eyes. Guilt for bringing up the subject and an overwhelming need to comfort him crashed into Nadia. Before she could check the impulse, she reached across the table and wrapped her hand around his larger fingers, mimicking his earlier actions. After a slight hesitation, he reversed the hold and his hand gripped hers. As if holding on.

"My older brother died six months ago from a brain aneurysm. It was sudden and so damn unexpected. One moment, he was healthy and strong, the next..." Grayson shook his head, not finishing the thought, though he squeezed Nadia's fingers tight. "My parents, they took his death hard, as you can imagine. Jason was their firstborn, the heir, their favorite. And he should've been. We were thirteen years apart and weren't close, but I still admired him—loved him. He was a good man. Smart. Respectable. Commanding. Perfect."

"No one's perfect, Grayson," she whispered.

"In my parents' eyes, he was," he said. "They adored him. And when they lost him…" His full lips firmed into a harsh, straight line. "I've never seen them so broken. They'd not only lost their child, but their favorite."

Again, she countered him, leaning forward across the table. "Not their favorite. Maybe they had the most in common with him since he was the oldest. Or spent the most time with him since he would one day take over the business. But parents love their children equally. Even my mom did, although that's not saying much. They would've been just as devastated if, God forbid, it'd been you who'd died. Or your sister. Their love is the same."

A grim smile curved his lips even as he lifted a hand, and after a pause, cupped her jaw. He rubbed the pad of his thumb just under her bottom lip, and she fought to contain the sigh that tried to escape. Her lashes fluttered, her body liquefying. It was the first time he'd touched her outside of their charade. And other than when they'd been stuck in that dark hall. If she were thinking, if she were smart, she'd pull back. Instead, she leaned into it, turned her head slightly so her mouth brushed the heel of his palm.

Even across the distance of the table, she caught his ragged inhale. His gaze lowered to her mouth, studying it as if he would receive a PhD on every curve and dip. She trembled under his inspection, and when his eyes lifted to hers again, she shivered harder from the flash of fire there. That stare promised things—things she knew damn well he could deliver on.

"How is it possible that you, who has every reason in the

world not to see the best in people, still believes in things like a parent's love and fairness?" he murmured. With one more caress over her skin, he released her, dropping his hand to his glass of wine. He raised it, sipping, but his scrutiny never wavered from her.

She didn't have an answer for him. But then again, he didn't seem to expect one.

"But to answer your initial question, at this point, I can't tell my mother to back off because no matter our history, I have to be gentle with her. She's been through enough these past months. And other than those first couple of weeks, I don't believe she's allowed herself to fully grieve. Instead, she's focused all her rather formidable attention on other endeavors—one of which happens to be finding me a wife. I think if Jason had married, if he'd had children before he died, her desire to see me settled with someone wouldn't be this...passionate. She would've had a piece of him to hold on to, to cherish. I can only imagine she doesn't want history to repeat itself. And it might be selfish, but I'll suffer through her annoying attempts rather than see her broken again."

Selfish? There were several words she could use to describe him—arrogant, demanding, high-handed, sexy as hell—but selfish? No. Not when he would create an elaborate fake relationship just so his mother wouldn't sink back into dark grief.

Grayson Chandler was...complicated. Playboy. Gentleman. Sometimes asshole. Seducer. Selfless son. Enigmatic stranger.

And with every layer he exposed, she wanted to peel away another. And then another. She longed to find the core of this man, see who lay beneath. See the truth she suspected he revealed to no one.

In other words, damn her, she wanted to be special to him.

Maybe she was more of her mother's daughter than she acknowledged.

"Sir. Ma'am. Can I interest you in dessert or an after-dinner coffee or drink?" Their waiter appeared next to the table, saving her from more enlightening and terrible revelations about herself.

"I'm fine. Nadia?" Grayson asked.

She summoned a small, brittle smile. "I'm through, as well."

Minutes later, table cleared and check paid, Grayson escorted her from the restaurant, a hand placed on the small of her back.

Warmth from his palm penetrated her dress to the skin below. The clothing between them might as well have been invisible, because her imagination convinced her she could feel every hard curve and plane of that hand. Lust, bright and ravenous, curled low in her belly, and every step forward, every brush of her thighs against each other, cranked up that need until she shivered with it.

Oh yes. She'd fallen so far down this rabbit hole. But did she want to climb out?

She didn't know. And that indecisiveness spelled one thing.

Trouble.

Eleven

Grayson curled his fingers tighter around the steering wheel as he guided his black BMW i8 toward Nadia's blue-collar Bridgeport neighborhood. Within the interior of the car, he couldn't elude her wind and rain scent. Couldn't block out the memories of how that scent was denser, richer on her skin—between her thighs.

Sometimes he woke up at night imagining that so-damn-addictive flavor on his tongue. And his hand wrapped around an erection.

Chaining down the growl rumbling in his chest, he kept all his focus on the road in front of him. Because glancing over and glimpsing the long, lush legs molded by her dress might be his undoing.

When he'd purchased the clothing, he'd imagined how it would slide over the full mounds of her breasts, skim over the wide, feminine flare of her hips and cling to the thick perfection of her thighs. Both regal and sensual. Powerful and sexy. But he'd underestimated how the material would caress every dip, arc and curve like a lover's hand. How the dress would have him desperate to peel it from her and expose the walking wet dream of her body that he'd had the pleasure of only once.

Given her mother's history with men, the truth of why Nadia most likely dressed in drab, ill-fitting suits had struck him like a fist to the gut. Finances undoubtedly played a part, but a woman with her looks, her siren's body, had probably deflected more than her fair share of advances. Especially if the opinion in her town had been—how had his own father put it?—that she didn't fall far from the maternal tree.

Yet, he'd harbored no regrets for buying her the dress or the new wardrobe crowding his trunk. As he'd told her, she deserved it all.

Dinner had been a test of how long he could pretend to be civilized when all he hungered to do was climb over her like a stalking, starving beast and consume every god-damn inch of her.

Yes, it'd been a trial, but one he'd passed, and not because of his own strength. She'd successfully kept him in his chair with her vulnerability.

God, she humbled him. With that sliver of trust and with who she was.

His father's report might have included all the bullet points of her history, but it hadn't captured her determination, her fire, her fighter's spirit, her loyalty to family.

Something grimy slid through him. How would Nadia, who'd sacrificed her education, her time and own comfort for family, feel about his refusal to sacrifice for his own family? Had it been his fear of seeing disdain etched on her lovely face that had trapped his confession about leaving KayCee Corp for Chandler? This woman had placed everything on the line for her brother. But Grayson refused to do the same for his father and mother. For Jason.

"Thank you for dinner," Nadia said into the silence that suffused the car. "It was the loveliest anyone's ever taken me to."

"You're welcome," he replied quietly. Then, because an unhealthy curiosity to learn more about her rode him hard, he added, "You're a beautiful woman, Nadia." And sexy as hell. "So while I understand that you came from a small town, I don't comprehend how there weren't any men who didn't want you, shower you with dates to fine restaurants, offer you the world." He risked a glance over at her. Noted the delicate but strong line of her profile. The proud tilt of her shoulders. The thrust of her gorgeous breasts. "Were they all blind?"

"No." The word, though soft, held such an aching note that he battled the urge to jerk the car to the side of the road and look into those deep chocolate eyes. To demand she tell him what lay behind that bleak tone. "They weren't blind."

She didn't say anything more, but Grayson didn't miss how she also hadn't replied to his first comment about whether or not there had been anyone who wanted her. The omission grated, burrowed under his skin.

He wanted all her answers. Her truth.

He wanted her naked in the way he refused to be for anyone else.

He was a hypocrite, and he didn't care.

Minutes later, he pulled the car to the curb outside her humble home. Dark windows stared at them. He should turn off the car and walk her to the door. Make sure at least one of those windows was glowing with light before he drove away.

Instead, he continued to sit behind the wheel, engine idling. Beside him, Nadia didn't make a move to exit the car, either. The silence that had joined them for the ride from the restaurant settled between them again, but this time tension, thick and alive, vibrated within it.

"Is your brother home?" he asked. The thought of leaving her inside the empty house unsettled him. She hadn't mentioned a lack of safety in the neighborhood, but still...

"No," she said. "He texted me earlier. He's staying with a friend tonight."

On edge, Grayson removed his hands from the steering wheel and settled them on his thighs, digging his fingers into the muscle. Reminding himself to keep them there and not reach across the console and touch the soft flesh on the other side.

"Is it sad that the most real relationship I've had is this pretend one with you?" Nadia rasped into the dark. "I've built this...this wall around myself because I've had to. I've learned to. It's how I've survived. But other than Ezra, it's also kept me from getting close to people. The only time I've lowered my guard in years was the night of the blackout. With you. And it felt so *good*. Such a relief to, for once, not have to protect myself because, even though we worked at the same place, I didn't think we'd come into any meaningful contact again. I felt...free. You asked me once if I ever wanted to just let go. Hand over my control and let someone else take care of me for a little while. I did in that hallway, and I want to again. Tonight." She turned to him, and frozen by her admission, he met her gaze. "I don't want to be alone tonight."

Need—a deep, hungry yearning—stretched inside him. It expanded, twisting and tangling until he breathed it, became it. And all because of the woman across from him and seven words: *I don't want to be alone tonight.*

He understood loneliness. Often battled it. But was it him she wanted to keep her company? Or would anyone do? Was he just convenient?

I don't care.

The confession pounded against his skull, the truth reverberating in his chest.

He wanted her—no, *craved* her. Had since first seeing her in that mansion's hallway. If she wanted to use him to push back the isolation, the dark, then he wouldn't question why or who he was a temporary replacement for. He'd give her that. And take some for himself.

Because, damn him, he wanted to take.

"If you go home with me, I can't promise I'll be able to keep my hands off you. Right now, it's requiring every bit of self-control I have not to stroke my hand under that dress and reacquaint my fingers with the wet warmth my dick wakes up hard for," he ground out as a warning. The only one she'd get tonight.

"I didn't ask for your promise," she whispered. Her lips parted, and her gaze dropped to his thighs. To the unmistakable imprint of his erection. When she returned her eyes to his, they gleamed with the same arousal that coursed through him. "I don't want your promise."

With that husky avowal echoing in his head, he eased the car back into Drive and pulled away from the curb. Neither of them spoke, not for the entire journey to his downtown condominium. They didn't exchange words as he parked the car in his reserved space under the seventy-story building or on the swift elevator ride to the penthouse apartment. The doors opened into his large living room, and, cradling her elbow, he led her inside.

Sweeping a glance around his home, he attempted to see the place through her eyes. Vaulted ceilings, floor-to-ceiling windows that encompassed three walls, an open plan where each room flowed seamlessly from one to the other. The Chicago skyline, Millennium Park and Grant Park seemed to crowd into his place, a beautiful vista of lights and shadow.

It'd been this view that had convinced him to purchase the property. Not the paneled library with its stone fireplace, or the chef's wet dream of a kitchen with top-of-the-line appliances. Not the three luxurious bedrooms with en suite bathrooms or the twenty-four-hour doorman service or exclusive rooftop club.

None of that could compare to the panorama of the city he loved. The city that had welcomed him with open arms, offering him the chance to prove he was more than just the Chandler spare.

Dragging his attention from the glittering skyline, he focused all of it on Nadia. On her face. Her body. Studying her for any hint that she'd changed her mind. That she regretted accompanying him here. From their conversation over dinner, he'd detected her opinion about men with money. They were users. Opportunists. Selfish. Her experiences with rich men hadn't been positive, and with him waving three-quarters of a million in front of her for her "services," she'd no doubt lumped him in the same category as those men who'd exploited her mother.

But maybe she hadn't painted him with the same brush.

Because she stood here in his home, and as she shifted her espresso eyes to him, they didn't hold contempt or remorse.

Just desire.

A groan rolled up his chest and throat, but he trapped it at the last minute, tamping it down. One more chance. He'd give her one last chance to opt out of this before he touched her. Because once he put his hands on her, all bets would be off.

"Are you sure, Nadia?" he rumbled, voice like a poorly maintained engine. "If you've changed your mind, I'll take you back home, no questions, no pressure, no anger. This is your choice, and yours alone." God, those words scraped his throat raw as he uttered them, but they needed to be said. She needed to know he didn't expect more from her than she was willing to give. "Another thing." He allowed himself to cup her jaw even though that small caress sent a jagged bolt of lust ripping through him. "This has nothing to do with our agreement. Whatever happens here—whatever doesn't happen here—is between us alone. Understand, baby?"

She nodded, and as she'd done in the restaurant, slightly turned her head and brushed her lips across his palm. And like then, his body turned to stone, his erection pounding like a primal drum.

"Tell me something nobody knows. Something that will stay here," she whispered, the moist heat of her breath bathing his skin. Her gaze flicked up to meet his as she pressed a sweet and sexy open-mouth kiss to his palm.

Through the almost painful grip of arousal, he recognized the request. They'd asked it of each other the night of the blackout. The past collided with the present. On a dark growl, he lifted his other hand to her face, caging her in, holding her steady as he lowered his head until just a bare breath separated their mouths.

"No one knows that I haven't been able to erase you from my mind since that night in the hallway. You were supposed to be a one-night distraction. But instead, you haunt me. You, this fucking need that grinds my gut to dust, won't leave me alone. And I resent and want you in equal measure."

Her hands clutched the waistband of his pants, holding on to him.

"Your turn," he damn near snarled, a little angry with himself for admitting all he had. "Tell me something nobody knows and that will stay here."

She encircled his wrists, rose on her toes and crushed her mouth to his. With a groan, he parted his lips, welcomed the thrust of her tongue, sucked on the silken invader and dragged an answering moan from her. Jesus, she tasted like his happiest memories and his darkest moments. Like every decadent treat he'd luxuriated in and every indulgence he'd denied himself.

Like addiction and temperance.

Like everything.

The alarming thought whispered through his head, and he mentally scrambled back from it. This—his mouth on hers, her tongue tangling with his—was physical and so goddamn good. But still temporary and simple.

There was nothing simpler than sex.

"Tell me, baby." He ground out the order against her lips.

"You're American royalty, one of our princes," she whispered, her nails biting into the thin, sensitive skin on the inside of his wrists. "And you make me feel like the Cinderella you called me." She paused, bowing her head until his lips pressed to her forehead. "More, I want to be your Cinderella. Just for a little while."

"You dream of being a princess, Nadia?" He thrust his fingers through her hair, fisting it and tilting her head back so she had no choice but to meet his gaze. He needed to see her eyes. "Is that who you'd like to pretend to be?"

"No." Shadows shifted in her brown gaze, but so did the truth. "I want to pretend to be wanted."

The groan he'd imprisoned before barreled out of him, and he claimed her mouth. Took it. Voracious for it. For her. He thrust his tongue past her parted lips, conquering. No, not conquering, because she opened wider for him, laying down every defense and surrendering.

Pleasure quaked through him. Pleasure and acceptance of her gift.

Bending his knees, he dropped his arms and gripped the undersides of her thighs. With a swift movement, he hiked her in his arms. Her short, sharp cry reverberated in his ears, but she encircled him with her arms and legs.

Damn. All that soft flesh and strong muscle pressed against him, embracing him. Her position shoved her dress up her thighs, and the material bunched high. He glanced down between them, catching a glimpse of black lace. Clenching his teeth against a curse, he swiftly strode forward toward his bedroom. But each step rubbed her exposed, panty-clad sex against his hard-as-steel dick, and he fought not to stumble and slam them back against the wall.

"I can feel you, baby," he muttered against her lips. "Soaking me through my pants. Already telling me how much you want me. Good," he damn near snarled. That's how much his control had deteriorated. "Because I need you. I haven't stopped since you let me inside this sweet, hot body."

In response, she opened her mouth over his throat, licking a path up the column and sucking the skin right under his jaw. Pleasure charged from that spot directly to his erection, hardening it even more. He inhaled a sharp breath, his grip on her tightening.

"Go on and play," he warned her. "Because when I get you naked on my bed, I fully intend to." She stiffened in his arms, and he gently nuzzled her hair, though he didn't bother to prevent his irritation from leaking into his voice. "No, Nadia," he snapped. "Whatever thoughts just crowded into your head, get rid of them. They don't belong here."

He carefully set her down on her feet in front of him. Once more he burrowed his hands into her hair, cradling her head between his palms and tilting it back.

No hiding from him. Not tonight.

"They don't belong here at all." He gently tapped her temple. "Every curve—" he slipped his hand down her shoulder, brushing the backs of his knuckles over the mound of her beast "—every valley—" he swept a caress over the dip of her waist, the slightly rounded swell of her stomach "—every inch—" he slid his hand between her thighs, cupping her drenched, warm sex "—deserves to be seen. To be worshipped."

A whimper escaped her and in the sexiest, earthiest show of abandon, she grabbed onto his shoulders, threw her head back and ground herself against his palm.

He growled. "Do it again. I want you to do just that again. But on my mouth."

With hands that should've been gentler, less hurried, he quickly stripped her of her dress, her boots and underwear. He refused to leave a scrap of clothing on her.

In moments, he jerked back the dark gray bedspread and laid her out on his silver silk sheets. In the place where he'd woken up sweaty, straining with his throbbing, aching erection in his hand—dreaming about her. But now he wasn't fantasizing. This was vivid reality. And so much better.

Unable to tear his gaze from her, he crossed his arms in front, gripped the bottom of his sweater and tugged it over his head. Toeing off his shoes and peeling off his socks, he stalked forward, not stopping until his knee dented the mattress between her thighs and his hands bracketed her hips.

She tried to close her legs, but his knee prevented the action.

"Open for me," he encouraged. "I need to see you."

He smoothed his hands up her thighs, his thumbs meeting at the juncture. Exerting easy pressure, he waited until her muscles relaxed, then she opened her legs for him. His flesh pulsed behind his zipper, and he groaned at the sight of her glistening, swollen sex. He hadn't even touched her yet, and he was ready to come.

"Damn, Nadia. You're so pretty. So beautiful. I want to…"

He didn't finish the statement. He couldn't with his mouth covering her flesh. With her heady, delicious taste filling his senses. On a growl, he licked a path through her folds, hungry for more. Beneath his hands, her thighs tensed, tightening around his head. A long, high cry erupted from above him, and it only spurred him on. That, and the insatiable appetite her decadent flavor stirred in him.

He feasted on her. Like a man starved who sat before the most sumptuous of feasts. He discovered and tongued, sipped and worshipped every part of her sex. The plump folds, the small, fluttering entrance, the hard little button of nerves at the crest. Wet, open-mouthed kisses; lush, greedy licks; tight, pointed thrusts. He didn't let up, didn't stop until a litany of cries poured from her, and the legs he'd hooked over his shoulders shook.

Focusing on the engorged, quivering nub at the top of her sex, he circled it, sucked on it. And below, he slowly drove his fingers into her soaked, clenching core. He moaned into her flesh, his dick flexing and aching as it remembered the perfect clasp. The clawing need to feel her sex pierced him. He pulled his fingers free and drove them harder.

She exploded.

Satisfaction roared inside him, and he didn't stop pleasuring her until the last tremble rippled through her body. Only when she went limp did he withdraw, jackknifing off the bed and ridding himself of the remainder of his clothes. He retained enough control to yank open his bedside table drawer and remove a condom. In seconds, he sheathed himself and returned to the welcoming haven of her body.

Nadia's eyes, slumberous and deep, met his as he crouched over her, his arms braced on either side of her head. He lowered his head, captured her mouth, and she didn't flinch away from tasting herself on his lips. Giving him one of those whimpers he loved—the ones he counted and hoarded—she slipped her tongue between his lips, dueling with him. She curled a hand behind his neck, holding him to her, and trailed the other over his shoulder, his chest, across his abs and down. He hissed into her mouth as she wrapped her slender fingers around the base and guided him to her entrance.

He jerked his head back, his eyes closing at the first brush of her wet heat against the swollen head. Letting her take control, he followed her lead. Allowed her to feed him inside her, inch by inch. Claiming him with each tiny pulse and arch of her hips. And when she slid around to his ass, cupping him, pressing against him, he sank fully inside heaven.

Curses, praises, prayers—they scrambled up his throat. But he clenched his jaw, locking them behind his teeth. Bowing his head, he blinked against the sweat rolling from his brow and stinging his eyes. He stared, captivated by the view of her folds spread around his staff, hugging him as her silken, tight flesh sucked him deep.

"Grayson," she breathed, lowering one hand and lifting the other until both gripped his shoulders, her short nails biting into his skin.

God, please let her mark him. He wanted to glimpse those little half-moons denting him in the morning.

"Gray," he corrected, lust and his almost nonexistent restraint roughening his voice to the consistency of churned, broken gravel. "Say it, baby. Gray."

He'd ordered her to say the shortened version of his name before in the hallway. And she hadn't uttered it since that night. Hearing her say the name only those close to him used—he didn't analyze why it was damn near vital for him to hear it. He just did.

"Please… Gray," she whispered, levering up and brushing her lips across his damp shoulder. "You feel so…" She rolled her hips, her tight core spasming around him. "I can't take…"

"Yes, you can, baby," he ground out, battling the lust threatening to tear him to shreds. Wrapping his arms around her, he held her close, pulled free of her body, then thrust back inside to the hilt. "You are taking it. Taking me."

Any more words were beyond him. He reverted to that caveman who'd preceded all of his blue-blooded ancestors. Claim. Brand. Possess. Those were the defaults he flipped to, and he lived only to ride her body, plunge into her, mark her as his own. If he wasn't consumed by pleasure, that thought might scare him. And later, maybe it would. But now, with her cries blanketing his ears, her nails marring his skin, her sex pulling at him, urging him to drive deeper, pound harder...

He was an utterly sexual being created to pursue ecstasy.

Nadia clung to him, chanting his name—Gray—again and again, sharper, higher. He couldn't hold out much longer. Not when electrical pulses crackled and raced down his spine, sizzling in his lower back, his balls and even the soles of his feet. He was alive, so much more alive than he'd ever been in his life—except for the last time he'd been balls-deep inside her.

"Give it to me, Nadia." He reached down between their sweaty, twisting bodies and rubbed a firm caress over the stiff nub that peeked out from between her folds. Once, twice...

A keening wail erupted from Nadia, and she bowed so tautly in his arms he almost feared she would snap in half. Her sex clamped down on him like a vise, squeezing hard, milking him, coaxing his pleasure.

And damn, he surrendered to it. To her.

Release barreled down on him, and with a hoarse, ragged growl, he slammed into her, riding it out, at the same time giving her every bit of the orgasm still rippling through her. His senses winked out, leaving him in a space where nothing existed but her and the pleasure she gave him.

Air rasped out of his lungs as he fell over her, at the last second tumbling to her side so he wouldn't crush her with his weight. He curled around her, still connected, still buried deep inside her.

And for this moment, there was no other place he wanted to be.

Twelve

"Why am I feeling a sudden affinity to the poor lamb about to meet his Maker?" Nadia grumbled under her breath as Grayson opened the passenger's side car door and extended a hand to her.

Grayson snorted. Apparently, she hadn't been as quiet as she'd thought. She smothered a sigh and slipped her palm over his. With the other hand, she gathered the skirt of her dress—another gift from him—and stepped from the car. Grayson didn't release his hold on her as the valet drove the vehicle away, instead intertwining their fingers.

It's pretense. Act 2 of the Grayson and Nadia Show.

The cool but frustrated voice of reason whispered the reminder inside her head, and she heeded it. Even repeated it. But it didn't stop her heart from thudding or the slow heat from pooling low in her belly at the casual sign of affection.

Of connection.

Walking into this glittering lakefront mansion where the guests ranged from senators to billionaires like Grayson to celebrities, she needed that connection. This anniversary party thrown in honor of his parents by a family friend was a whole different animal from the smaller cocktail parties and dinners she'd attended by Grayson's side. There'd already been mentions of them in a few society columns, blogs and sites. And while some had been kind toward her and others hadn't been as charitable, the same thought had echoed through each—what was the Chandler heir doing with an unknown like her?

Unknown. That had been the nicer name. The not-so-nice names had included "nobody," "the wide-hipped ingenue," and the ever popular "gold digger."

She didn't like Grayson's world. It was beautiful, but cold, petty and cruel. Her mother, who had perfected the art of "nice nasty," had nothing on Chicago's social elite. In the month since they'd started this charade, Nadia had lost count of how many times she'd chanted "It's for Ezra. It's for Ezra..." to herself. Her brother's future was the only thing keeping her from bailing, returning to her plainer, poorer but kinder world.

Well, Ezra...and Grayson.

She glanced at him as he guided her up the marble steps and past the stone arches soaring high above them. Mounted sconces and strategically placed lamps lit the porch—if that's what rich people called it—illuminating the majestic beauty of the foyer beyond the grand front door that wouldn't have been out of place on a palace.

Grayson fit this place. With his regal male beauty and sexy confidence that he wore as naturally as his perfectly tailored Italian tuxedo, he belonged in this place of wealth and prestige. In this moment, she felt like a girl dressing up in a costume gown. She was a fraud, while he was the real thing.

And yet... Yet, she continued the charade.

Because as unbelievable and impossible as it might

seem, Grayson needed her. And not just to avoid his mother's matchmaking schemes. But in the weeks they'd been spending time together, she noticed he showed people the playboy or the charming businessman. But not *him*. Not the broody, sometimes dark, sharp-minded-and-tongued man who existed beneath the veneer. He granted her peeks, though. Glimpses she suspected he didn't allow anyone else to see. He needed someone with whom he could shed the personas. Even if only for a little while.

And she would be a liar if she didn't admit, if only to herself, that she hungered for those moments.

Stupid. Stupid to want more. Have you learned nothing?

"Are you okay?" Grayson murmured in her ear as they entered the mansion.

"Yes." She pasted a smile on her face that she hoped appeared serene. Or at least normal. "Why do you ask?"

"Because you have my fingers in a stranglehold," he drawled, arching a dark eyebrow.

Immediately, she loosened her grip. "Sorry," she murmured. "I didn't realize."

A tall man in a black suit complete with a bow tie approached them. "Can I show you to the ballroom?" he said, extending an arm toward the rear of the foyer.

"Give us a minute, please." Grayson didn't wait for the staff member's agreement, but cupped Nadia's elbow and guided her toward the fireplace on the far side of the room. A fireplace in a foyer. Jesus, she really had entered another world.

"Nadia." Grayson's fingers pinched her chin, raising her head so she had to meet his blue-and-green gaze. "Tell me what you're thinking."

She tried to quell the tingle that zipped from her face down to her breasts and lower still. Tried. And failed. It'd been two weeks since they'd had sex at his penthouse. In that time, he hadn't touched her more than their pretense required. Part of her understood why. After their discussion that night at the restaurant and what she'd revealed to him about her past, he probably didn't want her to feel as if she were pressured to make sex part of their bargain. He was respecting her boundaries.

But the other part of her… That half wondered if he no longer wanted her. If the novelty of sex with her had worn off. If he didn't find her desirable…

She shook her head, trying to dislodge those destructive words from her head. But the movement inadvertently removed his hand from her. Grayson frowned. And didn't return his hand.

"I'm thinking that I'll be lucky to not embarrass either one of us. This night is on a much larger scale than a dinner party," she said. Not a lie. Those *had* been her thoughts earlier.

His frown eased, and his gaze softened. Once more, he touched her, this time cradling the nape of her neck. A charge sizzled down her spine, and she barely smothered a groan.

"You have the prettiest eyes," she blurted out, desperate to distract herself from her short-circuiting body. But then, her own eyes rounded as what she'd uttered rebounded against her skull. *Oh. Hell.*

Surprise flickered in his stare, before it became shuttered. "What?"

She waved a hand in front of her head as if she could shoo away her words. "Don't mind me. I told you I was nervous. Let this be a forewarning of what I will be like once I enter that ballroom. If I have the chance to meet Cookie or Lucious from *Empire*, I'm just letting you know right now to expect more spouting of random crap."

He didn't chuckle. Not even the corner of his mouth quirked in amusement. "So the comment about my eyes was just…crap," he stated, voice flat.

Now, she frowned. "No, I meant it. Your eyes are gorgeous." She studied the carefully bland expression, heard the monotone timbre. "You don't believe me," she concluded.

When he didn't reply, but just continued to peer down at her, she wavered between being curious and offended. Hell, no one said the two had to be mutually exclusive.

"Present situation aside, I'm not in the habit of lying. Care to tell me why you don't believe me?" She thrust up a hand, palm out, when his lips parted. "And don't you dare say you don't know what I'm talking about."

His mouth firmed into a straight line, and his eyes narrowed. Silence beat between them, but she was raising a teenager; she could out-stubborn him any day.

"My eyes are weird, not pretty. You should save the meaningless compliments for when we have an audience. They're wasted when the two of us are alone," he stated in that same aloof tone.

He'd meant to shut her down. Hurt her feelings and force her into dropping the subject. And oh, goal almost accomplished. Her chest throbbed where that cold arrow had taken a direct hit. Maybe if she hadn't caught the thread of hurt beneath the steel, she might have let it go.

"Ouch," she drawled. And something that could've been regret flickered in his eyes before the shadows shielded it. Risking more rejection, she shifted closer and clasped his head between her hands, tilting it down so this time she was the one forcing him to meet her gaze. "You listen to me. I don't know what asshole put it into your head that your eyes are weird or anything less than unique and beautiful but screw them. No," she snapped, when he covered her hands with his and tried to remove them from his face. "They are beautiful. Gorgeous. Intelligent. Different. Bold. *You.* In this pretentious world of yours where conformity is mistaken for perfection, you are utterly *perfect*. And anyone who says differently can get fucked."

His eyes flared with shock, a heartbreaking and maddening uncertainty and…delight. Joy that should've terrified her—and God, it did—swelled behind her ribcage. Afraid of what her face might reveal, she dropped her arms and turned away, taking a step in the direction the staff member had indicated.

But a muscled arm wrapping around her waist drew her up short. A hard chest pressed against her back, tuxedo jacket lapels brushing the skin bared by her backless gown.

"When you greet my father, I'd suggest you not tell him to get fucked," he drawled. Before it could fully sink in that it'd been his own parent who'd criticized him, Grayson tightened his hold on her and pressed his lips against her hair. "Thank you," he whispered.

He released her, took her hand in his and guided her forward.

Silently, she exhaled a deep, slow breath.

Okay. Still feeling the imprint of his arm and the caress of his mouth, she straightened her shoulders and hiked her chin. Tendrils of hope cautiously bloomed within her.

Maybe this night wouldn't be as bad as she'd assumed.

You know what they say about assuming.

The taunt floated through her head as she stood near the huge balcony doors of the ornate ballroom. Massive crystal chandeliers provided more than enough light for her to glimpse the elaborate gardens beyond the spotless glass.

Sighing, she turned from the temptation of the great outdoors and surveyed the grand room filled with Chicago's wealthiest, most famous and celebrated. For the first hour after she and Grayson arrived, he'd stayed by her side, refusing to leave her alone. And she'd appreciated his solid presence. It'd been easier to maneuver these choppy society waters with him.

But ten minutes ago, his father had cornered him and practically yanked him away to speak to business associates. Since then, she'd smiled and murmured hellos to those who didn't stare right through her, floating through the crowd like a ghost.

She strolled to one of the many framed photographs of Grayson's parents and family that were mounted throughout the ballroom. Pausing before the one that included all three Chandler children as well as Daryl and Cherise, she studied it. Grayson's parents sat on a white settee, while Grayson, Jason and Melanie formed a semicircle behind them, Jason in the middle, standing a couple of inches taller than a younger Grayson.

Her attention, almost of its own will, focused on Grayson's older brother. In this picture, he appeared to be in his late twenties. Handsome, refined, a little reserved. But he was the only one who touched his parents. One hand settled on his father's shoulder and the other on his mother's. Cherise had one arm lifted, her bejeweled, slim fingers covering her son's.

That the only sign of warmth in the picture was between the oldest son and his parents was…telling.

And sad.

"We make quite a spectacle, don't we?" a cultured voice laced with amusement and a hint of deprecation said.

Nadia glanced away from the photograph to Melanie, who stood beside her. Nadia had been so caught up in her scrutiny of the image, she hadn't heard Grayson's sister approach. The older woman had been the only person to warmly greet Nadia this evening, and a rush of relief washed over her.

"It's very dignified," Nadia said, opting for diplomacy.

Melanie snorted, a favorite sign of disdain she shared

with her brother. "Stuffy as hell is what I think you mean." She smiled, her blue eyes gleaming. "What you can't see is Gray goosing Jason, trying to make him break his austere demeanor. Only by sheer force of will did Jason maintain that expression. Dad and Mother had no idea what was going on behind them."

Nadia laughed, seeing the picture with new eyes now in light of the story. She picked up the twinkle in Jason's eyes, the barest of bare smiles on Grayson's mouth. And the slightest hunch of Melanie's shoulders as if she were silently midlaugh.

"You remind me of my brother and me," she mused, smiling with real warmth for the first time that evening. "We are always teasing one another, too."

The light in Melanie's gaze dimmed, but the love as she stared at the picture remained. "Jason, Gray and I, we had a…complicated relationship. But we did love one another. And there were times like this one where we enjoyed one another. In those moments you realize there's nothing more important than family."

"I couldn't agree more," Cherise Chandler interjected, appearing on the other side of her daughter. She glanced at the photograph, and for an instant, grief flashed in her eyes. But in the next moment, the emotion disappeared; her blue gaze, so like her daughter's, was hard like diamonds as she turned to Nadia. "Family is the most important thing in this life."

Did she refer to life, in the abstract, or "this life," as in the world of Chicago's elite? Since this was Grayson's mother, Nadia was going with the latter.

"I missed the opportunity to wish you a happy anniversary earlier when I arrived, Mrs. Chandler. Congratulations," Nadia said, offering the other woman a smile.

And as she'd expected, it wasn't returned. "Thank you." Cherise nodded. Once more, she glanced at the picture of her family, but this time resolve hardened her features. "Forty-five years of not just marriage, but family, shared experiences, commonality. Yes, loss but also strength and loyalty. Above all loyalty."

"Mom," Melanie murmured, but her mother shot her daughter a sharp glance.

"This needs to be said, Melanie," Cherise replied before returning her attention to Nadia. "Six months ago, this... dalliance Grayson has with you wouldn't have mattered to me. You would've been one of many. But now you're like that company of his—a lark, a distraction from what's important. While he should be focusing on what's best for this family's legacy, he's playing CEO with a business that won't be around in another few years. While he should be considering his own future with a wife who will benefit him both socially and financially, he's wasting time with you. You and that company of his are amusements, diversions for a man who doesn't have responsibilities, who doesn't have a duty to his family. Amusements and diversions none of us can afford."

Each word struck Nadia like well-aimed, poison-tipped darts, and she nearly shrank away in pain and humiliation.

But damn if she would allow Cherise Chandler to witness her wounds. Later, she would curl up around her battered pride and try to regroup. But right now? She would never give the other woman the satisfaction of watching her crumble.

"That's enough, Mother," Melanie bit out, anger vibrating through the frosty reprimand. "Nadia is Gray's choice and guest. This disrespect is beneath all of us."

"You're wrong," Nadia interrupted Melanie, her gaze meeting Cherise's without flinching. And though, inside, Nadia still trembled from Cherise's verbal slap, her voice didn't waver. "Grayson isn't *playing* at CEO—he *is* one. And his brilliance and boldness have propelled the company into success. They've already changed the landscape of technology and finance. And KayCee Corp will continue to do so—years from now."

The passion that swelled inside her and throbbed in her voice was disproportionate for a fake fiancée, but she didn't care. Everything she stated was true. And it was a damn shame his mother didn't recognize his accomplishments.

"And you very well could be right about me. Maybe I'm not the woman who will—how did you put it?—benefit him socially and financially. But who do you believe that woman to be? Adalyn?"

"She belongs here. In our world. Unlike you," Cherise snapped. "They are the same."

Nadia shook her head. "There's so much more to him than how many generations back he can trace his family tree, the blue of his blood or the number of zeroes in his net worth. He's a man, flesh and blood. He needs someone who understands him, who sees beyond the social masks, who will support and love him unconditionally."

"And you actually believe you're that woman?" Cherise scoffed.

"I don't know," Nadia answered honestly. "But he doesn't think Adalyn is. And my heart breaks for him, because it doesn't seem like you are, either." She stepped back, glancing at Melanie. She reached for a smile and failed. "It was nice seeing you again, Melanie. If you'll both excuse me."

She walked off, not glancing back, her hands trembling in the folds of her dress.

When she'd made that bargain with Grayson, she should've asked for hazard pay.

Grayson charged down the hall. Away from the study where he'd allowed his father to lure him with the promise of "It'll only be a couple of minutes." A couple of minutes had turned into damn near thirty. His father had ambushed him, arranging for several board members to join them, where he'd come just short of announcing that Grayson would be returning to the Chandler International fold.

Only respect had locked down his vitriolic tirade. Respect and the ever-present guilt that Chandler International was his duty. That he owed his father and mother this because the son they'd wanted, the son they truly loved, had been snatched from them. No, it wasn't his fault that Jason had died so suddenly, so nonsensically. But still, his parents had lost their *son*. Even if Grayson was the booby prize, didn't he owe them this?

A Chandler to replace a Chandler. A son for a son.

Rage, powerlessness and grief churned in his gut, surging to his chest and up his throat until he had to swallow convulsively against the bellow of fury that clawed at him, demanding to be loosed.

The noose of obligation, duty and love tightened around his neck, choking him even as it dragged him inexorably closer to a future that had been meant for Jason, not him.

"Grayson?"

He didn't contain his growl at the sound of the soft, feminine voice calling his name. Drawing to an abrupt halt, he slowly pivoted, facing Adalyn. Any other man would look at his ex and see a beautiful, confident woman of class and sophistication. Any other man would notice the lovely green eyes, the delicate facial features and the slender body exquisitely showcased in a gown that undoubtedly bore a label from a coveted designer.

What they might miss would be the calculating gleam in those emerald depths or the smile that carried the barest hint of cruelty. When Grayson had been in love with her, he hadn't caught those details, blinded by loveliness and charm. But now, as she neared him with a sultry stride, they were all he saw.

"What do you want, Adalyn?" he demanded. "And let's skip the part where we pretend this meeting is by chance."

Anger glinted in her gaze for a second before her thick lashes fluttered down, hiding the emotion. Hiding the truth. "I don't mind admitting I've been waiting all evening for the opportunity to have you to myself. You've been so—" her mouth twisted, that cruelty making more of an appearance before her smile returned "—occupied of late that we haven't had time alone to talk."

He sighed, thrusting his hands into his pants pockets. "Because we have nothing to talk about," he ground out. "We broke up over a year ago. Anything you deemed important enough to converse about could've been accomplished in that time. Since you didn't search me out, and I damn sure didn't go looking for you, I'm going to assume whatever it is you suddenly have to say can't be vital."

"I've missed you," she whispered, shifting closer to him.

If not for the two years he'd spent as the star pupil in the School of Adalyn Hayes, he might've fallen for the soft longing in her voice. For the lovely pleading in her eyes. But not only had he walked away with a degree in disillusionment and pain when their relationship ended, he'd left with a heart made of stone. And it pumped mistrust and scorn rather than blood. Rather than love.

Obviously, taking his disdainful silence as encouragement, she moved nearer until her floral fragrance filled his nose, and she laid a hand on his chest. Over the heart she'd betrayed.

"We had good times together, Grayson. I wish you would let yourself remember them. I do," she said, tilting her head back. "I remember how we laughed. How we were nearly inseparable. How you treated me like a queen. How you touched me, giving me more pleasure than any man ever had before or since." Her breath quickened, and she trailed a fingertip over his jaw. "We were so good together. You can't deny that. And you can't deny that you loved me."

No, he couldn't deny it. But then, he hadn't been aware that sex had just been another tool in her arsenal. A way to make him fall in line.

"And this return of memories has nothing to do with the business deal between your father and mine?" He arched an eyebrow. "The timing is just a coincidence?"

She shrugged a shoulder. "Our families have always been business associates. At one time, you didn't see anything wrong with making that bond even stronger with marriage."

"You're right. At one time, I didn't," he agreed. "But that was then, and right now I'm thankful that I didn't marry a woman who found me—and my bank account—interchangeable with any other man."

He stepped back, allowing her hand to fall away from him.

Fury tightened her features, hardening them. "So do you think that *cow* out there is better than me? Everyone is laughing at you, at her. She's a joke, and you're the punch line."

"And here's the real Adalyn. I was wondering how long it would be before she made an appearance," he drawled, then shifting forward, eliminating the space he'd inserted, he quietly snarled, "And you go on believing you're untouchable. That because of your face and your father's name that you're beyond reproach. But I'm more than willing to be the one to show you differently. And if you insult Nadia one more time, if I hear you even utter her name with anything less than delight, I'll take you down. Strip you of the so-called friends you surround yourself with. Destroy that sterling reputation you hold so dear. I'll take the gilded cage of your world apart bar by bar and, Adalyn? I'll enjoy the hell out of it."

Leaving her staring at him in shock, he pivoted and stalked away from her. With every step, weariness slowly replaced the anger, the gratification.

God, he was just…tired. Tired of the machinations. The games. The agendas.

He needed to escape this hallway. Get away from Adalyn.

From the reminder of how false beautiful faces could be. How relationships weren't based on love, trust or respect but were barter systems, founded in how much one party could cull from the other. All he had to do was examine the evidence in his own life.

His relationship with his parents.

With Adalyn.

With Nadia.

They were lies built upon a foundation of greed.

And he wanted to raze it all to the ground.

Thirteen

Nadia glanced at Grayson, the shadows from passing streetlamps whispering over his sharp features like ebbing waves. When he'd returned to the ballroom and located her over an hour ago, something had changed in his demeanor. Oh, he was still polite and charming, the playboy and charismatic businessman both making appearances, but he'd been…colder. More distant. Tension seemed to vibrate within him, and it set her on edge.

What had happened between the time his father had asked to speak with him and his reappearance? Even now, tucked in his town car and nearing her house, the question lodged in her throat. As if part of her were too afraid to ask. Afraid of the answer.

Turning from him, she gazed sightlessly out her window. Though it'd only taken a little over a half hour for them to leave the lakefront and reach her Bridgeport neighborhood, the change in worlds might as well have been light-years apart. No majestic mansions, huge iron gates or long private drives. Just weathered storefronts, parks abandoned for the night, brick greystones and bungalows and quiet streets caught between its industrial past and its rejuvenating, diverse present. It'd been her home for only a little over a year, but it felt more welcoming than the town where she'd spent most of her life. And definitely more welcoming than the entitled world she'd just left.

The world Grayson belonged in.

You and that company of his are amusements and diversions for a man who doesn't have responsibilities, who doesn't have a duty to his family. Amusements and diversions none of us can afford.

Cherise's words rang in her head, reverberating in her soul, rattling loose the ghosts she'd convinced herself had been exorcised. She'd been an amusement, a diversion for Jared. This engagement to Grayson might be a sham, but his parents didn't know that. His friends didn't. Those columnists and bloggers didn't. So to the world, she'd once more become what she'd promised herself she wouldn't ever again.

Someone's "for now." Because she wasn't worthy enough to be his "forever."

She sucked in a shaky breath, clinging to the tattered remnants of her pride and wrapping them around her like Cinderella's ash-stained rags. Only this didn't end in a fairy tale. When this pretense with Grayson concluded, she would be two hundred and fifty thousand dollars richer, but she would still be on her side of the tracks, and he would return to his glittering, privileged tower.

The car slowed to a stop, and she blinked, glimpsing the familiar houses on her street. Grayson exited the car, rounded the hood and pulled her door open. He extended a hand to her like he'd done when they'd arrived at the mansion hours ago. Like then, she placed her palm over his and let him help her stand on the curb bordering her house.

"I'll walk you up," he said.

"That's not necessary. Ezra's home," she objected, suddenly needing this night to end. She had wounds to lick, emotional armor to reinforce.

"I'll walk you up," he repeated in a tone that brooked no argument.

"Fine," she murmured, and led the way up the short walk to her porch. She removed the key from her clutch purse and slid it into the lock. As she turned it and grasped the doorknob, a hard chest pressed into her. She gasped. Even through the layers of their clothes, Grayson's heat burned into her, warming her against the cold November night air. He pressed his forehead against the back of her head, and with her hair swept over her shoulder, his breath bathed the nape of her neck. "Gray?"

"Let me come in," he rasped. Except for his forehead and his chest, he didn't touch her, but the quiet desperation in his voice grasped her as tightly as if he'd wrapped his arms around her. "I…" He paused, audibly swallowing. "I need you."

The ragged tone, the harshness that seemed heavy with loneliness didn't speak of physical desire—well, not only that. It was thick with more. With a hunger that exceeded sex. A hunger for connection, for…her.

"Please."

The entreaty shuddered through her. She squeezed her eyes shut and twisted the knob. And pushed the door open.

They walked through together, and she reached behind her, blindly searching for his hand. Locating it, she twined their fingers together and led him to her bedroom. For a moment, nervousness over how he would view her tiny room with its secondhand, scratched furniture, queen-sized bed and threadbare rug washed over her. But then Grayson's hands were cupping her shoulders, turning her and pressing her against the wall next to the closed door.

His big body curved into her smaller one, and he surrounded her. Covered her. And then his mouth crashed to hers, consumed her.

She moaned under his lips, and he crooned, "Shh." Warning her to keep quiet, not to disturb Ezra.

Nodding, she tilted her head, opened her mouth wider to his voracious kiss. He was…ravenous. Barely granting her time to breathe. But, God, every lick, every draw on her tongue, every pull on her lips… She didn't need air. Not when he fed her his.

Greedy hands shoved her coat from her shoulders, jerked down the zipper at her side, dragged the dress off her. He didn't even leave the scrap of thong on her body, leaving her bare and vulnerable. Trembling.

With equally quick movements, he rid himself of his clothes, removing his wallet before casting his pants aside. Hauling her into his arms again, he backed her toward the bed, but enough of her senses remained unclouded by lust to shake her head.

"Not there. The bed squeaks," she warned on a pant.

On a growl, he yanked the bedspread off the mattress and threw it on the floor. Then, he sank to it, taking her with him. Once more, he covered her, notching his hips between her legs. She encircled his shoulders with her arms, holding him so close she swore she could feel every muscle, tendon and beat of his pulse against her. They kissed, tongues tangling, breaths mating. He nipped at her lips, chin, throat. And she fought down a whimper when he levered off her. But he only left to sheathe himself, returning, bringing his heavy, delicious weight back to her. Again, she wrapped herself around him, her legs joining the embrace.

"Please, Gray," she pleaded. Unashamedly. This might have started with him needing something from her, but she was just as desperate for him. Craving those moments where she didn't feel so empty. Only Grayson had given her that.

She buried her face in his neck, drowning in the physical pleasure and refusing to dwell on why Grayson could give her the peace and sense of safety she'd never found with anyone else.

He slipped a hand behind her neck, cradling her as he pushed inside.

She waited, breath suspended, expecting him to destroy her with the fierceness of his passion like the two previous times they'd come together. Like his kiss and touch since they'd entered her house.

But instead, he held still above her, his big body balanced on his forearms, his face hovering over hers. Slowly, so slowly time seemed to stutter, he dipped his head. Brushed his lips over the corner of her mouth. Swept another barely-there kiss to the other side.

He was still set on destroying her. But with tenderness instead of fury.

Give me the storm, her mind railed. She could get lost in the storm. Could be tossed and plundered by it. But this gentle rain... This she wanted to let bathe her, creep beneath skin and bone to quench a thirst born of a neglected girl, a rejected woman. A thirst she could usually deny existed.

Except when he kissed her with rain.

"What are you offering me, Nadia?" he asked, taking her back to that night of the blackout when he'd asked her the same thing. When their time had been limited to a few short hours of pleasure. Before she'd known this beautiful, powerful, flawed man.

"Me," she whispered. "All of me."

Her answer was the same—but different. Then she'd added, "for tonight." This time she didn't add boundaries, an expiration date, although they had one. And from the narrowing of his eyes and the harsh rasp of his breath, he'd noticed the omission.

He withdrew from her, slow, deliberate. And thrust back into her with enough power to yank a gasp from her throat.

"Quiet, baby," he murmured, covering her mouth with his palm. Bending his head so his lips grazed her ear, he whispered, "I need you to keep quiet for me."

Then he consumed her.

She strained beneath each plunge, taking each piston of his hips as if it were her due, her reward. He rode her, branding her flesh with his cock, marking her.

And God help her, she let him. She welcomed it.

And when pleasure crashed over her like a wave determined to drag her under, she welcomed it, too.

Because he came with her.

"You're doing this because of your brother, aren't you?" Grayson murmured.

Nadia stilled in tracing random patterns over Grayson's bare chest. They hadn't moved from the floor, and with her limbs weighted down with satisfaction and lethargy, she didn't want to. Not with his large body under hers, his warmth radiating against her, and the sheet he'd dragged from the bed covering them.

He didn't expound on his question, but he didn't need to. She understood what he meant by "this." Her mind waged a battle against her heart over answering. He'd seen her naked, had touched and kissed every inch of her, but somehow admitting this would bare her even more. And she wrestled with giving that to him. What if he used the information against her? Did she trust him?

In the end, her heart made the decision. And won.

"Yes," she said. "How did you know?"

"I didn't at first," he admitted. "But I never stopped

wondering why you would agree to my offer when you first turned it down. Given what I've discovered about you, money in itself wouldn't be enough to motivate you. Not when you have an issue accepting even a dress from me. But for your brother? You've sacrificed so much for him already. You would do anything for Ezra. Including pretending to be my fiancée. And enduring everything that comes with it."

She hesitated, but then nodded against his chest. "Ezra was accepted into Yale. I found out the afternoon after I left your office. He was awarded a partial scholarship, but without going into debt, we couldn't afford to send him."

"The two hundred and fifty thousand," he said softly.

"The amount of tuition for four years," she confirmed.

Silence fell between them, only the hushed sounds of their breaths filling the room. But he didn't doze off beneath her. Though his fingers sifted through her hair, tension stiffened his body. The urge to comfort, to soothe whatever bothered him rode her. Gathering her courage, she pushed herself up on her elbow. But before she could question him, Grayson lifted his other hand to her jaw and lightly traced the line of it.

"I'm ashamed when I look at you," he said, and she flinched at the disgust in that confession. Disgust that wasn't directed at her, but at himself. Even in the shadowed confines of the bedroom, she glimpsed the glitter of anger in his eyes. "You awe me, humble me. And I feel guilty for touching you, for taking what you give without reservation, without holding back, when I'm not worthy of it."

Stunned, she sat up, uncaring of her nudity. She stared down at him, blinking. Shock, like an ice-cold slap to the face, sent her reeling. "What?" she rasped. "Why would you say that? Think that?"

That familiar shuttered expression settled on his face as

he, too, rose, the sheet pooling around his hips. Anger, sadness and frustration welled within her. She wanted to take a hammer to that mask. Splinter it to pieces so he could never hide from her again.

Why do you care? Three more months left, and it doesn't matter.

It mattered, dammit. It. Mattered.

"You would give—and have given—everything for your family. Even your mother. You raised your brother, provided for him, and never left either one of them. You forfeited your own education so your brother could have his. You put your dreams on hold to make sure he could pursue his. Putting his needs above your own. That is you. It isn't me." He bit off the last words, a muscle ticking along his clenched jaw.

"When Jason died," he began again after several seconds, "it became my responsibility to take up where he left off. Chandler International isn't just a family business—it's a legacy. A heritage. And a Chandler has always headed it, leading it into the next generation. Without Jason, that falls to me. Even though I've received this birthright by default. Even though I'm considered second-best. Loyalty, duty— they come before personal needs. I should be honored to helm this company. But I'm not. I don't want it. I'm not selfless like you, Nadia."

"What do you want, Gray?" she whispered, finding no pleasure in his compliment since he meant it to condemn himself.

"To be free."

She understood the desperation in that quiet statement. How many times had she prayed, begged God to liberate her of her mother's tainted shadow, of people's low expectations, of the chains of responsibility?

"Gray, I love Ezra with all my heart. But I wasn't ready to be mother and sister to him. I wasn't ready to drop out of high school to get a job and provide for him. I wasn't ready to leave childhood—such as it was—behind and enter adulthood way too early. If I'd had a choice, I wouldn't have. And there's no guilt or shame in admitting that. Given the same circumstances that I faced, if I had to do it all over again, I would. Because he was more defenseless than me, more vulnerable. But if I'd been offered a different existence, a kinder one, I would've chosen that for both Ezra and me. One where our futures were our own to shape and forge." She lifted a hand, and it hovered above his thigh before she settled it on him. "You have a choice. That's power—your power. And you shouldn't let anyone steal it away from you with their expectations and demands. They can have them, but you don't have to live by them."

A humorless half smile ghosted across his lips. "You make it sound so simple."

She released an impatient sound that was something between a scoff and a curse. "Of course it's not simple. Disappointing those we love and respect is never easy. But…" She squeezed the thick muscle of his thigh. "What are you afraid of?"

He shook his head, a slight sneer curling the corner of his mouth. "I'm not—"

"You are," she insisted, interrupting him. She slashed her other hand through the air. "Forget that macho, masculine bullshit. What are you afraid of?"

An internal battled waged over his face, in his eyes. Though part of her braced for his rejection, she curled her fingers around his. And only long moments later, when he flipped his hand around and gripped hers, did she exhale.

"Killing what little pride in me my parents have left," he finally rasped. The harsh timbre of his confession rubbed over her skin like sandpaper. And she cherished it. "Losing their love. Losing them." His eyes closed, and the dense fringe of almost absurdly long lashes created deeper shadows. "But just as much, I fear who I will become if I give in and return to Chandler." He lifted his lashes, and his blue-and-green gaze bore into hers. She met his stare, though the stark pain in it was almost too hard to glimpse. "I fear being trapped."

"Gray," she breathed. On impulse, she climbed onto his lap, straddling him. Cupping his face in her palms, she leaned forward, pressing her chest to his, her fore-head against his. "Oh, Gray." She sighed. Easing back just enough so she could peer down into his eyes, she mur-mured. "You are…" *Everything.* "So worthy of your par-ents' unconditional love and acceptance. Just because you are their son. But also because you're beautiful, brilliant, a testament to the same pioneer spirit that started Chan-dler International, and devoted. Not surrendering to their demands doesn't make you disloyal. It makes you the man they raised you to be. A man who thinks for himself. Who is successful. Who thrives in difficult situations. Who stands by his commitments, his dreams and his decisions. And if they can't see that… If they can't be proud of the person you are, *their son*, then that's their issue, not yours. Never yours."

She wrapped her arms around his neck, ordered herself to stay quiet. That she'd said enough. Any more and she might reveal more than she intended. More than she could afford. But then she smoothed her thumbs over his sharp cheekbones. Swept them over his full, heart-stopping lips. Gazed into his beautiful eyes.

And she couldn't stop the last words from slipping free.

"I've only known you—truly known you—for weeks. And, Gray, I'm proud to know you," she whispered in his ear. "I'm proud of you. If no one else tells you, I will."

She brushed a kiss over the soft patch of skin beneath his earlobe. Another to the bridge of his nose. One more to his chin. And one to the center of his mouth.

As if the last caress snapped a tether to his control, his arms whipped around her, hugging her so tightly her ribs twinged in protest, but she didn't ask him to release her. Instead, she clasped him closer, as well. And when his mouth took hers, she opened to him. Surrendering. Giving.

Falling.

Fourteen

Nadia stepped off the elevator onto her floor Monday morning. Greeting several early arrivals like herself, she made her way to her desk.

You can't just walk around smiling like a ninny. Jeesh.

The exasperated admonishment echoing in her head didn't dim the wattage of her soft grin at all. Not when the most nonsensical, bright joy glowed in her chest like a lamp on the highest setting.

All because she'd woken up next to the man she loved Sunday morning.

Yes, she loved Grayson Chandler.

More than a little panic simmered beneath her happiness. Somewhere in the last few weeks, she'd ignored every warning to herself. Had broken every promise, disregarded every cautionary tale and fallen for the man she'd sworn would remain off-limits. The last time this sense of excitement, fear and hope had trembled in her heart over a man, the demise of the relationship had nearly destroyed her.

But Grayson wasn't Jared.

Yes, Grayson had initially thrown money at her to get his way, but his motives had been altruistic, to avoid causing further grief to someone he loved. Yes, he was arrogant and domineering, but he was also selfless, generous, a little broken but possessing a beauty even he didn't recognize.

So, yes, she'd fallen for him.

And she couldn't decide if she was foolish as hell…or taking a wondrous leap of faith.

She could still feel the phantom press of his body as she dozed after making love—

She rolled the phrase around in her mind. Had they made love? On her part? Yes. On his…

Her belly knotted, pulling taut. She didn't know. Grayson certainly enjoyed sex with her, but did he see her as more than his fake fiancée and occasional bed partner?

Could he love her?

That damn, flighty hope shivered inside her again, and she dumped her purse on her desk with one hand and rubbed a spot on her chest with the other. Directly underneath her fingers, her heart beat out a nervous tattoo.

"Good morning, Ms. Jordan," Mr. Webber greeted, stopping in front of her desk.

His gaze dropped to the big rock on her ring finger before lifting back to her face. Ever since it'd become office gossip that she and Grayson were "engaged," her supervisor had been a little guarded with her. As if unsure how to treat her—a regular employee or *his* future employer. Either way, there hadn't been any more requests for weekend work.

"Morning, Mr. Webber," she replied with a smile, opening her bottom drawer and storing her bag in it. She reached for her computer and booted it up. "Is there anything I can get you?"

"Could you email today's schedule to me?" he asked.

She fought not to roll her eyes. Because she sent him

the next day's schedule every evening before she left. He'd had it sitting in his inbox since Friday night. But instead of telling him to check his mail, she nodded and murmured, "Sure thing."

Her boss entered his office, and she lowered into her chair, ready to get the day started. Speaking of today's schedule, she needed to check her phone to see if Grayson had added anything for them to attend tonight. Weeks ago, he'd synched their calendars so if he added an event, the notification would pop up. But first...

Swallowing an irritated sigh, she opened her email and composed a new message, attached Mr. Webber's schedule and sent it off. She moved the mouse to the minimize button when a bold message in her inbox from an address she didn't recognize snagged her attention. Curious, she clicked on it.

Then frowned. Not understanding what she read. But if the words took moments to sink in, the pictures that populated the email did not.

Her heart pummeled her sternum so hard it hurt her chest. Air that had moved in and out of her lungs so easily just seconds ago jammed in her throat. Thank God. Because it blocked the pained whimper from escaping.

She scrolled through image after image.

Grayson and Adalyn standing close in a hallway, her hand curled into his tuxedo jacket.

Adalyn touching Grayson's jaw in a lover's caress, wearing a sensual smile.

Grayson with his head bent low over Adalyn, their faces so close their mouths nearly brushed.

There were ten in all, revealing a couple caught in an intimate moment.

From the clothing, the pictures were taken at the Chandlers' anniversary party. Where had Nadia been while Grayson and Adalyn met? Had she been defending herself against his mother while he cuddled up with his supposedly hated ex? Had Cherise been a distraction while those two arranged to meet?

Question after question bombarded her, and she wanted to cry out with the onslaught. She shoved to her feet, her chair rolling back to hit the wall behind her. Ignoring the curious glances thrown her way, she flattened her palms to the desk, unable to tear her gaze from the images. With trembling fingers and humiliation blazing a path through her, she moved the mouse, scrolling up to the message above the pictures.

I didn't want to have to resort to such measures, but you didn't leave me another choice. If you won't believe my words, then maybe you will believe pictures since they're supposed to be worth a thousand of them. Grayson has never stopped loving me, as you can very well see. Whatever you think you have with him, it's not real. You're doing nothing but making a fool of yourself. Find your dignity and walk away with at least some of your pride intact.

There wasn't a signature, but one didn't need to be included. Adalyn. She'd discovered Nadia's email address and blindsided her at work with proof of the unresolved feelings between her and Grayson.

Wait, wait. Grayson had been adamant, when they first struck their bargain, that he'd never reunite with Adalyn. If something had happened between then and now to change his mind, he would've told her… Wouldn't he?

Yes.

The part of her that stubbornly clung to belief in his integrity hissed out the agreement. There had to be an explanation for the pictures. For the emotion and intensity that seemed to vibrate from them.

Before she could reconsider her decision, she hit Print on the email. Moments later, she snatched up the still-warm papers and headed toward the elevators. Though Mr. Webber would probably reprimand her if he exited his office to find her gone, she was willing to risk it.

She needed answers.

Minutes later, she stepped out on the executive floor of KayCee Corp and strode towards Grayson's office. Mrs. Ross, his administrative assistant, glanced up as she neared, a polite but welcoming smile curving her mouth. Nadia forced herself to return the gesture, even if it felt brittle on her lips.

"Good morning, Mrs. Ross," she said, surprised by how even her voice sounded. "Is Grayson, I mean, Mr. Chandler in?"

"He had to step out of his office for a moment." The older woman swept a hand toward the closed double doors. "But I'm sure he wouldn't mind if you went in and waited for him. He should return shortly."

"Thank you," she murmured, heading toward his office. Once inside, she closed the doors behind her and exhaled, leaning against the wood.

Just ask him. I'll just ask him. He'll explain and everything will be fine.

She nodded as if someone else had offered the advice and pushed off the door. There had to be an explanation. She'd encountered Adalyn Hayes only a handful of times, but they'd been enough to tell the woman was manipulative and wouldn't be above trickery to get what she wanted. Which, in this case, was Grayson.

The cool logic of the argument blew on the flames of hurt and humiliation burning inside her. She crossed to Grayson's desk to sit in one of the visitor chairs to wait on him.

"What the hell?" she breathed.

She stared down at the manila envelope with her name typed across the label. The email printout floated from her numb fingers to the top of Grayson's desk. The thought of respecting his privacy and not opening the file didn't occur to her. And before she could convince herself it wasn't a good idea to snoop, she already had the flap opened and the thin sheaf of papers freed.

Stunned, she read the private investigator's report.

Marion Jordan, town drunk and whore. Children by two different men.

Nadia Jordan's arrest record.

High school dropout.

Everything about her past—about her—in black-and-white. In startling, stark detail.

Anger. Pain. Shame. They all seared her, rendering her to a pile of ash. She couldn't breathe, couldn't think, couldn't... Oh God, she just *couldn't*.

"Nadia."

The papers fluttered to the floor as she slowly pivoted at the sound of the deep voice that she adored...and now resented.

Grayson watched her, his unique eyes hooded. Examining. He knew what she'd discovered, what she'd been reading.

"You had me investigated," she stated, amazed at the flat tone. Shouldn't her voice be a pitted, ragged mess from all the internal screaming? First his ex's email, then this report. Both of them had emotionally flayed her, and she should at least sound like it. "You pretended not to know about me, about my mother, my life in Georgia, when you knew all along."

"I didn't order that report. My father did," he said, that inscrutable, aloof mask firmly in place. Except for his eyes. They remained alert, bright.

"But you didn't tell me about it, either," she accused. Releasing a chuckle that abraded her throat, she shook her head. "And all the way here, I was telling myself that you wouldn't lie to me. That if you had something to tell me, you would be upfront about it. Not hide anything from me. Then I find that."

Like a movie reel cut to the slowest speed, she replayed all the moments she'd shared with him. How she'd showed him her heart. And the whole time, he'd already known. Had already been judging...

"What are you talking about, Nadia?" he demanded, eyes narrowing as he advanced on her. "I haven't lied to you. That thing," he flicked a hand toward the report scattered on the floor, "doesn't mean anything to me. My father had you investigated to prove a meaningless point. I don't care where you were born or who your mother is. I care about the woman standing in front of me. You should know that by now."

"Then about this?" she whispered, picking up the pictures from where she'd dropped them and thrusting them toward him.

He didn't remove his eyes from her until his fingers closed around the papers. As he read the email and studied the pictures, his features darkened until his scowl could've incinerated the whole office. Finally, he lifted his head and fury lit his blue and green gaze.

"Where did you get these?"

She shivered at the barely leashed rage vibrating in the question. "An email from Adalyn, I'm guessing. It was waiting for me when I arrived at work this morning."

"This is BS," he growled, tossing the email to the seat of the visitor's chair. "I don't know how Adalyn arranged for those pictures to be taken, but they're misleading and false." He thrust a hand through his hair, disheveling the thick strands. "She cornered me at my parents' party, and we argued. She did get close to me, touch me, but what those pictures don't show is me pushing her away. They don't contain an audio file of me telling her there's no way in hell there could ever be an 'us' again. Of me threatening her about insulting you again. She's a vindictive bitch who's seeing dollar signs in her future and refuses to take no for an answer."

Nadia couldn't speak, the hurt from the email and the report too fresh. She'd arrived at work hopeful, cautiously happy. But now, she'd curled back into her protective shell, too afraid to place her bruised heart on the line.

"Nadia." He sighed, again running his fingers through his hair, gripping it before dropping his arm to his side. "Do you know why I ended my relationship with Adalyn?" He glanced away for a brief moment, before returning his focus to her, shadows darkening his eyes. "The night of the anniversary party, Adalyn told me that I loved her. And she was right. I did. With everything in me. When I thought of my future, I couldn't picture it without her in it. Did I know she wasn't perfect? Yes, but who was? She was everything to me. Until she wasn't."

He stalked across the room toward the floor-to-ceiling window behind his desk. She stared at his back, the tense set of his shoulders. A part of her wanted to urge him to continue. But a greater, more fearful part, didn't want to hear it.

"Just after we were engaged, we attended her friend's engagement party. I stepped outside to take a phone call, and when I finished, I heard Adalyn and her friend on the far side of the balcony. I headed in their direction, but then I heard snatches of the conversation. It was about me. And Jason. She told her friend that she'd managed to catch me, but only because my brother turned her down. She'd tried to seduce him, but he hadn't been interested. So she pursued me and won me. In her words, one Chandler brother was as good as another just as long as she landed one of them. The man didn't matter—the inheritance did. I loved her, but she loved my money and the lifestyle it would afford her."

"Gray," she breathed, pain for the man he'd been weakening her legs. Reaching out, she steadied herself on the edge of his desk. "I'm so sorry. No one deserves that kind of betrayal. Especially you."

"It's over with. In the past," he said, his tone abrupt as he spun to face her with his hands stuffed into his pockets. "The only reason I'm going into it is so you can understand that however those pictures might appear, there will never be anything between Adalyn and me again. I haven't lied to you."

She believed him. But that didn't beat back the sadness, the foreboding and the buckling sense of loss that swept over her, threatening to drag her under. Because while she accepted the truth about Adalyn, she also couldn't deny another certainty.

He couldn't love her.

She would never be more than a buffer between him, his mother and ex-fiancée.

The death of that resurrected hope stabbed her, and she sucked in a breath, willing the pain to recede. But it wouldn't. She'd been a fool twice. And this time, it was much worse. At least with Jared, she hadn't known he was using her. With Grayson, she'd entered their bargain with eyes wide open. He'd even warned her against falling in love with him.

...I don't want to hurt you... Protect yourself from me...

And now she understood. He could never trust another woman with his heart. Not after Adalyn had betrayed him so deeply. Yes, he'd been upfront about what he'd expected from Nadia and their bargain. She'd been the one to forget the consequences of dreaming, of hoping...

She forced herself to straighten away from the desk. Though agony seemed to pulse through each of her limbs, she would face this like she hadn't faced Jared.

Head held high.

With pride.

And walking away.

"You told me once that your greatest desire was to be free," she reminded him softly. "But as long as you're holding on to the past, you will never be completely free."

He frowned at her. "I'm not holding on to the past. After everything I've just said, you still think I want Adalyn?" he demanded, removing his hands from his pants pockets and splaying them wide. "Nadia—"

"No." She shook her head. "I believe you. But that doesn't mean you're not still trapped there, locked to her." If she were smart, if she possessed even an inch of self-preservation, she would leave now. But she couldn't. Not until she'd laid herself out there. She'd walk away, but it would be with no regrets. "You shared with me, so I'll do the same. I have an Adalyn in my past, too. His name was Jared. He was a couple of years older than my twenty-two, the son of a town councilman, rich, handsome. And he said he loved me. I believed him. I *wanted* to believe him. That someone like him could find me beautiful, desirable…"

"You are beautiful and desirable," Grayson snapped.

She smiled and didn't try to mask the sadness in it. "He was the first man to make me see it in myself. Until, like you with Adalyn, I discovered the truth. I was his dirty little secret. Stupid me had thought we were in a real relationship, that he didn't care about who my mother was, about my past, that he just loved me. I found out way too late that he'd been dating the daughter of his father's buddy and planned on marrying her. But I shouldn't have worried," Nadia continued with a bitter crack of laughter. "He still intended to keep me, even though another woman would be his wife. In his eyes, I was supposed to be flattered that I would be his side piece."

"He was a bastard, Nadia," Grayson growled. "A little boy masquerading as a man. You didn't deserve that kind of disrespect or pain. That speaks more about him than it does your worth."

"I couldn't agree more," she said quietly. "I promised myself then that I would learn my lesson. That I would guard my heart, demand better for myself and never give my body or my soul away to someone who didn't earn it. Who wasn't worthy of it. In the last few weeks, I've broken my vow. Jared might have betrayed me years ago, but I've betrayed myself now."

He stepped toward her, his frown deepening. "Nadia. What are you saying?"

She dragged in a breath, and it sounded ragged and painful in the room. "I'm saying that I've fallen in love with you. Against my better judgment, I have. And the man you are…" She pressed her palm to her chest, over her heart. "God, Gray, you're so worthy. But so am I. I deserve to be honored, cherished, valued…loved."

He stared at her, his face etched out of stone, carefully aloof. "Nadia, you don't mean that."

"Oh, but I do," she countered, pain lacing every word. She didn't have the strength to mask it. "I also realize you can't give me what you don't have. And maybe, a few years ago, I would've been okay with that. Taking crumbs. I'd like to think I wouldn't have been. But then again, I've never met a man like you, Grayson Chandler. You've made me believe in love again." A wistful smile curled her lips. "But being by your side these last few weeks has shown me what I could have. What I dream of obtaining one day. And I'm not willing to settle for less than that. For so long I've settled for half a life, desperately trying not to become my mother while raising Ezra. And though I have zero regrets about my brother, I've never focused on who I am. Who I want to be. I want more. I deserve more. In who I am and who I'm with."

"Goddamn it, Nadia," he snarled, advancing on her a

step, before drawing up short. "What do you expect me to say? That I love you, too? I've been honest with you about what I want from the beginning. Is this bait and switch supposed to be some kind of guilt trip?"

His accusation slapped at her. But instead of flinching and cowering away from the impact, she hiked her chin higher. "I never asked for your heart or your love, Grayson," she said, purposefully using his full name. "I'm not even offering you mine, because you can't care for my heart. You can't protect it. And I can no longer afford to put myself— or my heart—in the care of someone who doesn't value it like it deserves. Not again."

She turned then, and though it cost her, she strode away from him toward his office door. Only when she grasped the knob and paused, did she speak again.

"The night of the blackout, I didn't tell you my identity or that I knew you because I wanted to have that night for myself. Ever since I started work here, I've been attracted to you. Crushed on you, as silly and immature as that sounds. You were always a gift to me. And for one night at least, I let myself have that gift. But that'll teach me to reach too high. The fall, the breaking, isn't worth it."

She opened his office door, and without glancing back, walked out on him.

But not on herself. For the first time ever, she was walking toward herself.

Fifteen

Grayson jerked his tie loose then off as he strode into his living room. He paused long enough to fix a Scotch at the bar before striding to the window. Before, the view of the Chicago skyline always soothed him. The strength, beauty and grit of the city with the soothing calm of Lake Michigan's waters. They balanced each other, and they balanced him.

Usually.

That was before Nadia had walked out of his office a week ago after announcing she loved him. But didn't trust him with her heart.

His fingers tightened around the squat tumbler.

Not that he'd asked for her heart. Or wanted it. Because he didn't. He'd been down that road and had no interest in traveling it again. Only an idiot or a masochist would eagerly court that kind of disaster. That kind of pain.

And he was neither.

But when Nadia had said she loved him… He sipped the

lcohol and relished the burn as it slid down his esopha-
gus. The path of liquid fire distracted him from the precious second when a flame of joy had flickered in his chest
when she'd admitted her love for him. Then, he could deny
its existence. And in the long, brutal hours he'd put in at
he office since she'd left, he could pretend he hadn't felt
that second of incandescent delight. Before he ruthlessly
snuffed it out.

While recounting the ending of his relationship with
Adalyn, he'd relived that moment when he'd overheard
her lies, her careless disregard for his love. Reexperienced
the pain. The humiliation. Feeling that again...and with
Nadia...

He threw back the rest of the drink, closing his eyes.
Adalyn had damn near destroyed him. Nadia would finish the job, if he let her.

And he couldn't.

The intercom near the elevator doors buzzed. Shaking
his head, he strode over to the entrance and pressed a button.

"Yes?"

"Mr. Chandler," the lobby security guard said. "There's
a Mr. Ezra Jordan here to see you. Should I send him up?"

Nadia's brother? Grayson's heart thudded against his rib
cage. He should say no. Nadia had left his office, then quit
her job, walking away from not just him but his company.
She'd ended their association, so what could he and Ezra
possibly have to talk about?

"Send him up, please."

He was a glutton for punishment.

And yet, he waited next to the doors and stood there
to greet Ezra when he stepped from the elevator a minute
later. Grayson didn't say anything, just watched the teen
stalk toward him, anger tightening his handsome features
and vibrating off his frame. Ezra stopped directly in front

of Grayson, shoving his locs out of his face as he glared
at him.

"You hurt her," he barked, fury gleaming in his dark
eyes. "You promised me you wouldn't, and you did. She
won't tell me what happened between you two, but she's
not the same. She quit her job, man. So something must've
gone down. You should've left her alone if you—"

"She left me." Grayson interrupted Ezra's tirade, impatience brimming inside him. He needed this boy with
Nadia's eyes to leave so he could return to his obsessive
brooding.

"But you must've done something to make her do it,"
Ezra snapped in return. "You're the first man she's opened
up to since that asshole Jared. She doesn't trust easy, and
she damn sure doesn't love easy. And I'm not blind. She
loves you. But you just threw it, and her, away."

"I understand you want to defend your sister, Ezra. And
if I was in your place, I would do the same for mine. But
you don't know all the details about what happened between your sister and me," Grayson said.

"I don't care," the seventeen-year-old snapped at him.
Admiration swelled in Grayson for Ezra. Due to Grayson's
power, position and wealth, most men wouldn't dare speak
to him like Ezra was doing. But Ezra didn't give a damn.
Just like his sister. "I don't need to know the details. The
only thing that matters is Nadia has been through a lot—
too much. She's given up too much. She deserves the world.
And if your head is too far up your ass, then it's your loss.
And that's what I came over here to tell you. She's the best
thing that ever happened to you. If you're too stupid to hold
on to her, then that's your bad. Not hers."

Jerking his chin up, he pinned Grayson with one last
glare then spun around and marched back to the elevator.
Grayson didn't move as he disappeared behind the doors.

Didn't move as the minutes ticked by and the teen's adamant and proud words echoed in his head.

She's the best thing that ever happened to you. If you're too stupid to hold on to her, then that's your bad. Not hers.

How long he stood there, he didn't know. He couldn't move as the truth bombarded him, pummeling him and rendering him frozen.

Frozen except for the rapid beat of his heart.

Images of the past few weeks passed before him at light speed, and he locked his knees against the dizzy sensation that almost pushed him to his knees.

From the moment they met in that hallway, locked for the night in the blackout, she'd seen him—*really seen him*—like no one else. Not even his family. She'd challenged him, gone toe to toe with him, shielded him, teased him, encouraged him...loved him.

Gray, I'm proud to know you... I'm proud of you. If no one else tells you, I will.

In this pretentious world of yours where conformity is mistaken for perfection, you are utterly perfect.

I've never met a man like you, Grayson Chandler. You've made me believe in love again.

Oh God. What had he done?

What in the *hell* had he done?

He loved Nadia.

It'd been there all along, but he'd been so busy guarding his heart that he hadn't recognized it. When the truth was, she'd captured his heart the night of the blackout. The night she'd called him a protector and offered herself to him, trusting him.

She'd called him noble, and then he'd been too much of a coward to strip away his fear and tell her she didn't have to ask for his heart. She already had it.

But he still wasn't worthy of it. That didn't mean he

wouldn't move hell, heaven and earth to earn her heart her belief that he would protect it, cherish it.

Where once he'd been afraid to risk his pride and heart that fear no longer trapped him.

For Nadia, he would risk it all.

Sixteen

Grayson entered his parents' home, a sense of urgency tingling under his skin. Weeks ago, he would've been riddled with guilt, his shoulders weighed down by the heaviness of disappointment or even failure. But now, as he strode to the informal living room where his family often gathered, only determination and impatience flowed through him. This was a task he needed to get over with so he could move on to the more important business ahead of him: Nadia.

The scene that awaited him was one he'd pictured in his mind. His father seated in his armchair near the fireplace, a book opened in his hands, flames dancing behind the iron screen. His mother, a planner splayed wide on her lap, settled on the love seat. And his sister sitting on the opposite end of the small couch, her laptop perched on her thighs. Yes, the scene was expected—and a little sad. They all sat in the same room as a family, but no one interacted, no one laughed or even lovingly argued. If he just replaced his father and mother with him and Adalyn, this would be their future.

And he wanted none of it.

His father glanced up from his book, noting Grayson in the living room entrance. "Grayson," he said, a faint frown creasing his forehead. "This is a surprise. What brings you by?"

His mother and sister looked up from their work, and Melanie stood, setting the laptop on the coffee table. She came over and planted a kiss on his cheek. "Good to see you, little brother."

He smiled, squeezing her shoulders. "Thanks. I came by to talk with all of you for a moment." Not willing to beat around the bush, he leaped in. "It's about assuming the CEO position of Chandler International."

At the announcement, he'd won his parents' complete attention. A hint of satisfaction gleamed in his father's eyes and slightly curved his mouth. His mother nodded, as if his decision to helm the family company had been a foregone conclusion.

"I'm not returning to be CEO or take over when you retire, Dad."

A deafening silence filled the room, and his father blinked, staring at him. Seconds later, red mottled his father's face, and he pushed to his feet, his eyes narrowing on Grayson. His mother also rose, her hand pressed to her chest. Beside him, Melanie touched his elbow, and that small show of support beat back the force of their disappointment and anger.

"I know this isn't what you wanted to hear, but it's my final decision. I know the history and importance of Chandler International, and I respect it. And you may not see it this way, but I'm honoring that history by creating my own legacy with my company. The same hard work, spirit and determination that went into creating and building Chandler is going into KayCee Corp. It's mine. It's something I can leave my children along with Chandler International. This is my path, and I won't abandon it out of guilt or a misplaced sense of loyalty."

"This is unacceptable, Grayson," his father snapped. "Completely unacceptable. And I won't hear of it."

"You're going to have to, Dad," he murmured. "And it might be unacceptable to you, but you must accept it. I'm not Jason," he added quietly. "Heading Chandler was his dream, not mine. And I won't be—I can't be—a substitute for him."

His mother's gasp echoed in the quiet.

"That's not what we were trying to do," she objected, voice hoarse. "We just needed to impress on you the importance of this family's tradition. It's our strength, our power."

"No," Grayson contradicted, shaking his head. "The people in this room are the strength and power of Chandler. All of us. Dad—" he turned his attention back to his father "—you've been so focused on me taking over the company that you overlooked the one Chandler who has worked hard by your side for years. Who knows the company just as well as Jason, and most importantly, wants to be there. Who enjoys being there, but hasn't received any recognition." He glanced down at Melanie, and his sister's eyes widened as his meaning sank in. "Yes." He nodded. "Melanie deserves to helm Chandler International, not me. And if you don't announce her as the incoming CEO to the board, then I promise you I will do everything in my power to persuade her to leave Chandler and come over to KayCee Corp."

His father sputtered in outrage, but Grayson wasn't finished. He pinned his mother with a steady gaze.

"And Mother, I love you. I freely admit, I haven't confronted you about quitting all the matchmaking attempts because I didn't want to hurt your feelings or cause you more pain. But, no more. Not with Adalyn or any other woman. It ends here. I'm in love with Nadia Jordan. She is everything to me, and I won't stand for any more disrespect thrown her way by you, Father or Adalyn. You need to accept this decision and her. Because if you don't—if you do anything more to hurt or malign her—then you'll lose a son. Like I said, I love you, but when it comes to Nadia, there isn't any divided loyalty. She's my first and only choice."

"She's a lovely, good woman, and I'm happy for you, Gray," Melanie said, taking his hand and squeezing it. "We'll welcome her, won't we?" she said, studying their parents.

Neither his mother nor father answered, but the disappointment, the shame he'd anticipated, didn't appear.

"Well, it seems you've made your decisions, and we have to live with them," his mother said, ice dripping from the words.

"You do," he agreed. Kissing his sister's temple, he nodded at his parents. "One day, I hope you'll understand my choices. In the meantime, I need to go win back the woman I love."

Seventeen

Nadia stared at the numbered buttons in the elevator as they lit then dimmed as floor after floor slid by. Finally, they arrived on the fifteenth floor, and she stepped free of the elevator. She'd been on this level only a couple of times. And both had been in her early days at KayCee Corp. But what could Human Resources possibly want to see her about now as it'd been almost two weeks since she'd quit and walked out?

Nerves plagued her belly, and she surreptitiously glanced around. As if Grayson would appear around every corner or stride out of a closed office door. Which was ridiculous. The president of the company did not just hang around the HR floor. Still… She'd gone nine days without seeing him, hearing his voice, inhaling his sandalwood and mint scent. In time, she hoped to stop dreaming about him, waking up hurting in her heart and body over the loss of him.

But today was not that day. And glimpsing him, even

from far away, might break her into too many pieces to recover.

No, distance was her friend now. Distance and denial.

Not that she regretted her decision to end their "relationship." She didn't. Yes, every breath seemed edged in an ache, but for once, she'd chosen herself. She'd placed her well-being, her heart, her worth first. She deserved to be valued. To be loved.

And she refused to settle.

Inhaling a deep breath, she approached the executive assistant's desk for Marsha Fowler, the head of Human Resources. Another mystery. Why the head of HR would ask her to come in and talk. How many employees who quit without notice were invited back? Not that Nadia intended on working for KayCee Corp again. The company was phenomenal, but she just...couldn't.

"Hello," she greeted the young blonde on the other side of the desk. "Nadia Jordan. I have a nine o'clock appointment with Ms. Fowler."

"Yes." The assistant smiled and rose from her chair. She rounded the desk and gestured for Nadia to follow her. "They're waiting for you, Ms. Jordan."

They? Unease twisted and knotted her stomach as she trailed the other woman down a hall. Who...? She didn't have long to wait to find out the answer. The assistant knocked on a closed door, then opened it.

"Ms. Jordan is here." Smiling at Nadia, the blonde stepped aside so she could enter.

"Thank you," Nadia murmured and moved into the large office. And drew to an abrupt halt. Shock. Confusion. Anger. And God, so much love, slammed into her with the force of a flying hammer.

Marsha Fowler sat behind a wide desk. Melanie Chandler sat in one of the chairs in front of it. And Grayson stood next to the other.

Though it pained her to look at him, to soak in the beauty of his chiseled face, lovely eyes and firm, sensual mouth, she couldn't tear her gaze away. She was a starving woman plopped down at a table overflowing with the most succulent food and drink.

Leave. Self-preservation kicked in moments too late, and just as the words "setup" whispered through her head, Ms. Fowler waved her inside. "Ms. Jordan, please come in. And thank you for coming by on such short notice."

"Hello, Nadia," Melanie greeted with a warm smile. "I can imagine you have a ton of questions. I promise we won't hold you up long."

"Hello, Nadia."

That deep voice of velvet night wrapped around her name had her nearly closing her eyes to luxuriate in it. But she forced herself to meet his gaze and nod.

"Grayson."

His blue and green eyes burned into hers, and in them she saw her broken hopes and foolish dreams. Unable to bear them, she glanced away and silently ordered herself to focus on the two women in the room. That had to be the game plan if she intended to make it through this meeting and leave unscathed.

"Please have a seat." Ms. Fowler waved to the empty chair. Nadia obeyed, sinking down into the seat. "Well, Ms. Jordan, I know you left the employ of KayCee Corp almost two weeks ago, but I also understand the circumstances were...unusual." She cleared her throat, briefly glancing at Grayson. "Mr. and Ms. Chandler asked that I call you in so they can present you with a counteroffer."

"I appreciate this, Ms. Fowler. But I'm afraid my mind is made up—" Nadia said, preparing to stand once more, when Melanie laid a hand over hers.

"You're under no obligation to accept, but please, just hear me out," Melanie requested. Nadia hesitated, but nodded. "It's come to my attention that you have an interest in nursing."

Nadia jerked her head toward Grayson, who hadn't uttered a word after greeting her. His steady contemplation of her didn't waver, didn't flicker to his sister or the HR director. Heat flooded her face, and she couldn't determine whether it was anger or embarrassment. Both. Definitely both. And the fault rested firmly on the wide shoulders of the man several feet away from her.

"Yes, Gray shared that info with me," Melanie continued, drawing Nadia's attention back to her. "In the spirit of transparency, he's also told me why you were working here instead of pursuing a degree in your preferred field. Several nonemergency urgent care chains fall under the Chandler International conglomerate. I would like to offer you a position at one of the centers as a receptionist while you enroll in a nursing program. Chandler will cover the expenses for those classes, of course. That way, you're pursuing your degree while actively working in the field and gaining experience."

Stunned, Nadia stared at Grayson's sister. Shock barreled through her, and she couldn't speak. Could barely comprehend what she'd said. Going to school? An entry job in her chosen field? Paid tuition?

What the hell was happening here?

Bewildered, she once more disobeyed her own instructions and yanked her attention from Melanie to Grayson.

"Marsha, Melanie," Grayson finally spoke. "Could we borrow the office for a few minutes?"

Both women stood, and in moments, only Nadia and Grayson remained. Seconds ago, the office had been large, but now, with only him there, it seemed to shrink, his presence filling it to overflowing. Unable to remain sitting, Nadia rose. But the sense of vulnerability didn't dissipate.

Suddenly, she felt naked, bared to him. And she hated it. Resented the effect he still had on her.

Feared that it, too, would never disappear.

"Why?" she asked, her voice stronger than the whirlwind of emotions whipping inside her. "I know you're behind this. What is this supposed to prove?"

"What is it supposed to prove?" he repeated, shoving his hands in his pockets and cocking his head to the side. "Nothing. No, I take that back," he added. "It's supposed to prove to you that you're not only worthy of good opportunities but deserving of them. That you shouldn't always have to be the provider, protector and sacrificial lamb. Someone should do the same for you. Cover you. Shield you. Give everything to you. This isn't a handout, Nadia. Because there's no one in this world who has earned those things more than you."

She choked back an inconvenient sob, refusing to shed one more tear over this man. At least not in front of him.

"That sounds pretty. But we're over, remember? I don't need those sentiments. Especially since no one's here to witness them."

His eyes briefly closed, and if her own hurt wasn't coloring her judgment, she might believe pain spasmed across his face. "You want to lash out at me? Fine. I can take it. You're more than justified. Not only was I an ass for rejecting the most beautiful gift you could ever offer me, but I was a willfully blind ass. Which makes my crime worse." He blew out a breath, then his mouth firmed into a straight, grim line. "You told me that as long as I'm holding on to the past, I'll never be completely free. At the time, I didn't want to hear that. Didn't believe it. But you were right. I might have been over Adalyn, but I hadn't let go of the anger, the pain, the fear. I was in a prison of my own making. And rather than escape it, I just locked more chains on the bars. Keeping myself in...and you out."

He took a step toward her, removing his hands from his pockets. He raised them, bowing his head, as if studying the palms. But, moments later, he dropped his arms to his sides. Then he lifted his head, and… *God*. Her breath stuttered in her lungs, and her heart slammed against her chest, as if trying to break free and fling itself at his feet.

Gone was the inscrutable, aloof mask. Gone was the shuttered gaze that hid his thoughts and emotions. Gone was the charming, affable smile that had been his playboy persona.

Loneliness. Pain. And love. They all creased the bold lines of his face. There for her to see, his shield completely torn down. For her.

Tears stung her eyes, clogged her throat. She balled her fingers into fists and held them over her chest, caught between wanting to—needing to—protect herself and reaching out to him.

"Nadia, you told me that you couldn't offer me your heart because I couldn't care for it or protect it. And again, you were right. Then. But now…" He moved forward, those big hands palm up again in supplication. "Now, I can. I will. I don't have the right to ask you to trust me with the most precious gift you have, but I am. I'm begging you to believe in me one last time, and give me your heart, your dreams, your future. I'll guard it with my life, keep it from harm. I love you, baby. With you here—" he pressed a fist to his chest "—I don't have room for fear or bitterness. If given the choice between living in the past or walking toward a future with you, there isn't a choice. It will always be you, first and only. Please, Nadia." His voice roughened, and he stretched a hand toward her, his fingers stopping just shy of her chin and jaw. "I don't want to be in prison any longer."

On a gasp and cry that erupted from her, she took the last couple of steps that brought her into contact with his hand. She clasped his with both of hers and turned her face into it, pressing her lips to the palm. And because she was touching him again after being starved of him for nearly two weeks, she kissed him again. Then cupped his hand over her cheek.

"My love—my heart—is yours," she breathed against his skin. "It always has been. And there's no one else I'd rather have keeping it safe."

"You'll never spend another moment of your life doubting if you're loved, baby," he whispered, lifting his other hand to cradle her face. In seconds, his lips molded to hers. Then he shifted them to her jaw, the bridge of her nose, her forehead. "I love you."

"I love you," she whispered.

Hope, it turned out, wasn't foolish.

Or only relegated to fairy tales.

Epilogue

One year later

"Now there's a sight I imagine no one would believe they'd ever see," Shay Knight mused.

Nadia followed the direction of the other woman's gaze. But besides the couples crowding the DuSable City Gala's dance floor, she didn't notice anything different.

"What?" Gideon asked, slipping his arm around his wife. Grayson's business partner and Nadia's former employer appeared as impassive and intimidating as ever, but she'd spent a lot of time around him and his wife. The man might scare the hell out of other people, but not her. She'd witnessed how much he adored Shay, and that kind of scaled down his scary factor from a ten to a three and a half. Okay, four.

"Darius King and Isobel Hughes together. And the Wells family, too, all in the same room, and no open warfare," Shay teased. Catching Nadia's confused frown, she grinned. "Oh, Nadia, I have to bring you up to speed on all the gossip you've missed out on. That group used to make the Hatfields and McCoys look like bosom buddies. Now, Darius and Isobel have two children together, and the Wells are doting grandparents."

"Speaking of grandparents..." Gideon dipped his head in the direction of the back of the ballroom. "Mom and Olivia just arrived. Since Shay told them she's pregnant, Mom has been a helicopter grandmother," he drawled. But his affection for the women in his life shone brighter than the light from the crystal chandeliers.

"We'll catch up with you," Grayson said, clapping a hand on Gideon's shoulder. "You know your mother loves me best, so if I don't come say hello, she's going to be crushed."

Gideon slid him a cutting glance, but the smile playing about his lips ruined the threat in the look. Grayson laughed, and Nadia snorted.

"So, Cinderella," he said, turning to Nadia and lifting her hand that he held clasped in his. The laughter in his eyes warmed her, as did everything about her husband. They'd been married for nine months, and she still lost her breath around him. Still pinched herself that she could call her longtime crush her spouse. The name he'd once called her in this same place a year ago fit. She was Cinderella come to wonderful life and had the most beautiful man as her Prince Charming. "Will you honor me with a dance?"

She scrunched her nose, pretending to think it over. "Depends. Do I get to lead?"

"Always." And with a grin and a heart-melting kiss to her ring finger, and the smaller, princess-cut pink diamond in an antique setting that replaced its ostentatious predecessor, he led her among the swaying couples. "Just in case I haven't told you tonight," he murmured, drawing her close into his arms, "you look amazing."

"Thank you." She cupped the nape of his neck. "But

since you picked this dress out, I think you're really just giving yourself a backhanded compliment."

He chuckled. "Possibly. But in my defense, you did tell me to pick whatever. I love when you're neck-deep in work. It allows me to get away with so damn much."

"Something tells me after I graduate, it's going to be hard as hell to rein you in," she grumbled, but the words ended on a bark of laughter. "Between you and Ezra, I'm going to have my hands full."

Ezra, in his freshman year at Yale, still called her regularly to compare class schedules, homework and tests. He also checked in with Grayson almost daily. Those two had become as close as brothers, and she couldn't be happier that the two men she adored most also loved one another. Between work at the urgent care clinic, school, her husband and her brother, her life had never been as full.

Or as blessed.

As perfect.

"Just think," she said, tangling her fingers in the shorter hair above his neck. "This time last year we were trapped in a hallway—"

"Having sex," Grayson interjected with a wicked grin.

She playfully slapped his shoulder. "And yes, having sex." She laughed. "A lot has changed since then," she said.

"In the best ways, though," he murmured, placing a kiss on her lips. "I've found the love of my life. I'm happier than I could've ever imagined. Melanie is already growing Chandler. And my mother actually smiled at you last week."

Nadia grinned. "Cherise is coming around." Okay, so she was being generous, but Grayson's parents were thawing toward her. But their acceptance of her didn't matter when their son stared down at her as if she were the most precious jewel he'd ever seen. It wasn't just enough—it was everything. "After all we've been through, we're definitely going to have stories to tell our kids about this gala… And we can start in about seven months."

For a moment, Grayson's face blanked. Then, seconds later, joy so bright suffused his face, it was almost hard to gaze upon.

"You're pregnant," he confirmed, voice hoarse and thick with the blinding love that gleamed out of his mismatched and beautiful eyes.

"I'm pregnant," she said, grinning.

With a shout, he lifted her in the air, twirling her around, heedless of the people around them. "She's pregnant!" he shouted.

Heat poured into her face as applause broke out, but she threw back her head, laughing. And when his mouth covered hers, she lost herself in it. In him.

Out of the darkness of a blackout, she'd found the shining light of love.

Happily ever after wasn't just for Cinderella.

It was for her, too.

* * * * *

COMING SOON!

We really hope you enjoyed reading this book. If you're looking for more romance, be sure to head to the shops when new books are available on

Thursday 6th March

To see which titles are coming soon, please visit
millsandboon.co.uk/nextmonth

MILLS & BOON

Desire

Indulge in secrets and scandal, intense drama and plenty of sizzling hot action with powerful and passionate heroes who have it all: wealth, status, good looks… everything but the right woman.

LET'S TALK
Romance

For exclusive extracts, competitions
and special offers, find us online:

f facebook.com/millsandboon

🐦 @MillsandBoon

📷 @MillsandBoonUK

Get in touch on 01413 063232

For all the latest titles coming soon, visit
millsandboon.co.uk/nextmonth

JOIN US ON SOCIAL MEDIA!

Stay up to date with our latest releases, author news and gossip, special offers and discounts, and all the behind-the-scenes action from Mills & Boon...

 millsandboon

 millsandboonuk

 millsandboon

It might just be true love...

MILLS & BOON
MODERN
Power and Passion

Prepare to be swept off your feet by sophisticated, sexy and seductive heroes, in some of the world's most glamourous and romantic locations, where power and passion collide.

Julia James — Heiress's PREGNANCY SCANDAL

Jennie Lucas — Chosen as the SHEIKH'S ROYAL BRIDE

Kim Lawrence — A WEDDING at the ITALIAN'S DEMAND

Sharon Kendrick — The SHEIKH'S SECRET BABY

MILLS & BOON
HEROES
At Your Service

Experience all the excitement of a
gripping thriller, with an intense romance
at its heart. Resourceful, true-to-life
women and strong, fearless men face
danger and desire - a killer combination!